PRAISE FOR *SALLOWSFIELD*

"Wyatt Sallow travels to the town of Sallowsfield in the United Kingdom in search of himself, modest fame, family history, and possible and imagined loves. Cliff Hudder has created a funny, hapless, befuddled, and creepy character in a sprawling novel that will surprise and entertain you about what we seek at middle-age, what confuses us, and what consumes us as we try to turn a 'will to lose' into a quiet victory."

SERGIO TRONCOSO, author of *Nobody's Pilgrims, A Peculiar Kind of Immigrant's Son,* and *From This Wicked Patch of Dust*

"From the moment Cliff Hudder's characters enter his novel, you have the sense that the author is not so much writing about them as introducing them to you; that they are real citizens wandering around the town of Sallowsfield and living their real lives. He portrays them with insight, a deep awareness of their desires and struggles, and a benign tolerance for their inevitable failings. By the time you finish this book, you'll know these people like your own relatives. Or maybe even better."

ELIZABETH CROOK, author of *The Which Way Tree, The Night Journal, Monday, Monday* and *The Madstone*

"With hints of Lodge's *Campus Trilogy,* Joyce's *Ulysses,* and even Swift's *Gulliver's Travels, Sallowsfield* deftly and repeatedly defies expectations. Hudder arranges a meta chessboard and moves his characters with the sure hand of a master storyteller. You're going to fall as hard as I did for his imperfect hero and the misshapen figures he meets in the wonderfully drawn, bizarre world of *Sallowsfield.*"

DAVID SAMUEL LEVINSON, author of *Antonia Lively Breaks the Silence* and *Tell Me How This Ends Well*

"From the Pantheon of Picaresques stumbles Wyatt Sallow on his Pilgrimage to Sallowsfield. His Quest—for X, Y, and Z—is the Quest of the Great Wanderers—Todd Andrews in *The Floating Opera*, Binx Bolling in The Vieux Carré, and Leopold Bloom in 'The Lotus Eaters.' And as we accompany him on his sallow search, we both recognize and discover ourselves."

GLENN BLAKE, author of *Drowned Moon, Return Fire,* and *The Old and the Lost*

SALLOWSFIELD

SALLOWSFIELD

A Novel

CLIFF HUDDER

The Sabine Series in Literature

TRP: THE UNIVERSITY PRESS OF SHSU
HUNTSVILLE, TEXAS 77341

Library of Congress Cataloging-in-Publication Data
Names: Hudder, Cliff, 1957– author.
Title: Sallowsfield : a novel / Cliff Hudder.
Other titles: Sabine series in literature.
Description: First edition. | Huntsville : TRP: The University Press of
   SHSU, [2024] | Series: Sabine series in literature
Identifiers: LCCN 2024008718 (print) | LCCN 2024008719 (ebook) | ISBN
   9781680033571 (paperback) | ISBN 9781680033588 (ebook)
Subjects: LCSH: College teachers—Texas—Fiction. | Market
   towns—England—Fiction. | Genealogy—Fiction. | Superstition—Fiction.
   | LCGFT: Novels.
Classification: LCC PS3608.U3 S25 2024 (print) | LCC PS3608.U3 (ebook) |
   DDC 813/.6—dc23/eng/20240304
LC record available at https://lccn.loc.gov/2024008718
LC ebook record available at https://lccn.loc.gov/2024008719

FIRST EDITION

Front cover image courtesy: iStock | CSA-Printstock
Author photo courtesy: Magda Berg
Illustrations courtesy: Brandy Beucler
Cover design by Cody Gates, Happenstance Type-O-Rama
Interior design by Maureen Forys, Happenstance Type-O-Rama

Printed and bound in the United States of America
First Edition Copyright: 2024

TRP: The University Press of SHSU
Huntsville, Texas 77341
texasreviewpress.org

The Sabine Series in Literature
Series Editor: J. Bruce Fuller

The Sabine Series in Literature highlights work by authors born in or working in Eastern Texas and/or Louisiana. There are no thematic restrictions; TRP seeks the best writing possible by authors from this unique region of the American South.

BOOKS IN THIS SERIES:

Cody Smith, *Gulf*

David Armand, *The Lord's Acre*

Ron Rozelle, *Leaving the Country of Sin*

Collier Brown, *Scrap Bones*

Esteban Rodríguez, *Lotería*

Elizabeth Burk, *Unmoored*

Cliff Hudder, *Sallowsfield*

For X. For Y. Not for Z.
Fuck Z.

*So fare thee well, poor devil of a Sub-Sub, whose commentator I
am. Thou belongest to that hopeless, sallow tribe which no wine of
this world will ever warm; and for whom even Pale Sherry would be
too rosy-strong; but with whom one sometimes loves to sit, and feel
poor-devilish, too; and grow convivial upon tears; and say to them
bluntly, with full eyes and empty glasses, and in not altogether
unpleasant sadness—Give it up, Sub-Subs! For by how much the
more pains ye take to please the world, by so much the more shall
ye for ever go thankless!*

~HERMANN MELVILLE, *MOBY DICK, OR THE WHALE*

*. . . which made up the whole of the 2011 UK census where we at
Buzzcall uncovered the rarest surnames: unusual names that have
lingered for centuries but are on the brink of extinction in Great
Britain. If you see your surname on this list of rare and presumed
extinct names—we'd love to hear from you!*

*Birdwhistle, Berrycloth, Combs, Dankworth, Fernsby, Loughty, Mira-
cle, Relish, Sallow . . .*

~BUZZCALL BRITAIN BLOG

Sallowsfield *is a small to medium-sized market and university
town[1], the 22nd largest in the United Kingdom, with the fifth-largest
urban area in the metropolitan borough of _____ and a population of 80,949 at the 2011 census[2][3]. The town is known for its role in
opposing the Industrial Revolution and as the birthplace of Off to
the Planets co-star Henry Scott. A town of mixed contemporary and
Victorian architecture, the Sallowsfield railway station is a Grade II
listed building described by Carlton Woodson as "not a bad looking
railway station."*

~WIKIPEDIA

CONTENTS

PART ONE

1
The dog. The man.

The dog snarls. The man hears through the cicada-like thrumming of chronic tinnitus its teeth when they *clack*, sees incisors streaked with yellow, gums red and black as slobber flies and dampens his wrist and palm. He feels the dog's hot breath on his right hand and smells that breath: wet and unhealthy, like canned lunch meat when the lid is first pried. Yes, he yanked the hand away in time—*just*—but his notebook falls open, drops to the ground for the second occasion on this trip. His itinerary is visible, neatly hand-printed with block letters on its last page: LIBRARY – UNIVERSITY – HILL – MUSEUM.

Today is HILL.

The dog attacks for *no reason*. The man, who *did not do anything* to this dog, rocks on the iron bench to distance himself from its clamping jaw. The bench is positioned at what might be called a scenic overlook, but the man overlooks no scene. He is frightened. Scared shitless. No fair! The man is far from home and wearing tweed and being attacked by a big dog.

A woman he at first thinks he knows—and around here, by the way, there seem to be so many women he thinks he knows, one right after another as a matter of fact; it's quite notable—this woman has gotten hold of the dog's black vinyl leash, pulls at it fiercely, leans to keep Sallow from ripping out Sallow's throat, then another woman who's with the first takes up the leash, too, gets serious, screams, "Sallow!" This second woman (with much longer hair, streaked—both sides—with shock-grey strands flying from her bloodless face) wraps her right forearm in the vinyl strap with difficulty, yanks, puts her back into it. "Unnngh!" The leash creases pink flesh on her forearm but her weight makes the difference and the two women together, backward-leaning, pull the Shepherd-mix up the path where it digs its paws, lowers its flat head, remains aimed at the fleshy, middle-aged, dust-covered man on the bench beside his dust-covered pack or suitcase.

Wyatt W. Sallow, MBA, sniffs, adjusts his glasses, wriggles his fingers against his lapel as the women pull the dog away. He makes sure each finger is attached and functioning. All of them damn well better be, or . . . wriggle one, wriggle two three four five.

It's over. Probably. Though the dog continues to bark and snarl.

Wyatt looks to the women for some kind of apology or explanation as the dog continues its expressions of hate. It won't let up. The two women holler his name (he knows why now), "Sallow!" and say other things. They're either warning him against "getting bit" or the canine against "taking bits." Wyatt can't be sure. Their accents are thick, Northern. Their words bounce down the hillside like scattered softballs. He can't unravel what these words intend before they roll away, into the valley.

He was not bothering their crazed fucking dog!

Sarah Marsden and Annie Graves exchange glances. They make ready to move away, retreat without returning the "Hello!" this man had offered just before Sarah's dog attacked. They're being rude perhaps, but there it is. They pull the leash and head up the path, finally persuading the dog to follow after much coaxing. Best to go. Although Wyatt Sallow can't know it, the wordless glance between Sarah and her friend and co-worker Annie after Sarah's dog attempted to assault and possibly take a piece out of the stranger on the iron bench . . . this wordless glance had only confirmed an implicit though silent agreement they'd made—instantly—even before closing in on the bench where he sat. That agreement had been to forgo their usual plan (one often followed when encountering any stranger) to ask this gentleman wearing tweed where he acquired his mobile network service, inquire as to whether he was happy with his mobile network service, inform him (along with the offering of a pamphlet) that there existed now a limited offer and deeply discounted opportunity to switch to Interfone Connect. This offer they presented to strangers most weekdays while standing at a portable display outside an electronics store, the side door of which opened onto a shopping arcade across from Boots. Being an American, or a Texan anyway, and only in the area for eight days, Wyatt Sallow would not have been able to make use of their offer, but this, his place of origin, they would never learn, despite more than one opportunity.

No matter.

They no longer desire to approach him with the offer, and so feel no impediment to simply moving away. Sarah and Annie can just tell. He's no dice. Obviously, a guy with a poor attitude. Determining this (and at a glance) is a skill, an ability obtained via multiple daily encounters with people while standing outside electronics stores next to a card table full of Interfone Connect promotional swag (pamphlets, but also memory stick lanyards, key fobs, pocket-sized bottles of hand-sanitizer) . . . it was the arrival, for them, at a "knowingness" which delivered the strong certainty (even before Sarah's dog had directed such a dislike . . . no, *unexpected disgust* towards him) that here is a man who does not care about Interfone Connect.

Sarah glances back, sees him examine his hand. He appears to grin ironically, but Sarah cannot know how, especially when he squints through his thick lenses in harsh light, a corner of Professor Sallow's mouth rises habitually, not consciously, resulting in a muscular spasm that only resembles a smile and should probably count more as a sneer. Stout and stoop-shouldered, his clean-shaven cheeks shine, his facial hair expresses itself mainly in bushy eyebrows. Just as bushy: dishwater brown hair that springs from what he does not so much consider a receding hairline as an expanding forehead. A rash encircles his throat. There the skin is reddened and sags in rings like a leg in loose stockings. Sarah considers that he is "crookedly" attired, his oversized jacket with the frayed elbow patches canted at an angle, the entire package ending in a pair of spindly legs sprung in front of him, his body still recoiling from the dog's attack.

It is, in addition, a fact that people often remark on Wyatt Sallow's somewhat unnaturally tiny feet (one of his off-white sneakers now touches the gravel path tenderly in an unsteady rhythm). When he peers down his own frame, along the length of his legs—as he might, say, when leaned back in a dental chair, nervously awaiting the ministrations of a hygien-ist—the smallness of his feet creates nearly a forced perspective effect, and his shoes appear to be very, very, very far away.

Wyatt Sallow's wife is a dental hygienist, incidentally, but not his dental hygienist.

Sarah doesn't notice his feet at all, nor will anyone else, at least not in this book.

2
Also Open on May Bank Holiday (though not explicitly listed).

He'd had to bring the baggage/pack/duffle with him to the remote scenic overlook as he'd wanted to see the hilltop during his visit—it was prom-inent on his itinerary—yet he couldn't bear to part with his belongings. Not if they were unsecured. His new room wouldn't be available until 3:15 pm. Earlier, his taxi driver had brought him to the top of this historically important hill and dropped him off.

After four days of exploring the region—half of the total time Wyatt had allotted for his trip, his first non-work-related travel from Turner, Texas, in more than twelve years—after this number of days he considered Hussein to be *his* taxi driver. But he'd neglected to make any arrangement for the man to return and carry him back *down* the hill: a positional blunder.

"I can watch that for you," Hussein had said, eying the luggage, "until your room's ready. I'll keep it at the office."

Wyatt felt a creeping unease. "I'll hang onto it."

"It's no trouble," said Hussein. "It's huge! You're going to carry it around? Here?" He smiled. "You don't trust me with your . . . bag. After all we've been through." A statement, not a question.

"That's not it."

"I told you I'm Kashmiri, right?"

"Yes."

"Not Iranian or something."

"That's not it."

But the luggage/pack/bag contained too many important items to risk a parting. Wyatt thought quickly. "I might need something in it."

Hussein surveyed the gravel car park on the hilltop with its slanted rubbish bin a few yards from the shut up Victorian Tower, looked beyond into a hazy horizon and surrounding hills that seemed so, so distant . . . impossibly far away from this elevation. It was a moment when many would have lowered the sunglasses from the top of their heads to cover their eyes, but Wyatt noticed that Hussein—although he always had sunglasses on his head—never used them as sunglasses.

"I might need my notebook," Wyatt said and shrugged. He already held the notebook clamped under one arm. He considered unknown actors in this "office" Hussein mentioned, perhaps unable to contain their curiosity, who might examine the contents of his bag. He imagined them pulling out his vacuum constriction device (with its long, looped tube). He'd never admit such a suspicion to Hussein. He, like his driver, also turned to look into the distance, down the valley and towards the nearby town.

"Unknown actors in this office of yours would go through my stuff, wouldn't they?"

Hussein frowned. "Hilarious, Dr. Wyatt."

Wyatt made it a point in his life not to correct mistaken assumptions that he'd earned a PhD. Those degrees, after all, were a dime a dozen. He could have gotten one. There were, at that moment, over 4 million persons on the earth with doctoral degrees. (He'd Googled this.) There were, on the other hand, only 1,721 chess grandmasters.

Not that he was a chess grandmaster.

"And you haven't seen her at all?" Wyatt asked Hussein.

The woman who'd come down the steps of the train station. He had even sent Hussein a picture of her via his phone so the driver could be on the lookout. He somewhat regretted sending that particular picture, but . . .

"You asked twice. I have not. But if I do, I'll let you know."

After exchanging a few more words, Hussein started the taxi that shuddered, the engine making its familiar, unspooling fishing line sound, its gears cracking like knuckles. Then the vehicle rolled to the steeply descending road at the edge of the car park and dropped from sight.

Wyatt considered only then the return trip. Hussein—thoughtless of him—had driven off without mentioning it.

A circuitous path lined with informative signs began at the Tower, a structure that appeared to Wyatt's eye as a kind of squared rook with another, shorter, roughly crenelated rook fixed on top. The Tower could be entered and climbed, or so it said in his guidebook (that didn't say much when it came to this region, truth be told) and offered an even more bird's-eye view of the surrounding valley. But not on the day he arrived atop the hill. A sign near its front, iron-reinforced door displayed an arcane formula for those relatively few days of the year the stairs might be ascended to the viewing gallery.

Open 12 noon to 4:30 pm
Every Sat/Sun from: 8th Sept to 21st Oct
Inclusive of
October Half-Term Holidays:
27th Oct to 4th Nov (every day)
In addition to
Christmas Holidays:
15th, 16th, 22nd, 23rd, 27th, 28th, 29th, 30th Dec
Closed 24th, 25th, 26th Dec
And February Half-Term Holidays:
12 noon to 4:30 pm
Saturday 16th Feb to Sunday 24th Feb

Turning away from this tightly sealed structure, he'd begun his explorations along the hilltop's circular path. Soon his luggage's lower parts revealed a skein of dust picked up as he'd traveled the commanding overlooks, reading the hill's history on informative signboards, learning of its featured archaeological hallmarks. The signage included maps and schematics that sliced the knobby rise into layers and produced a kind of ant-farm visual of the tribes and clans that had inhabited it over the centuries. Wyatt leaned, out of breath, put his weight on the wheeled suitcase's handle as he thought about buried castles, defenses, even a possible connection to an ancient famed epic romance that thrilled him although he wasn't sure he believed it possible. He had studied *Le Morte d'Arthur* as an undergrad, twenty-odd years before. A lot had happened since, but what had not happened was Wyatt imagining Camelot as a place he could visit pulling wheeled luggage.

Considering it, he felt the new layer of dust on the suitcase/duffel/pack gave the thing a satisfying "travelled" look. And why not? On his fourth day, he'd begun to feel "travelled," too.

After more than an hour of circumnavigating the hilltop, he'd come to rest on the bench at the scenic overlook to consider his next move. A stiff wind gusted. Clouds feathered against a washed-out backdrop of pale blue. He spent some minutes resting uncomfortably on the gluteus-creasing (though thoughtfully provided) bench. Sitting was something he knew of from his coaching duties at Taylor State College. ("Another aspect of mastering fundamentals," he often descried to his team, "is *planting the fundament.*") Below, in the valley, a cow bellowed, the creature itself hidden by blocked and broken terrain. A black crow, or raven, made an appearance on a grassy rise to his right, then exited, the bird large enough to warrant a notebook entry. He pondered, tapped his teeth with his ballpoint. He breathed in the fresh hillside air, moved his shoulders in his oversized jacket with its corduroy patches. He felt after some deliberation that the bird was big enough to warrant a concrete comparison in the form of a simile. He balanced his personal notebook on one knee, leaned over it.

As big as a shoebox he wrote on a white page.

Thinking more, below this he inserted: *As big as a dictionary.*

Not bad.

The hillside wind blew against his cheeks.

Wyatt considered other concrete comparisons connectable by "like" or "as," but couldn't think of any. In parentheses he added:

(Raven?)

Farther below than the invisibly bellowing cow (nearly 1,000 feet to the valley floor according to informative signage atop this stark hill) the landscape spread in green sward—farm *this*, road *that*—all the way to the horizon's edge. Beautiful. And for someone from East Texas, an inconceivable vista. Wyatt sat, notebook closed on his right knee, his notation about the crow (raven?) safely secured. He kept his ballpoint in his right fist, gripped the extended handle of his suitcase/luggage/pack with his other hand.

He minded his own obscure business. This mainly had to do with a particular person he often obsessed over at odd moments. He watched as two women, strangers to him, approached through slanted, knee-high grass. To his astonishment, while they approached, they began to call his name. They did this several times, in fact, repeatedly and loudly.

"Sallow! Sallow!"

Did he know them?

He'd squinted through his progressive lenses, swiveled his head to improve the focus. Were these, against all odds, people he knew from East Texas? Wouldn't that just figure? Yet it seemed impossible. The uncomfortable iron bench where he sat had been installed on a hillside 4,700 miles from his home and a pretty much equal distance from everyone that he knew on planet Earth. Yet he'd already encountered someone he knew from Turner, Texas, in the town that nestled in the valley behind him, so he couldn't discount the possibility. On the first day he'd arrived, in fact. The love of his life! Of all people. Yes. His life's great love, that is, coming down the high steps of the train station and turning down a cavernous lane in her white ... uhm ... *slacks*.

In Sallowsfield? Yet there she had been.

The two women were following a large dog, trying to leash it. They were middle-aged, their plaid shirts untucked, with dark wind-threaded hair just going grey that spread like wings beside their rosy faces, and their dog was big. They were big, too. Possibly sisters. As big as ...

He couldn't think of anything.

"Sallow!" they called. "Sallow!" They did not appear to look at him, unless, perhaps, stealing occasional glances. Both mainly attempted to attract the attention of the dog that trotted with high steps in the grass. Wyatt had enjoyed his trip, despite some shocks, and now—to add to these traumas—this, the sound of his surname, ringing in his ears across the rolling bluffs. But soon, their intention grew clearer.

"Sallow! Saaaaalow!"

Ah.

The dog had his name.

By the time the group approached, the animal had been successfully leashed by one of the calling women, who pulled at this canine Sallow tightly to steer him away from the bench and the human Sallow, although the dog inched closer against her wishes. The dog smiled at him. Wyatt was of the opinion that some dogs could smile in a friendly manner. Perhaps he, Dog Sallow, had sensed their cognominal connection. Dogs were excellent judges of character. They had incredible olfactory powers. Had he sniffed out Wyatt's patronymic? And so, he reached to pat Sallow's square head and prepared to ask the women about the name.

We know what happened next.

Not his fault!

3
A Kind of Algebraic Factor

After the canine assault, Annie and Sarah continue to move quickly away, the troublesome Samuel still exerting himself against his leash, straining towards the man after having for some unknown reason developed a visceral, even molecular-level dislike of him, his strange luggage, or both. "Samuel" was the name the women had called across the hillside as they'd attempted to fasten the leash. After the custom of the region, they pronounced this name with three syllables, so that Wyatt would hear it as is own was trebly odd. It had something to do with his reasons for making the trip, no doubt, which amounted to a search for his family roots. A very disorganized yet frantic search, the arrangements made at the last moment, as if the window for this long-desired journey might close forever did he not act immediately. Book the ticket. (Houston to Manchester, non-stop.) Make the trip.

If not now, would there be another chance?

Perhaps he misheard the dog's name because the women's voices had been broken by the wind, their words altered by reverberations from the landscape, or buried under Northern accents of the type that often fell thick and strange on foreigners' ears. At any rate, all of this—influenced heavily, no doubt, by his amateur genealogical reason for being there— had caused Wyatt to hear, in the aural confusion that hillside sounds at times take on, his own surname rather than the dog's actual moniker.

Wyatt waits for them to leave. Then he waits longer. Finally, he gathers his notebook and his ballpoint from the gravel. He squeezes the pen once, twice. He feels a kind of residual bite across the fingers of his right hand, a ruler-straight ridge where the dog *could* have gotten him with its sharp teeth, digging in the flesh, pressing bone. Blood everywhere. His right hand is difficult to flex as a matter of fact when he makes a fist, though the teeth never made contact: stiff, like muscles or nerves had been damaged when, in fact, his hand is fine, just feels a little warm.

The dust and gravel path shows the track of his two-wheeled luggage up to the bench. A row of shrubs along the foreground frames the sweep of the landscape. He's used to looming pines, impenetrable dark underbrush, gloom. Here, fields as regularly shaped as quilt panels hug the hillsides, their borders marked by what he would be very interested to know are called "hedgerows"—a word he had familiarity with but had never seen illustrated in the wild. (He has noticed an affinity in himself for dividing lines and barriers of various kinds.) After occupying the bench another quarter of an hour, settling his nerves, he decides to adopt a structure below him in the long valley as his ancestral manor home. Why not? It's a personal fancy, and it wasn't like he'd uncovered any other, actual ancestors on this sudden, misguided trip that had drained his savings. The building is rustic, like many of the decayed mill structures he'd encountered in the region. Such edifices projected a seductive beauty for someone teaching in the Applied Business Department of an American college: brick and mortar symptoms of economic disease. Not all is business with him, however, as Wyatt has a poet's nature, and—in his luggage/backpack/suitcase—nineteen copies of his short, poorly reviewed, yet award-winning collection of verse in chapbook form, also grabbed at the last moment to take across an ocean.

Wyatt's heart rate returns to its steady *tap, tap, tap.* His sparse hair feels damp for some reason. Guidebooks and historical treatises (a weighty example of which, *Sallowsfield: An Undeniably Admirable Place*, he hauls in his luggage) call attention to the hill where he presently sits, notable for its "distinctive shape," as well as for the tower atop its plateau that serves as a recognizable landmark as far away as the central streets of the adjacent town. The elevation's oval aspect has made it a candidate (along with approximately forty other locations that claim the possibility) for the location of Camelot, as is another nearby site presently covered by a golf course. Home of Arthur, his questing knights. Crafty Merlin. Lancelot and Guinevere, who destroyed a kingdom with their adulterous behavior. (Wyatt begins to recall that class from twenty years before.) He does not consider himself a man who has experienced a great life-altering love that derailed him, darkened his heart, destroyed all he'd spent great effort piecing together as Guinevere had done to Arthur. Well, except for that one time. The police report, his letter of resignation (not accepted!), and even editorials on the *Turner Tribune* opinion page could attest to the effect of womanhood on Wyatt Sallow. He recalls the person he'd seen at the train station in the town below the hill but files that for the moment. Hussein is keeping an eye out for her. Hussein has a picture. An inappropriate picture.

Embarrassing, but Wyatt flattens his heart, as per his training.

He rises, shaky, maybe from hunger, or from the trauma of the snapping dog he (incorrectly) believes has his own name. "Some lesson there," he says to himself, analyzing. "Some analogy. Attack of the self? On the self? Identity . . . something?"

He pulls his luggage/pack behind him down the center of the gravel path towards the car park and the Tower where he'd begun exploring the hill. Terrible things were always happening. It didn't matter where you went.

Wyatt Sallow strides onto the car park, constructed on soil overlaying ash and burnt matter that harkens back, down into the clotted soil, to before Roman occupation. A father and son team flies a drone across the narrow plateau, a new toy for both. It struggles against the wind, spends much of its time speared in the ground at alarming angles, but these mishaps don't keep it from rising, struggling against the wind again, the man and the little boy frowning over their control box. "Wonderful," Wyatt says. "Wonderful." A handful of other cars are in the lot. Over there, looking down into the town, a slender blond woman stands in an ankle-length dress. Her skin is milky white. Maybe if she, or someone, were heading down anyway, or if he asked politely . . . but that sets a high bar as Wyatt dislikes asking for things, especially help. (He recalls, suddenly, an incident in the deep end of a swimming pool when he was a child and how "help" had been exactly what he'd gaspingly requested. He had not done so lightly.) The day before he'd met someone at the university who might consider driving up here to pick him up. But too bad, as in fact he'd disposed of this person's phone number.

Did his cell even work outside of the United States? Also too bad: Sarah and Annie were gone, as they could have explained that if he was relying on its map function (he was) and had texted his taxi driver a topless photo of the love of his life (regrettably, he had), he must indeed have an operational international plan.

Closing the circle of his hilltop journey as he drags towards the tower, it flashes on him that considering this flat-topped elevation rising from the valley a kind of "Round Table" makes the claims of the informative signage less of a stretch. Home of the troublesome Guinevere.

Wyatt wonders if there is a path he could use to descend into town. He doesn't want to walk the narrow, winding pavement Hussein's taxi had disappeared down so rudely. At the tower, he begins to seek a way down the hill on foot. Or, perhaps he shouldn't rush into anything. How many players lost—though far ahead in material advantage—by pushing forcefully, squandering clear advantages, not taking time for simple, strengthening moves?

Guinevere. Perhaps her relentless spirit lurks nearby . . . or lurks at the nearby golf course. Scholars, he recalls, considered her as she appears in narratives like Malory's, as symbolic. "The Woman Force" or something. On this hilltop, he wonders if they had neglected her flesh and bone humanity to create a mythological variable or placeholder, forgetting for the moment how this describes exactly the way he tends to think of people important to him. Not by their names. The woman he'd sent Hussein to look for (she had a cleft chin and had once said she would, should he die, sneak a cutting of her hair into his coffin so that a piece of her would "accompany him through eternity"), that woman he thought of as "X." Not a name, but a kind of algebraic factor. Something to be solved for.

There are three women he identifies with these algebraic variables.

Wyatt feels at his own paunch under his tweed jacket. Walking the circuit of the gravel path has tired him. The boy and his father continue to fly the drone into the wind and the ground. Two young people help an older lady in a skirt and heels descend some steps, revealing one way down the hill. They lightly steady her by an elbow, the boy crooking her cane over his forearm. Wyatt doesn't particularly want to be stuck behind that trio, nor ask to go around them, nor clomp his heavy suitcase/pack down each of the steps. Clouds scud the sky where a small single-engine plane circles and dry twigs rustle at his feet. A candy wrapper of a chocolate brand he's never seen before in his life scuttles past the wheels of his luggage, caught in the wind. Below, down the long slope of the hill towards town, the familiar circular roof of a house stands out from the regular square and rectangular varieties. Hussein had pointed out its unusual architecture driving him to the summit. That direction must be the way he had come.

Leaving the path he sets off, cross-country, down the hillside, his progress followed by the lithe blond woman at the hill's rim with straight shoulder-length hair in the long dress who, despite this mode of attire, is not a hippy but a now-retired teacher of elementary school children. She is not the spirit of Guinevere. (Her name is Rachel. Rachel Shrimpton.) No figure of literary myth, sylph or siren, nor a star-maker scouting agent seeking talent.

Possibly a co-star-maker.

With her left hand shielding her brow Rachel Shrimpton watches the stranger begin his descent into Sallowsfield.

4
Bollards Loom.

It is said of some that there is an "irresistible attraction in their manner," immediately obvious to any with the good luck to be "admitted to their intimacy."

This is not said of Wyatt Sallow, but especially not now as his tweed jacket, like his thin, unkempt hair, contains brambles and twigs, the shirt-tail of his blue cotton Oxford is untucked, and a splotch of dampness rises along both trouser legs, soaking particularly one knee.

He says: "It's a wonder that I didn't break my damn neck."

Wyatt Sallow, MBA, knows fulfillment. As in, knows about it. His expertise is for the most part of the legal kind: *performed completions of obligations as set forth in a documented contractual agreement.* For now, Wyatt feels he should wait until he reaches some innocuous location, possibly finds a garden wall to crouch behind, before fulfilling his desire to open his suitcase/pack with its twisted corkscrew handle that he drags along one clogged and useless wheel. He needs to dig out a pair of shoes. Or a shoe, to replace the one he'd lost in a murky ditch as he fell, tumbled, and careened down the side of Tower Hill.

Wyatt believes it's possible he isn't thinking straight. He'd taken some hard slams against the hillside. Anyone seeing him with a wet flopping sock worked three quarters off his foot, his hair unkempt and, unbeknownst to him, studded with twigs and grass . . . anyone observing him dragging his pack on its now single serviceable wheel by its now mangled joke of a handle might also believe he's not thinking straight. Thankfully, there aren't many people around, only the occasional car on the road he slowly parallels in his limping fashion.

Unfortunately, there are bollards ahead.

At the bottom of the hill, he had landed, finally, along a shrub barrier he would have been happy to learn was yet another hedgerow, close enough to a house to be considered part of its backyard, so that didn't seem like a good place to be digging into a suitcase. Instead, he trudges towards town, looking for a better location to arrange himself. He feels aches in muscles he hasn't felt aches in for a while, a sensation similar to one he'd experienced returning to snow skiing after a decade's hiatus. Wyatt says out loud much what he'd said to himself returning to the lodge in Aspen that afternoon with his flattened wine bladder, bruises, and an imprint of a jumper buckle on his belly from a particularly hard landing. He'd rejoined a dozen of his more athletic colleagues who'd made up the package tour that frigid Winter Break. His wife (now estranged), six and a half months pregnant with their boy, Wyn, had stayed at the lodge with

"Cousin" Yuri, who had enjoyed so much the novelty icicles that formed in his thick mustache as he strolled outside. At any rate, here, Wyatt repeats again what he had said on those icy slopes in Aspen, and does so out loud, and for the second time.

"It's a damn wonder I didn't break it, my damn neck."

On this grassy hillside, occasional misjudgments of foot placement had meant that he'd jammed his leg and knee several times, though he had planned to skip, lightly, crabwise, down and across the sloping terrain. He'd kept his center of gravity high, attempted to remain upright, but nonetheless spent so much time on his back, on his now crushed *again* shoulder, on his ample backside, that—especially there towards the end—he'd wondered if it might not have been better to crawl down the hill on all fours. He doubts doing so would have covered his jacket with any *more* twigs and straws than the halting method he'd adopted. Probably if he hadn't felt those people on the hilltop watching he might have tried it. As it was, he'd barely missed bashing his brains against a sharp grey stone. (More likely his leg, truly.) Stone the size of a dictionary. Except for that trench full of fetid grey water, and the general embarrassment of making a spectacle, the worst had been the falls. "You have to block *through* the other fella," Evan Gonzalez, a student, a linebacker on the Taylor College football squad had once told Wyatt (Taylor State had Division III status—largely because the NCAA had decided against a Division IV). The student explained to Wyatt the technique of strong defense on the field, although this was a different kind of field, and he had little hope of blocking through that hill. From another perspective, these had not even been falls the way he'd experienced them, but more instances when the uneven ground had risen up to ram into him. Hard. He fears a turned ankle, a stressed knee, wonders at an aching calf muscle, but this is by no means the worst, as the whole experience has reminded him of a bad shoulder injury he'd sustained while doing the stupidest thing he'd ever done in his life.

Maybe second stupidest.

At the bottom of the hillside, skirting the backyard of a tile-roofed residence where he'd rolled to a stop, Wyatt had stepped over a fence made of rusted pipe, then situated himself on a vaguely familiar-looking road. He felt certain a nearby intersection led into town. A well-proportioned and neatly trimmed house with brick flowerbeds went past as he lurched along, then another after that, and another. As always when he saw such living arrangements he was reminded of his present home: not the one he owned in the trendy outskirts of Turner, Texas, called Carlson Ridge where he'd once lived with his wife, but the place he stayed now in the seedy trailer park. These homes he slowly passed were color-coordinated, well kept, and the nice cars occasionally passing on the road convinced him the area was not private or secluded enough for him to do what he needed to do as far as breaking into the suitcase/pack, but with relief he recognized ahead that place where Hussein had turned right to take the narrow lane up the hill, so he clopped across—careful, by his fourth day, to look both ways, but most careful to examine the "wrong" way—and warily stepped to avoid broken glass or other sock-piercing debris of the kind roads often contained.

The luggage/pack he now drags behind him contains several pairs of shoes, two sports coats, books he had brought to read on the eight-day trip, books he had recently purchased in this or that shop on his trip, all packed away to read later. The pack/satchel holds nineteen copies of his verse collection chapbook. There is zipped into its interior a heavy volume on the Luddite movement that had been the subject of his graduate school thesis, something he'd bought from a backstreet bookseller in a small nearby town, purchased mainly out of habit. He doubts he'll read it at all. *Sallowsfield: An Undeniably Admirable Place* he'd obtained from the bookstore of the historical association on the second floor of the town library—a closet space, basically—for a reasonable price. The library had been instrumental in convincing him that, despite its name and his name, he personally had no family connection to the town. Disheartening. Also packed away is his somewhat embarrassing vacuum constriction device with its coil of tubing. As for the suitcase/bag itself, he'd bought it especially for his eight-day journey.

The thing could be called "luggage" only by accepting a broad-minded notion of the term. Deciding to embark on his first trip of any kind east of the Sabine River in a dozen years, Wyatt agonized over transporting his clothes, supplies, toiletries, and personal items in a foreign land for eight days. His resources were limited. He haunted stores specializing in travel

gear in Turner as well as nearby Athens and Marshall, hit every department store in the mall on the bypass, even visited a mom and pop variety/
antique shop on the outskirts of town that touted "used trunks and cases"
(accessible via a dirt road through a pine thicket), but Wyatt could find
nothing to fit his needs. For one, he had difficulty imagining these needs.
He could not easily project in his mind what travel to Sallowsfield would
be like. For years his voyaging had been limited: driving to the college,
driving back to his fifth-wheel recreational vehicle parked in the Tranquility Park RV Camp, occasional side trips to the Pizza Shack on Academy
Boulevard. Wyatt took up but then eliminated aluminum wheeled cases,
rolling spinner soft-sides, lightweight polycarbonate carry-ons, systems
with room to hang jackets and pants . . . eh . . . *slacks*, luggage with bum-
pers, cases with runner rails and corner guards, weatherproof tarpaulin
rucksacks enclosing a nest of pockets and internal compressor straps. . . .
His Dean, Nick Zepeda, had unexpectedly come to his aid with his suggestion of the Sisyphus/Granite website. The Dean was, in addition to his
celebrated self-confidence when it came to guiding their department into
an uncertain future, his fine mane of silvery hair, and his reputation as an
"all-or-nothing-kind-of-guy," an accomplished traveler. "They only make
one thing," said the Dean. "And it's the best thing ever."

A hybrid device, the Sisyphus/Granite was banded by four flat straps
that cinched tightly around its polyester/nylon shell, these held fast by
clever plastic latches. The luggage/pack contained in its folds a system
of hidden shoulder pads with supporting waist belt that converted it to
a backpack after a few adjustments, meaning Wyatt could bypass using
its oversized road-treaded wheels should the terrain prove treacherous.
Unfortunately, Wyatt could no longer lift the thing to his shoulders
because of the weight of the shoes, eight days' worth of clothes (some now
needing washing), the sports coats, accumulated books, vacuum constriction device . . . to contemplate it caused his spine to ache. The sturdy
telescoping handle with comfortable handgrip thus had been greatly
appreciated, as were the seven external storage pockets that meant he
didn't need to crack into the main cavity to get to maps, the guidebook,
occasional snacks. The front panel displayed its maker's logo: a silhou-
etted figure leaned against a giant oval stone.

But one of the oversized road-treaded wheels now being gone and the other clogged with dirt, Wyatt has little recourse but to drag the thing behind him, a somehow inverted version of Sisyphus in profile.

Bizarrely, he had encountered, as mentioned, a narrow ditch filled with viscous water in the middle of his hillside descent, this being the landscape feature that had felt itself entitled to his right sneaker. With the flopping sock and barely mobile pack/suitcase he drags behind him like a native travois . . . it's all quite the picture. Although he's lost the shoe, he retains his notebook, which he carries at his side. He's not at all sure of the location of the ballpoint pen. Wyatt lumbers in a halting gait that adds a final touch to the overall impression of a person who's off his medication, but he pats the side pocket of his jacket to make sure the plastic tubes with child-proof caps click firmly together. They do.

He's happy to have both socks. "You want to murder your mother," his wife had said to him once upon seeing him walk inside the house with only one—a Ukrainian folk superstition. He certainly did not want his mother dead, and as far as he knew, she lived on at this moment in a suburb of Houston known for fast-food franchises, multiple dollar stores—some right across the street from each other—and toxic chemical plants. He no longer lives with his wife, although look closely as he lumbers towards town after his scrape with that towered hillside and you'll see he still sports a sterling silver wedding band ordered from the catalog of a jeweler in Kerrville. He also still carries in his head many of his wife's statements concerning the world, collected in a lifetime of meandering between nations, careers and faiths, including time with an Eastern European sex cult that attracted new members by wearing thigh high skirts in airport lobbies, a nature worshiping group that set up conical Native American tepees on the outskirts of a park in Kraków where they ate mushrooms and gnawed pemmican that came vacuum sealed in packages from Hayward, Wisconsin, and finally the religion she'd settled into recently: a stripped down version of Buddhism that featured hours of repeating a monotonous phrase while contemplating how what appeared to be one world was really ten worlds—and how careful you had to be when choosing which to live in.

To judge by the lack of traffic, the road he travels is little used. Removing his phone to examine its map feature, he finds that it miraculously does not present a screen crisscrossed by cracks or a web of fractures after its repeated hillside bashing. The map that rises from blackness on the screen indicates a dogleg ahead veering left then connecting to another road that is a straight shot into town. Wyatt pauses to examine his surroundings, especially the broad fields of grass to his right where a man in a yellow shirt strides over low hills and throws a Frisbee to a dog. He nearly feels the tiredness he imagines hikers experience after strenuous but healthful exertion, then remembers how uncomfortable his foot is in the damp sock.

There's no real cover, but Wyatt determines he can't go farther on a single shoe, and—worse—bollards loom.

More on those later.

Wyatt pauses along the plank wall, removes the tight straps from the heavy pack/bag, begins to dig for a decent pair of walking shoes. It being his fifth day of travel, he's filled much of the pack with unwashed clothes from the previous four, and these serve as a wrinkled and somewhat odorous obstacle to locating the footwear packed farther down. Wyatt groans, dumps soiled items onto the sidewalk in a heap (making sure to slide the vacuum device under this heap should anyone pass), locates a pair of dress shoes he'd brought in case of formal emergency. They would have to do, but at that moment—had there been a traffic light somewhere that changed from red to green? —a car arrives, a woman eying him from the passenger seat. No, it would have to be the driver's seat. For a moment, he believes it might be X. But no. He often feels he sees her in unlikely places as she is a woman given to appearing in unlikely places. *This* woman, with short black hair, focuses her green eyes on him, watches where he kneels on the pavement, bent over his pile. It occurs to him, a professor of ethics, that an ethical person might render aid to a poor traveler, but certainly she doesn't realize he's from out of town. Rendering aid to every derelict encountered would set up a different kind of ethical problematic. Besides, he's a professor of *business* ethics. The paradoxical issue of aid to derelicts seldom comes up in his curriculum.

To save time he abandons the idea of changing shoes and removes the one sock, wipes the bottom of his foot with it, finds another dirty sock in the pile to serve as replacement, then affixes a dress shoe to his right foot. He pours the pack's other contents into its cavity with both hands, wonders at the possibility of now affixing it all to his back like a backpack since the wheels have been so harshly misused, but his muscles cry out just from the effort of bending over the clothing pile.

Attempting to zip the contraption closed—not having latches, the duffle/case features a thick black zipper around its entire perimeter—he finds he can't. A sleeve and then a cuff of his Tuesday blue button-down impedes the progress, then the shortened leg of a pair of unwashed boxer briefs does likewise. Next: the lining of a dark sports jacket he's brought but hasn't worn. Each of the items in turn snags the zipper as he tries to clear them from its converging path. His pushing them aside works to no purpose, for the soiled items as a whole—not replaced in the same manner with which they'd been carefully packed—won't allow the matching zipper seams near one another. Wyatt sits on the luggage/pack, finally, a last resort. Three cars pass in succession, each with drivers who glance his way, each glance managing to deliver astonished scorn. Then: a bicycle club. Seventeen, no . . . eighteen cyclists speed past in racing and touring gear, including those special shoes, tight, multicolored . . . leggings? . . . and teardrop-shaped helmets of festive hue. Their tires rub the pavement, chains click through sprockets. Each cyclist manages a helmet-pivot towards Wyatt atop his pack where he sits with bandy legs splayed, one foot in dirty sneaker, the other in cognac-colored wingtip. He watches them from the position he's assumed: half-bent, struggling with the zipper, beginning to sweat. Forcing the thing closed with his weight doesn't work, and, with a glance skyward he pushes his glasses up his nose—they've fallen when he hung his head between his legs in momentary defeat.

He cradles his head in his hands, closes his eyes. Finding X. Encountering her in this town. An unbelievable stroke. But would it affect his life in a positive or negative way? Here, on another continent, away from the context where they'd had so many problems. Insurmountable really. Court-order-to-maintain-twenty-foot-distance-type problems. Here was a chance to get it all back. A theory explaining her presence begins to formulate in his mind. Details accumulate. He knows that—if she's arrived here to do what he suspects—he could help her with that as well. What might they accomplish together! A new world.

A strange new world.

Rising, Wyatt flings the pack open, empties its contents, starts over. He raises some white boxer briefs to fold them in half (a traditionalist in most things, with underwear and luggage he's embraced a hybrid modernity) as if holding them out for an angry-looking young man who approaches just then, on foot. Wyatt is surprised to see the man, but his eyesight has suffered in recent years, though the college refuses to make accommodations. This might have been an explanation for his falling FIDE rating (there were others). The man's lips are chapped. Hands in pockets, he wears what Wyatt's students and the youthful players on his team called a "hoodie." The jet-black garment hides his hair and that the young man's jeans and shoes are also black gives him a cat-burglar aspect. Wyatt has seen many individuals in the region traipsing aimlessly, as if without employment, even in the early afternoon. Many looked unwashed, like this man who leans into his brisk walk. He carries in the crook of his arm a soiled-looking, torn, plastic Tesco bag, and—gosh—a black notebook also under his arm, one that looks much like Wyatt's notebook.

Wonderful! It seemed so many people around here carried black notebooks. What did it mean?

The man nods as if he knows Wyatt—or knows him well enough—and without pausing in his gait, shifts his gaze across the clothing items spread in his path and the white boxer briefs in the professor's fingers, the white emptiness of the yet untouched, breeze-blown pages of the open notebook on the grassy verge. Wyatt resists the urge to corral towards himself all the belongings he's brought from a distant continent (plus some favored books from this side of the ocean). Their eyes meet.

"Three pair." Wyatt raises the underwear an inch. "Three dollars."

The man nods, says nothing, steps carefully around the piles and continues towards Tower Hill. Whoever he is, Wyatt can't help but respect someone who keeps a journal notebook, as he feels such persons are becoming rare where he lives. Here they seem to be on every lane and sidewalk.

After a few moments, he thinks he should have said, "pounds," not "dollars." He hazards to turn and see which way the man had gone, but, glancing behind, can't locate him anywhere.

5
Amelia.

Wyatt's failing eyesight, or the quickness of the encounter, leaves him with the wrong impression. While the notebook is of the same color and style as his own, it's not a journal at all. The unlined pages had been one-third filled with pencil sketch drawings, along with, yes, the occasional odd note or paragraph concerning these, but mainly sketches. With the journal (better to say sketchbook) shut securely under an arm, there would have been no way for Wyatt to see the drawings or know this. The passing figure noted only the blank white sheets of the other notebook that lay along the sidewalk, and so assumed it also contained drawings.

What Wyatt more properly gets wrong is that this is a man. Amelia Davies had dressed that afternoon in a black sweatshirt with a hood pulled over her hair, snugged to her brows by its drawstring. Her baggy tracksuit bottoms likewise reveal little gender-wise. She moves uphill, swings left stiffly across knobby fields, heading towards an outcropping of abandoned buildings along the flank of Tower Hill called, locally, the "Armitage Pile." Amelia wonders what kinds of pictures the odd and somewhat frightening itinerant salesman spreading his goods on the pavement along Hare Road might be drawing.

As she has most afternoons this week in the hours before her husband returns from working with his uncle, she hikes into the nearby hills to draw. Amelia is an artist. Or: she's a person who has decided to teach herself the skill of drawing, which makes her an artist after her definition of one. She's learning this skill. Amelia has checked several books out of the library to help her do so. The hiking part is wearing. Not only is she low on energy—the euphoria she'd often come to rely on wearing off in recent days as she feels her health beginning to improve again—but her limbs are stiff. At times she believes, walking uphill, that she can discern ligaments that hold her knees together, stiff rods along both sides of her legs. Walking downhill is not so bad.

Amelia, thirty-two years old on the day she steps around the stranger's sidewalk display, has decided that for the duration of a year she will perform the exercises in the popular book *Natural Drawing the Natural Way*, following the directions (though not religiously), then seeing at the end of that time whether she's improved and deciding what to do with this new ability (or even talent). So far, she's lasted a week and a half. She is bored with drawing already, true, but can discern a growing sense of accomplishment as she fills the sketchbook's pages. Maybe that's all it takes. The addition of material. While her euphoria is waning, she also no longer feels pains in her back and suspects—although she's afraid to check it on, say, a bathroom scale—that she must currently be topping seven stone, reducing that annoying ache in her kidneys. If she *knew* she was topping seven stone, that could be . . . but the point is, Amelia feels that this approach to a new career—*artist*: a new way of thinking of her-self—makes sense, at least as much sense as the way she's approached her marriage, having also given it a year to see if it improves.

And the drawing, to her, shows progress.

This artistic program of hers she's carried out for the past week and a half has already resulted in her filling the first third of the pages in her sketchbook, although she has the self-awareness to be alert to flagging enthusiasm, a concept she's familiar with. It's nearly impossible for her to cast her mind back to, for example, the thrill she felt at that first dinner date with Graham, the way she had found him so interesting, full of ambition, and—above all—easy to talk to. Such a good listener. Played the acoustic guitar! (He'd put his foot through that recently, though, for reasons that might or might not have anything to do with Amelia.) Good looking, too. Built solidly across the chest, with powerful arms. Amelia felt no embarrass-ment when seen with him in public, novel given the arc of her dating life. (The terrible state of his hair these days, though. Oh well.) She hasn't both-ered to tell him about her drawing ambitions, as she figures it will evince the by now usual noncommittal response. Graham appears to believe that the more time he spends away from home the less friction he will develop with Amelia, but this isn't helping with the *fiendish cycle* of mistrust that's started up since she found out about the German woman. (In a history class, she had once misheard *fin de siècle* as *fiendish cycle* and when she realized it, decided she liked it better than the French phrase anyway so used it a lot.) Amelia is sure—relatively sure—that when Graham says he is absolutely finished and through with the German woman, he means it, truly and literally. But has someone perhaps taken the German woman's place? How could that even be known, except by asking? Or following him around town, spying on his movements? Which she had tried, by the way, yet she'd discovered nothing by that effort. And she can tell by the silent treatment she gets every time she's *about* to ask him if there are others that knowing anything for sure about this husband is problematic. Graham has become secretive and resentful.

Resentful, she supposes, of having been caught.

She has made it her habit, then, to turn to the sketchbook only when he's at work, which is a great deal of the time, and that way her new career can be a secret, too. Everyone, in fact, gets to have secrets, don't they, Graham? Like German women. Or there's the secret stack of magazines in the understairs. At any rate, Amelia has made improvements with the drawings over the past week and a half, at least to her eye and considering she'd never tried drawing before, not even in school. The pictures aren't bad.

Amelia turned to teaching herself drawing after having soured on the notion of more standard instruction, like from teachers. Like that jewelry-making workshop that appeared to her merely a good way to blind herself with a flying metal shard, not to mention the "Fun with Power Saws" class she saw promoted on the Borough Library notice board. What had she been thinking? Amelia felt lucky to have got out of that one with her fingers and three sides of a jewelry box. *Natural Drawing the Natural Way* is full of precise exercises which she's worked through, although not sequentially, but randomly, flipping along until she finds something she wants to try on a particular afternoon. Nor does she follow the instructions to the letter. Some of the principles of draftsmanship (like holding that pencil at arm's length to gauge relative sizes)—yes, she'd looked carefully at those parts. But if the book asked her to draw her hand from memory, then Amelia—in direct contradiction—*looked at her hand* as she drew it. Not with a few sidelong glances, either. And not without quite a bit of erasing along the way. Her artistic productions all showed ghostly outlines of previous artistic production in their margins and backgrounds. But Amelia had made a point of laying her hand on the table and depicting it "from life." Glaring at the hand, in fact. Like giving it the full eyeball. A sneaking-up-to-a-neighbours-window-after-midnight sort of stare. The book also suggested to write on the back of the drawings what she really thought of them, her "true and objective impressions," but instead she abandoned this and began to write on the drawings themselves, at times effacing them with her words but generally just filling in the page's white margins (most of these showing as a smudged background those faint traces of erasure) with things like "My real feeling is that this hand has a certain 'weight'—as if it's pressing down on the page, pressing down hard. Like it's about to clench into a fist to be shaken at an uncaring sky or husband." It appeared to her, then, an evocatively drawn hand although not fine draftsmanship, the thumb nearly as big as the other fingers combined and in large part ravenously consuming the foreground. Amelia began to conclude at the end of the week and a half that she did have an eye for sketching, though not for scale.

When the book demanded that the drawing pupil sketch a real chair and an actual friend's face—that is, not from photographs—she purposely found a magazine with a picture of a chair or face instead and worked from those, besides which she had no friends to speak of aside from her old friends in Hull whom she never gets to see anymore since her husband moved her to the outskirts of—Jesus Christ—Sallowsfield, and she didn't much like any of her chairs or, for that matter, the rest of the furniture, all of which—a house *full* of it—had been given to Graham and Amelia by his uncle who "knew someone" in the furniture business (Graham's relatives always turned out to "know someone"), although Amelia had to suppose he actually knew someone in the *ugly* furniture business. Graham, having lost his job at a tyre store, works for his uncle and nephews, who speak of "business connections" in sales though she has never seen any product they're selling, which makes her suspicious. The latest enterprise they'd embroiled Graham in had something to do with a fish and chip shop. Okay. But he never brought home any fish. Or fish smell.

Amelia had followed Graham into town just the previous Monday, stealthily moving from doorway to doorway along narrow Station Street, turned sidewise which—she grinned ironically—she supposed made her nearly invisible these days. She'd done this though it involved strenuous walking and even an understanding that she might discover something unpleasant that would just kick her off again. But Graham never got near any chip shop that she could tell, just wasted time playing with a stupid flying toy—some kind of spinning aerial top—on the square. In the year since she'd found the credit card receipts, she has steadily been able to trace—from that very day in an app she keeps on her phone—her plummeting weight, bad enough at one point to land her in the emergency department where she lay on a wheeled cot, her eyes thrilling to the bright swaths of light on the ceiling. This, Amelia felt to be a vastly underreported aspect of the whole thing: the exhilaration ... exultation even, once the body began to consume ... well, the last thing it could find in the house to consume, she supposed.

But she feels better now. Self-confident. Amelia has no trouble setting aside the drawing book's directives because she considers that she's been following orders a *little too much* lately, especially Graham's concerning how she "shouldn't worry" about the hours he keeps, or how she's "daft" in thinking he's brought home some other woman's scent on his shirt: why that's the cleaner they used at the chip shop, isn't it? She's been a little bit too obedient, in other words, and—as a person with self-awareness—does understand how ridiculous it sounds to criticize the stray scent here or there considering how she'd cheated on her husband, too. And this after only the one year of marriage. That Croatian student it was who'd done the roof repair in March. But the Croatian student was over now, and she was branching into other kinds of transgressions. She keeps her library books (lately these are about drawing, mostly) far past their due dates, for example. But her husband is a burk without the sense to pay cash for gifts to perfumed German women, and the library has other books, so ... What she *really* feels is that she's been too obedient in general, especially when she shouldn't have been (like that time she simply hadn't been able to see past hurting the feelings of someone—someone pretty good looking, true—who'd asked her to marry him).

Amelia's at home most days and can probably sneak down the lane even without the black clothing, the hoodie, baggy tracksuit: nobody would notice. Nobody cares, and her failures are buried, Amelia thinks, snapped shut like when she closes the sketchbook's covers or drives a Croatian to a train station—gone like any sandcastle she might have made with her father on the Scilly Isles. (Her father had always had a real job. One. One at a time. He would call her onto the back steps just to look at particularly unusual sunsets.) So, she hikes off in the afternoons to the foot of Tower Hill, to the "Armitage Pile." It's a place she'd noticed once when Graham had driven her to the cricket pitch north of town for what she considers one of the most interminable days of her life, by which she means a day of cricket.

Again, the book had "recommended" a study of the Great Masters by taking a famous landscape painting like might be found in a book of historical art movements and making a drawing based on it. This was all the encouragement Amelia needed to pull on her black hoodie, go outside, and find a landscape by *actually looking for one*—not a Great Master but a Great Pile, there on the flanks of Tower Hill. She'd already done the drawing of the chair and a girl from a magazine: she's way ahead of the book, in a manner of speaking, and she'll begin this drawing of these nineteenth-century farmhouse ruins—roofless, the Pile consists mainly of undergrowth, stones, and a few standing walls (one even with a framed window)—she'll draw this ruined farmhouse against a blank sky, is the thing, place it on the page across from the drawing of the girl. She'd found the girl, glancing coyly over her bare shoulder at the camera, in one of her husband's magazines she'd uncovered while cleaning the understairs a few months back, another discovery she'd never bothered mentioning. She's not sure why she hasn't said anything about this growing stack in the back of the understairs. Not for the same reason she hasn't mentioned the Croatian, though somehow related, and just as energizing—to know about it yet not let on she does. "This does look like a girl," she'd written on that page with the drawing from the magazine. "Not the girl looking coyly over a bare shoulder in the porn, but she does look like some other possible, actual, randy girl. Wanting it. Near vibrating with wanting it." (To be fair, the shuddering lines of erasure marks that surrounded the female in the drawing added to that particular nymphomaniacal tremble.) "But has a cartoonish, large mouth, poor thing," Amelia added with her stubby drawing pencil. "Needs a dental hygienist."

This afternoon she would draw the ruins, then, and possibly write in the blank margins around this rendering when it was finished: "These do look like some ruins and now I'm going to go home before Graham gets back, and have a wank: see hand with giant thumb, previous." Other pages featured drawings of her own feet with slightly enlarged big toes, a well-executed knee or sperm whale snout (hard to say), a face that didn't look like the face of an old lady wearing a hat she'd seen walking through the arcade in the town center, but does look like *some* old lady (this, Amelia's version, giving the impression that a hat is the last thing this grizzled old drawing wants to wear), and a shaded portrait from memory of the author Lewis Carroll. This, of course, was supposed to have come from a drawing already included in the pages of *Natural Drawing the Natural Way*, but she ignored that and drew him from memory instead, though she could not for the life of her imagine what Lewis Carroll might have looked like nor recall ever seeing a picture of him. If the book wanted to suggest she use her memory to draw something so near to hand as a hand, she figured: "How about a challenge?"

Amelia's already grown tired of this project, feels like the Armitage Pile might be a kind of last-ditch attempt to kindle some interest before she leaves it for good. Though only thirty-two, she feels winded going up the slight incline across the fields, keeping her "appointment with the muse," as *Natural Drawing the Natural Way* suggests (strongly) because "if you tell the muse you'll be somewhere and don't show, then why should she bother to be there the next time?" "Disloyal bitch muse, then," Amelia replies, "that's you—coy, off staring over cunt shoulder at somebody else with a sketchbook before I even..." She pauses to catch her breath before plodding farther, leans forward more. "Used to get over twelve-foot fences to swim in rich fuckers' pools." She recalls the breeze on her naked, firm (but unribbed) torso as she and her friends used cupped hands to squirt water at each other and squeal in stoned delight. "Now I can't get over how rude that waiter was at Gurkha Sizzlers."

And here. Finally. In a field, she locates a flat stone the size of a two-seater sofa and sits. Removes her pencil case from her wrinkled Tesco carrier bag. Pulls off the hood and shakes out her long brown hair. She lowers her pencil to the sketchbook. The pencil is a stub, the rubber almost gone. She could throw it out, but it's like a race. Amelia grins, grips the stub in her bent bloodless fingers. What disappears first? The part that leaves the marks or the part that rubs them out?

She places the side of her hand on the white paper, raises her head and there it is.

The Pile. The Pile. The Pile.

Wyatt hurries, wants to be up and moving towards town. "It's a wonder I didn't break my . . . leg. Could have hit that sharp rock, cracked my skull." The rock, jagged, brutal, half-hidden in the grass is highlighted in a jumble of imagery imprinted on his brain by the tumble down the hill. He had been downright airborne for a second there. He shudders. "Could be up there now. Bleeding out." Wyatt can't believe a hill, especially one so far from home, could treat him like that. Then there was the mysterious hooded figure. Where had he gotten to?

He replaces everything, manages to seal the zipper around the pack/luggage's perimeter. He rises, uses his arms to hoist himself from the sidewalk, shakes his jacket from which twigs dislodge, then resumes his walk, feeling—save the occasional passing cars—he could be miles from civilization. The man who'd travelled more than four thousand miles to spend only eight days in Amelia's town and whose life had intersected with hers for twenty three seconds, limps, unevenly shod, slowly toward central Sallowsfield, considering the ten worlds his ex-wife had told him about, and. . . *which* world did this place represent, he wonders? With its fetid streams. Its missed connections (including familial). Its roving bands of jobless? This certainly was not—okay—the lowest world (hell). It was not an upper, higher world of enlightenment either, unfortunately, but . . . but, something else. A realm of pure impulse like those of the animals? That would be harsh. Yet it seemed not even partially enlightened, like perhaps the world of the voice hearer or the teacher could be, those who at least attempted to see the world for what it was.

A featureless bank of weeds and grey soil rises to his left across the two-lane road, a wooden plank fence separates him from open fields to his right. In the distance some kind of atmospheric smudge hangs over the town that shares his name but none of his ancestry, spreading to fill a wide vista as it lifts. Resigned, he works his way towards the smudge that comes no closer as he struggles forward and decides it is perhaps best described, the grey scene, as that realm that featured mostly insatiable torment, spiritual and physical craving: the life state his mean Ukrainian bitch of an ex-wife, during her Buddhistic phase, had called the world of hungry ghosts.

6
"What? Might someone come by expecting the previous structure?"

Cars continue to pass him by in interrupted but more frequent bunches as the afternoon progresses.

Following the dogleg curve to the left, over a grey hedge rises the odd roof of the round house Hussein had shown him, and—of course. He recalls this now from the taxi drive to the hill. As the lane straightens ahead of him it reveals a row of homes that snake towards the roiling horizon, a residential neighborhood. Several of these rows of houses are aligned, one behind another, across the landscape. In contrast, and across from the round house, stands a square, dark grey structure that announces itself in foot-tall letters over an ancient door. TOWER HILL SCHOOL ~ REBUILT 1890. In front of this school are the bollards.

He's noticed these (he always notices these) in several locations across the town, although he can't fathom their use in this location. They don't seem to be protecting anything, as they often did in his home-town: erected to ensure no one parked in front of a bank of elevators in a parking garage, for example. He knows these bollards—short posts used to ensure the protection of an architectural perimeter, block vehicular incursion, or provide resistance to impact forces—trace their etymology to maritime mooring devices, but can be found as far back as Roman times, the nineteenth-century variety often employing decommissioned cannon barrels sunk into the ground. Wyatt, almost of necessity, had availed himself of all this knowledge that most people don't even bother to take for granted, bollard-wise. These located in front of the school (located there for some reason he can't fathom unless it is to inconvenience him: *especially* him) resemble those cannons with their dome-shaped tops set on thick, galvanized pipe. For safety, pedestrian traffic direction, bicycle parking, and general asset protection, they had come into widespread global use.

These, basically:

Unless you've clipped a fender on one backing out of a parking space on a busy trip buying holiday gifts, you've probably never noticed them.

They are everywhere.

You're welcome.

The bollards on the road in front of the old school are—the worst part—spaced regularly. Had they been positioned with random distances between, it wouldn't have had anything to do with poor Wyatt. He still isn't sure they apply. Does he have to do that here? Does he *have* to slalom between them, touching each with an alternating palm as he weaves his way to the end? Was this, uhm . . . policy even enforceable after an injurious tumble down a tall hill that had left him battered and sore?

While pulling luggage with only one wheel?

Plenty of rationales arise to justify his forgoing these particular aligned posts with the oval globules on top. Since—unlike some other health issues—there isn't anything diagnosable about what's wrong with him when it comes to bollards (like ADHD, for example), then this is merely an act he performs as a kind of "lucky move." He engages in it when he comes on any set of standing aligned posts, traffic cones, or other objects evenly spaced (irregularly spaced, as said, *do not count*) just for grins, as it were . . . an act he does every time he encounters them, without fail, more or less the same way people, without overthinking it . . . the way people walk around rather than under ladders, let's say, or avoid sidewalk cracks when they note sidewalk cracks are even there at all. But that does not mean he has to navigate through these bollards in the same way this particular afternoon. Does it?

On the other hand, if it's a habit, done for luck, one would have to say his luck wasn't running high, so what might befall him if he went around?

Wyatt touches the first bollard with his left palm, skirts to its right, tugs at the luggage/duffle behind with the other hand and pulls in with an elbow, resisting the centrifugal force his curving step makes as he rounds the galvanized pipe and prepares to pass the next (there are five) on its left whilst cupping its top with a right palm, having switched his hold on the resistant handle. These are sturdy, motionless, permanently installed, do not budge even given the full tugging weight of his moving body. (The less sturdy "temporary bollard" makes up an entire specialized genre of bollard-related architectural engineering, generally with some kind of removable bolt structure at its bottom, employed on pathways where bollards are useful for discouraging traffic, but where access might at some point be required. Like:

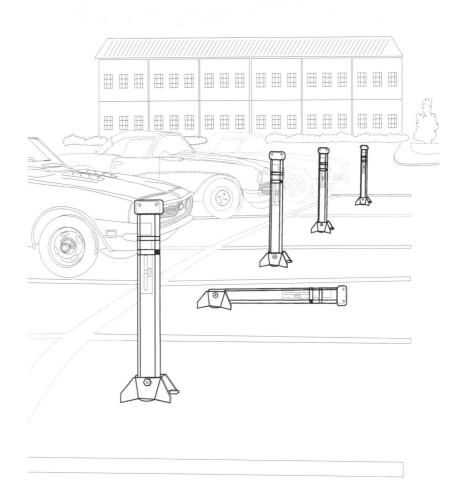

You're welcome.)

The thrumming of Wyatt's tinnitus—a sound he's carried with him across an ocean—increases in volume as he swings between these structures, as it often does in times of stress. Wyatt's glasses again slip down his nose, his hands too busy to adjust these as he manages the five bollards, first the touching and then pulling, then the pulling and touching, so he tips his chin, examines the next bollard's approach through the bottom of his lenses in a way that looks haughty, no doubt, to casual observers. Wyatt isn't old by most measures—forty-five—but they had been forty-five years spent sedentary and, let's face it, angry. Disappointed. Reading dense text for hours out of the day, squinting into computer screens, hunched over a 64 square playing surface deep in calculation, pondering tactical choices, engaged in strategic planning. Just forty-five years, and he was falling apart. Sad. The fourth bollard approaches—almost there!—but *Oh, no!* When already clearly past this fourth one it inexplicably snags a corner of his bag/pack, and "Sure as shit," he growls, the bollard yanks the twisted handle roughly from his hand. Wyatt stops, turns, retrieves the handle from the concrete sidewalk.

Not fair.

Because, come on, what does this mean? Must he go back to the *start*? Effect a complete *do-over*? Must he?

He knows. He knows what it means. Or: is it enough to merely back the luggage between the third and fourth pylon once again, make another, cleaner run at this next to last one, rather than plodding all the way several feet and . . . ? That would be good enough, surely. In fact, it wouldn't matter. It never matters! But as one voice tells him this is ridiculous to debate, another, in a clearly audible tone he can replay at any moment, snarls, "*I think you heard me.*" This voice always arrived in the guise of the notorious "Retro," a character in the animated film series his little boy, Wyn, had watched countless times (*Rocket Cadets*), so many times that Wyatt could recite long scenes of dialogue nearly by heart, though he hadn't been consciously listening to it the last few thousand times it played on the flat-screen in his living room. Wyn's favorite: it involved talking rockets and their race to Pluto to win the Planetary Cup—passing eventfully through every other major feature of the solar system in an astronomically improbable but no doubt educational-for-its-age-group fashion. Count on it being that cheating scoundrel "Retro" who resounded in his head when he felt a wrong move imminent.

"*I think you heard me.*"

Considering resounding head voices makes him also recall the humorless staff of over-reactors at the facility—called "Cypress Pines"—where he'd spent some eventful weeks after his undergrad days. He rattles the pills in his jacket pocket.

Wyatt decides he's doing enough. Fuck "Retro," who's the least reliable character in the whole *Rocket Cadets* franchise anyway. Wyatt is a visitor, and following the rules as best he can, so makes the quick backup maneuver, then proceeds, rounding the fifth bollard with relief.

He feels justified in leaning on the school's iron fence railings a moment. No one would have put such a large sign reading TOWER HILL SCHOOL ~ REBUILT 1890 on any structure they didn't want paused before and perused. Mainly he wants to collect his thoughts. Wyatt pants slightly, wipes his forehead. Running his fingers through his hair to, in some manner, groom it, he removes from the sparse follicles a thick black twig he'd picked up in his slide, clamber, and roll down the hill. He stares at the black twig. He considers the TOWER HILL SCHOOL ~ REBUILT 1890 and wonders why anyone would hang such a giant sign to indicate not when the school had been built but *re*-built.

Rested, he moves on.

7
The Island of Dilemmas and Quiz Nights

The homes on this route are new, jammed close, and appear to Wyatt to be of semi-detached design as judged by their bilateral symmetry. Cars fill the short driveways and spill onto curbs. In one window hangs a flag of Brazil. Something to do with soccer, no doubt, or maybe an actual Brazilian living in the outskirts of Sallowsfield. The professor had labored years with a pre-impression of the town that had been built, misconception by misconception, from decades of family oral history and mythology. None of it is borne out by the place's reality. He'd imagined a kind of hamlet, full of persons related to him. He'd fantasized, right up to getting off the train from Manchester, about entering a sea of racial recognition, each face looking like someone who could be family. Or better: looking like himself. His late father and one of his half-siblings had mentioned—no insisted—that any of the Sallow clan, were they to travel to this town across which he now limped—his hair tousled, his luggage wrecked—they would be "treated like a king." It had been a not unpleasant sensation to hold in his mind as he'd finally managed to buy the ticket, fly across the ocean, and (against Dr. Than's advice) make his visit. He'd done it because someone had suggested he go, years before. "See what you find. You keep talking about it. Don't research it, just go. Promise me you will."

That had been "X."

One of the offerings in *Water Take Me Down and Also Burn Me* (Wyatt's volume of verse published in stapled, chapbook form) titled ". . . To Sallowsfield!" had been an homage exactly to this nonexistent, chimerical town he had created whole cloth in his mind. The poems, written twenty years before he had ever left Texas let alone before he had set eyes on the place itself, infused everyday activities with the desire to escape, travel, voyage away to that point of nurturing, familial, original acceptance. That is: ". . . to Sallowsfield!" A character, known in the poem as "the exile," moved from scene to scene in a genre-crossing work that touched upon both the epic and the picaresque traditions. There is an unsuccessful fishing expedition ("nor hooked those bass the rippling shallows yield"); the accidental espying of, for some reason, a group of overweight women skinny-dipping in a pond ("their nakedness no hedge of mallows shield") . . . and so on. In other words, each ottava rima stanza ended in a multisyllabic couplet paired (somewhat) in a rhyme with the town's name, as in the stanza where "the exile" bests some youths from a neighboring street who invade his own lane by showering these miscreants in a hail of flying dirt clods ("And taking to their heels, those callows yield"). It was, perhaps, this singular poem's features that had most persuaded the judges for the Texas Tech Younger Poet Series to make their award in what must have otherwise constituted a slow year for poetry in the Panhandle. With its enjambment ("in avian reverence even swallows/ kneeled . . ."), synesthesia (lighted candles described as "beacons through the night whose tallows pealed"), imagery that had been shaped to match with rhyme-sound much as spinal columns are shaped through the use of chiropractic methodology (boys in a gym removing those fabric pieces used to dry after a shower: "and laughing from this sport, their towels peeled") . . .

...well, the book was perhaps awarded by the committee for its adventurous and comprehensive inclusiveness of poetic devices. No one went so far as to suggest that the school printed the chapbook ironically, no one except for that scathing anonymous critic who did suggest exactly that, and Wyatt regretted that the single review of his work, in the student-staffed Daily Toreador, had savaged its "rhyme so relentless, it's as if sound were a stalker, or a shark cutting towards a beach packed with weekend bathers."

At any rate, Wyatt became disabused of his longstanding yet unrealistic and somewhat vague impression of the town immediately upon entering the railway station and encountering there, first off, a Tandoori chicken stand. A trip to the local genealogical room at the borough library had taken this disabusement and disabused it further. The trip has now left him inconsistently shod, weed stained, foul-ditchwater-dipped, and limping in a residential district through which he drags his single-wheeled, bulging, zippered portmanteau by its twisted handle. But X is here. In this town. Shocking. After some purpose of her own, no doubt, that has to do with her own obsessions, and he thinks he might just know what those could be.

At one point another road interrupts the line of relentless home fronts, entering the main thoroughfare at a 45-degree angle. On the resulting triangular island or isthmus, a pub has been constructed, its architecture of vague mock Tudor pedigree with crossed brown timbers against white stucco. It, like the rest of the neighborhood, appears new, lacking even rings of damp glasses on the picnic tables out front. Wyatt steers to one of these, lowers himself onto the attached bench, rests a moment. A mural of The Queen decorates the space below a second-story latticed window frame—her skin so yellow she looks nicotine stained. "The Elizabeth Hotel," says the signboard, although it's definitely a bar, not a hotel, with another sign offering

Live Music
Pub Games
Quiz Nights
Pool

... and warning that vehicles and their contents parked in the small diagonal carpark do so at their owners' risk. Wyatt risks it for the moment. He considers a beer or ale would be a great comfort, but his head swims. He has pretty much established himself at a different bar, the Top and Tail annexed to the train station, and momentarily feels a sense of betrayal, yet from the door comes the unmistakable beery aroma he loves, along with its beckoning warmth and tobacco drenched staleness that had nearly disappeared from such places at home. Music (not live) plays from invisible speakers within. There are only a few cars in the lot, so he considers that while he looks flummoxed and even disrespectable, an establishment needing business might overlook this and his unmatched footwear, too. On the other hand, after a couple of drinks, could he even make it back into town? If he buys a glass of lager, or two, will he be too groggy to find his way across the map to his new hotel? He rattles the bottles in his side pocket again. His medicine? He'd skipped it that morning. Could he wash the pills down with an alcoholic beverage?

His morning dose of two, round, yellowish tablets warded off what his doctor—that moron—described vaguely as "tendencies," while the elongated pink one each evening worked more against the appearance of "predispositions"—predispositions Wyatt did not truly have faith he even possessed any more, but Dr. Than gave him such a hangdog look when he asked to titrate off of these substances he continued to fill the prescriptions and keep to the dosage schedule. "And if you stop taking them?" asked Dr. Than. "And if when you stop taking them you cannot sleep?"

Sleep. Yes.

Much more straightforward: the single 10-mg diazepam before bed ensured that before he could say *pam, pam, pam*, he'd go out like a light, sleeplessness being the most direct trigger, according to Dr. Than, of both the tendencies and the predispositions Wyatt felt he no longer had.

Though he did need to sleep.

And what about the suitcase/pack? Can't really cart that into a pub. Perhaps stashed over there next to the recycle bins? But were it to be lost? Or stolen?

The days and hours that he would carry the pack as opposed to when he could safely deposit it in a hotel room had been planned out on the eight-day itinerary outlined on the last page of his notebook. It had been based on research of check-in times of his already booked rooms, a strategy he'd crafted as carefully as any move over the board. Hussein's insistence on the premier quality of the hostel he'd stay in that evening had ruined all this foresight.

Should he stay, or should he limp towards town? Will they ask him to move if he doesn't purchase something? It's a kind of dilemma, which means Wyatt should have been at home with it, as his livelihood depends not so much on commerce as dilemmas. Such were the ethics of business, at least at the undergraduate level. For example: when operating in a third-world country, is it better to maintain a stance against corruption and lose market share, or go ahead and pay the culturally common bribes that allow for local hiring, steady commerce, improvement of working conditions, environmental and sanitary rehabilitation? Discuss. Wyatt himself had never worked for any kind of business other than Pizza Shack during high school, nor drawn a salary from anything but an academic institution—but solving the dilemmas was not the goal. The goal boiled down to getting students to produce essays. His present circumstance appears to call for a different approach.

Perhaps if he goes inside, a taxi could be called.

A white taxi pulls to the curb. Hussein opens the door of the low vehicle, climbs out, leans on the roof.

"I thought I'd find you here," he says.

Wyatt's chest grows tight. "Did you locate her?"

"A joke, Dr. Wyatt. I took a fare down New Leddy and saw you here."

"I've arrived in this place due to a series of unfortuitous accidents."

"You look it. I haven't seen her. Yet." The taxi driver walks before him, his sunglasses, as always, atop his head. Wyatt still isn't sure why anyone would ever need sunglasses in this continuously overcast region. "You look a little worn," Hussein says.

"I wish you'd been there to bring me back down."

"You walked? Down that road?"

"Sort of."

"I gave you my card!"

Wyatt removes the cellphone from his jacket. "Aren't there country codes or . . . something. I don't know."

Hussein sits beside him on the new picnic bench, leans forward, and takes up Wyatt's phone in his long fingers. He punches what seems an interminable string of numbers and his own mobile rings melodically in a falling xylophone tremble in his breast pocket.

"It does work," says Wyatt.

"You paid for international. Must have. Hey, you texted me the picture. It's the same system."

"Ah."

Now he knows. What a ridiculous oversite. A blunder. He needn't have taken that tumble down the hill at all. He'd missed one crucial detail out of the universe of details. That's all it took. That's all it ever took.

Hussein points a finger. "You know what? A lady."

"Anyone I know?"

"Doubtful. A lady. She left her baby in a car in a car park. It was Sainsbury's. She was just going to run in, so she left the baby, but she forgot and left the keys, too. That car was stolen, Dr. Wyatt."

"When was all this?"

"It wasn't found until days later, abandoned in a field. The baby was dead."

"Jesus Christ!"

"And covered in ants."

"Hussein! Please!"

"Ants. Crawling all over the baby when they found it." He looks sideways at Wyatt. "You know the point of this story?"

Wyatt thinks he does. He hates dead thing stories. "Call a taxi?"

"Call a taxi."

Hussein returns the phone to Wyatt's breast pocket, rises, takes up the suitcase/pack, hesitant to touch the mangled handle so grabbing it, finally, at a webbed handgrip on the body of the luggage/bag itself. "Absent-minded professor. Your room must be ready."

Wyatt uses his arms again to push his battered frame from the bench. He's a little sorry he has to leave the rich atmosphere pouring from the airlock of the Elizabeth Hotel. "You haven't seen her, but what did you do with the picture?"

"I've enlisted the help of friends."

Wyatt isn't sure he likes the sound of that.

Before he bends his body into the back of Hussein's taxi, he glances above the odd roof of the round house and looks one last time at Tower Hill.

1
The Direction of the Game

His airplane mechanic father passed away in bed at home of heart disease on a sad Friday the 13th when young Wyatt was himself thirteen years old. A superstitious person, he does not worry when that confluence of weekday and date arrives on the calendar, reasoning—apropos of a superstitious person—that his father's demise soaked up all possible ill-luck a son could accrue in a lifetime of Friday the 13ths.

To be expected, as an only child, Wyatt spent the rest of a bookish adolescence taking up an enormous percentage of his mother's attention. An English major as a baccalaureate, he subsequently overcame this achievement through the five-week stay in the modestly grim mental institution ("Cypress Pines"), and by the new millennium—finished with his MBA and landed on the tenure track at tiny Taylor State—he had turned to the "bridebasket of Europe" to seek a partner. He'd had enough of American women, and doubted he'd find a suitable one anywhere on the continent anyway. Wyatt had tried. He'd dated an American woman, after all, or at least gone on a date with one. It had been a one-time tryst (of a sort) with another English major during his BA years, a girl who believed that evolution, if not an all-out hoax, certainly got more credit than it deserved. This date had consisted of his going to her home, accompanying her on a walk that encompassed her block and one adjacent street, then returning to her door, the young lady talking Jesus the whole circular trip. Chastened by this experience as to how love worked in his own culture (i.e., as a frustrating runaround cloaked in facile spirituality)—the "traditional foundations" and "family values" that online websites promoted for the women of Eastern Europe and the Ukraine sounded comforting and ideal. In fact, during those early, heady days of Ukrainian matchmaking, the agency he chose (Dnipro Girl) was still only partly a criminal enterprise, and Wyatt settled on the last woman he met in the organization's office near Independence Square in Kyiv, a tall and angular girl he came to think of as "Z." She received this designation because while he hadn't gone through the entire alphabet of possible matches on his trip, by the time it was over he felt he had. "Z" was the only Ukrainian spousal candidate who'd brought him any presents (a t-shirt that featured the iconic American recreational trailer, the Airstream, and also a small stuffed unicorn). "You are rare," she told him. "Like this mythical beast."

In the United States, Z had quickly (too quickly?) given birth to a son who Wyatt loved unconditionally no matter his parentage, but congenital myotonic dystrophy plagued the little boy who did not live past the age of eight, nor did the marriage last beyond the final hymn in young Wyn's memorial service. Professor Sallow never again saw his gangly bride with the prominent nose, this despite the fact she said, "It's not that I want him removed . . . like a tumor."

Or so she is reported to have said.

Z, Wyatt is certain, loved little Wyn very much as well. She had kept a three-ring binder on all aspects of his condition. It had, over time, grown thicker and thicker with records of hospital visits, pharmaceutical records, the years-long battle with the boy's eczema. But she appeared to have no use for Wyatt, now. Which was fine. Fine.

Fuck Z.

Our man Wyatt, now a bitter, hoary, forty-five, holds the opinion that he could, whenever he wanted, backtrack, retrace his steps, start over entirely, life being, for him, a series of . . . well, bollard-like obstacles: a route that could be run again. This faith had no doubt been underscored by the harsh reality of, in his chosen sport, the impossibility of going back: the one act that could not be performed. Every piece, once touched, had to be engaged. Each engagement, once made, had to be accepted. Pawns quite literally could move only in one direction, but an even more profound expression of the arc of time had been woven throughout the foundations of the game. Upon a win, a loss, or draw, one could go to the next opponent, even face the same opponent again, or—since the advent of affordable software such as OtterShark—face the same *something* again, but going back, backtracking inside the same game, no. No takee-backees.

The game was not life. Despite its oft-recurring sadnesses, ironically enough, life could be bent to the will much more easily. One miscalculation, or inaccuracy, a single—worst of all—blunder could not determine the outcome of an entire existence. Could it? No. There were second chances. There were third, even fourth acts. Wyatt could yet, for example, he firmly believed, if he had the opportunity, achieve the level of grandmaster if he decided to try. (No, he couldn't.) He could be a successful Dean of the Applied Business Department of his college. Zepeda was making a hash of it. (Demonstrably true. But people liked Zepeda.) Or, as stated, he could, by applying himself develop into a successful poet (Hah!). Or so he believed. To make a start at this latter project he'd brought the stack of chapbooks.

He would drop by the university during his visit. Wyatt could think of nothing better than to spend a summer conducting writing workshops in a place that shared his name. He imagined already the exoticism his students would conjure for him. He would be, like the unicorn plush toy he had wrapped in a plastic bag and tossed into a dumpster one rainy April afternoon along with many of the other books and possessions he associated with his marriage . . . he would, that is, no doubt present to students in this country as a true "mythical beast." Why, the jokes he could tell. ("When they said they'd name the school after me . . .") As for a strategy to make it happen, he had none. The lack of design to his journey had come about by design. It had been, in fact, suggested by X. "Don't research, just go," she'd said. "See what you find." She'd said it nearly five years before he stepped off the train and saw his name imprinted against the blue national railroad hue on the rectangular station sign. Of course, it wasn't his name, exactly, but as happens to many who spend years with a terminally ill child, Wyatt had learned to slip easily into whole matrices of subtle denial. But the point was, the game was not life. One could go back. One could.

2
For Those Who Need Their Chronologies Chronological

For instance: let's go back to his arrival in the region the previous Monday, the train ride from Manchester.

A low-ceilinged overcast darkened the hooded ridges and spine hills in the distance as an impossibly green landscape moved past the rail car windows. Seeing this for the first time shocked him. For some reason, Wyatt had not anticipated all the green. This, perhaps, gives some notion of just how little research went into his trip.

Clearings between the trees showed close-cropped, heaving hillsides. He had not expected it to be hilly, either. Some were gently rounded hills, others fat like bursting barrels. There were unevenly shaped bare mounds scarred like scraped knees. As the train raced the countryside, more distant, more majestic rises appeared, bald as burial cairns, some topped by lone, finger-thin towers. He understood that Sallowsfield—the name of which he heard announced aloud for the first time over the train's square black loudspeaker during a clear and lilting female intonation of stations that approached—featured its own hillside tower. He wondered if he'd notice it from the window when he arrived.

He would not.

Forested islands of green swept past separated by carpet-like sward. To live within these rises and folds must give a feeling like ... Wyatt pondered it, his notebook open, his giant pack wedged in the seat beside him. He planned on writing some poems during his stay. The part of East Texas where he'd spent the last nineteen years without a vacation had few majestic vistas. In fact, it had none. His home contained no overlooks framed by hills or rolling plains, only enclosed, claustrophobic regions of pine walls and heat, the sky glimpsed as a rare novelty between branches, voyeur fashion. He noticed this most profoundly returning for a conference one year to the open spaces of his alma mater, the locus of his poetic distinction: Lubbock, Texas. Though he had not taken a vacation in a dozen years, Wyatt did not feel the loss for he had traveled on several faculty excursions, plus the journeys necessary for dealing with legal matters pertaining to his wife. He'd also attended business education conferences across the United States: so many that their logoed book bags hung from his office doorknob to the point that only the addition of another office doorknob could accommodate more. But in Lubbock, the flat dish of the horizon surrounded the viewer who stood at any open vantage place—a vacant lot or soccer field—and a scream-blue sprawl washed into every corner of the overhead vault. On his present trip, the rushing train skirted the realms of the claustrophobic and agoraphobic in a comforting balance. He watched the landscape slash past the window with his chin crooked in his hand. Yes. East Texas had smothered the poetic urge in him. He would resuscitate it here.

The wheels of the train carriage thrummed below him, and he heard the voice of Kitty Canaveral, the love interest of heroic Bobby Booster in *The Rocket Cadets*: "Why, you have more talent in one chamber nozzle extension bar than a lot of rockets have in their whole multi-stage body tubes."

He heard the voice of Wyn repeat: "Tooobs."

In the seat in front of him, a man drank juice from a can. Across the aisle, a kid with rolled-up shirtsleeves read *Northanger Abbey* through a screen of blond hair. Two South Asian guys chatted behind him. He glanced at them quickly once he had a line on their conversation. They appeared to be—wonder of wonders—academics who taught business. Wyatt raised his bushy eyebrows. One of them announced himself "tired of this post-doc contingency thing," while the other denounced "Reader Rubbish" for hogging all the positions. Although he wanted to join in, as "Tenure Trash" himself, avoidance made more sense. Their discussion moved from "buoyancy unions with tiers and standards," to "commodities markets with dynamic pricing." The terminology caused him to conclude they were not only academics complaining about part-time appointments, but also engaged themselves in business of some kind. Wyatt overheard them contemplate "the cost in euros of a kilo of potatoes in Austria."

He believed firmly that working in business destroyed the objectivity required for teaching business, just as dancers in ballet companies made terrible ballet critics. He had become a fan of objectivity in group therapy sessions at "Cypress Pines." There he had worked hard to pretend to withdraw into himself while others sniped at each other and at the therapist/facilitator, airing grievances over everything from the lunch served at the facility, to the channel played on the television bracketed high on the wall, to fierce arguments, apropos of nothing, concerning the marriages of Ava Gardner. The chaos of the facility convinced him of the merits of paying attention to all relevant details but doing so through a method that favored distanced examination over personalized participation. A kind of feigned apathy: that was the ticket. Or at least he attempted this. At times Wyatt, true, could not resist adding to the commotion himself. ("She never *married* Bogart, just starred with him in *Night of the Iguana* while with Sinatra, and . . .")

This seldom proved helpful.

During his interview with Dean Zepeda at Taylor State, Wyatt had expressed in nearly passionate terms what he considered his somewhat unique faith that professors in the College of Business should avoid any position in any enterprise that "engaged in transaction-seeking or transaction-execution for the purpose of creating profit," the definition of business in his book. Better to say this was the definition in the book he had taught from for the past nineteen years, a title so familiar to him that he had at some point forgotten half of it, namely everything after the colon. He did keep track of editions to avoid confusion on his syllabi. Wyatt now tended to think of the textbook as *Business Ethics: Important Sounding Subtitle*, 10th Edition.

Wyatt Sallow's one experience with work—still prominent on his CV—had been in high school: a cook and delivery driver for a Pizza Shack restaurant near his home. There he'd come under the leadership hand of Assistant Manager Tod Guidry. Assistant Manager Tod Guidry had been a certifiable asshole. Studying business was fine. Taking part in it could be a chore.

Another reason he did not join in the conversation occurring in the seat behind him: Wyatt could not knock tenure. His academic position had kept a roof over his family and provided the insurance that covered otherwise staggering medical charges. His wife wanted to finish her American licensing and take up her career as a dental hygienist, but Wyn's illness kept her at home. Wyatt at times weighed the balance of whether the life-saving income from Taylor State made up for the federal and state aid it disqualified Wyn for, but, in general, he'd lived in terror of anything that would threaten this salary and health coverage. Without his appointment, he could not have kept his little group together. No. Not even to the limited extent he had.

Even after everything had changed, he didn't want to think about that horrifying possibility.

At a stop in a sizeable station that signboards labeled "Manchester Piccadilly," several passengers boarded. At the last moment a couple came into the carriage who Wyatt noticed not because of their outrageous dress, but more just their attitude. They sat across the aisle and a few rows away, facing him because of the arrangement of the seats, and exchanged no words with each other. To Wyatt they gave an unmistakable appearance of being locked in mutual animosity. The man was tall, had a black vest over his Hawaiian shirt, wore a pork pie hat and dangling earring. One tightly rolled sleeve revealed a barbed wire arm-band tattoo. His partner, a pale brunette in a white blouse, clutched at a gift bag from some shop, scowled in a creased line downwards across one side of her face with an expression that spoke of broken promises, the kind it had been stupid for the man in the pork pie hat to have made in the first place. Wyatt felt certain they were partners, though he'd never seen them before. He slipped into what used to be a common exercise for him, although it had been set aside for years: constructing a narrative matrix for the "characters" he encountered, like these, and forming an instant crystalline story synthesized from lies and associations originating in his own head. He couldn't remember when he'd last tried it. But . . .

"I am the man in the pork pie hat," Wyatt said to himself. The man seemed the kind of intriguing guy Wyatt always wished he could get to know, someone with poise and presence like a creative artist or musician. (The sort X so obviously favored.) He attempted to picture whole the disappointments delivered on this partnership. Resentment over her family's attempts to borrow money, perhaps. Or: dental hygienist career not going as promised. Anger that he couldn't comprehend the vital importance of her needs (including many she hadn't told him about). That profound betrayal of her refusing to stay the person who had climbed down from the chair, steadied her hands on his shoulders while he held her hips, kissed him firmly in a surprise move one Spring Break.

The woman looked out the window without joy and the man in the pork pie hat glanced for a moment around the car, then zeroed in on Professor Sallow, his eyes narrow, as if disbelieving anyone wore tweed anymore, or as if desperate to signal in some way. "Did my best. Not enough." Or was it more like a question? "How did I survive a battle across a grid of chaos only to find myself on this train? *Looking at you?*"

Wyatt turned, realized he had not fabricated a narrative matrix at all—not even close. He'd just been caught rudely staring. "I am *not* the man in the pork pie hat," he mumbled, "and fuck him anyway," then returned to flipping the pages of his guidebook.

After three-quarters of an hour, the train steered into and then out of a dark tunnel before executing a sweeping right arc that Wyatt figured would lead to other sweeping curves, occasional tunnels, paths through the shocking green landscape, but the trajectory continued in its same fashion a few seconds only, then the carriage slowed, and the clear and lilting female intonation of "Sallowsfield" came from the square black speaker. He admired the stately red-brick train station that appeared on the right, but as all movement halted, he noted its high arched windows had been covered with plyboard so that, no, maybe that wasn't the station. A low-slung affair with a sheet metal arched canopy over a disembarking area stood along the other side of the tracks. The brick edifice, he learned later, was a common and recurring architectural element of the town: an abandoned textile mill.

Leaving the car, he lugged his pack down fifteen steps (had they heard of disabled access here?) and through a damp, puddled passageway under the rails. A young man with more earrings than Wyatt had ever seen, wire loops clustered along both the lobe and wing of the right ear, passed him going the same direction. He hadn't expected to see that sort of ear in Sallowsfield. A breeze moved in this tunnel lined with tile that featured framed posters advertising a concert and a Medieval fair. They hold concerts here, Wyatt thought. Medieval fairs. He rose again, clomping the pack against fifteen concrete steps back to platform level, approached the station lobby, watched a crowd bustle behind glass windows. He paused, uncertain, before crossing the threshold, past the Tandoori chicken stand, then came up short among a gaggle of uniformed train personnel standing before a troubling bank of turnstiles. He didn't see any other way to go. Unsure, Wyatt remained in the doorway of a snack shop momentarily, its shelves ransacked like there'd been an approaching hurricane he hadn't heard about. He examined a few bottles of water and the sparse offering of magazines and newspapers he wouldn't mind purchasing—any glance through the doorway of his office at Taylor State would attest to his love of printed paper products—except for the displayed prices he couldn't figure out. The currency in Ukraine had given him trouble, too, years before—the *hryvnia* and *kopiykas*. Something about the empty, echoing atrium opening to his left, also with puddles on the floor, likewise reminded him of Kyiv and its multiple transitional zones—colorless places that seemed firmly in between other places rather than possessing free-standing identities of their own. Here the walls displayed photographs of the arched station and its overhead awnings, some in color; other pictures captured the impact of the metal and fiberglass much more effectively in black and white. On an opposite wall, a nearly bare bookshelf held a folded card: "Leave what you've got, take what you'd like to read." Wyatt made a mental note to deposit a copy of *Water Take Me Down and Also Burn Me* on his return departure.

One copy.

Finally, he asked, and a uniformed official explained, without rancor—as if the train service had set him there to deal with just such lost souls—that he needed to feed his ticket into the turnstile to exit the platform.

His hand went to his breast pocket. "I was going to save it."

"It won't work again." The official grinned.

"It has my name on it."

The man wrinkled his forehead. Another, younger, similarly dressed railroad employee drifted over from a few paces away.

"As in, my name is Sallow."

"That's a name?" The official appeared perplexed.

"Never heard it," said the second, younger man. "Not around here." He had a Russian lilt to his speech.

Wyatt wondered if he'd imagined the accent and if he'd have to dig his passport from his carefully concealed and boxer brief-covered money belt to offer proof of identity.

"If you lost the ticket somewhere in transit," the first man said as if reading from a policy manual, "we can let you through that last barrier." He winked. "It does happen that they are lost sometimes."

Wyatt removed the ticket from his breast pocket. "It's right here."

"Ah."

He felt uncertain. "It's just. You know. Like a keepsake."

The first man examined the printed information on the ticket. "I see that you do have it, yes."

"There are t-shirts," said the second, younger man, indicating a high-ceilinged lobby beyond the turnstile. "Cups."

Wyatt grew at that moment childishly thrilled. Of course, there were cups. He had one in his office—a winter scene in Sallowsfield he'd found on the internet. This very station might serve as font and source of all the town's promotional glassware. He had not considered at all the possibility of a gift shop. Perhaps he could purchase a shirt emblazoned with his own name. Y would be impressed.

In addition to having an "X" and a "Z," Sallow had a "Y."

"A Sallowsfield t-shirt," he said. "Alright. I'll put this in the turnstile, then."

"In the slot," said the first man.

"Then to the shop, on your right," said the second. He tipped back his official-looking hat.

Wyatt, unable to figure out the method of it even after agreeing to give up his keepsake, ended by handing the ticket to the younger official who looked at his coworker, shrugged, and slid it into a not terribly obvious slot in the turnstile.

"But . . . not a Sallowsfield one," said the older man.

"Never seen that t-shirt," said the younger. "Not around here."

"Station Cat t-shirt. They have those."

Wyatt felt caught, wanting to move through the open gate, yet somehow tricked if there wasn't going to be a shirt.

"Gary," said the first official, who leaned to clamp a hand on the gate, keeping it from closing so Wyatt could exit, "has shirts."

"He's not here today," said the younger man. "But he's not dead."

"Still alive," added the other. "His day off."

"He's fine. People don't see Gary for a few days," the other man added, "and they start to ask."

Wyatt stepped through. "Gary the Sallowsfield Station Cat?"

The older official got a far-away look as if he could just make out the shirt for sale from there, although the shop remained hidden around a far corner. "I believe it just says 'Gary.'"

"He's fine," said the younger one. "Best not to start rumors."

A corner table in the station proper groaned under the weight of pamphlets and handouts about what to see in the region, although a thorough scan of these indicated no publication that concerned the town specifically. He did find a glossy three-fold concerning Gary, a black and white and very furry feline wearing headgear much like that of the two men at the turnstile. Possibly it would have made sense to have done at least a little research before arriving. He could see no cups in the gift area, nor t-shirts save Gary's.

Able to put it off no longer, he prepared to leave the station. Wyatt took a breath, dilating his nostrils. He probed with his hand for important weights on his person. Wallet. Heavy ring of keys (which he had absolutely no reason to carry across the Atlantic). Heavy rectangular phone in the inside jacket breast pocket. In the side pocket, his pills. Twirl the sterling silver wedding band. Journal notebook in hand, ready to record any impressions at a moment's notice. Satisfied, he pulled his Sisyphus/Granite luggage/pack behind him, moved towards some astonishingly tall doors—taller than any twelve-foot-tall person would need as far as head clearance went—and clenched his hand around the large brass handle.

3
Paul

Far from spending his days worrying over commodities trading or the price of potatoes, Wyatt occupied much of his waking time with concerns about the collegiate team he coached and instructed, attempting to ingrain in his charges deeply the basic principles of tactics and strategy so that they—the tactics especially—found a home in the group's subconscious. The trick was to lodge these at such a depth that when examining a position on the board, ideas about moves, plans—*what to do next*—appeared even if the students lacked any strong foundational sense of from where those ideas originated. His approach, he knew, flew in the face of more programmatic "menu item" considerations such as candidate moves, checking the *role* of pieces before and, then, after a proposed action, memorized opening repertoires, and so on. Wyatt himself when he played—or when he *had*—calculated profoundly as he sought a path across the field of squares, the way often unclear, the 8×8 landscape at times an apparent jumble. To compete in this sense became more a cultivation of personal qualities than an application of knowledge. Winners had certain things in common, he knew, qualities that he cultivated in others and himself, although he had little evidence that the cultivation had taken hold. OtterShark, the chess computer software he used, often indicated it had not. Still, attitude mattered. He insisted to all who would listen that he was not an advisor to a club, but a coach to a team. The 8th ranked collegiate chess team in East Texas.

Recently he had returned to beginnings, to the recorded games of the seventeenth-century player "Greco." Wyatt found himself enchanted by their perfect beauty. That is until a friend pointed out Greco played only white, that many of his opponents' moves were illogical, and that perhaps "Greco"—with such a literally one-sided mastery—had not truly existed at all beyond a sort of pedagogical demonstration of tactical possibilities. This caused him to feel again a revulsion towards the game that took hold from time to time, nearly as strong as its obsessive pull. This same friend, however, had told him about the five-hundred-dollar flights to Manchester from Houston that summer (the two metropolitan areas linked by petroleum interests), and a quick trip to the internet indicated only a short train ride could take him from there to the town he'd heard about his entire life, and that his life's great love had told him to visit. Those words of hers. "Just go. Promise."

Would there ever again be such a reasonably priced offer? That coincided with his summer break? That—if he were careful—the accumulated funds in his savings account would *just* cover?

So he had come.

Wyatt pulled the massive exit door towards himself by its bronze handle (heavy!) and peeked out onto a scene that revealed not so much revelation and recognition as it recalled the doubts he often encountered at the board. Then those doubts intensified. What registered at first was a random situation, one that presented no clue as to how to proceed.

The confusing tableau unfolded below him, as to exit the station meant walking onto a large, pillared porch platform situated at a surprising height over the town's central square, a broad stretch of pavement that seemed sunk into the earth like an amphitheater. Wyatt leaned against a vertically ribbed column and paused before considering the steep concrete stairs. He didn't see a handrail. He wasn't fond of descending steep stairs without handrails. His medication, he knew, and its vertiginous side effects exacerbated this distaste. Overhead a banner had been fastened across the columns. It fluttered and waved like the sail on a cutter, although he couldn't read it from below. His town had banners. Out on the square itself, he had not expected the pavement to squirt jets of water. Spigots or valves in rows had been inserted into the flagstones, and children ran and splashed, though it was fifty degrees, chilly for a Texan. (His town had water jets in its paving stones.) The children might have considered it chilly as well, as most splashed in jackets and leggings. Ovals of dampness stained the rectangular slabs that paved the square, and water in occasional puddles whipped and frothed. Wyatt checked his phone, its digital map. He couldn't get straight in which direction to set out to find his lodging: the Town Central Hotel. He didn't know if the line of white taxis to his right was the answer, either. If this hotel were close, he could walk, and he'd had unpleasant surprises in taxis in unfamiliar places before, mainly the surprise of their unpleasantly high cost. Nearly criminal.

From the elevated stage of the porch, he had a three-quarter view of the Henry Scott statue, the actor imagined in the role he had made famous, the android, Matrix, on the long-running *Off to the Planets* series. People milled in all directions around it, the figure gesturing towards its own bow tie (the character's favored communication device) like a bronzed, ignored mime. A muscular, lightly red-bearded man stepped across the base of the station steps, strode in unlaced boots directly in front of Wyatt, picked at his teeth with one of those plastic prods that held a tiny length of floss in a u-shaped crook. He made good progress with it before tossing it to the pavement trailing a damp string of tooth gorb. Wyatt paused, lifted his notebook across his left forearm, removed his ballpoint from his jacket pocket.

Tooth gorb in my town.

Another man in a zippered jacket with racing insignia had a flying top—colored red on one side, white on the other—that he spun along a cord between two sticks, then tossed in the breeze. Wyatt couldn't tell if this was a vendor, a street performer, or if the man had simply sought an empty space to play with the toy. He seemed to be telling an onlooking couple about the device, both of them holding their hands out to wave him away. The top sprang high, hovered momentarily before drifting back to where the still talking man caught it once again on his cord. Around Wyatt, the yawning square contrasted with the close buildings and narrow streets that surrounded it. Rough-bricked Victorian structures spread from the square down corridors that seemed a labyrinth or warren. He prepared to scribble out his impressions of the square from his high perch, and as his pen hesitated over the mostly blank white pages, he grinned to himself.

An entertainment venue attached to the station cranked up loudly in the late afternoon, and Wyatt could detect the signature seedy club sound of over-driven music through bad speakers. Well-dressed women headed toward that space having been poured into their outfits (occasionally over spilling them) in ways that shouldn't have been sexy yet were. Out for a night, they tottered across the pave on high heels in a way that expressed swagger, not imbalance. Wyatt gripped the handle of his luggage. He put away his pen but hefted his notebook, felt its weight. He wiped at his mouth with two fingers.

Amid this assortment, dancing spumes from the valves choreographed themselves in random bursts. Wyatt had since childhood, whenever he imagined the mythological square, pictured a green common, thatched roofs, perhaps a hilltop manse for the Lord's residence (Lord Sallow). He sensed the strong unreality of the real town. Like sex the first time: not a bad experience, but not the one expected.

All this was aurally overshadowed by a band on the far side of the plaza where tents and booths had been aligned along a thoroughfare. A saxophone wailed from that direction, separating itself by a few octaves from the other instruments under a central yellow tent. They played an unfamiliar tune with a driving, climbing bass line. He'd have to check that out. He began to feel surer of himself.

The man with the dental device reappeared, stopped, as if interrupted by a realization, then rose up the station steps. He paused near Wyatt, who for some reason felt—as he often did when strangers approached him in a public setting—that he was about to lose money. The man offered his hand immediately and silently, which the professor—unsure of what else to do—shook.

"Paul McBride," he said. He stood stiffly as if at attention, bending forward slightly. The man's palm was calloused and dry.

"Wyatt Sallow." He waited for the name to sink in. "Like the town."

Paul McBride didn't comment on this. He leaned in more as if to share confidential information. "The new style," he said quietly. "I don't have it."

"Oh well. It's . . . that is, my family is . . ."

Paul withdrew something from his windbreaker pocket, his elbow crooked. If he'd been in Houston, Wyatt might have flinched. In Turner, for that matter. Here he couldn't imagine trouble. But if the town could contain flying top hobbies, entertainment venues, and personal dental hygiene devices, it could contain trouble, too, and of a kind Wyatt might not recognize until too late. Paul, however, pulled out a flip phone, the kind Wyatt's students had made fun of recently. *"Dr. Sallow, you're so 2014."*

He had laughed, good-naturedly. He had not reminded them he was not a doctor.

"Not like yours." Paul indicated Wyatt's newer model that he still had open to its map function. "How old do you think I am?" Paul asked. "Guess."

Ruddy complexioned with short red hair, Paul didn't look like a gypsy, but Wyatt wanted to avoid guessing games. They so easily sidetracked into betting games. He could have said, "I don't think so," and walked away. Even stalked away. Rude, but when would he ever see Paul McBride again?

On the other hand, it was a pretty small town, and he'd be here eight days.

"I don't think so." He grabbed the telescoping handle of his duffle/pack.

"How old?" Paul insisted. Insisted so sincerely, it seemed for a moment that maybe he didn't know his age and needed advising.

"I'm terrible at ages." Wyatt did know it generally made sense to low-ball. "Twenty-one?"

"I'm twenty-eight!"

"Ah." The man looked fifty, easily. Maybe he "slept out." His boots alone looked twenty-eight years old. Wyatt shrugged. "How old am I?" he asked in return.

Foolish.

Paul did not hesitate, as if reading from a card. "Forty-five."

"That's . . . How did you . . . ?"

"You look like me dad. What's your job, Wyatt?"

He toyed with the various answers he gave when asked this question. "I'm in education," was good. "College professor" was a safe bet, offering up a kind of respectability in most contexts. "Coach" would depend—mainly on how many questions he wanted to follow up with. *What sport? What team?* It could lead only to long discussions and occasional arguments. There were answers suitable for airplanes—which he generally only rode when going to conferences. Other responses worked better in bars. He enjoyed bars but rarely made it to them these days.

A good answer for someone who appeared to be a homeless person in front of a train station escaped Wyatt for the moment. He couldn't encounter such people without thinking of his little boy. A whiff of some nearby trash bin's organically charged contents brought a wave of nausea.

Momentary, but enough that he bent, rested his hands on his meaty knees. Fuck. He groaned.

"I'm a poet," he tried.

"College professor! Good one. Visiting uni?" Paul appeared to take no note of his distress.

"You . . . that's . . ." So many hours on the plane. So much travel. "I'm doing something over at the university, yes."

"I want to go," said Paul. "I will. Someday. Make something of meself."

Bent over, Wyatt nodded. "You should. Can. You will, Paul."

"Look like you're afraid."

Wyatt had difficulty keeping up. "You're fine. You're fine, Paul. I'm just new here. Maybe you can tell by my . . ."

"Not afraid of *me*." Paul snorted. Nodded toward the square. "Got t'station but can't go down t'steps." He leaned closer. "See it from time to time, *as they say*."

The man's intonation was so strange. "I . . ."

"Spot a man for a lager?"

"Pardon?"

"Change on you, Wyatt?" Paul Kelly held a large can Wyatt hadn't noticed before. It was certainly of noticeable size. Paul rattled the minimal liquid in the bottom of the can.

He did have some change in his pocket—had exchanged dollars at a kiosk in the airport—but retained some confusion concerning exactly how much money the coins represented. "I don't have anything on me at this time."

Paul raised a finger. "*At this time*, Wyatt, is the only time you *could* have it." He looked very serious.

Something about the guy. He was so threatening initially, striding across the square with his boots, dirty teeth, . . . beer can as it had turned out. Wyatt reached into the change pocket of his trousers, pulled out some round coins. "Not sure . . ."

"Hah. This is a lot, Wyatt." Paul flipped the coins in his cupped palm, nodded down the steps again, towards the square. "Take a look." He leaned in close. "You should . . ." He held up two air quotes, one still attached to the empty can. "Go."

"What?"

Paul turned. He cut diagonally downwards across the steps and to the right, towards the Top and Tail, a pub at the end of the station opposite the music venue. Paul fingered the money. Wyatt had given him ten pounds. Two five-pound coins. "Good on Wyatt," Paul thought, grateful, though he didn't look back at the man. When he'd said *At this time* was the only time Wyatt could have given him ten pounds, he'd meant it. Paul often told people, including those he cornered in front of the station, about time. He stopped halfway down the tall steps. "Dr. Wyatt!" He looked straight at the pub, though addressing the visitor with the oversized case over his left shoulder.

"Yes?"

Paul surveyed the square. "A stitch in time," he said.

"Yes?"

"Is stupid." Then Paul swung into the Top and Tail.

4
"Be not conformed to this world."
–Different Paul

When his stomach settled some, Wyatt moved away from the fetid trash can and carefully negotiated the non-hand-railed steps. The pack/bag/ suitcase hindered mobility. He could explore the richness of the town but needed to secure this burden first, so he aimed initially at the arc of white taxicabs. Maybe he could walk to the Town Central Hotel, but if he didn't know where it was, proximity didn't help. He steered around puddles and the misty squirts of water that caught in the breeze and sprayed his face, his nausea draining away completely in the invigorating coolness. He nearly shivered. Wyatt made his way to the front of the taxi line, where a man in a turban stood with one leg on the rear bumper of the first car. "Town Central?" Wyatt asked.

The man made a shape with his lips as if whistling, but no whistle came. "This is a town. You are at the center of it."

"A hotel? With that name?"

"A short walk," he said.

"I have this . . ."

"Not worth it," the driver said. "Not worth it for my nephew." He raised his head, indicated the next taxi in line with his white-bearded chin. There, a younger man, dark-skinned but turban-less, raised his fingers from the steering wheel in greeting. A pair of sunglasses on top of his thick head of hair reflected the skylight of the open square.

That seemed to foreclose Wyatt's inquiring at the next cab. "I don't know where it is, though, so . . ."

The man indicated with an open palm, as if offering a snack, the tents and the raucous music at the edge of the pavement, spun on a heel, and walked to the other side of the cab.

Wyatt tugged at his luggage/pack self-consciously. Was the hotel on the plaza? Or several blocks in that direction? "I don't guess you have a brother-in-law in the next taxi who might . . ."

The man, without looking at Wyatt, shot his arm again in the direction of the street fair.

As he had not, on Monday, yet taken it cross-country through rough terrain, Wyatt's pack glided over flagstones in a satisfying way, its thickly treaded wheels emitting a not too attention-grabbing *thrum thrum* (pause) *thrum thrum* (pause) over the concrete. He aimed in the direction the cab driver indicated, passed a brunette girl with long hair and ragged flared jeans who walked with hands in her pockets. A guitar fretboard rose from the unzipped top of her backpack. Henry Scott appeared to turn his profile slowly, a more direct gaze as Wyatt walked past the bronze. Sure enough, the statue's eyes showed no pupils, giving it a believable resemblance to the character Scott played in *Off to the Planets*. Wyatt assumed the actual actor needed contact lenses or special effects to achieve that look.

The statue was generally ignored by passers by, save a middle-aged man who stood in an orange vest of the sort road workers sported, a duffle bag at his feet. The man gazed into the blank pupils in a restive fashion, as if attempting communication. Wyatt felt there was something else about

Henry Scott he should know or had forgotten. Something besides the TV show. What was that? He really had been foolish to travel all this way after so little research, but he let it pass and continued towards the tents the taxi driver had indicated.

At the street fair, banners displayed messages urging bystanders to IGNORE HATE, CHANGE THE WORLD, and, more mysteriously, KEEP CALM AND HAVE A BALLOON ANIMAL. A houndish dog lay with its head on crossed paws under a blue cloth-tented table beside pictures of other dogs, each AVAILABLE FOR ADOPTION. A lot of the signage had been safety pinned to overhead cords and fluttered, unreadable, in the cool air. A bubble machine had been set up and emitted large floating globules like those that usually come from blowing the liquid in a bottle through rings. A stream of these spheres floated over the entire festive scene, and Wyatt closed his eyes to their transformative gyrations in the air as they attempted to become rainbow hued.

He maintained an uneasy relationship with bubble machines.

"What brings you?" A tall youth with close-cropped hair holding leaflets in his fist stood before Wyatt.

"Just arrived." Wyatt tried.

"I feel the same!" This young man had to shout above the sound of the group with the soaring saxophone. He glanced at Wyatt's luggage. "Why in town? Where from?"

Wyatt, with some trepidation, attempted to explain. In the shortest possible version he could craft, he gave his name. Something of the family stories. Roots. A friend, a very good friend, had suggested he fly over to see . . .

The tall youth nodded. "I'm Raymond. Just Ray." He shuffled his leaflets, spread them like a hand of cards. "Sallow. Never heard that name." He shook his head. "Not around here. Kevin! This is Wyatt, Kevin. He's from Texas."

"Texas!" Kevin, bearded and wearing shorts despite the chill, hauled a hand cart stacked with water bottles. Leaning back to counter its weight, he settled it on the pavement to give Wyatt his full attention.

"From Texas to Sallowsfield. Today!" said Raymond.

"And doesn't know anyone here!" Kevin said.

"Doesn't know a soul," said Ray.

While true, Wyatt wasn't sure why they'd made that assumption. He began to feel once again he was going to lose money.

"How wild is it you're here?" Kevin had a voice that boomed from behind his beard. "Has anybody in Texas *heard* of Sallowsfield?"

In fact, in Wyatt's experience, no one he'd told about the trip, none of his colleagues, believed there existed such a place with such a name. "I don't think so."

"Nobody in Texas has *heard* of it!" Kevin glanced around the square as if taking it in for the first time, only now discovering the town's awesome obscurity.

"Says his last name is Sallow," said Raymond.

"Sallow?"

"Sallow."

"Never heard of it," said Kevin. "Around here."

According to a website Wyatt had found, on the continent of North America there were fewer than forty individuals with his surname, a name he personally never saw associated with anyone save himself and two half-siblings he exchanged Christmas greetings with but had never met (Jack and Judi). Bizarrely, here where the square fronted a row of Victorian-era structures with street-level businesses, he could find his name multiple times: very possibly more times than he'd seen it publicly displayed in his life. Over Raymond's elevated right shoulder, the name dominated the district: Makeover Sallowsfield. Sallowsfield Central Apartments. Dragon's Tongue Tats—Sallowsfield. Farther towards an intersection were signs for the Sallowsfield Cocktail Lounge and Sallow-Botafogo, Brazilian Cuisine. This didn't count places he saw the name listed next to covered bus stops, or truncations like Sal Royale Teen Fashion. (His dean, Dr. Zepeda, sometimes called him "Sal," although Wyatt dearly wished he wouldn't.)

He had never seen the name on any building or street sign in Turner, Texas—or any other part of Texas for that matter. He had never met another person with the surname aside from his estranged wife ("Z"), and his son, Wyn.

Raymond and Kevin offered him tea in a paper cup if he would step over towards a table under a pavilion tent where this was being freely poured, then Raymond ("Call me Ray") pointed out on the flyer he'd been shuffling how there'd be a church service the next evening, and that Wyatt should come. "You are invited. Ask for Ray."

"Get him to his hotel!" Kevin boomed. "Don't you think we could get him a lift, Raymond?"

"I feel like we can get him a lift to his hotel if he can wait a bit." By this time, they had picked up, from his scattered story, that he taught at a college. "What subject, Wyatt?"

"Ethics."

"He teaches ethics!" Kevin hollered.

Raymond pressed the flyer into Wyatt's hand. "When you get there, ask for Ray," he repeated. "Look, Wyatt, you're a philosopher. Consider the canal boat."

"It's Business Ethics."

Raymond brought his own hand down his throat as if soothing it. "A problem. In engineering. Do you know about the canal boat, Wyatt?"

He considered. He had heard of canals. He had heard of boats. He noted that a third guy had come up, obviously familiar to Raymond and Kevin, which he could tell by the pointed way they did not look at him. This guy had a dark goatee, the creased bruise of a black eye above his left cheek, and, soon, under his arm, a Black friend who stepped up and moved close. The young Black guy grinned and squirmed, his eyes darting from side to side.

"The locks they go through are narrow," said Raymond. "The boat has to be narrow as well."

"That's why they are narrow," put in Kevin.

"I may have seen one." Wyatt meant in a TV documentary he'd watched, possibly in the 1990s.

"Never seen a canal boat!" Kevin announced.

"God, they're awful," said the young Black man. He didn't have the sort of accent young Black people had in East Texas.

"People live on them, Wyatt," said Raymond. "Families. Go to the Italian Restaurant in Firmwood and you'll see the canal. The boats. Without principles, like the principles, Wyatt, that go into canal boat construction . . ."

"Yes?"

"It can be hard to, well . . . you might feel like you didn't fit. Have you ever felt like you didn't fit?"

He would have answered had the goateed man not taken that moment to enter the conversation.

"Fitting in is what your 'faith'"—and here he removed an arm from his friend's shoulder, lifted both hands in the universal "air quote" Wyatt had just seen Paul utilize for the word "go"—"What your 'faith' basically consists of."

Wyatt tried to remind himself that he needed to be getting some of this down. He wasn't in town on a lark. He wanted to make a note concerning the incessant utilization of "air quotes" in Sallowsfield. He figured it would be truly rude if he took out his journal.

"Look," he said. "Do you mind if I take out my journal and . . ."

"Evan," from Kevin. "Don't start that."

Wyatt felt he might have some trouble setting this conversation in his notebook, what with the similarity of the names "Kevin" and "Evan," to highlight only one difficulty. But as the first conversation of any kind he'd had in his own, surname-connected town, he felt setting it down had some importance.

He opened his journal, took up his pen from his pocket, listened. The young Black man's hair, dyed white (nearly silver) at its tips, grew out in otherwise jet-black dreads that spread like an explosion from the top of his head. He had a nose piercing.

"Conformity," said goateed Evan. "Follow the crowd. The rules."

"The rules!" Kevin laughed his booming laugh.

Raymond appeared stumped. "There are always . . ."

The young Black man spoke up. "Fit in. Can't fit anything in them boats." He spoke directly to Wyatt. "Spent a week on one."

"Thank you, Philip." Evan seemed sincerely appreciative of this addition. "'Be not conformed to this world,' says the Apostle Paul in Romans," he continued. "'But be transformed by the renewing . . . of . . . your . . . mind.'" He pointed here towards his own head, the slicked-back hair. "Especially these days, Raymond, don't you think a Christian—a true one—would have to stand out from the crowd?"

Wyatt scribbled down this question.

"That's not in the Book," said Raymond. "You made it up."

"Christians are nonconformists. Not narrow, like canal boats. I mean, were you popular, Raymond, when you told your friends about conforming to the Lord?"

"It's not about being popular. Or conforming."

"Behold this man." Evan framed Wyatt with his hands as if setting him for a master shot in a TV series. "His problems. Here, from across the sea. Come to seek his identity."

Wyatt raised his ballpoint. He hadn't said that, exactly.

"Come to find meaning. Did you find it?" Evan asked him. "Did you find your meaning or your identity, sir?"

"I've been here twenty minutes."

"Identity!" Boomed Kevin.

"Them boats!" said Philip. "I mean narrow."

"Which he won't," said Evan. "Some name no one has heard of."

At that moment a bus turned in front of the square, its illuminated signboard read "SALLOW 240."

5
Philip

"Boat smelled of petrol," Philip said. "Sandwiches *tasted* of petrol."

Philip, the only native son in the group, possessed the longest town pedigree. His grandfather had been of the *Helpinstill* generation, a group that arrived from Jamaica in a ship of that name to work as laborers, a role in which they'd been exploited for several decades, establishing families the whole while. And so, Philip had grown up in the Springton district, five square blocks above Springton Road that was still home to jerk chicken, reggae shops, and the Empress Ballroom across from the Tres Chic hair-dressers. A Bailey-Higgins Brothers grocery was there, where a person could find yellow yams, plantains, bulla cake, and Matouk's pepper sauce. Raymond, Kevin, and Evan, by contrast, were *comer-inners*: landed in town after failing admission to Cambridge, Oxford, Nottingham, or other, even less prestigious universities. Philip's father was a noted regional figure for his Caribbean restaurant but, more publicly, known for yearly high-profile local TV chat show appearances promoting the carnival parade and food festival. Philip, however, was no chef, and sadly had absorbed only one habit of his father's, who, when tickled by something, laughed in a way comically similar to Santa Claus's Christmas mirth making: "Ho, ho, ho."

"Ho, ho, ho," Philip would say, and think of his father.

It might not seem much, but not everyone can get away with dropping "Ho, ho, ho" into general conversation. Philip's father (who no longer spoke to him) had the gift, and his son had picked it up.

Philip didn't begrudge the newcomers. Well, that Texan. He seemed odd. Taking notes. Like he was an anthropologist or something, but Philip had seen that kind of desperation before. Wyatt. This Wyatt. Had the same attitude as the old men. Men too old to go to clubs but who go to clubs anyway, trying to be what they weren't because they were too old. Sad. But Philip put up with the comer-inners and, frankly, loved Evan. Philip had never encountered anyone like the skinny boy with the satanic beard and swept-back hair and—today—that sexy black eye that gave him such a wiry, streetfighter look. Evan hadn't gotten the eye in a street fight, but during their fucking when Philip accidentally brought his knee up simultaneously with Evan bringing his face down ("*Sorry! Sorry!*" "No problem. No problem.") In addition to being muscular, hard—*hot*—Evan had what Philip considered to be "aspects." Something like "qualities," or even "facets," but, in the case of Evan, more angular. While Evan always displayed these, to appreciate them, really see them, you had to get close, live with them. Hang around Evan, maybe when he'd had too much coffee. Especially when he'd had too much coffee. I mean, *canal boat analogies* for fuck's sake. No way that kind of tripe could sneak past the steel trap that was the mind of Evan.

During times when Evan had too much coffee, he'd start in on what Philip thought of as his "loops." Tell the same story over and over. And over. Ask the same questions. Even present the same problem, but each time . . . *modulated.* A performance, really, not some smirking act, and it went along with his lean sexuality as far as Philip was concerned, though he often had trouble convincing others. Like convincing them how Evan was a thrill in bed, which was hard to get across. Probably you'd also have to fuck Evan to appreciate his ingenuity, and Philip burned with jealousy over the potentiality of someone doing that. Philip had had sex before.

Three times, in fact. But these days he had to ask himself if he really had—before Evan, that is. He wouldn't be going back to that old stuff, would he, nor could his father make him. Or, maybe the thing was . . . it was the foreplay. *That* made the difference. What had been missing. It made sense Evan would be good at that as he was so skilled a practitioner of a looping and pointless—better to say *not pointed*—performance repertoire.

At uni, every Wednesday, Evan and Philip wandered into the cafeteria in the Lowery Annex. Every Wednesday after their Applied Economics lecture and by the same route, they moved through the concrete garden, past the auto-sliding glass of the Student Center. They'd order the same lunch at the Chinese portal. Better to say Evan ordered the same (Chow Mein plate), while Philip went in some Wednesdays for Szechuan Chili Chicken, others Shitake Fried Rice. Most important: first Evan would address the servers in pinny aprons and paper hats behind the steam tables. "Would you crew take all of the offerings that you have (That was rich: *offerings*) . . . the offerings that you have here, and kindly rank them?"

These servers were young locals and high school types engaged in part-time work—doing it with an enormous turnover for that matter—so most of them, not knowing better, took him seriously, an aspect of customer service instilled in them by their supervisor for however many weeks or even days that they'd likely keep the jobs.

"Rank them?"

"On a scale of one to ten."

Commonly they would stop and think it through. Ponder it. The workers who were taking classes already at the college might go so far as to inquire if he meant by affordability or quality, but usually, they just launched in. "The steamed vermicelli rolls, definitely a seven. Definitely. The Crab Rangoon, more a five."

"Ah," Evan would say.

"Even a four."

The line behind them grew as Evan listened to the ratings, absorbed the data. He nodded, ticked the items off with his fingers as if to help remind him which dish held which rating, which was ridiculous, as he was ordering the Chow Mein. He always ordered the Chow Mein. Every Wednesday after Applied Economics, before making this inevitable selection, however, after he'd heard the menu as judged on the scale of one to ten by the cafeteria workers, he'd point out the plates under the display light on an aluminum shelf. Not a warming light, mind, just display, the meals there covered in cellophane, marked with prices, often indicating daily specials.

"And this one? How much is this one?" Evan would hold up a Styrofoam plate of Sweet and Sour with egg roll starters, let's say, artfully arranged under a cellophane wrap and labeled with a white A6 card. Six pounds fifty.

"Six pounds fifty."

"Not this kind." Evan tapped the cellophane. "This one. That I'm holding."

"The one for display?"

"How much?"

"We can't sell it." By this time someone had no doubt come over from the cash register, usually a rose complexioned girl, but, again, Philip never recalled seeing the same person working the register more than one consecutive Wednesday over the course of a term, the turnover in the college café being fierce, or—who knew? Maybe Evan drove them into other lines of work?

After a few minutes discussing with the staff how and why some item that had a price tag on it wasn't available for sale, Philip would get his Stir-Fried Tofu or whatever, Evan his Chow Mein, and they'd find a table, favoring the ones against the wall or in a corner. Evan had a variation on this routine for wherever they went.

Who else could have such an effect on people? Well. His father, maybe. His mother had passed away unexpectedly in 2012. A heart valve problem that took her in the night. Philip had felt his categories shift, his position in the *scheme* change. Profound, *right*? No longer the son of Janet Howell-Baptiste, the community organizer, also a force of nature, who'd been the actual logistical power behind the yearly Caribbean festival that had brought Philip's father so much prestige. But Philip and his dad, Jacob, had kept it up. Kept it together. They'd *done* it together, and now Jacob was a staple on local TV, known for his signature Santa laugh. But he didn't want to speak to Philip anymore. "You sicken me," Jacob had said to Philip. This year he'd be putting on the festival without his son.

That Evan.

Yes. Yes and . . . Evan . . . Evan was a graduate assistant in the Econ Department, a role that provided him office privileges in a space he shared with other assistants, each of whom now knew not to walk out of the room and leave their computers open with email activated, as he—*get this*—continuously sought opportunities to create miscommunication, is the thing, as soon as they wandered away from their desks. Evan had sent an email to Earl's statistics professor, for example, using Earl's account—a message to the effect that Earl had decided to no longer do the assignments in the statistics class, as he found them "disruptive to my psyche and emotionally draining." *Ho ho ho.* Earl couldn't figure out why the professor requested a meeting. *Ho ho ho.* Other grad assistants in the office space they shared with Evan didn't know why they always received strange packages for no reason, like a videotape promoting a high-speed grass strimmer that ended up in Karen's box, or advertisements for items like see-through toilets addressed to the literature major, Darren (who had particularly bad skin), or . . . or that promotional copy of *Horse Fancier* magazine that ended up on David's desk—all of which had been sent off for by Evan under the recipient's name, each of which allowed him to ask his victim bizarre questions in a tone of seriousness such as: "David! Is that legal now?"

Philip would occasionally indulge in similar jokes, but always with random people over the phone: much safer. Evan performed his bizarre rites in the open, face-to-face. That was the difference between them. That was the performance element. That was the wonder of Evan.

Wyatt Sallow's own practical jokes and prank phone calls were more targeted.

6
"X"

Raymond and Evan continued their heated discussion as the young Black man with the silver-tipped braids listened on with a wry grin and bearded Kevin, having strolled a few paces from his hand cart and water bottles, occasionally re-broadcast their words to anyone passing through the square. Wyatt, glancing at his journal, found a page of disconnected topics, a circumstance he attributed mainly to Evan who, tugging on his dark goatee the while, maintained the better part of every exchange, nudging anything Raymond said into a different association. While the notes began with scribblings that fell under the general category of "conformity and its discontents," Wyatt saw after a while that his entries had drifted and slid into subjects like "the aggressive qualities of pacifism," then the "relation between church and state," and—after a good half hour—"the problematic destiny of the unevangelized." Wyatt began to step backward. There was something of the Dean Nick Zepeda aura in this Evan: a tendency towards what his friend Professor Wickham (Renaissance Literature) called "argument for argument's sake, not inquiry for knowledge's sake." Time was passing. Wyatt mumbled something about getting that "cup of tea" after all (air quotes included. When in Rome . . .), then moved away from them, towards a row of festival awnings, closer to the band under its tent. Soon, the music smothered the conversation, and he could no longer see the group or the young Black man who took it all in with a vague smile, the only one who nodded at him when he left. For the period since he'd exited from the station to standing on the steps with Paul McBride to the discussion with Raymond and Evan and the pronouncements by Kevin, the whole while the talented band in the tent had played a song. That is, they'd played the same song, the one with the prominent saxophone and driving bass. It was either a very, very long tune, or they'd repeated it many times over the past three quarters of an hour. A casual observer might conclude it was the only song they knew.

Wyatt found a metal bench away from the spraying spigots on the square. From a distance, he examined the familiar countenance of Henry Scott, deciding after a while that the bronze worked well, harmonized with the actor's metallic appearance in the role of the clever android in *Off to the Planets*. The same figure with the duffle bag and orange vest stood before the statue, as though transfixed by it, though Wyatt could no longer see this man's face. Pulling *The North: A Tough Guide* from his pack, he considered its rudimentary map of the town. He'd purchased the guide mainly because of its sketchy information on Sallowsfield, all owing to the suggestion from X: no research. "Go in cold, Wyatt. Nothing preconceived. Just see what happens and write about what you find." Whatever gumption he possessed to lift the luggage/duffle, strap it to his back, go in search of the hotel was impeded by the poor map, and the—as far as he could tell—unmarked streets. He didn't know in which direction to launch—the boulevard leading away from the station to the right, or another, very similar street to the far right. In addition, the square appeared much smaller "in person" than it did on the map. Was there some other central town square? But there stood the famous statue. He wondered again if there might be some sporting goods store or even a novelty shop which might have apparel that featured the town's name. A t-shirt. A scarf. Perhaps a simple knit cap with SALLOWSFIELD incorporated into the woven threads. When he glanced up from the guidebook, he could discern from this new angle the banner stretched across the columns of the station, an advertisement for an art and architectural design festival at the university. Below this, a group disembarked from the tremendously tall station doors, and these people walked down the very steep steps into the square, and one of these people was the woman he had designated as X.

7
Nasty, Brutish, and Short

"Again," said the turbaned man when Wyatt approached him a second time. To all appearances, the cabs stood in the same positions they'd occupied earlier. He couldn't see why they wouldn't take him even a few blocks to the Town Central Hotel Sallowsfield rather than sit without fares, but this didn't matter anymore.

"I have . . . a different one."

The man gave the impression of not noticing Wyatt. It was as if he were reading a newspaper, and not taking the trouble to glance up, only he held no newspaper. "The Town Central Hotel is still too close," he said. "It has not moved."

"I have another..."

"You have. You have moved. You walked to that fair." The man cranked his head towards the blaring saxophone. "You were halfway to the Town Central Hotel when you got to that fair."

Wyatt glanced down the long lane, at X's white pants disappearing into the unknown reaches of a bustling street.

"I want you to help me catch a woman," he said.

The man lowered his foot from the bumper.

"That is, I need you to ... follow a woman."

"Woman?"

"The one I'm pointing at, down that street." This didn't seem to be going well. "To see where she goes. That's all."

The man looked more interested. He peered down the street between the buildings where Wyatt pointed.

"The white pants?" Wyatt went on. "It's nothing weird. I'm not a stalker."

"The what? So say all stalkers."

Wyatt considered the restraining order. But this man was oversimplifying the relationship alarmingly. "I'll never catch up with her dragging my pack."

"And fetishists. You know this woman?"

"I can tell you about it as we go."

"Go? Go to chase a woman through the streets?" He peered more intently. "In white trousers?" Oddly, at this point the man giggled like a child, then narrowed his eyes.

Wyatt panted. "Who's getting away."

The man crooked his leg, placed his foot on the bumper again. "This does not interest me."

Wyatt glanced toward the curled and wave-like accents at the tops of the Victorian structures around the square. "She's getting away." He felt rising desperation. "And then the Central Town. Town Central. How about that? Both!"

"You're starting to enter a zone."

That didn't sound good.

"A zone that does not interest me," the man said. He steepled his fingers. "Or realm. A zone or realm that while it doesn't interest me, because there's a chase for a girl that will not be successful . . ."

"Not at this rate!"

". . . that will not be successful. Just yet another distressing girl chase on yet another day."

"Yes?"

"And . . . and not a big enough fare . . ." He leaned towards the second cab in line. "Possibly it does interest my nephew."

By standing on his toes and craning his neck, Wyatt could just make out the white pants.

"Only now he's not here."

"Where is he?"

"My nephew is much hungrier than I am. He's broke, basically." Placing his teeth over his bottom lip the man emitted a shockingly loud whistle that shrieked and reverberated from walls of nearby buildings.

Wyatt winced from the piercing volume. He glanced towards the station, the spurting water streams on the square, a restaurant across the street that called itself "The Sallow Corner." He tried again. "Where is he?"

"Where's who?" The young man who'd waved from the steering wheel earlier came from behind his uncle, his sunglasses perched on top of his head.

"Fare," said the man in the turban. He aimed a flat palm towards Wyatt. His eyes returned to their reading-a-newspaper-without-a-newspaper stare.

At the bench when he first saw her, Wyatt had not hesitated nor bothered with the energy required for disbelief. X, the love of his life, had come to this town. His town. He did not raise questions of how or why, though deep in the somewhat difficult to navigate lobes of his calculating mind the glimmer of a theory began to form. He had watched as she reached the bottom of the stairs, then turned to her right quickly, such that he didn't see her face for long, but long enough. X was not mistakeable. Her turning away, perhaps, made him more certain it was she. The straight back, the lively, compact step, the firm buttocks in the white jeans. She had, at one time, been a contestant in muscle-building contests, and this had left her with a not particularly feminine physique. In outline or silhouette, she was, perhaps, not a beauty. As for her physical form, X appeared almost relentlessly unremarkable, but a type of un-remarkable that—Wyatt believed this—could not be duplicated in any other woman. This despite the fact that Zepeda, department Dean and asshole, seeing her on campus one time and not realizing Wyatt's connection, had—within his earshot—described X using Hobbes' summary of the life of mankind in a low, chuckling murmur.

Wyatt's first view of her on the square was one he knew. She had, in fact, the last time he saw her, been turning away, receding into a distance, although at that time police lights had also flashed against her white robe.

Wyatt had been left with a simple task. By showing him her back, he knew, objectively, that she distanced herself from him: usable knowledge. He knew her speed. She was not, it was true, particularly quick, but she would also be, he understood, reliably steady once she attained cruising velocity. Here, on this fountained square, a time/space pattern recognition problem arose, nothing more. From this distance (too far to see if she carried a notebook; she would almost have to be carrying a notebook)—the distance between the metal bench next to the Christians and their raucous song that started up again—same song, same saxophone solo—the distance from there to the steps of the station . . . he knew catching up with her, choosing the correct angle across the pavement before she left his sight, could be achieved in only a limited window of opportunity. Something like the Rule of the Square applied: a law that delivered—much in the same manner as inexorable fate—the verdict on any King's prospects chasing down a pawn racing for the eighth rank and promotion.

He muted his heart. There were, yes, bollards between himself and X, but from the iron bench only one that crossed his path. Win! He rose, tugged at his luggage, palmed the single upright post that stood as an obstacle between himself and the curb and stepped into the street as a soapy bubble, a shiny spinning globule, silver-ish at its perimeter, floated overhead.

The horn blasted in his ear, the brush of the truck's surface turned him slightly to knock his journal from his grip. Inside the lorry, the driver (named Charles Ryan, Sallowsfield native, or—as he often referred to himself—yes that Charles Ryan), dressed despite the temperate day in a quilted ski jacket and baggy corduroys, a blue knit cap pulled low to his brow, (the town's name, SALLOWSFIELD woven into the blue fabric with white

letters) "snicked" his wheel rightwards with the barest of cranking movements from his powerful, Popeye-like forearms. It was just enough to avoid
flattening a mindless pedestrian dragging a giant suitcase who'd stepped
off the kerb and into the lane without looking, the stupid dog-eating bastard. Charles' "snick" had taken up about an eighth of a turn: the difference
between grazing the fibers of the man's corduroy elbow patch (Who wore
those anymore? Corduroy trousers, fine. Elbow patches?) versus a body
in the street, broken spine, shit-ton of paperwork, late delivery, late home.

Wyatt caught himself before landing on the pavement, searched the
crowd for X as the truck's horn dropped in tone, the insistent and accusatory sound speeding away. A logo painted across the lorry's closed back
doors indicated that a brand of ice cream packed into a large-box-like
vehicle had nearly killed him, and also that this month's featured flavor
was something with a ridiculous name he caught from of the corner of
his eye. Wyatt had stepped into the street without looking, at least not in
the right direction, and so had nearly been flattened by a few metric tons
of Sweet Minty Choco. Not the end he'd imagined. His heart—rather than
flattening—had leaped into his throat upon seeing X unexpectedly, then
vaulted into his mouth after the brush with death. ("That was a close one,
Kitty," Bobby Booster noted after the narrow avoidance of an asteroid collision.) White circles in his swimming vision pulsed to his blood's Taiko
drum solo, competing with the Christians' brassy orchestra. Wyatt leaned
on the handle of his luggage to retrieve his notebook, felt his head wobble
when he rose, perhaps having done so a little too quickly. He had to move.
There was no time to ponder broken spines, as she was getting away. He
tried to brush street grime from the notebook's pages while looping his
arm through the luggage/bag/pack handle and he moved towards the
inexorably receding X. He had the idea then. He'd aimed back towards the
line of cabs, his eyes on her white pants.

But even after the ride had been arranged, the nephew appeared in no
hurry to get started. He strolled to the rear of the cab, lifted its hatchback,
reached for Wyatt's luggage. "Who is this woman did you say?"

"I'll tell you everything, but we should go."

"Of course. Oooof. What do you 'ave in here?"

"I'll tell you that, too. She's someone I loved. Love."

The nephew peered down the street. "Maybe you should call."

"What?"

"She doesn't have a phone?"

Wyatt realized that he and the taxi driver did not occupy the same theoretical space. In the cosmos of his consciousness (... which everyone possesses, by the way. When any pedestrian is flattened in a road, we lose a universe... just saying ...), there lurked no possibility of calling X, besides which she had changed her number, as he knew from experience. The driver clearly saw this as some kind of normal relationship.

"I ... no, she doesn't have one."

Paul McBride strode past, lowering his lager can, wiping his chin. "Now!" he called out. A bubble formed on his lips.

"Please!" said Wyatt.

8
On Interludes. (An interlude)

Time trouble. Clock running, flag about to drop, and Wyatt, with X getting away, felt the moments begin their inexorable curve towards a new phase. That homeless person, Paul, inserting himself into the fold of this precious second like that, upset him, although unfairly. First Paul held strong convictions that time possessed no physical texture or fabric, and so could not be folded, explaining why one cannot have a "stitch in" it. Mainly, however, Paul wasn't a homeless person but lived with his father on the Oatland Road. The bubble machine, too. Among his toys—though to Wyatt's mind they didn't qualify as toys, being so ephemeral—Wyn favored most the bubbles blown by himself (Wyatt Sallow) from those plastic rings attached to the underside of caps that enclosed bottles of soapy water. Those bubbles fascinated Wyn. At a children's fair in Turner Centennial Park, he and Z once pushed Wyn's chair near a spewing bubble machine, much like the one on the Sallowsfield Square. The device emitted bubbles in a constant stream. They'd approached it innocently, and Wyn had pointed at each of the emerging spheres, using his favorite identifying phrase. *"That one!"* Then: *"That one!"* Soon, his delight grew frenzied. Wyn began to cry (they had to assume, at first, for joy), then labor at breathing in an alarming way until his mother, Z, (fuck her) distancing the chair from the bubble machine, had to examine his temperature, readjust his nasal tubes, clean around his feeding tube and inspect his diaper while he continued to wail, helpless against an onslaught of bubble after bubble after bubble.

Wyn knew bubbles. He also was very pleased with his own birthday and recognized it with some glee whenever it came around.

As for Paul, he'd had a promising HVAC career derailed by drink. A single weekend escapade—just one—had left him debilitated. In a stupor, he'd slipped from the sofa where he'd been watching Manchester United flatten Arsenal. He fell over onto a low table. The crease of this table's edge hit his arm, pushed his elbow also into his left side, his unconscious mass serving to pinch a nerve in the limb. The combination of randomly combined physical forces reduced a good percentage of oxygen flow to his brain and did so until his father shook him the next morning. He'd been there hours, although it seemed to Paul an instant. "An instant can be longer than you think," he discovered. On the square, he still fingered the coins Wyatt had given him. The accident against the edge of the living room table had left him injured in the arm but—thankfully from his own perspective—had also planted a realization in his frontal lobes. He often told people, including those he cornered in front of the station, that time does not *pass.* That time, for that matter, does not *march on.* "What is here today," Paul pointed out to them, "is not gone tomorrow." Here he paused for effect. *"Necessarily."* "Also," he would occasionally throw in, "it is impossible to pause *for* effect. Every pause *is* an effect."

Time is not *of the essence,* nor is it *on our side.* It does not care enough to choose sides, and you're a fool if you depend on it to stroke your ego that way. (There, he might have had something.) It is not *money,* and so cannot be *well spent,* although the ten pounds Wyatt so thoughtfully handed over certainly could be.

These kinds of statements drove his father crazy. Such a little thing. So stupid. To fall a certain way, across a certain, cheap living room table, and end like this.

Paul to his father: "You could not be *in time,* let alone *on* it, not even *once upon* it. It will not *tell,* and you cannot bide it, be ahead of it, have better luck the next of it, achieve anything in the fullness of it, get by barely in the nick of it, or live on it—borrowed or not. Most definitely time does *not* fly, Dad, when you are having fun." He emphasized this by coming close to his father's face. "It cannot fly no matter what you are having."

"Fine, Paul, fine."

Sometimes his father, listening to this, after Paul had gone to bed, sat on the floor in the kitchen with his legs in front of him and held his hair, struck, but…just look at them all now, Paul thought. And…*now*. The white taxis, the station steps, the stone lion above the bank, that street fair, that bubble, that bubble, that bubble, that figure disappearing down Station Street in white slacks, they were missing it all. So sad, Paul felt, for good old Wyatt and the turbaned man and the kid with the sunglasses on his head, so sad they were missing it, and then it was gone, and then…aw for fuck's sake…they'd missed it again, hadn't they? All of it gone once more.

9
On Interludes Following Interludes (Another one)

As for X, the trim and compact brunette who had once performed in female muscle-building contests had entered Professor Sallow's life through the collegiate chess team after he had separated from Z (moving out to his fifth-wheel camper in the Tranquility RV Park on Caddo Road, while Z remained in their home on Linden Lane with "Cousin" Yuri and he, Wyatt, labored to avoid seeing the pair of them in a town of fewer than 40,000 souls). X, an unhappy wife and devoted mother of two with a neglectful petroleum well recovery engineer for a husband, at the age of thirty-six found in tiny Taylor State a workshop for exploring new passions. In addition to chess, she held interests in Native American culture, music, and writing, and found the attention given her by a winner of the Texas Tech Younger Poet Prize heady enough to agree to "writing workshops"—meetings at the coffee shop on the second floor of a mall bookstore chain where once a week after lunch Sallow labored at his verse while X began what would become the first chapters of a romance about a New Orleans pirate ghost working in the *Vieux Carré* as a musician and short-order cook. (If that sounds familiar—it being such a popular work, later turned into a Netflix series—you no doubt already know the name behind the "X.") And, no, she and Wyatt had never really been serious, although she had kissed him once in his office, then again a few other times, then relented after complaining to him that her breasts "used to be *jewels*, Wyatt, but are sad and flat as bananas now," to which he had answered: "Why don't we let me be the judge of that?"—had relented, that is, and emailed him a picture of herself sitting in her bedroom on the express condition that he agree to delete it immediately, which he had not been able to do because he loved X. Her enthusiasms were so quirky. Her skirts were so short. Wyatt Sallow, devastated by the whole transcontinental Z fiasco, considered X to be the love of his life and, so, had given her that lettered designation, as she seemed, yes, a kind of missing factor or quality to be solved for, but more *the solution itself* given his miseries otherwise. X was "the woman force," and the whole thing hadn't ended well at all after she explained she was leaving her husband but for somebody else, and he, Wyatt Sallow, broke down her front door, but fortunately X did not press charges.

It's not hard to see why finding her 4,700 miles from home had delivered such a profound shock, nor hard to understand his desperation to catch up with her, confront her, try to explain, try again . . .

10
Versatile Hours and Decent Earnings but You Never Find the Girl.

"Now!" Paul called out. A lager bubble formed on his lips.

"Please!" from Wyatt.

Paul passed on, and seconds spilled before our poor Wyatt was in the back of the cab, and the nephew, who introduced himself as Hussein, turned the ignition key. "That's Station Street. Do you see her?"

Wyatt had poor vision, inherited from his mother. There had been that issue at work. He'd attempted to have the administration recognize failing eyesight as the sort of "condition" the Americans with Disabilities Act had been created to address and acknowledge that "they must by all accommodation" move him to classes that required less reading, more Scantron multiple-choice tests, fewer essays. But he habitually only requested the Scantron-heavy BUSI 4071 Principles of Business Ethics sections anyway, courses that appealed to no one else in the department at all, so no changes had come from his eyesight complaint. Still, he had over the course of a career gathered so many theoretical resources pertaining to Aristotle on virtue, Hobbes and the social contract, not to mention Kant on duty, and Bentham and Mill's utilitarianism . . . so many brittle and yellowed lecture notes . . . that it now required little preparation on his part to teach Business majors about ethics (not the same as *teaching them ethics*) to the extent they wanted to know about it, and this lack of necessary preparatory time left him free for his faculty advisory role as coach. "I'm not sure if I see her," he whined.

"And she's not your wife?"

"I was . . . am married." He had to think about it. "But not to her."

"Uh, huh."

"But I'm separated, though. Let's go, right? I'll tell you *everything*, but I want to catch her."

"Give me something if we're to head her off, sir. Does she live here? Is she a visitor, too?"

X couldn't be living there, could she? How perverse if so. "She's visiting. She must be visiting."

"What hotel?"

Wyatt hadn't thought of that. When X left the station, she carried no bags. Was she in a hotel? "What hotels are on this street?"

"Station Street?"

"Yes, Station Street."

Hussein scratched the inside of his ear using a little finger. On this little finger, he wore a small oval amethyst ring. "None," he said.

A nagging auxiliary root breaking from the seed of Wyatt's theory explaining X's presence began to unwind. If correct, she wouldn't necessarily have just arrived, and she wouldn't necessarily have any luggage. Or even be staying at a hotel.

She probably would have been carrying a notebook journal, though.

As they pulled from the station, Wyatt felt a claustrophobic enclosing of the cab as buildings loomed on both sides. Brown brick walls blocked the afternoon sun. He could discern no trace of X, but also no clear location where she could have exited this featureless street. It seemed to let mostly onto the backs of businesses. There were no shop doors or signs. For not the first time, his mental image of thatched roofs and a village green was usurped by that of a cramped mill town. A "Purveyor of Fine Meat" went past, but Wyatt, though he looked through the plate glass, couldn't imagine X having gone to such a purveyor, not straight from the station.

Wait. *Wait!* There, a black journal notebook, sure enough. But carried by a fragile-looking woman with unkempt brown hair who kept close to the featureless bricks along the street, dipping into the occasional doorway like a spy tracking a terror suspect, peering back towards the square. Odd.

"It might help if I knew who we were looking for," said Hussein.

"White jeans."

"Have you a picture? And who is she?"

He had a photograph of X he'd saved on his phone. One in particular. At random times he would pull up this image. Square his shoulders. Pretend he was seeing her in person. She'd emailed this picture, sitting on the bed in her bedroom. Or better to say the room she had once shared with her husband. It was, after all, difficult to inflict self-torture without torture instruments.

In this image her breasts were bare. As hinted before, as for X's body, her figure, her naked chest—as a beauty, she would have to be called undistinguished. Yet the attraction he felt towards her was powerful (olive skin, freckled neck, her deeply impacted dimples), and he'd spent a lot of time poring carefully over this picture, including its background. Behind one tantalizingly bare shoulder, for example, X was reflected or paralleled, in a way, by a framed Art-Deco print of a nude dancer, or one-third of such a print. In this drawing, an arm and a calf along with a neat, pointed foot frozen mid-step were tastefully framed to one side, although the rest of the drawing had been cut off by the limits of the photo's border. X's own feet were hard and dry, an artifact of her intense training and the dehydration required for muscle tone and contrast under stage lighting. Her toenails were long and pointed, and hash marks of tiny black hairs crowned the joints of her toes. He knew all of that, amazingly, from a single encounter when she'd removed her shoes in his presence. Her forearms—and just touching one of these had been enough to drive him to a frenzy—were not expressive like in the art print, but firm and also forested in black hair that flowed in discernible waves across her skin. As for her nudity, X, mother of two, had always claimed to have "working boobs," red-nippled and close to her chest. Our Wyatt loved these. He enjoyed nothing more than to lay his head against her belly, smell her skin, consider her breasts, neck and chin from that angle, although, again, this stemmed from the same single encounter in his office, the time with the shoes, and she'd been fully clothed. Except for her feet. In the picture, however, X's oval-shaped and medium-red nipples were turned on their sides rather than horizontal. Wyatt felt they were exquisite.

Her motive in sending him the photo remained obscure, aside from the fact he had asked her to. She agreed on the single condition he deleted it immediately. This was something, now five years later, he still someday planned to do.

Also, in the picture, below the fraction of cheap wall-hung art—the furnishings of the entire bedroom no doubt bought at an outlet store—a lamp stood with white shade rimmed in cotton-white balls. Behind X's other shoulder it appeared that molly bolts had been drilled into the sheetrock of the room, although nothing had been attached there, at least not at the time the photo had been taken. Two of the plastic molly disks showed with their central, pupil-like holes, flat to the surface. X, Wyatt recalled, had just gotten a new laptop and was trying out its camera. Her hair, in this picture, was so straight she must have recently come from her favorite stylist, the one who applied the iron, which delivered to her an Asian look for about a day and a half until her hair resumed its usual loose curls. Again, as to why she'd agreed to send it, perhaps that new haircut had tipped the scales. Her tan lines formed peaked triangles that pointed upwards—dunce caps shaped like her bikini top. And there: the squinched, dark eyes. That chin. Those dimples. Her smile. She was a Cajun.

She'd sent it after she'd broken his heart, but before he'd broken her door.

"Do you have a picture?"

Wyatt had been thinking of his head on the fabric of her blouse and smelling her skin. "If we can drive for a while. She must be in this direction." He swallowed. "I have a picture, but I can't really show you."

"Really?" Hussein laughed. "Well, now you *have* to."

"No."

"Look! You've now told me of the existence of this picture. A picture I knew nothing about until I heard it from your lips. I get it, now. She's the girl of your dreams," said Hussein, nodding. "I see it."

"Well..."

"The love of your life. You caught a glimpse of her today, unexpected. And don't want to lose her again."

Wyatt pondered. "You're figuring it out."

"Cab drivers work it out. You don't seem like a weirdo—or not the usual kind."

"Thank you."

"Very good! Yes. This happens to mushers." Hussein leaned over the steering wheel, looked both ways at a cramped intersection. "What's your name?"

"Wyatt." He didn't want to get into the other part. "I'm a ... (*don't say poet, don't say poet*) university professor from Texas." He winced. "Cab drivers, then, are always looking for these girls?"

"That's it."

"Because of men who jump into the cabs and say ..."

"*Follow that girl.* Until you get to be like my uncle, and stop taking these fares, and start giving them to younger drivers."

"What's wrong with these fares?"

"They're depressing, Dr. Wyatt." The man looked at him in the rearview mirror. "We never find the girl."

As per usual, he let the "Dr." pass. "Oh."

"Ever. But that's not the point. You've done the right thing."

Wyatt smiled grimly. "No matter, keep up the chase?"

"Keep up the chase in a *taxi*, Dr. Wyatt. A friend of mine, for example. When we were at school, he was leaving a party, and this girl . . . well, she really wanted him, see? She leaped into his car as he was driving away and demanded a ride!"

"Moxy," said Wyatt. He had no desire to hear this story.

"Then, there was a terrible crash!"

"Oh. Geez."

"A terrible crash, and she was turned into a vegetable."

"Good God, Hussein."

The driver shook his head. "What a terrible thing to have to live with. My friend, he escaped unscathed, of course. Which is a word that interests me. I mean, you never hear about people being *scathed*. But *immediately* after this, he became a Jesus Freak. So that's not unscathed." Hussein tapped the steering wheel, considered it deeply. "So, later, another girl married this friend of mine, though all her friends tried to tell her not to, that it was a mistake, but she wouldn't listen. Do you know what, Dr. Wyatt?"

"No."

"He's a Jesus Freak to this day."

"And the other girl? Is she still a vegetable?"

Hussein shrugged. "The point is: *when it comes to love, call a taxi*."

11
Smell Matters. Smell matters.

"I'm afraid you might take this wrong," X said to him one day. It was their best day. The banana day of their relationship. "So, I'm not going to tell you."

That old ploy had frightened him. It could be something disappointing. It was most likely something disappointing, but he had to know, so used the same response Hussein had. "I believe it's as good as told when someone says that," he insisted. "I won't take it wrong."

On that day she'd come to his office to help him organize it. So much had happened on that day.

"If you ever die . . ."

He laughed.

"My plan is to cut some of my hair and burn or bury it with you."

He had no good response for that. X was about ten years younger than Sallow, so he could certainly "go" first.

"Since I don't know if you'll be burned or buried."

As someone who had been morbid all his life, the possibility held some attraction. His poetry—though most of it had been written in his youth—tended towards the brooding. *Water Take Me Down and Also Burn Me*, in addition to its homage to the tiny, Brigadoon-like Northern market hamlet that served as the rich font of his family name (and as he could see by the somewhat grimy, grey-bricked buildings that glided past the window of Hussein's cab, did not exist), featured for the most part verses haunted by recollections of bitterness and loss, the kind that had permanently alienated "the exile" who spoke from its stapled pages; isolated him from the beauty of the world. This was all the more noteworthy when you considered he'd had only about nineteen years' worth of recollections to work with when these poems were written. Wyatt had not experienced anything like his later levels of bitterness or loss at that point. The scathing review (for, in fact, *Water Take Me Down* and its author had definitely, back in those years, been severely *scathed*) in the *Daily Toreador* had referenced the "difficult to pin down, yet still somehow unearned quality of the imagery"—one of the milder barbs the reviewer had tossed.

"Have you got a plan for that?" Wyatt asked X. "Will you sneak it into my hand during the viewing?"

"Bribing the undertaker? Not sure. The point is, I'll spend the rest of time intermingled with you. But it makes me sad."

"From hair to eternity."

She did not laugh. She rarely laughed at his jokes, certainly not in the way he laughed at hers. But laughing with her made him feel good. It had made him feel good on both of the occasions it had happened.

"How *will* I get it in there?" She considered momentarily but then appeared ready to move to another project.

X enjoyed, when Wyatt knew her, partaking in the Native American custom of connecting with nature by sitting for hours in an enclosure with smoke and heat. Sweat lodges. This might have been something else that toughened her skin, made the pads of her hands dry and hard. When she'd come from one of these all-day rituals and he got anywhere near her, even across a chessboard, she smelled like a burning museum.

12
The Victim

Wyatt became disoriented as he and the cab driver prowled the streets, searching for X. They arrived at length where a large banner across a columned building advertised an art and architectural demonstration at the university. They had made a complete circuit of central Sallowsfield.

"We can keep looking," said Hussein.

Wyatt sighed. "Take me to the Town Central, I think."

Hussein made a semicircular loop around the station, the square, the statue, the Christian street fair. "So, she's the reason you're in town?"

He looked for Kevin, Raymond, Evan, the bemused young Black man whose name he'd heard but forgotten, tried to make out whether that saxophone played yet the same song. "I came for a different reason." He didn't want to admit to Hussein what that was. "If someone really wanted to know about this town, where would they go?"

Hussein listed out a few of the not-to-miss locations, including Tower Hill and a certain ice-cream store—Mrs. Donnelson's—in a district called Springton.

"Is the university far?"

"You'll go there?"

He stretched things a bit, as he had with Paul. "I have a meeting there."

"I'm studying business administration at uni," Hussein said.

Wyatt didn't want to get into that. "I teach . . . writing."

At the Town Central Sallowsfield, Wyatt got out of the cab at an alley ending in an elevated porch with a glass door covered with credit card logos. Hussein insisted they'd arrived, although Wyatt had difficulty seeing anything that looked hotel-ish. "They'll take care of you," Hussein said. The fare was cheap, even after the aimless wandering. Wyatt wondered if Hussein gave him an agreed-upon standard *Follow that girl!* discount. Trying to remember what sort of coins he'd put in Paul's outstretched hand, he was pretty sure the long drive around town cost less than his charitable contribution to the lager panhandler. He did not know if he should tip or not, so he added a few more pounds to the cab ride. "Listen. Maybe. If you see her. You're out a lot. Driving."

"I am. But I'm looking for white . . . oh, by the way. I think you're the victim of an Americanism."

Hussein explained to Wyatt how "pants" meant—to put it politely— "underwear."

"Really?" Wyatt thought back. "Your uncle. What does he think of me?"

"He no doubt considers you an exotic freak."

"I don't know how to get this picture to you. It's on my phone."

Hussein lowered his sunscreen, removed a business card from a clip. "Text me."

"If you can keep it to yourself. She's somewhat exposed."

"We will make it a part of our professional relationship," said Hussein.

Later, in his hotel room, Wyatt pulled up on his phone the shot of X in her bedroom. As always, he toyed with enacting the simple reflex of thumb against trash can icon in the screen's lower right: deleting the image as he'd promised. But he didn't delete it.

Wyatt texted the cab driver the topless picture of the love of his life.

CHAPTER THREE

CAPTURES AND EXCHANGES

1
"Y"

Wyatt Sallow came from a respectable family. His father had made his living "in Civil Aviation," although it was true that the elder Mr. Sallow hadn't gotten into an airplane since a stormy night in 1962 when he had looped his arms through a parachute's shoulder straps and paused in the open door of a high wing, eight-seater, nine-cylinder, air-cooled radial engined de Havilland DH-2 ("Beaver")—considered by many the "most reliable" aircraft in its class. The "Immortal Beaver" bucked, yawed, and slid sickeningly high above the Davis Mountains in West Texas, as Wyatt's father thought to himself "I'm doing something that is saving my life," and threw his body into the freezing night after the pilot had said to him and the two other passengers, "Gentlemen, leave." Wyatt's father had begun his career as an engine machinist working for the border patrol and along with two agents, the other passengers in the plane, managed to parachute safely into the desert after the wings of the "Beaver" iced up in an unexpected April blizzard. The encounter of his (also somewhat small) feet onto the frozen scrub-covered soil as the parachute deflated in the darkness above him like white milk in chocolate milk marked the end of his last sojourn away from *terra firma*. Mr. Sallow spent the rest of his career feeling it unnecessary to actually fly in any planes ("most reliable" models or not) in order to—with unlit Roi-Tan clamped in mouth—faithfully maintain their airframes, fuel systems and nine-cylinder, air-cooled radial engines. The pilot, Robert L. Grantham, had remained in the aircraft until the others safely departed, then strapped on his parachute. This, unfortunately, became entangled in a wing as he exited, upon which point he was, as the El Paso newspapers put it, "carried to his death."

Professor Wyatt Sallow, for whom names were important, always remembered that of Robert L. Grantham with gratitude. Without this man he knew he would not be there, rocking on a plyboard-hard mattress, assuming at times a fetal position, at other times covering his head with the Town Central Hotel's shapeless, scratchy pillows to block music from a rowdy karaoke session in a pub at the end of the alley, writhing in sleepless agony in the town of Sallowsfield on the other side of the globe from the Davis Mountains.

The pub (named the Boy with Bucket) funneled amplified vibrations of Monday night contestants directly against Wyatt's closed second-floor window frame. "Don't It Make My Brown Eyes Blue?" alternated with "I Will Walk One Hundred Miles" as Wyatt gritted his teeth and murmured *"No it does not,"* and *"Start now."* The music shook the panes and even the ceiling tiles in his small room. He swore he heard lyrics that sounded like "Show me the way to Amarillo," which was not possible, as he'd lived in Amarillo two years while in community college and never heard of such a fucking song. At some point, the pop tunes had been abrogated by what appeared to be a local sporting chant. "SAL. LOW. DUBYA-ESS-FIELD. FIGHT ON. NO QUIT. DO NOT YIELD." He considered uncoiling the vacuum constriction contraption he'd promised his urologist he'd employ at least fifteen minutes per day, but he despised the item (it resembled, especially at night, a torture instrument from a Fritz Lang film), so put it off. Although he had to admit, if X truly was in town, mightn't the device prove itself a godsend? In such a manner he lived and, let's face it, absurdly hoped.

So, the night before, despite diazepam, he had not slept well—a worrisome circumstance for him. In the morning, however, despite the karaoke setback, Wyatt perceived recognizable, undeniable signs he was about to experience a banana day.

He had gotten the term from "Y." He'd had a life-altering romance with "X," a soul-crushing marriage to "Z," but his relationship with "Y" was of a different sort. Wyatt trusted Y. A confidante. An administrative assistant at the college, Y had a head on her shoulders and his interests at heart. He nurtured a near-certainty of this. She was quite attractive, far out of Wyatt's league, and decades younger, this allowing him to replace the vicious necessity of pursuit with a more comfortable attitude of avuncular counsel. Ironically, X, who held such sway over him with an almost mystical vitality, though her trim figure had its attractions—drawing such labels as "compact," even "well-put-together"—would not be considered "attractive" by most Western societal standards. Then "Z," Wyatt's wife, had been gangly: her hair stringy, her nose long, and breath of questionable Ukrainian origin.

He had certainly never courted nor flirted with or propositioned "Y." "Banana day" came to him from her personal glossary. The term denoted a day of rare perfection. The sort one received only inside a narrow window of time after an alignment of conditions. (Paul McBride, had he been nearby, could have explained to Wyatt that time has no windows. Nor doors.) The banana day's arrival involved the same multifaceted criticality as an orbital launch. The analogy came from Y's understanding that bananas spent half of their existence on the kitchen counter unripe, green, fibrous, not tasty. Notably, pretty much the entire other half of their life on the counter was devoted to being past their prime: darkened, soft, neither flavorful nor of a pleasing texture. Somewhere in between came *the day* (or day and a half if stretched) when the bananas needed to be picked up, peeled, devoured. The banana day was a perfect pivotal few hours of sweet, flavorful firmness, not to mention unbruised goodness.

This was the day that a banana showed its true self.

It should not be thought that "Y" was an especially cheerful person just because of her banana theory. She had another principle she labeled functional denial. "I've faced more trauma than most, Wyatt," she said. "Not more than you."

"Of course."

"I don't see how you can stand up. But pain is pain. And that's why I implement functional denial. There are functional alcoholics, no?"

"And this is like that?"

"There are functional illiterates. The important part is the 'functional.' Not *how* you do, but *that* you do." She paused to look at him squarely. "That *you* do is undeniable, Wyatt. Seems like you'd be crushed."

He rubbed his forehead.

"Like an empty egg. You know one of the best ways to keep it up?" Y asked.

Misunderstanding, he was about to deny needing that kind of help, although he had no plan to attribute it to the vacuum constriction device.

"The functionality? To keep functioning?"

"I'm guessing that according to you it's denial, although . . ."

"Denial." Y nodded behind her desk alongside the entrance to the faculty offices. "You should consider trying it."

Wyatt felt he was way ahead of her there.

He hadn't always known Y very well. One day at a division meeting, she had risen and explained to the assembled faculty that one among them had lost a child, "his little boy," and that they would be taking up a collection to obtain a thoughtful gift for the family, and that they should see her about donating for this gift. To either side of him, Wyatt's colleagues stiffened. He had just returned to campus after his sad, sad hiatus. Y didn't know Professor Sallow well enough to recognize him or notice him where he sat, cross-legged, near the center of the day room. Or realize, for that matter, that the gift she solicited was for him and his wife. Or that this wife had told him three days before, via phone, "I see no future in it."

Wyatt, who until that moment had been starting to feel the possibility . . . had begun to imagine himself able to rise from a nearly bottomless gloom owing to the familiar surroundings, the friendly bookish sights and smells, the inexorable time-structure of his teaching schedule . . . the dogged normalcy of *another Tuesday at Taylor State* . . . well, he stopped feeling that possibility and jerked instead involuntarily hearing Y's announcement, then narrowed his eyes. Like a man entangled in a harpoon line buried in the fleshy back of a sounding sperm whale, he knew he was headed down, down. Wyatt recognized with some surprise that he would find them, the depths, here, even here, or they would find him. He stood, pressed his feet onto the floor, moved towards the hallway, nodded to those who slid past to either side as they made room and little eye contact.

Y, informed after his departure both of Wyatt's presence and his background by an entire academic department of helpful gossips, spent much of the afternoon crying in a storage closet behind her desk at the entrance to the faculty offices in Krall Hall. Wyatt hid in his own office until she'd left for the day, sniffling. He'd felt bad about causing such grief.

Later, they'd become friends.

Now, despite jet lag, a bad mattress, and the shock of finding X on the streets of an obscure market town that he had traveled to on a whim inspired by her (aided by a cheap flight offering on Singapore Air), Wyatt felt rejuvenated and soon walked with a light step down Barronsgate and towards the town library. The chronic pain of his hamstring injury— caused by leaping abruptly and awkwardly from a chair on rollers when a wasp entered the Taylor State library in November of 2012—had disappeared. Best, he had to admit, was the weather. It had been 92 degrees Fahrenheit when he drove to Houston Intercontinental Airport. Here—if he understood the calculation from Celsius, it was closer to 50 degrees, with a cleansing waft of air from the direction of a hillside he could see from the street. The rook-like Victorian tower Hussein had pointed out rose above the town against a blue sky.

On this important, auspicious day of all banana days, Wyatt unfolded the map he had been given at Town Central Sallowsfield by the very soft-spoken owner/manager Amy Ramsdale which, despite having the appearance of being a xerox of a xerox of a mimeograph, graphically expressed much more information than the one he'd found in the pages of *The North: A Tough Guide*. In that book, Sallowsfield warranted four paragraphs. The first advised how travelers could best save time by not bothering to read the other three paragraphs. In essence, it recommended maximizing any vacation allowance by bypassing the town altogether. "Driving into Sallowsfield," advised the guide, "you might at first think there is little to detain you. You would be correct." Energized by the weather, the excitement of shops along Barronsgate, the fact that *all* of the streets seemed to align perfectly with the roadways clearly labeled on the over-xeroxed map he held before him as he marched on the sidewalk like a tiny-armed *T-Rex* on the prowl, Wyatt turned exuberantly into an arcade that led to a central shopping market and nearly flattened an old man in a blue cap.

The man staggered but, thankfully, did not fall, and Wyatt attempted to apologize. To all appearances, the man wanted none of it, although his loud vocal response to the professor's "Sorry!" was indecipherable: a curse, expression of anger, incantation wishing death upon him … it could have been any of these. The man stood with fists clenched, arms bent to either side Popeye-fashion in a quilted ski jacket and baggy corduroys. Wyatt felt embarrassed, yet also fixated on the blue knit cap, pulled low to the man's brow. Woven into the fabric the town's name appeared in white letters: SALLOWSFIELD, the first he'd seen of anything that appeared purchasable presenting his family name since his rail ticket had been swallowed by the turnstile. He had, so far that morning, seen his name on the temporary lettered announcement board of a cathedral, most of the ticker-tape-like destination signs on the fronts of red busses, on the plate glass window of a pub and another on the windows of two other pubs and another on the window of a takeout restaurant offering both Chicken Tikka Prawn and Murgh Musallam (whatever those were). Wyatt pointed to the knit cap, wishing to speak, wanting to ask where the man had gotten it, but received a scowl, a hand wave that caused him to duck backward, fearful of being struck. The man emitted a growling mutter that sounded like "Close *you've* come," and then stalked away.

2
Charles

It might be said that the guy Wyatt had nearly run over and who had nearly flattened him with a lorry hauling ice cream the day before had a chronic attitude problem, especially when he felt he had not been treated with respect. He was, after all—as he'd attempted to explain to the fat dog-eating bastard who had almost run him down—Charles Ryan. Yes, *that* Charles Ryan. A known quantity. A *name* that *came* if you please: as in *with a story.* Local journalists, in fact, had batted his name about, and in his presence. He had been mentioned by them, nearly, in the local papers. Had opened for Cliff Richard once, too, but it wasn't that so much that had them talking. Now it was seventeen years back, almost—time's a funny thing, isn't it?—but still. And this, Charles Ryan's near-notoriety, had come about through no fault or action of his own, but fame worked just that way sometimes, didn't it?

Seventeen or twenty years back, it had been, he'd come home to find a random message on his machine (back when phones had machines). The message, that Charles Ryan replayed, listened to, even expected to hear on national broadcasts eventually when the scandal broke, went exactly like this:

"Charles, I think those guys we've been dealing with are rozzers. *Get out!* Get out of town as fast as you can."

Click.

They had the wrong Charles Ryan. Charles Ryan himself knew this. He knew the unlikelihood that he could have any involvement in anything that would bring him into the orbit of cops. At the time of the phone message he rarely dealt with anybody about anything save attic insulation. Now a lorry driver for an ice cream concern, Charles Ryan had worked long hours in hot crawlspaces back then. A good hand. None better—ask around. Possibly the phone book had more than one Charles Ryan in it, so this criminal element had just made a directory error. (He had never checked it out about the phone book, as he felt discovering more than one of himself would be too heartbreaking.) A woman who was interested in him back then (and that there was a woman involved had not been part of the police, newspaper, or local jornos' interest, something Charles long considered a serious omission) . . . this woman suggested that what a citizen should do, *the thing someone would do* were they *interested in their civic duties*, would be to call the police, probably speak to detective inspectors, and let them know . . . something. Their caper was up? Their undercover case had been uncovered? This woman (He believed . . . yes, was pretty sure that Becky was her name. But it had been near twenty years.) . . . this woman, Becky, watched lots of television, but he wanted to impress her (back then), so he did it. He thought—and it did seem reasonable at the time—that if they were "stinging" somebody named Charles Ryan, they might want to know if the "case was compromised."

He called first, talked to a nice enough lady, who asked that he come in and bring the tape. He took the bus to the closest nick on Kingsgate with its officious smell where—it would have to be noted—he got handled rudely. Charles Ryan brought the tape in and played it on their machine. The way they treated him, why, it was hard for him to shake the feeling he hadn't done something wrong himself. He'd received a recorded phone message was all. Two of the rozzers there questioned him forty minutes or two hours and forty minutes depending on who Charles told the story to. They took down his name. Address. Inquired of his place of employment. They asked if he'd ever had any dealings with someone named Chris Harris, and Charles said he'd never heard of him.

"Who said it was a him?" they asked. "Name of Chris, could be man or woman."

"I don't know if he's man, woman, or gelded goat," Charles said (repeating a phrase often used by his mother), "so if I don't know that I don't see how I could know him." He considered. "Or her."

And on like that, with more about his background, his first wife and her family in Hammersmith (a shady group, he'd give them that), a traffic violation they found on his record (but also a notice of how he'd paid the fine for it, so nothing there), and then they worked around to Chris Harris again, as in—*How long have you known Chris Harris*? To which he'd reply, *Who's she?*

Suffice to say he left with a bad taste in his mouth, an uneasy feeling about the whole encounter, although maybe he'd made the mistake, going around to his local nick rather than a bigger station, as it didn't seem they had a lot to do there on Kingsgate. They were maybe just killing time. He saw only one perpetrator apprehended and brought in the whole while that Charles sat talking with them, a teen he knew named Wallace who'd kicked over a refuse bin onto the Ring Road. The very scowl Wyatt Sallow had seen when he'd turned the corner into the shopping plaza and nearly knocked Charles Ryan on his ass no doubt had its birth that day during that very police inquiry.

Before they "cut him loose," the cops warned him over public mention of the phone call, that it was part of a "continuing operation," as if anything that might have been "compromised" could be traced only to himself, not their sloppiness. Thinking he would never do his citizen-like duty again if they were going to be that way about it, thank you, Charles Ryan left, went home, and that would have made the end of it if the woman he was interested in, Becky, hadn't dropped by that evening, said, "That's right, let it go, let them get away with treating you like scum. While the real scum, the other Charles Ryan, gets away." So, Charles Ryan, this one, asked, "Well what is it, then, woman? What is it, Becky?"

He never thought Becky gave him enough respect. After all, it had been Charles Ryan who'd first come up with the idea of the concept album. He hadn't actually made a concept album, but the *idea*, why, that had been Charles all over, long before *Sgt. Pepper*. "Where each song is, like a hit," he told his friends in the band The Conrads. He'd played bass in The Conrads in 1963. They'd opened, once, for Cliff Richard. Or had played at the Royal the afternoon before the night Cliff Richard played at the Royal. "Each song stands alone on this album," Charles told his mates. "But together, they're bigger than just their parts. See?"

If they'd done it, they'd have been the first.

He'd had quite a few arguments with Becky, he remembered now, about what to do about the tape, and whether she should just move in with him, and what to do once she'd moved in with him, and all of these arguments, oh yes, he did now remember well. He'd done a lot of begging, too, none of which he remembered at all. Where's Becky now? He wondered this from time to time.

"The citizen-like thing to do," Becky said about the tape, "would be to not let the cops get away with this, but report to the newspapers how they treated you, and you just doing the citizen-like thing."

Charles Ryan sighed, heaved himself up that Friday, dragged himself to the *Examiner* office in the shopping strip across from the library, where, sure enough, the stringers talked it over, gnawed it over amongst themselves, but had a hard-enough time figuring out: how could they even write about that tape without tipping off the *real* Charles Ryan?

"He's standing here," growled Charles.

One guy at a desk that had no accessories on it at all—more like a desk those folks at the *Examiner* let him use rather than something that could legitimately be called "his desk"—he said he'd become intrigued. "Intrigued, beguiled, and tired of this sort of thing," he said. "This treatment at the hands of the police."

"That's it," said Charles.

The guy for one had had enough. He was going to write an exposé and got Charles Ryan's story, the gist of it, then and there, wrote it down in a leather sheathed notepad. Then came to visit at Charles's flat, saw the actual machine the message had been recorded on. (The message tape itself now in the "hands of the police," confiscated. Hadn't paid Charles a farthing. "So tired of this!" said the guy.) Then the guy returned a week later and interviewed Charles one more time to fill in missing details. Asked about the bass guitar and amp leaned in the corner. "Opened for Cliff Richard at the Royal," Charles told him, and also about his concept of the concept album and Becky sat on the sofa beside him during the interview, at times interjecting things, touching Charles lightly on the forearm as she did. The journalist snapped a photo of them together, smiling.

Then the journalist left.

Charles and Becky, encouraged, went out for a lovely curry.

The *Examiner* came out the next day, but they didn't print anything, and they didn't print anything the day after. A couple of weeks went by and Charles Ryan wondered if he'd missed the exposé by then and what about that picture of him and Becky? So, he stopped by the *Examiner* office one afternoon to see what was up, and that guy wasn't there, and when they asked what guy Charles Ryan meant, he had to admit he didn't know his name. This had been the kind of guy who, if you missed catching his name initially, the situations that followed probably wouldn't lend themselves to finding out what that name had been, and—sure enough— Charles didn't quite catch it at first. Michael? David? So, he didn't know, and he went to show them where the guy had been sitting, but the desk was gone.

They never did print anything about it, and now twenty-five years or so had passed, Becky was gone (Still alive, just living in Leeds. That's right. He remembered now. It's not like he hadn't asked her to stay), and Charles Ryan, *the other* Charles Ryan, had no doubt got away with his ill-gotten gains or the mayhem he'd caused or—who knew? Maybe he'd gotten clean away with *murder*, and so no telling what Chris Harris, whoever he or she was, had pulled off. They never did print anything, but they almost did, and so Charles had turned to that chubby git who'd banged into him in the shopping plaza, nearly knocked him down and . . . who was that, behind that slob with his fluttering mimeograph? Leaned against the Clarks "50% OFF" sign. Was it?

But no, she'd be in Leeds, so he scowled, thought fleetingly of the nice curry, mumbled something in his growling manner, something that even he wasn't completely certain he might have said before he stalked away, although probably it boiled down to something like: "Close *you've* come," which could be even more accurately translated as: *Close you've come to knocking me down you dog-eating bastard I'm Charles Ryan nearly in the papers.*

3
Collapsed Across their Balsa Slab

So the man in the blue knit cap stalked away, which disappointed Wyatt because not in the train station gift shop, not the hotel lobby, in no store window down the whole of Barronsgate—nowhere had he found any item of clothing he could wear when he got back to Texas that included the name of the town. It was odd, as he understood there to be a semi-professional soccer team based there, and he had even seen a sports center during his cab ride the day before when searching for X. Without an article of clothing emblazoned with the town's name, Wyatt doubted he could convince colleagues at Taylor State the place existed.

His advance reservation at Town Central Sallowsfield had been a minor surrender to planning. Thinking it over that morning, with the map gripped firmly as he walked, referencing it often, he wondered if the location had been chosen subconsciously. Had he internalized, from his earliest training, the importance of seizing the center? Currently a proponent of the Colle-Zukertort opening, his approach tended to quieter, positional play that delayed, but did not eliminate, this impulse for centralization. Wyatt perhaps felt instinctively that the Town Central offered him access on his first day to the important focal point, the place where he would spend his first full day and, as such, fulfill the initial aim of his trip: the history and genealogy room on the second floor of the library building. That the hotel had turned out to be less than amenable was beside the point, and, probably, a few days getting accustomed to the shift in hours and an end to the karaoke contest would solve most of his discomfort.

He'd been checked into his room by a young strawberry blonde who had one of the kindest voices Wyatt believed he had ever heard in his life. She was almost the mirror opposite of the woman he'd seen at the station: that is, X, who had dark features and a South Louisiana Cajun family background. X had been a student at Taylor, though not his student, and not the usual, inexperienced, post-adolescent kind he commonly dealt with. In her mid-thirties, X was in the midst of "finding herself" when they met. She became a member of the chess team (a formidable player he'd persuaded to join the women's Rapid squad), and they'd also bonded over their interest in writing. She'd come to visit him in his office over Spring Break nearly five years before, and so had arrived when things on campus were quiet, basically deserted, in order to help him organize and clean the office which had, no argument, crossed an event horizon of chaos. X had gotten on a chair to arrange a stack of papers atop a filing cabinet, which Wyatt didn't think looked safe, so he'd gone to her, asked her carefully to step down. That had been the start of it.

Arriving at his office in shorts, a tank-top under an open-collared shirt, she managed to twist in a whirlwind motion upon first arriving in the tight space, removing a scarf tied at her throat simultaneously. Why she would need a scarf in Texas in March was a question it did not occur to Wyatt to ask. X sent out concentric waves of the Middle Eastern musk he would come to know well, as she pointed first with laser accuracy to two shelves loaded with *Business Administration Educator* journals, most of these stacked flat rather than vertically, many without identifying spines revealed. "Do you read them?" She didn't wait for an answer. "At all?" She draped the scarf over the back of his office chair. "Those go. That goes. Those. *This* is cute." Amidst the detritus, she beamed in on a marionette-like representation of *Romeo and Juliet* made of painted balsa. Dramatizing a scene in the tomb, pressing on the knob beneath its base caused the star-crossed lovers to collapse together across their shared slab. It was a gift from Stratford brought to him by Professor Wickham in English, a man who had plenty to say about Shakespeare. Wyatt enjoyed the company of such people though they did tend to go on and on.

X would turn out to be very much in the same category as Professor Wickham.

"Let's get to work," she said, then moving aside a stack of textbooks proceeded to lie on the floor, her arm over her eyes. "As soon as this headache passes."

Professor Sallow felt alarmed. At least partly he worried someone might pass by, see a coed's bare legs sticking out his office door into the hallway.

"Can I get you something?"

"I get her all the time." X's headaches, interestingly enough, were gendered. She peered at him from under her palm. "I know when she's about to leave." X prodded the shoes off of her feet, left-side toes peeling away the right shoe at the heel and vice versa. The shoes were silver, low, and thudded on the office floor, making a homey sound that reminded Wyatt of something. The campus was abandoned, else he might have worried more about her behavior, but he decided no one could make anything untoward about it, so he sat in the room's other chair reserved for visiting students and looked at her, his hands together, elbows on knees, index fingers over lips. He didn't know if he should comfort her or just maintain a soothing silence but felt compelled to examine her powerful legs, besides which the freckles on them were so tempting to count. Fifteen. Twenty. She crossed her bare feet. Her toenails were painted a crayon red.

Wyatt lost track of how long she remained supine before she blinked, rose by bending at the waist. "Now is the time for all good men to come," she said, "as my father used to say," and began to clear away the *Business Administration Educator* journals into a large, black leaf bag she'd brought. After those disappeared, X moved on to a stack of articles Wyatt had printed off the internet to read later, then never bothered with. "This one is from four years ago! If you haven't read it yet . . ." They disappeared into a second leaf bag.

X worked around to a stack on top of the filing cabinet that couldn't be reached without climbing up into the student visitor's chair. Wyatt didn't think it looked steady. "Careful," he said and put his hands on her hips to help her down.

She placed her hands on his shoulders. He stifled a desire to touch and even stroke the dark hairs on her forearm, grasped her more firmly to steady her, then she stepped into their first, surprising kiss. Surprising for him anyway. Much shorter than his towering wife, Z, Wyatt's hands moved from her shoulders to her back, which felt straight and powerful. She was like a creature coiled, ready to strike, an artifact, perhaps, of the time she'd spent as a bodybuilder. X had been, in her years, many things.

She grasped his wrists. "You're so dear. I'm afraid you might take this wrong, so I'm not going to tell you."

This frightened him. "I believe it's as good as told when someone says that," he pointed out, and she'd laid out her plan to sneak some hair into his coffin, to be there with him when he left. Romeo and Juliet, on his crowded desk, lounged across their slab as she spoke.

Incidentally, it was at that first and only office visit that X, while continuing with her dusting, found the cup he had sent off for: a snow scene picturing a corner in Sallowsfield where Barronsgate met Queensgate. He made his usual attempt to explain its presence and the family mythology.

"Oh, you should go," X told him. "Don't research it or build expectations. Experience it. Write about it. Promise you will. Promise you will." Wyatt, at that moment, was not yet aware how X was liable to say or do just about anything at any time.

4
Amy

But the woman who checked him into the Lodge Central Sallowsfield, while attractive, probably would not have stepped off a chair and into his arms. Wyatt sensed he would have in no way been her type.

Amy Ramsdale commonly found herself attracted not to academics but tradespeople with skills: an honest plumber, maybe a plasterer with those exciting stilts they wore (and the way everything looked so smooth after they were gone). Nor did she react when she saw his name on the reservation card, or on his credit card. "Room 212, Mr. Sallow," she said, and that was that. She happened to have the kind of voice that created those neurological waves science labels by the highly technical term "tingles": one of those voices that synapses have to call across the midline of the brain to other synapses for help in decoding. Wyatt felt the flutter of grievous impossibility, took his key—an actual key chained to a cork fob that resembled a float for a fishing line—followed her pointing finger to a steep staircase, and began his ascent.

Amy Ramsdale, from a family that traced its origins in the borough to the fifteenth century ("The Ramsdales," as the locals said, "are a force with which to be reckoned") would not have registered Sallow's name as anything having to do with *her* town at all, and this sense of regional ownership was a strong one for herself and her relatives. To attempt to put it into terms the professor could understand, she would no more take note of his name than a hotel owner in, let's say, Dallas might have commented upon a guest signing in with the surname "Dal." "Sallow" was to her a sound, possibly one representing a skin hue or species of tree, but not a name. As a supporter of the History and Genealogical Room at the Borough Library, and author of several articles in their quarterly journal, Amy would not have been impressed by any person who came to visit for a mere eight days set with the task of uncovering his "roots." She had, however—and Wyatt might have been surprised to learn this—stepped down from a chair and into someone's arms just seven and a half months before: a carpenter redoing the bar and dining room. At thirty-six, she had divorced a lowlife officer of Her Majesty's Coastguard Search and Rescue who had proved incapable of searching for any passion beyond snooker or rescuing any aspect of their marriage beyond her business income. After he bled the hotel dry (it would be more accurate to say "drank"), she saw the occasional cabinetmaker adventure as acceptable, even noble. Amy had also climbed off a ladder and into the arms of a Croatian student who'd been tiling the roof the summer before. (It is to be assumed that this student had plenty to say about Sallowsfield upon his return to Zagreb.) After she ran Mr. Sallow's card and pointed him towards his room, she returned to her laptop and its open spreadsheet, the previous week's paper receipts speared onto an upturned spike at her elbow. These receipts she removed and checked against the accounts one after another. With her chin on her fist, she carefully entered the figures with one finger, yet could not help musing about her most recent . . . encounter, a man who had been ambitious to please her, at least, and had his own business besides (an installer of fire and burglar alarms), yet it had turned out badly. Amy sighed. She wished she could find a helpful, rugged electrician, although that desire might have been influenced by a sketchy circuit breaker that tripped every fourth time someone warmed toast in the breakfast room microwave.

Preferably the electrician (licensed) would have a big cock.

The American tourist in the tweed jacket with the glasses and rolling suitcase that he *clunk, clunk, clunked* up the stairs no longer registered to her at all.

Amy's erstwhile alarm and burglary boyfriend had called her mobile three times that very day, but she had not answered. As far as she was concerned, they were no more. They'd had an issue. Their issue had occurred on a road trip to Whitby, returning from an extended holiday weekend. They'd been on the A64. It had been more than a six-hour drive, and dreary, and how much could someone talk about fire and burglar alarms and—more importantly—how long could someone *listen* to such talk? Past Malton, the event occurred that annoyed her. A little. Or: a little at the time. But it had annoyed her enough. Enough that when the necessity came to settle in on an actual annoyance, one large enough that it could spill over into anger, anger great enough to inflate into a worthy candidate for blowing out of proportion . . . yes, that event just past Malton fit the bill.

For three weeks she chewed it over. She returned in her mind to the occasion, each time illuminating it from a different angle. Amy succeeded, at last, in developing the incident into a "thing." An event to dwell on, obsess over, finally point the finger at when the time came. Yes. Well. This experience. Amy stewed over it nearly three weeks before having it out with Andy (the name of the burglar alarm man), and when she had it out with Andy, she explained that they couldn't see each other anymore. She was calling it off.

Not that there hadn't been good parts. They were, as the saying goes, "into it." The two of them left marks on one another. Not metaphorical or psychic wounds but scratches and gashes, several of which occurred during their extended holiday weekend to Whitby. Andy had returned to bed after washing off in a warm shower one afternoon and was about to climb in when he thought he heard Amy say, "You're back." (To be truthful, because of dealing with so many alarms, Andy's hearing had been affected, and the soft, whispering quality of Amy's voice that helpless men like Wyatt Sallow found so attractive he found to be merely a strain.) "You're back," he'd heard her say, like he'd been gone, transported overseas a while, not taken a quick shower.

"Your back! Look in the mirror."

Straining his neck, he could see she'd mauled him. He looked like he'd been jumped by a cat with a vendetta. More, when he stepped to the bedroom with a look of awe, she didn't apologize. "Don't let your mum see," she'd said, and examined her own nails in wonder.

Andy lived with his mother.

Amy didn't mention at that time, the time of the phone call where she explained she had decided to mutually end their relationship (unilaterally), didn't mention at all something that had nagged at her about Andy even longer than the incident. It was his name. Well, it was their names. The combination of them. "Amy and Andy."

Uh, no. Not going to happen.

As for the event that caused the issue, true, he had not begged. He had not even asked to initiate it. Especially if by "asked" one referred to a direct request made via direct questions. He had hinted, somewhat ironically. Then ironically taken back that hint, somewhat ineffectively. They'd taken his van for the trip. The back space contained fire and burglar alarms, wires, tools in bins along either side of a crawlspace, so Amy had insisted on a hotel, nixing his scheme of placing a sleeping bag between the bins and the tools.

Most accurately she would have to say she'd paid for the trip, including the hotel, all meals (with breakfast before leaving town), but they did take his van and he drove the entire way, not trusting her so much to do so because "this my livelihood, girl." And it was all fine, she supposed. Pulling up to a restaurant in a van with brightly colored advertising on its panels was not a problem for a practical woman who managed a business herself. Even if the panels had cartoonish red letters with shining light rays shooting from them and phrases like "BE ALARMED—HILLTOP FIRE AND BURGLARY SYSTEMS"—with one side of the van featuring the head of a man vaguely resembling Edvard Munch's *The Scream*, except Munch's figure didn't have "STOP THIEF!" rising from its anguished mouth in a dialogue balloon. On the other side of the van, a cartoonishly stunned man with a bag over his shoulder, black knit cap, and raccoon-like mask had been caught in the glare of a 500-watt outdoor yard lamp beside a funnel stack of words inside the graphic of, for some reason, a tornado, which read:

INTRUDER

ACCESS

CCTV

FIRE

It was all fine. Nor did she even mind so much driving up to the seaside parking areas and stepping down in her bathing suit from this brightly colored, brightly lettered van that, on its very top, featured not a practical rack for ladders or pipes, but a three-foot-tall medieval shield constructed from fiberglass, crisscrossed by a long plexiglass sword and similarly styled mace. The shield read:

HILLTOP FIRE

AND BURGLARY

SINCE 2012.

No problem. Andy, her boyfriend, had financial difficulties connected with his ex-wife's stay in a rehab center that he had been responsible enough to cover, so Amy had paid for petrol, too, though the thing did guzzle fuel, and, in fact, it wasn't even a difficulty in *doing* what he suggested or hinted at, there on the A64, just past Malton (a divided four-lane shielded on either side by dense forest, nearly deserted of a Sunday afternoon), but this thing he wanted, there at motorway speeds, with him driving, her slipping off her seatbelt to more readily bend over his lap, this thing he didn't quite ask for except cleverly and indirectly, well, it came back to her as a possibility, a rationale, and Andy was so easy to get along with otherwise, she had trouble thinking of any other possibility or rationale. So, she broke up with him over it, a pretty good reason to do so, she felt, after she'd worked it up a bit, and this kept her from having to even mention the better reason she wanted quit of him and that was Alan.

Alan, Andy's dog, a bull terrier, went all places with him, including weekend getaways to seaside resorts. Short-haired, he had no discernible smell, which bothered Amy: a dog should smell like a dog, especially a dog she didn't really live with but did have to share a hotel room with. He also had particularly almond-shaped eyes—just a result of his breed after all, yet Alan seemed at most times to be gazing at her narrowly and with suspicion. Though of even temper and not much of a barker, Alan represented an upsetting presence in her relationship with Andy, one of the reasons she'd allowed Andy into the hotel kitchen back door where he'd set her on the butcher's table and pulled off her trousers. She found the feel of gritty flour in her knickers the rest of the day less disagreeable than a romp on Andy's fine mattress at his mother's if Alan was going to slouch down on the recliner and watch like a Chinese bathhouse attendant.

Driving the A64 after their getaway had concluded, where they'd gotten away from everything except Alan, Andy was apparently quite happy after what had been, by his reckoning, a "perfect" weekend. "It really was perfect," he said. "I'm so glad it was perfect," and statements to that effect.

Amy agreed.

"Not so perfect it couldn't be topped off with a motorway blowjob."

She gave him, instead, a full sixty seconds of silence.

"That was a joke," he said.

Amy understood this as Andy's most common ploy. "You're going to say it's a joke now it's settled; I'm not giving you a motorway blowjob, whatever that is."

They cruised about ten miles.

"I'm so glad I finally have a woman in my life . . . the kind of woman who *would* understand that giving her man . . . her man a blowjob while driving at motorway speeds was just a joke. Although," he grinned, "joking aside, it would also be pretty much all I ever wanted out of existence."

This, interjecting that what he kidded at was, indeed, what he really wanted—no kidding aside—and doing so in what could only be called a joking fashion was Andy's second most common ploy.

"I shall not be giving you a blowjob in this or any service van, and definitely not at motorway speeds."

"*Nor would I ask you to.* As it would be tricky, wouldn't it?" He checked his mirrors, passed a Mini Cooper. "At motorway speeds. What with me driving, checking traffic. Staying on the road."

"Please do."

"Making sure no other cars come by that could see that you were giving me an A64 blowjob."

"Good God, Andy!"

"Although this van is pretty high," he went on. "It would be lorries we'd mainly have to worry over."

More miles passed.

Then more.

"And the occasional taller-than-normal delivery van."

"Alright!" She pried open her seatbelt and flung away its webbed strap.

"No way," said Andy.

"Don't say I never gave you ... well ..."

And it was fine. Standard. Standard with the added dimension of flying through space and time in a van full of tools and wires. All standard until, pulling aside for a breather, Amy happened to look into the back only to catch Alan's gaze. Those accusing eyes. The upturned chin.

It was as if Alan were about to say, "And ... ?"

Without going into other specifics, Andy did appreciate Amy for what she did, as he couldn't imagine anyone else he'd ever pulled pitching in like that. That Amy. A corker. He'd held up his end, of course. As in: carefully checked for cars, kept the van on the road, stayed alert for any vehicle tall enough that passengers could look in the service van's windows. But it had been that, the multitasking required to successfully choreograph a motorway blowjob, that ended up as his downfall. It was not Alan's fault, as in fact that had not constituted the final straw, the dog's expectant leering being a much bigger problem. But Andy's inability to keep more than one aspect of oral sex as performed in a motorway context lodged simultaneously in his mind was what provided Amy the "thing," and that was that. Relationship over.

In one way of thinking about it, most humans aren't good at doing more than one activity at a time. One of Amy's clientele at the Town

Central Sallowsfield, Wyatt Sallow, knew well that plenty of grandmasters, international masters, and even those ranked below had the capability of playing seven simultaneous games or more: sometimes blindfolded. They were good at it (Wyatt was not), but for the most part people—perhaps men in particular—were not built for that kind of multi-lane thinking. One could support two lanes at most, probably, and that second one would move along at a much-reduced clip. When it came down to it and Amy broke up with him, Andy could feel no culpability. He had simply not done something most people (i.e., men, see above) also would not . . . perhaps *could not* have done. Because what she said three weeks later when she parted company with him over the phone was that Andy had basically attempted to murder her, Amy, on the A64.

"And *that's* the last straw," she said.

Andy spluttered. Then did some additional spluttering. By three weeks later, in Andy's mind, this event had all come about because of a spontaneous offer from Amy to unbutton his jeans and suck him off on the motorway.

"I put myself at risk for you," Amy said.

At risk how and of what? Discovery? Probably that escapade on the hillside stairs a couple months back at Havril Park had been dicier, especially as she found out a few weeks later her friends used those stairs commonly for almost daily aerobic Step exercises with a personal trainer. They'd dodged a bullet there, alright (worth it). Surely, they'd had less of a chance of being seen by a passing lorry than by being stepped over by Becky Samson and Jane McGuire out for their morning constitutional, and faced fewer dire consequences as well as Becky and Jane's outrage would have amounted to simple welcome diversion for your basic lorry driver, wouldn't it?

"I put myself in *danger* for you," she insisted.

"Okay, this whole '*for you*' thing. First of all, it was a mutual act."

"Yes. I always get a lot out of sucking you off."

"It was . . . agreed upon, then, if not mutual. *Ach*, what's the word?"

"Putting myself at risk. While you were safe."

This hurt. By the time three weeks had rolled around, Andy had an entirely different evaluation of the event, especially concerning how he'd been thinking of her welfare the whole time. How she could, in her waning days, have that event, that moment—*accomplishment*—to look back on. After her looks were gone, maybe. Happens to everyone. "But hey. Once. *Once* I, Amy Ramsdale, had been a caution. A *caution*. Why, one spring on the A64 . . ."

Yes, Andy tended towards the long view. It had been, in the final analysis—this *motorway cum-guzzling road suck*—a thing he wanted for her.

"*Consensual*," Andy said. "That's the word. Thank you. Which you agreed to. And what? Neither of us was in danger."

"We could have crashed."

"We could have crashed at any . . ."

"And I took my seatbelt off. While you . . . left . . . yours . . . on."

Had she? Had he? Andy had no recollection but wouldn't have been too surprised to learn he'd done that—or not done that—with the seatbelt. One, given the overall danger inherent in motorway blowjobs, and the fact that they were both engaged in one, that he had managed to keep the van in the correct lane, stay alert for road hazards, keep a lookout for prying eyes in passing vehicles, all the while steering carefully and simultaneously keeping up a cruising speed . . . Seatbelt! He hadn't thought of it at all! It was one too many factors to give attention to. Unsnapping the seatbelt was a bridge too far, that is, for the reptilian male mind to grasp if it were already grasping the wheel (tightly—white-knuckled at one point) with both hands. He recalled that he had, it was true, managed to help her open his fly, then separate that part in the window of his boxer briefs (which were gaining in popularity the world over), then remove a particular priapic item for perusal and inspection as she leaned on the floorboards.

If he had to guess, he supposed that he had, indeed, left the seatbelt on.

Andy almost had time to formulate an apology, but unfortunately headed into another line of thought about a very good reason this whole forgetting to remove the seatbelt thing occurred. It was, after all, a long-standing . . . maybe *pastime* was the wrong word, but plenty who drove vans had come up with this, especially those living in one town, yet working in another. *Vansturbation*, it might be called: a way to fill otherwise empty drive-time. Andy considered . . . why, he'd always kept the seatbelt on then, too!

"So, I'm obviously a prat," Andy said into the phone. "Who longed for your death. But maybe you don't know . . ."

"Thank you for understanding and goodbye."

"What if . . . ?"

"There's nothing more to say."

"Who's in the real danger here, is what I'd like to know? I mean, what with the teeth and . . . "

She'd already hung up. Andy shook his head. Looked over at his mum's recliner. "She'll be back," he said to Alan.

Stewing over these kinds of issues, Amy did not so much as glance at the man in tweed who clumped up the staircase, lifting his bulging bag one step at a time. She ground her chin into her fist and continued to feed last week's numbers into the spreadsheet.

5
The Kind of Nevdakha He Was

Wyatt had spent much of the sleepless night fretting over irrelevant matters. It wasn't accurate to give them the full status of worries. The hotel, as he discovered after clumping up the staircase, had been cobbled together from a collection of three adjacent buildings, as the floors did not align, with another haul up a steep incline necessary on the second story to get to his room from the already exhausting stairway landing. He believed that Hussein had dropped him at some obscure back entrance, but a quick walk before sundown revealed that the Town Central had nothing but back doors, having been tucked away amid a warren of old warehouses, a good hike from the hotel to any busy thoroughfare. Its promotional website touted both "no ground floor rooms," and "no lift," but did highlight "stairs with a single landing," possessing "handrails on both sides." Something about the setup's irregularities—like a puzzle whose pieces had been mashed together rather than fitted—tugged at his irregular thoughts through the night. Jet lag could share some blame. Getting up from time to time he looked out his room's square double pane over the triangular, translucent sunroom roof below, then down the alley flanked by fenced parking areas, finally resting his gaze on the booming Boy with Bucket Bar that rattled both layers of the windows with its karaoke night blasts.

Mainly, he worried about what he might or might not find in the days ahead.

So later that crisp, banana day morning, after the grumbling man in the blue knit cap moved away, Wyatt followed the xeroxed xerox to an arcade, passing SALLOWSFIELD CENTRAL TV AND ELECTRONICS and a few iron benches where a trio of elderly retirees had already gathered, in the covered tunnel, away from the sun.

Wyatt had already, on this morning, seen several disabled persons, many with canes, or wheeled walkers, navigating the cobbles of the tunnel-like arcade with difficulty. He wondered if some combination of the steep hills and the fragility of ankles after age sixty made injury a regional way of life. As if to refute this insult, three busty young women turned into the passageway stepping towards him, each pushing a carriage, each carriage holding a newborn. *"Wooh, wooh, wooh,"* said one upon seeing him. She had been somehow crowbarred into a pair of tights and sported a fluffy orange jacket and bronze ear-ring loops that grazed her shoulders. *"Wooh, wooh, wooh,"* she said, not to the infant in the stroller but to Wyatt's face. He smiled, uncertain if a smile was the appropriate response. Behind him, the doors of SALLOWSFIELD CENTRAL TV AND ELECTRONICS—across from the Boots—unlocked, and Sarah Marsden set out a card table she'd stand beside with her friend Annie Graves, the table to hold pamphlets encouraging deeply discounted communication opportunities by switching from one's current mobile network to Interfone Connect.

Wyatt rested on a bench near the arcade's exit onto a plaza that he knew, thanks to his map, was home to the library and its historical archive. He checked the time on his phone, considered entering the coffee shop on this side of the arcade to await the library's opening. This tunnel, Wyatt would learn—known locally as "The Swale"—had a vague association with a low drainage area that had served to sluice offal from the meat and fish markets that once covered this part of town. Brick pavement and the addition of a frosted glass canopy had turned it into an attraction, and its long breezeway created an aural peculiarity that happened to be most pronounced at the very bench where Wyatt rested, waiting for the opening of the coffee shop.

Though he'd passed them nearly fifty yards before sitting at the other exit of The Swale, Wyatt could now hear the aged trio on the other iron bench much more loudly. Loudly, though not distinctly. To his ears their conversation ran:

Old man #1: There you (mumble echo)!

Old woman: You were (mumble echo) yesterday!

Old man #2: It's where I'll (echo mumble) tomorrow if you (indecipherable sound).

It was as if he had been given a can and a string, the other end of which had been tightly fastened to this central part of town.

Wyatt placed his notebook on his knee, removed his ballpoint pen, tuned in to the conversations of those passing through The Swale—like:

The girls with strollers and carriages who jabbered on after they'd walked away from him. In fact, the farther down the arcade they traveled, the more accurately he could decipher their conversation. Like plucking a butterfly from a flowering shrub, he captured: *"Rod got into a fight with Max because Max hit Rod's brother, Danny, in Danny's good eye."*

"Whooooo," said the girl in the fluffy orange jacket.

From a middle-aged woman carrying a net grocery bag to another middle-aged woman in an un-tucked shirt: *"He's really good, really good, at bodywork on cars. The more his life flies apart, the more he puts cars together."*

An elderly gentleman to a young girl who was a relative or caretaker—it was hard to say. *"I am no stranger to coincidence."*

A thin, collegiate-looking man in a yellow sweater into his phone. *"It's seven-thirty, some sort of day between the weekends. Call me. Please?"*

Sarah Marsden to Annie Graves, whom he would not recognize later atop Tower Hill as they propped Interfone flyers on tiny plexiglass easels atop their card table. *"Ask her a question you'll get the answer, when the answer was born, and what it's wearing."*

One more from the "Whoooo" girl a last time before she exited The Swale and entered Barronsgate with a light step. *"That is fuckingly sad . . . and funny."*

The girl behind the counter at the coffee shop had the reddest red hair Wyatt had ever seen: a Kewpie doll quality color. He chose a table and waited for coffee American (which sounded comforting, though he didn't know what it meant) and a scone. He felt out of place, it was true, onstage in an unpracticed role, a visitor to his own body and skin. Yet he often felt this way in Turner, Texas, as well, at the Pizza Shack, let's say, awaiting a pepperoni slice and cola that would be carried over by a student on a bright red, plastic tray. He had at least three meals a week at the Pizza Shack these days, which was, he had no doubt, turning his bones to chalk, but cooking for himself had never caught on after "Cousin" Yuri moved in with Z in the house on Linden Lane and he, Wyatt, had gone to inhabit his fifth wheel at the Tranquility Park RV Camp. Basically, he felt he put up with enough shit in his life, why add cooking (and cleaning) to the dreary list? He could picture Yuri's green, precious-stone eyes on the last day Wyatt spent in that house, eyes that swam towards him in the gloom, tracking him as the man leaned close to emphasize his sincerity. "Z" had already explained to him after the memorial for Wyn—in a phone call— that she wouldn't come home anymore. And that this cousin was much, much more than a cousin. Also, that she didn't want to hurt Wyatt but, "I'm tired. I'm tired." "And now," said Yuri, almost chummy, "so we can go forward, together, about the little boy," but Wyatt slid off his own sofa like it were the edge of a two-story roof. He headed for the front door in a kind of escape mode. "It has been so hard for her, you can imagine," said Yuri.

"Fuck her."

"She knows you have the trailer. The RV. We ask only that we can use it until . . ."

Listening to Yuri, his own tongue had taken on a papery flatness, so he didn't manage to croak out (as he later would) that he did not want to go forward together or that Yuri and Z could have the house, he would never bother them. He didn't want to see either of them again as long as he lived. Wyatt pushed out the front door, and by the time he had crossed partly to the outside he knew that the interior space under that roof had altered, was no longer his home. Wyn's departure had transformed and drained the place of substance or . . . or . . . maybe his *presence* had given it a quality now lacking. How long had it been since the July early morning when he'd taken Wyn out into the darkness of the back porch, less than ten paces from where he now struggled to distance himself from Yuri's voice? The boy had coughed himself awake, so Wyatt sat with him on his lap, the two peering into pine trunks that materialized in gathering dawn like photographs in developer. Wyn's mouth moved, uttering inexplicable expressions or conclusions—hard to say. Words as lost as buried runes. Daylight came as Wyatt smelled his son's blond wispy hair, felt the boy's limbs twitch as rare spoonfuls of morning breeze mixed with the stifling heat. He wished he had a cup of coffee to reach for but instead, uncharacteristic of him, he placed both hands on Wyn's shoulders and squeezed. In the high-pitched imitated voice of Kitty Canaveral, he pointed out "You have more talent in one chamber nozzle extension bar . . ." and Wyn giggled. Leaving the house, it was as if his fingers could still make out the armatures there under the flesh of the boy's shoulders as he'd felt them that morning the two Sallows watched while the sun filtered through the trees.

He rubbed these fingers against his thumbs as he pushed out the door on the day of the memorial, leaving it open behind him, and Yuri followed, barefoot, yammered on about "That terrible thing you said."

"I'm sorry about it. Goodbye."

Save a few trips to gather clothes and toiletries, he had not set foot in the place since.

Yuri, he understood immediately, would snap up this offer: Wyatt could see it in the floating, gem-like eyes. He'd take it, although it seemed to Wyatt an utterly unacceptable arrangement, but then one night after an argument Z had once scolded him as "the kind of *nevdakha* who won't steal even if you knew you wouldn't get caught!" and he did not need a dictionary to translate, but, of course, he had said worse things to her over the years.

Especially that one time.

Considering Z intensified his sense that his feeling on this morning—the feeling of being out of place in a foreign land—only added to the day's sense of perfect banana appropriateness, for in another country it constituted—finally—the correct way to feel.

Large plate glass windows on two sides of the café opened onto both the arcade and the plaza where the library hunched, a nearly corner-less silver-grey globule of Art-Deco surrounded by shops, newsagents, and bank branches, most of these displaying in one way or another Wyatt's relatively rare surname. He watched a sampling of humanity file past. A man with enormous jowls (some condition?). A teenager approximating David Bowie's Ziggy Stardust phase. Wyatt sat with his back to the café's restroom door and could not help himself from hoping to find among this crowd the instantly recognizable X. She would be carrying her black notebook, much like his. She would be walking in an erect manner, pointing her expectantly upturned chin at the shops and stores. She might well be coming to the library, too, if his theory proved correct. He remembered, for no reason he could associate with the moment (the aroma of baked goods, cocoa, tea?) X's distinctive smell. He discovered, over time, that she used a perfume or cologne her husband had procured for her in Dubai, possibly Kuwait. He worked as an engineer in petroleum recovery. The perfume, according to her, constituted a rare, impossible to replace fragrance, custom made in a Middle Eastern market stall. "When I run out, there will be no more. I won't smell the way you expect me to." No doubt, by now, she *had* run out, and if he located her in this town, he would have to find some way to sniff out this possibility, perhaps an innocent swoop at her cheek for a friendly peck. Or he could hover his nose momentarily over her head, breathe in her rich black hair with its grey threads.

She was pretty short.

No doubt her smell had gone past its expiration date, like everything in the universe. Wyatt just didn't know what date that had been.

Beside him, two women conversed at a window table. "He keeps going off for *coffee*," one said, leveling at the beverage a charge of unspoken betrayal. Outside, a man and woman, grey-haired, wearing matching windbreakers, exited from a wide clearance store doorway into the library square. Wyatt stared hard at the man's forehead, imagined himself as this passing stranger as had been his custom in the past, only as with the man on the train with the pork pie hat, a dread crept over him. What was the most likely case? This was someone (smiling, with large white teeth) who'd made the right decisions, and done so in a way he, Wyatt Sallow, MBA, had not. The man had lived a life without . . . short of saying it any other way . . . sitting on a counter in an RV with his boxer briefs around his knees, howling in animal grief.

But then, you never knew.

At a nearby table an elderly couple ignored the parrot-like screeches of a man or child in a blue jacket who sat with them, bent over, emitting as well occasional groans, barks, then simply laughing. For no discernible reason, he laughed. His hair was slick, his pale cheeks pocked with acne. No one in the shop took any notice of the noises he made.

"That's right," said the woman to the other at the window seats. *"Coffee."*

The man or boy in the blue jacket turned towards Wyatt, then turned away.

Wyatt rose, collected his day pack, left the café without the coffee or scone he'd ordered and paid for. He'd walk to the library to wait for it to open. The woman with the fire-engine hair might think him strange, but it wouldn't matter for, as with the Aroma Kava cafeteria on Khreschatyk Street in Kyiv, the elevator of the largest chain bookstore in Turner, Texas, and even like his own home where he covered the mortgage on Linden Lane, he'd never be in that place again.

6
The Sallow File

Attitude was all. Negativity constituted the worst approach that could be taken in any sport, game, or competitive activity. Wyatt encouraged his team to focus on winning, even when heavily disfavored, as when entered in a tournament attended by colleges with programs that specifically attracted those with chess ambitions. Against any odds, a fighting frame of mind had a way of unsettling opponents. The more he considered the probability that she'd followed him here—no, preceded him here—the more Wyatt realized he was going to have to work up some mightily feigned surprise and strong resistance when their inevitable meeting occurred. He would have to exude confidence.

Though in fact he had low confidence that he could pull off such an encounter, as coming face-to-face with X always produced in him a heart-racing reaction similar to looking over a mist-shrouded city from a skyscraper's observation deck. Of course, she might have changed, and the fact that she no longer matched the portrait he'd hung in his mind, let alone resembled the picture he'd sent to Hussein (*why?*), or even smelled the same, these incongruities and the effort he'd have to make to reconcile them might cause him to falter in his cheerful, bravely put-up front. Unlike chess, where imperfections, bad decisions, blunders remained on the board, haunted the game until it ended, *could not be taken back* (or not without cheating, and that included cheating OtterShark, which was possible, but always left Wyatt feeling sour) . . . unlike the game, time, in reality, did have a way of healing other endeavors in life. This idea would no doubt make Paul McBride howl in laughter, yet Wyatt did strongly believe that all people, sure, made mistakes, but those—life mistakes—had a way of submerging under the combined weight of existence, mingling with other actions, some right and true, others neutral but, for that reason, rendered harmless. This included even those kinds of mistakes that could only be contemplated at a distance, parked down the street with the headlights off, from a position slunk low, barely peeking over a dashboard, as first police and, soon afterward, an ex-husband arrives . . .

At any rate . . . the library represented a locus of attention that would attract both Wyatt and X, and should that attraction occur on the same day, he could encounter her very soon. He attempted to steel his nerves.

Ultimately, he stood in line at the reference desk in the second-floor historical and genealogical center, a cavernous and popular investigative focus of regional history and genealogy, a small crowd having gathered on the second-floor landing even before the room opened. He wrote in his notebook, "I am crazy," then closed that page over a finger to mark it should the entry require additional details. Judged by their easy familiarity with the two librarians on duty, most of the clientele had returned after multiple previous visits. They discussed specific items of record they sought to add to their growing portfolios of researched materials, many of these separated into accordion folders and vinyl binders, carefully labeled, carried in the crooks of their arms. Bookshelves and cabinets encircled the perimeter of the room, along with map drawers, newspaper sheets draped over wooden dowels, even the occasional architect's model. Windows looking onto the plaza were tall and arched at the top, each featuring a round oriel at their apexes, decidedly at odds with the early modern exterior. Four-bladed fans turned lazily against the distant ceiling and, below these, tables with rows of desktop computers occupied much of the center of the room. Couples and individuals of many ages bent over keyboards, tapped screens with their fingernails along tiny rows of numbers and names. Behind an area of reference desks, green filing cabinets rose in a stack nearly eight feet tall, a drawer just below shoulder height labeled, sure enough, "S-SE." Wyatt assumed it all to be there. Births and deaths. News items and clippings. He wondered if X hadn't gotten to the filing cabinet first, perhaps removed or reserved that material. As one way of looking at it, he had depleted his savings in a major fashion not to reach this town, but to reach that drawer. The tallest of the labeled cabinets required a wheeled stepladder for access, but "S-SE" was right there. No, not even just below the shoulder—more just above the elbow.

Outside the library, on the pavilion, he'd waited momentarily in front of a diptych bulletin board mounted on square posts, calendar notices sealed in its bifurcated glass case. One side of the display trafficked in "events," the other "Visitor's Information." He had difficulty discerning the difference between the two. Lectures were advertised, and musical evenings. A class called "Fun with Power Saws." Even arts festivals. Wyatt noted everything pinned to the board had occurred either the week before his arrival or was planned for the week after his departure. He had managed to arrive during a break in the town's narrative.

At 9 am by his phone's digital readout, he climbed the high concrete stairs, entered the oddly shaped building, browsed momentarily in a corner of the ground floor. As the Town Central map indicated, a rectangular area to the right of the entrance served as an "Information Centre," but this appeared to be mainly a gift shop, featuring a table similar to the corner of the railway station containing pamphlets of interest to anyone touring the region. All these points of interest were nearby yet outside of Sallowsfield, and included famous sculpture parks, homes of literary figures, museums having to do with the coal industry, textile industry, and industry in general. There was a promotional card for the Thornfield museum, an institution he'd read about in *The North: A Tough Guide*. Their collection featured historical overviews of the town, so he pocketed one of the cards. A man stationed at a cash register wearing a green shirt and matching green tie sold mugs and t-shirts, none sporting the town's name. There were library-themed book bags encouraging patrons to READ, and ENJOY BOOKS, and ENJOY BOOKS BUT IN THE MEAN-TIME—SHHHHH! One quote Wyatt found comforting, Twain's: "Outside of a dog, a book is man's best friend. Inside of a dog, it is too dark to read." Again, it occurred to him that without a souvenir, East Texas would have difficulty believing he had been here at all.

Arrived upstairs, Wyatt judged that the clientele of the day moved too slowly for his taste in taking up their business with the man and woman who manned the reference desk, only two persons on staff to manage the large crowd. He'd entered through a security turnstile, no doubt there to ensure no archival resource escaped the room unless properly checked out, but why have one going in? He attempted to choose which of the two reference staff he'd rather speak to regarding his inquiry. Standing behind two broad desks that gave them each their own, spacious, horizontal surface upon which to spread arcane materials, one was a birdlike, older blond woman, the other a tall young man with sun on his cheeks. Behind them loomed the tall green cabinets arranged alphabetically. Wyatt felt sweat trickle down the small of his back in the close, heavily heated hall of records. He stepped to one side of the metal reference desks to look more closely at the bank of filing cabinets, moved to approach the "S-SE" cabinet, adopted a serious demeanor (like the one his father managed without a hitch).

Wyatt held firm to the belief that he stood a better than 50/50 chance of succeeding at any endeavor if he acted boldly as if it were his right to do so. It's how he had arrived at the Boryspil Airport in Kyiv, like a man come to rescue someone . . . or, no . . . *secure* something he deserved. His father, who with little Wyatt in the car had once blown past a National Guard roadblock keeping the public from a seaside community devastated by Hurricane Otto simply by holding up his license, barking the word "Sallow" past his unlit stogie and driving through it, had that knack. This was no National Guard roadblock and, most likely, no one would notice him approaching the cabinet, register him pulling open the drawer, removing—with a nod of recognition that indicated "Yes! There it is!"—the Sallow File.

"You!"

The tone of the birdlike woman did not possess either a volume or timbre often associated with birds. Nor was it of the sort generally used to alert someone that a mistake had been made: more a sound that a policeman might employ to interrupt the actions of someone about to throw a brick through a jewelry store window. The woman did not bother to provide details as to why she focused the "You!" in Wyatt's direction, the word alone, plus her indication by eye only, sending him back to his position at the end of the line. He fell behind a pair of older people, the man of a decidedly Napoleonic look (though taller) with wet lips and a precise over comb; his partner, with her pencil poised, shook multiple bracelets that clacked down her thin forearm as she continually rolled up her sleeves, preparing, no doubt, to capture important genealogical data pertinent to her own identity. "Right. Of course," Wyatt said. He decided that the young ruddy-cheeked man might prove a better bet after all. The eyes on that woman. The voice!

When the lines had edged forward, Wyatt recognized that he hadn't apologized for stepping out of sequence, but it had become too late to do so as both the harsh, angry woman and the young man now busied themselves, absorbed with arcane operations in assistance to researchers, she with newspaper clippings from what appeared to be mid-twentieth century, he with a wide nostriled man who managed to peruse a reproduction of a medieval map with a look of astonished disbelief. Wyatt wondered if the map represented this region and attempted to feign interest in it. Although he often expressed the maxim "ask forgiveness, not permission," he did not, in fact, live by this rule in practice. Sure enough, in the case of his attempt to see the "S-SE" cabinet, he'd asked for neither.

His failure to reach the cabinet drawer gnawed at him, yet he had to consider it a temporary obstacle. Whatever apology he might express could still be done loudly, perhaps stretched out, including as one rationalization his never having been there before, so not realizing "behind the desk" was forbidden—not in a smart-aleck way, but sincerely. This sincerity he could no doubt sell more readily by only slightly increasing his Texas accent, making obvious, at least, his North American origins. *Not from around hey-yah.*

Simultaneously chastised and piqued at being chastised (though he had arguably deserved to be), Wyatt stewed over the circumstances of life and the uneasy way desires struggled against barriers of doubt.

This crowd might take an interest in his unusual surname, even if the vicious, angry, and no doubt dissatisfied-with-life woman who had unleashed the tirade against him—the tirade of "You!"—did not. Same with that ruddy-cheeked fellow. Chastised, then, but also growing angry as the line edged forward, angry at himself that he hadn't spoken up ("I'm sorry about what I did fifteen minutes ago" would not fly now). Wyatt stiffened, drew back his shoulder as if brought to military attention. This woman did not know him. Not just the family name thing. She didn't know he held an academic position: one in a system far larger, he supposed, than this public library. But then why should she? He was obscure. His obscurity increased every day (his shoulders slid into a more "at ease" posture) with every poem he did not write and white paper on the ethics of masking reserve bids he did not publish. (One of those, unfinished, lay untouched in his suitcase/pack. He had brought it on the trip, feeling he might have time to work on it, as people do.) Wyatt had to admit none of his tax dollars supported this public library, although his own name hung over the door outside. Perhaps he shouldn't be there. The man or the woman might point this out and, since he was not a resident, a citizen, a library cardholder, perhaps he would be turned away. The general ethical admonishments concerning treatment of guests, including clients and, in this case, visitors, might be invoked against that rude, wren-like woman, but he felt a lack of certainty. He waited, sweating, which allowed him to feel better, at least momentarily, for he tried not to let unethical people get to him: there wasn't much to be done about them if they were that far outside the norms of civilized social discourse. It had all happened so fast, although aside from an intuitive sense that it would pay off eventually, he didn't know what had gotten into him to make such a move in the first place and escape from his position in line. He should wait his turn. A moment of self-reflection might have reminded him that his "intuition," his hand waving, his "oh, hell, let's try this" approach seldom worked over the board either, even when he'd played against people rather than software, although flesh and blood opponents were subject to similar acts based not on calculation or sound principle but guesswork. "Feelings." The disastrous effects of his own guesses often became nullified in that way. That he had such a nearly obsessive interest and even knowledge of the game, however, was often worthless when he played people of skill or—here he shuddered—talent. Those who had in relation to the game what he believed X had. Even when she had broken his heart, he'd tried to remain in her orbit, drawn in by her aura. Even after she told him he was "not the third man," he had gone to her house to feed and walk her dogs, Bert and Ernie, when she had to be away. In fact, he'd done that twice.

Persistence. Might not those efforts still pay off?

A truly large young woman with uncombed hair arrived before the bird-like lady, who nodded, saying nothing. The girl began pulling on white cotton gloves wordlessly as the librarian bent below her desk, stood again with an ancient looking volume crooked over one arm, the book complete with a closed bronze clasp and tiny triangular lock, like a medieval bound illuminated manuscript. The work's leather cover had been carved with loops and whorls. The reference woman offered the heavy item along with a key, and the big girl held out her arms to receive both items.

Relieved when the man motioned him to the metal desk, Wyatt stepped forward. Cleared his throat. Tried to come up with an introductory statement that might encompass everything he'd been considering while waiting his turn.

"I'm from Texas," he began.

The young man made no movement.

Wyatt waded into laying out, at least superficially, his purpose, lying only a little bit in doing so, though he sounded unconvincing even to himself. "Just in the North for an academic conference" . . . "decided to come over" . . . "family name" . . . "a lark" . . .

The young man asked his family name, and he obliged.

"No."

"Yes, it's me." The young man's disbelief would be easy to assuage with that passport from the money belt below his own belt, trousers, and boxer briefs. A Sallow. Come to Sallowsfield.

"I mean we don't have anything on it. Never heard that name."

The trickle down Wyatt's back became more like two trickles, one for either side of his spine. Why heat this place so oppressively? "Not in those . . ." He indicated the filing cabinets.

"You're looking for records?"

"Records." He nodded.

"Which?"

Wyatt knew he'd need a better reason than the one he was about to give. "That tell about my name."

"Nothing here. Not for that. I've never heard it." He turned to the angry woman. "Have you heard of it?"

"Heard of what?"

"Sallow. As a surname."

"Never heard of it."

"Could it be . . ." Wyatt moved his chin towards the filing cabinets again. His mind raced. Somewhere, under the surface of his thoughts, he should have wondered if the young man had seen every name, every file, scrap, even, that might be in such a large bank of cabinets. And if not, the only way to truly say "we have nothing on that" would have been to engage in pulling out that drawer over there and doing some rummaging.

"You've looked into it?" the man asked.

"Just over on a lark. Didn't get a chance."

"Most look into it," said the young man. He indicated the cavernous room. "Before getting this far."

Wyatt was close to nodding. Very close to indicating that he really should have done just that. He leaned forward, on the brink of telling the young man that he'd be back later. Of course, it had taken him several decades and a suitable fraction of his savings to stand there on that day. He would not be back later. He was forty-five. Damn that X. Where was she? "I'm sorry," he began.

"After they've checked the digital records, they come here."

"Was there a woman before?" Wyatt brought his hand below his shoulder to indicate X's height, although he considered he might be holding his hand too high. She always loomed in his memory. "Brunette. Swarthy. Also, American."

"I haven't seen her," said the young man. He turned to the angry woman. "Have you seen her?"

"Seen who?"

The reference librarian copied Wyatt's height indication with his own hand. "American. Swarthy. Brunette."

"Not around here."

"Asking about that surname?" Wyatt added.

"I'd remember that," said the young man.

"Sallow!" said the blond woman. The big girl with the huge leather volume having moved away, the librarian now dug through a box of index cards for another client who worried at a button of her grey sweater, carried a purse that resembled an Easter basket, and, judging from her manila folders, had done research before arriving.

"That's what he says."

"Not around here," she said. "No."

"You've never heard the name, *Sallow*?" Wyatt asked.

"You could check the digital record," said the young man.

"I can't say that I *have* ever heard it," said the woman. "It's not usually a name."

"Not usually," agreed the man. He rushed, politely, to add: "Although I do believe it's your name."

"Sounds like one," said a balding man in line behind him. He wore a Polo shirt and had a face as square as the clock Wyatt's grandmother kept on top of her upright piano. "A name."

"Thank you."

"I think so," said clock face. "*Sallows*field, right?"

"That's it," said Wyatt. "I'd have thought . . ."

"Around here," said the woman, "the big names, the historical ones, are Ramsdale and Booth."

"Lots of Booths," said the young man, who Wyatt noticed had a name tag. His name, spelled out in large and reassuring block letters, was "Jon."

Wyatt withdrew a few more random noises and phrases from his vocal cords, aimed mainly at Jon, about how he'd so unexpectedly, by a kind of coincidence or even whimsy, found himself in Manchester and realized, looking at a map, that the town his own father had told him about was only a short train ride away. And—"So I asked . . . Was there any place around where, *on a lark*, I might be able to look into local records? Historical books on the region or . . ."

"Just here," Jon said. He indicated the room, which made up most of the second floor of the library. "You could look into all that here. If there was anything. It's not a common name, though. Not in this town. Not like Brooks."

"Brooks?"

"Or Lowery," said the birdlike woman, who wore no name tag.

"I was thinking about the university . . ."

"University records and college archives. No genealogy over there."

"Bad luck," said the man behind Wyatt. He held a full accordion folder under his arm, wore a look of hope this would wrap up soon.

"As for the records, they've all been digitized," said Jon.

"I see." Wyatt only wanted to leave the stuffy room at that point. Maybe he could flip through some of those volumes along the walls. Look in their indexes.

"Town was founded by a royal grant to the Lowerys," said the woman, closing one box of index cards, looping a rubber band twice around it, opening another. "That's why all those buildings are named after the Lowerys."

"Like the Lowery Building," said Jon.

"And Lowery Annex," she added.

"I'll be back after I've looked at some records." Wyatt didn't see any point in telling the pair he'd failed to check records or historical treatises about the town on purpose at a suggestion, made five years before, by the very woman he had asked about and who he expected to have already been there. Or to be showing up soon.

No doubt she would find similar disappointment.

"They've all been digitized," said the woman. "The records."

It was as if the pair had so profoundly never heard of the name that it was not required for them to check the massive bank of cabinets behind them, their familiarity with local names, local buildings, being so complete that "Sallow" could be removed from the list of possibilities encountered in those files.

Wyatt paused before walking away. "What do you think is the best way to see those? The records."

"We have them here," said Jon.

"*You what!*"

"Do you have a library card?"

"Chuffin' 'ell," said the man behind Wyatt. "He can use mine."

Of course, he had no card, but this turned out to be no impediment, as for a few pounds Jon issued him a slip of paper with a temporary password for use with the databases. Coming from behind the metal desks, he took Wyatt to a computer where the Texan removed his tweed jacket gratefully, felt a cooling dampness under his arms as he draped it over the back of a hard oak chair. Jon stood over him, made a few keyboard passes and brought up a screen. "This is one we use for family names."

"This looks familiar," Wyatt said.

"That woman you mentioned."

He perked up. "Did she use this?"

Jon nodded, but not in agreement, more a pondering movement of his head. "Probably. It's advertised a lot."

Wyatt recalled now where he had seen TraceYourAncestors.com. It was advertised almost hourly on television and cable news, especially late at night. The online subscription featured DNA analysis in addition to record access. Jon, in other words, had connected him to a service he could have purchased membership to for a few hundred dollars, or less, then examined from his office in Turner, Texas, or perhaps on a laptop, on his mattress, in the comfort of his own fifth-wheel RV.

Jon showed him how it worked. He typed "Sallow" into the only available field (one labeled "try here first"), then stood back. A list appeared.

Wyatt pointed to the first entry. "That's my father."

"*Really!*" Jon bent to look at the indicated ancestor, then at Wyatt. The Texan suspected that until that moment, the librarian hadn't believed him at all.

"You know, what sometimes happens is families name themselves after towns. People come here . . . well, not *here*. You're the only one that's ever asked about this name that I've ever met. But immigrants think the town was named after a family, and so take the name."

Henry W. Sallow. Date of death, 13 September 1985. The record showed his father as single, but that wasn't the case. He'd been, in fact, on his third wife, Wyatt's mother, Anne, now living comfortably in a Houston suburb. He prodded the name with an index finger. "All my life . . . he told me the town was named for the family."

"Maybe the opposite. Could be your family were immigrants and came through."

"He told me this was our home."

7
Maria, Daughter of Ingham

Jon left him to spend what amounted to a restful if not revelatory morning with the database. Wyatt glanced occasionally at a nearby couple who'd discovered a long pull-out drawer containing a map of their family estate going back to the twelfth century. "Absolutely," said the man to Jon, stomping and shaking his head. The woman grasped Jon's arm. "Ab-so-*lute*-ly," she added.

The large young girl had opened her ancient book, planted her elbows to either side of it. Wyatt noticed she was so overweight the skin at her wrists overlapped the fabric of the gloves she wore, the two hands bulging in the white cotton like drowned corpses. The girl did not appear to read the bound black-letter text at all, nor turn its open pages, merely raised her head with closed eyes, smiled, nostrils flaring.

As it turned out there were Sallows in Sallowsfield in the 1600s, listed on the parish records of St. Peter's Church. That is to say, there were two. Maria, the daughter of Ingham, was recorded baptized on September 11, 1642. Wyatt located this on the typed digital printout, though when he pulled up a photo of the parish document itself, he wasn't sure how they'd gotten "Sallow" from the smear of archaic script recorded in an angular, rune-like hand. He couldn't tell where they'd gotten "Maria" or "Ingham" either, and was "Ingham" even a name? Uncertain, Wyatt scribbled the information into his notebook as best he could. At least he had found a room where he no longer appeared strange and out of sorts sitting and writing in a notebook. Everyone in the room transferred information from computer screens or original documents onto their own paper with serious concentration. His ballpoint pen had not been allowed, however. Jon had given him a pencil with the library's logo embedded in the wood.

A few scant traces he could connect with his recent relations, but not many. At the end of several hours, Wyatt felt the massive temporal weight of a place—unlike East Texas—that had a history reaching back centuries but recorded in a mongrel and capricious language during eras in which most people had been illiterate anyway. He began to sweat again. A gaping chasm existed for the name "Sallow." The family name evaded all records during the years between Maria and Ingham and one Joshua Sallow, who appeared on a ship manifest when he left his home of Torquay for Newfoundland in the 1890s. Joshua appeared, as it were, unexpectedly, like flowers from a low-rent magician's sleeve. The name and the Canadian connection Wyatt recognized from his father's stories. Definitely his great-grandfather. But where had Joshua come from? Did he represent a long line of ancestors from the region, or an itinerant who'd seen a name and adopted it?

Wyatt considered those years, the empty ones, between Maria's baptism in 1642—if that had been her name—and himself, voyaged across an ocean to arrive here on the second floor of this library.

8
Alfred

He spent much of the day with the database before wandering in the afternoon through the business district, into the northwest reaches of town such a distance that he could see the new student services building of the university (one eye seeking his X always in the passing crowd). He turned back towards the Town Central Hotel, stopping for an hour at a Chinese restaurant that specialized in takeaway orders, but provided counter-tables. From his stool, as he mostly speared pork and noodles with the chopsticks he'd foolishly requested, he could see the cathedral steeple below which Maria (Somebody) had been baptized. (Well, an earlier steeple, the first cathedral having burned to the ground in the eighteenth century.) He felt no overwhelming connection. By the time Wyatt left the reading room, Jon had taken him to a closet across from the hall of history and genealogy. It turned out the library had a publishing arm and had produced an anthology of historical articles Jon felt was excellent, and on sale for 5 pounds. Wyatt's eyes widened when he hefted the volume. He knew that he'd need this book, though it would add to what he carted already in his luggage/pack. *Sallowsfield: An Undeniably Admirable Place* represented the culmination of a decade's worth of essays produced by local amateur historians who formed a society under the auspices of the library. (He did not notice Amy Ramsdale's name beside Chapter 16, the owner of the Town Central Hotel having authored "Guest Houses, Boarding Houses, Inns and Hotels in 19th Century Sallowsfield.") It had been professionally done, with maps and black-and-white photographs from several eras of the region's history. Two early chapters were devoted to "Tower Hill," mentioned to Wyatt already by Hussein as a not-to-be-missed attraction. One article explained the blood-and-entrails-soaked origins of "The Swale" where he'd rested in the morning. A scan of the index revealed there did not seem to be anything in its contents about Mrs. Donnelson's Ice Cream or his surname. For that matter, he could find nothing at all about how the town itself had come to be named. The introduction indicated that a traveler in the eighteenth century had summed up Sallowsfield with the pronouncement "It is undeniable that I have found here nothing to admire," hence the somewhat strident counterargument inherent in the anthology's subtitle. He closed the cover. There in the Chinese restaurant, he dug deeper into the carton with a single chopstick. "Man, the tool user," he mumbled, which tickled him, so he smiled, angling a slice of stringy barbecue from the rice and chopped vegetables.

While not a drinking man, per se, he felt the need for fortification. Wyatt left the restaurant, entered the street like a stranger from an obscure, only barely parallel world—the sole visitor from that other Sallowsfield that existed in shadowy corners of his family's myth-memory, a town with its own history, library, university, canals . . . canal boats . . . although to the best of his recollection, this mythic Sallowsfield contained no ditches for scraps of offal. Amidst these musings, he stumbled upon The Angle Pub located in the L-shaped corner formed at the intersection of two shop rows by the mercantile plaza. Its door opened directly upon a rising staircase, so he imagined it as a second floor, smoky, dark recess. A printed list of "ales and ciders" hung beside the door. None struck him as recognizable. After the events of the library, Wyatt decided there was no place he would rather be than upstairs in The Angle with all of its ales. Yet he hesitated.

That place, that bar, would no doubt be different from the way he imagined it. Should he climb the stairs, announce himself as a Texan, a Texan named "Sallow," a hale fellow well met, seeking the best ale in town? He remained standing beside the door. Wyatt possessed enough self-knowledge to recognize it would not go well. The indifference, most likely, would be palpable. This, the gap between his expectations, here at the bottom of a flight of stairs, looking over a drinks menu, and the reality of whatever existed on the upper story, tore at him, delivering up the sort of projection of inevitable disappointment he wished he'd processed before investing in plane fare and hotel reservations. He could make the effort to at least poke his head into The Angle, but a man descended the stairs then, paused at the door, leaned against its frame, and lit a cigarette, considering Wyatt through eyes narrowed against the smoke. So, The Angle probably wasn't a smoky bar at all if it didn't allow tobacco upstairs, but worse, the man looked unfriendly. The sort who, if crossed, might resort to violence. Wyatt felt small, retracted in comparison, like a telescope snapped together into a squat tube on the bridge of a frigate. The Angle might well be full of such threatening, clannish, and—worst of all—indifferent men, who wouldn't appreciate an outsider.

He kept walking in the general direction of the hotel.

The smoking man, Dr. Alfred Combs, head of Creative Writing at the University of Sallowsfield, finished his cigarette, crushed it under a shoe, climbed the stairs to rejoin his friends, thinking, for some reason, of the Saturday morning he'd learned of his father's death. He began to climb, and the old football injury (hamstring) worried at his right buttocks as he rose above street level. He considered that it could have been that fellow gaping at the menu, the one in the ragged tweed. The man's face reminded Alfred of his father, no question. His own face was flush from ale, exertion, end of term duties. Still, he felt good. His personal mortality didn't rise to any immediate concern. Aside from that man, he could imagine no other reason to consider death as a topic, let alone the death of his father, although, as a poet, he did have the ability to recognize how he'd worried over that particular August Saturday multiple times in the past, written about it, even. Such a day would inevitably represent a recurring theme of interest for a poet, much as a loose tooth couldn't help but be a recurring theme of interest for a tongue.

At age thirteen, waiting outside his viola teacher's home, he'd stood with the instrument case leaned against his buckle after a lesson. (Dr. Alfred Combs was, despite flushed appearances, not dangerous. He'd taken viola lessons.) And, bugger. How strange his father had acted the night before. His father and mother had argued in their bedroom. These weren't the happy noises they commonly made—"arguments" of the euphemistic, earthy kind they would kid each other about the next day ("Quite the kerfuffle, eh?"), publicly even, much to Alfred's mortification. Instead, his father had been ill, short of breath and cross. Cross about being ill, basically. He despised doctors, his dad did. The night before, he'd been lashing out, even, which was not his way. Uncharacteristic. Insulting the lot of them—his sister's weight problem, Alfred's propensity for dreaminess.

His father would never see him make an actual career from that dreaminess.

With his sister safely tucked into her room, young "Alfie" had taken advantage of the confusion to stay up, watch a Friday horror show he'd been forbidden to see, broadcast after his usual bedtime. The program that night featured a story about a brain in a jar. Yes, that had been it. Dramatically lit, the brain glowed on the screen. In Alfred's memories, the story had been broadcast in black and white—high-contrast scenes like *Citizen Kane*. Although perhaps he merely misremembered the pickled brain's eerie luminosity. At thirteen, he felt he'd spent too much of his life waiting to get old enough—for an opening, just the chance—to stay up and watch this frightening Friday evening program. Yet when he saw the brain in the jar, he'd regretted this ambition. Chuckling to himself in the empty living room as a way of indicating (also to himself) that missing this program was not such a big deal, he turned it off, his parents' tense voices filling the sudden silence. He retired to his bed queasy and uncertain.

The next morning outside his viola teacher's house, he watched a car slowly, far too slowly, approach, then mysteriously stop beside him at the kerb. His father had not come to pick him up, nor had his mother. Melissa, the teenage daughter of the neighbors, just with her license, arrived in the ugly orange Cortina her parents had handed down to her after they bought a Morris Marina. Like television star Henry Scott with whom he shared a birthday, Dr. Combs considered himself a respected native son: a professor and published poet, although he doubted he'd get a bronze on the square. It had been a long, strange journey, from this town to Oxford then back to his position at the university, and he wondered at times if he'd have become a poet at all had Melissa not arrived to pick him up that day in the orange Cortina.

He'd written a poem about it. "The Beginnings of Melissa."

On occasion, he had, crouched low with only his eyeballs above the sill, watched her from his upstairs window. These had been times when she wore loose-fitting shirts that, from that raised angle, provided a view that could only be called revelatory. On this day when she picked him up, Melissa had characteristically mixed high-waisted flared jeans and plat-form shoes with a ragged denim waistcoat over an Anarchy t-shirt. It was the uniform of disaffected Sallowsfield youth in the mid-'70s who weren't completely sure how far into disaffection they wanted to sign up for. The smallest pooch of belly skin showed over her wide belt, and—obvious under the waistcoat—two pinched rises through the t-shirt fabric indicated she wore no bra. "Alfie," at thirteen, had only recently become aware that women possessed such things as bras, an awareness followed by another that while they did wear them, not all did, and, among those that did, some did not at all times.

It was, frankly, a dizzying concept.

Dr. Alfred Combs rose halfway up the steep stairs towards The Angle. The walls to either side were narrow. There was no handrail as anyone could easily steady themselves by applying pressure to the walls, wedg-ing themselves securely as they rose upwards or descended the stair-case. Even in the poor light of a single overhead cone, the plaster showed oil from palms and fingers that left a stain at about shoulder level. He reached at the stain and recalled how the car Melissa drove featured a gear lever, and Melissa One, as he now on occasion thought of her (there'd been another Melissa, of a different kind, in his navy years)—Melissa One moved expertly through the gears, her legs and left arm weaving a dance that advanced the speed of the car in accelerating bursts as her other hand steered. She spread her legs incrementally, tenderly pressing the clutch to one side, manipulating the accelerator to the other. The soft underpart of Melissa's thin arms jiggled when she advanced through second to third, and she didn't speak at all after she picked him up, just nodded, smiled in a thin-lipped manner. Alfred sat in the passenger seat, taking her all in at first, her wriggling flesh and slightly spread legs in the flared jeans. Melissa's cheeks were scarred—imperfect, though only slightly.

The car moved down the hard, straight surface of Hare Lane, through undeveloped property at the edge of half-built houses. Melissa drove and didn't say anything, only looked straight with her eyes unlevel, steering with one wrist on the wheel. Her thin fingers nail-tipped the top of the gear lever. Alfred didn't know why she'd come to pick him up but had a feeling of unease. It could have been her silence. It could have been lingering effects of the brain in the jar. He stopped stealing glances at her pores, though to look was so enticing. After a while, like Melissa herself, he simply stared out at the road, as if they were seated beside each other on a sofa, watching a late-night television program, possibly an upsetting one, ignoring each other, engrossed in some scene that passed before their eyes, and each pretending—for the sake of the other—not to be scared.

She'd shown up unexpectedly to give him a lift at a place his mother or his father should have come to retrieve him. Dr. Alfred Combs was certain to this day that she still stared straight ahead, not looking at him, when she said, "They told me to get you, Alfie. And not to say anything. I can't do you that way."

Hare Lane slipped to either side of the car. A tall woman in a black skirt and pearls strode the pavement, her high heels making her appear unstable. A house door sailed past. Alfred knew that house door well, one where the owners had painted eyes and a nose over the letter slot. When the postman came, he must have felt he was feeding the house.

"Your father. When we get there. It's your father."

At the top of the stairs, Dr. Alfred Combs shook his head like a dog drying its shaggy coat. He turned into the doorway, the only doorway at the end of that long climb. He walked into The Angle, which was not at all dark, certainly not smoky, and included along with taproom items and ciders a menu featuring tapas and Mediterranean cuisine.

In addition to teaching the craft of poetry, Alfred Combs served the university as coach of the intercollegiate chess team.

1
The Mole

With her back turned, seated at one of the low sofas by the gigantic panes that let onto the concrete garden, he couldn't tell for certain. It was her or it wasn't. Of course, he had to find out but considered also waiting. Seeing what developed. If she left the Lowery Building, he could follow, possibly across campus. Seeing her walk would settle the question. Wyatt had memorized her walk. Then again, as he concentrated on the small mole on the back of this woman's neck, revealed by her uncharacteristically short haircut, he had to recall if X had such a mole. He probably should have known that. Surely, he would have seen it in one of their nine elevator rides. If it wasn't her, Wyatt had even less certainty concerning what might happen next, as his trip, his journey "... to Sallowsfield!" had otherwise lost its point after his library research. He might as well catch a train to an attraction like Stratford, the Lake District, London museums.

But what satisfaction derives from reading a work of narrative art or even, let's say, watching a movie, if the ax-wielding psychopath veers from the garage of cowering teens at the last moment, distracted by a yapping chihuahua? Who would waste time with the story of a luxury liner that scrapes past—*missing by inches*—a massive iceberg and reaches its destination, unscathed (as opposed to sinking, *scathed*, into the depths, as Hussein the taxi driver might say, pointing his index finger skyward). Where's the loss of 700 souls in that scenario? The mounting of multi-million-dollar salvage operations complete with deep-sea submersibles? Where's the *story*? Of course, he must talk to her, and, even so, Wyatt's encounter at the university with the woman he took to be X skirts perilously close to just such narrative non-misadventure, but the ending of this encounter is itself salvaged, finally, by his own misjudgment.

Thank goodness. Thank goodness.

2
"One. Uhn. Two. Uhn. Pheeeeeeeew. Pheeeeeeeew."

Wyatt decided on Wednesday morning after a restful night (no karaoke channeled down the long alleyway) to explore the university, though in essence, his reasons to do so had diminished. He enjoyed a Full Yorkshire in the Town Central's breakfast room (minus waved-away black pudding) and nodded to young, calm-voiced Ms. Ramsdale at the front desk, who returned his gaze with a frank smile. (She could not place him.) After breakfast, stuffed but uneasy from the day at the library (and . . . how strange to be here. To have been lifted from his usual place, moved to this place. Far from home. And why?) . . . after breakfast, he hiked to the street, turned right towards the cathedral, right again at the corner, and at the McDonald's found a taxi stand, where the turbaned man from the station stood, his foot on a front bumper. Hussein lounged in the taxi behind him, reprising their positions from Monday.

Hussein opened the car door while the uncle made a few indecipherable comments and laughed. The driver, chuckling, got behind the wheel. "Want to know what he said?"

"Do I?"

"He has a name for you."

"Exotic freak? I don't suppose you've seen her," Wyatt asked.

"I have not. Are you feeling low?"

"I don't know."

"You probably don't want to know his name for you," Hussein said. "But here it is. He calls you 'Breakfast, Lunch, and Dinner.'" He laughed. "*Breakfast, Lunch, and Dinner.* Don't take it wrong."

"The university."

They drove, Hussein mentioning that his uncle was from Kashmir, and had that characteristic and somewhat difficult to appreciate (at times) Kashmiri sense of humor. Then Hussein appeared to recall he was dealing with someone who'd lost the love of his life. Lost her, apparently, on Station Street when her white . . . *slacks* disappeared into the warrens of Central Sallowsfield.

"I once picked up a fare, Dr. Wyatt. A woman. She had six fingers on one hand."

"Let me guess. One of her fingers got entangled in a steering wheel and she crashed."

"Nothing like that."

"A terrible car crash. She should have called a taxi."

"No, no. She said she was from Texas. That's all. That's what made me think of her."

Wyatt did not comment. The air in the streets had cooled and rejuvenated him despite his mood. At a stoplight, he rolled down the window by its manual crank to feel the breeze. A middle-aged South Asian man stepped off the curb where a younger man unloaded boxes from a hatchback. He could hear their conversation.

"Let me help," said the older man.

"No!"

"I don't want anything from you!"

"Always you want to help. Then you do too much. Then you want something."

The older man reached into one of the boxes. "What's is this?" He held up a thick blue ring.

"A giveaway."

"I can give it away."

"No."

"What is it?"

"Masking tape."

"You're giving free tape?"

The younger man took the roll from his hands, placed it back in the box and removed the box from the hatchback.

The light changed and Hussein drove on. "Do you think you know her?"

Wyatt frowned. "Her?"

"With six fingers?"

"Because she's a Texan, you think I know her? You think all Texans know the woman with six fingers?"

Hussein frowned. "I sense frustration. Look, I'm sure you'll find your love. You know, there's a fairy tale, Dr. Wyatt. An old drunk is found in the road."

Wyatt burped and tasted egg and sausage. In some ways he did wonder what this hexadactylic Lone Star female had been doing in Sallowsfield. "Is this a Kashmiri fairy tale?"

"So, some guys, they take him, clean him up, put him in the prince's bed. When he wakes up, they tell him his life as a drunk was a dream. He's really a prince." Hussein looked at Wyatt in the rearview.

"Then what happened?"

"That's it. Or all I remember. But see. Isn't that what everyone thinks? Here I am, a taxi driver, but really, I should be a businessman. That would be my true self. We're all princes in our own heads." He indicated his skull with the jewel-ringed little finger. "And so forth."

Wyatt sighed.

"It's Shakespeare," Hussein said. "*Taming of the Shrew*. Also, Emerson talks about it." He nodded down Queensgate towards the university. "I won't drive this taxi for my uncle forever. Distraction of love, right? The wife. The kids." He thrummed the steering wheel. "For them, I drive the cab."

"How many kids?"

"Two boys, one girl."

Wyatt shook his head. "Wonderful."

"I'm thinking, have been thinking, this is the way love works. With this person, whoever it is, no matter what you happen to be, really, when you're with them, you're the prince. When they're gone, or they leave, you're back where you were."

Wyatt watched the brown buildings glide past. "In the gutter."

"You're just . . . *anybody*. Or nobody. Think, maybe this way about your woman, Dr. Wyatt," Hussein said. "The big, big love is the X-Factor."

Wyatt raised his eyebrows.

"That's how a mathematician would say it. Right? The missing element? You plug that in, and everything makes sense."

Two blocks passed in silence.

Hussein: "Like, *I'd be okay if I only had X.*"

"Okay. Okay. Yes."

"Better to just . . . you said you were married?"

"I am married."

Hussein cocked his head a quarter turn towards the back seat.

"At least I think so." Wyatt shrugged. Sighed. "My wife . . . Maybe she's had me . . . whatever. Annulled."

"I see. I see. Maybe."

Hussein didn't ask if Wyatt had kids.

He got out at the curb of a parking circle near a university information kiosk, the counters themselves unstaffed at the moment, although stacked with catalogs. He'd arrived during a testing period, end of term, something Wyatt, coming from North America, had no way of knowing. He saw no students on the sidewalks. Near the kiosk, he surveyed the buildings as Hussein drove away. Again, he'd nursed expectations that had not panned out. He'd imagined old structures with well-worn bronze door fittings. To enter them was to encounter the smell of academia as it used to be: ancient with the papery aroma of old books in bindings held together with decaying paste. Scholars would be bent over these, breathing in the varnish of the paneled walls while above stairwells, murals in homage to students who'd fought and fallen in wars displayed toga-ed figures raising crowns to angelic blond women.

To his dismay, the buildings were too new for any of that. The only mural he saw consisted of black and white painted block letters and numerals signaling the offices of student broadcasting: RADIO SAL. A short walk from the information kiosk, a fabric barrier stretched across an access road, behind which construction of an elevated parking garage proceeded noisily. "TEAM SAL Works for You," the fabric banner insisted. This disconcerted him given the aforementioned nickname from his colleagues, that elbow-in-the-ribs, informal, secretly critical without coming out and saying it critically, shortened *version* of his name that appeared to be favored on this campus. Dean Zepeda even called him, on occasion, "Ole Sal," which he detested, silently, although Y often called him "Sallie," which he accepted without question as a term of endearment.

He found himself dwarfed by the largest campus landmark—an edifice he'd seen from the center of town the day before, the multi-storied red-brick "Lowery Building." He glowered at another banner—its fabric slit with holes to allow wind passage funneled from a breezeway that actually was very breezy—its lettering an invocation of, Good God, THAT OLD SAL SPIRIT. Close alongside the red-brick behemoth, the new "Lowery Annex Student Center" appeared to be the love-child of a secret affair between a cruise line and the Sydney Opera House and showed off its multi-layered interior through glass and steel girders wrapped across three massive sides. The whole Lowery complex stood beyond a flagged courtyard, and Wyatt paused to sit on one of the benches there before realizing it was not so much a bench as a large and uncomfortable block of concrete, similar to the pavement he'd been walking on, and cold to the touch. Bending, he could read at its base encouraging carved phrases from historical and literary figures (one, he noticed, was—like himself—an American poet), and after considering these a few moments on the uncomfortable, chilling surface, it occurred to him that these were, perhaps, not seats at all, but modernist works of art. He shot up quickly enough to aggravate the hamstring sinews he would strain nearly to their breaking point the next day, tumbling down Tower Hill. Wyatt hoped no one had seen him sitting on this potential cultural treasure, straightened his jacket, pretended interest in the catalog he'd picked up at the kiosk, and strolled towards the student center. The wind blew fierce through the courtyard.

Walking through glass doors that were difficult to pull open against that stiff breeze, he sensed that, in a mysterious interior transformation, "The Lowery Annex" had become no longer triangular, but oval, leaving odd marginal spaces around a shaft of emptiness that rose for four . . . no, five floors. The building was hollowed out, classrooms and offices circling the inside of its shell, the center wastefully free of anything but a column of air. Oddly fashioned spaces had been filled with customized, irregularly shaped furniture arranged at contrary angles. It seemed a perfect mix of the non-utilitarian with the unattractive. Helpful signboards beside a bank of four elevators indicated that, by chance, he'd come to the building that housed the Department of Creative Writing (4th floor), but he needed to tend to another matter first.

Not an experienced traveler, Wyatt's bowels were affected by entry into novel climes, even civilized ones. It was like Montezuma's Revenge, but Wyatt did not have to venture south of the border to fall victim. He'd come to expect it anywhere he went, like for a conference: Washington D.C., San Francisco, Dallas. "Where to crap?" became the question, as well as its corollary (or perhaps they were the same): "Where to crap comfortably?" Often, a hotel room was not the best option, owing both to issues of water pressure and the inability to walk away quickly from a crisis of one's own manufacture. Conference centers in even the finest hotels often had small and dingy facilities, sometimes requiring long hikes to uncover, and featuring queues that meant more pressure to get in, get done, get out. This was not Wyatt Sallow's way. In the Lowery Annex—brand new and modern, with a straggling crew in hardhats still pushing a cart to apply finishing touches to skirting boards and light fixtures—he discovered something truly magnificent.

The door into the men's room opened not onto a single chamber with toilet, trash-bin, and washbasin, but instead revealed as a kind of optical surprise a lengthy hallway of stalls, the perspective on the many doors converging nearly to a vanishing point. Wyatt grew dizzy contemplating it. Each stall door stretched from floor to ceiling with no space beneath revealing trouser legs telescoped onto shoe tops: a sure sign of attention to detail. Going to the third door (as entering the first seemed presumptuous, walking to the fifteenth slightly unhinged), he raised a palm to touch its surface. "Magnificent," he said, then entered. Upon closing the door to this stall Wyatt felt a comfort and privacy he hadn't encountered since embarking for Houston from Turner. He felt that, in his career, he'd had offices that were not as nice as the new restroom stalls at the University of Sallowsfield.

Seating himself, his sense of security felt a minor nudge as a sign on the back of the door indicated facilities were liable to be cleaned at any time, and "by workers of either sex." He did not fear this as imminent but still noted that it introduced an element of imbalance to an otherwise peaceful respite. Removing his phone, he opened an app that allowed him to play solitaire, the rectangular cards snapping across the screen as he moved or double-tapped them with an index finger. Wyatt no longer played chess on the phone, though he'd downloaded a mobile version of OtterShark. He found playing on the tiny screen *not* restful and, in fact, possibly harmful to both his classical game and his regularity. He felt it difficult to seriously consider candidate moves on such a small device. He nearly always lost was the main problem, no matter how low he dialed the abilities of the program. It reminded him too much of Blitz chess, at which he by no means excelled.

Wyatt tried to keep it from being generally known that he no longer played people over the board, only OtterShark on the computer. He found the software opponent enough. He at times considered that he was, as Botvinnik himself used to say, not terribly at ease with the competitive element in the sport.

He admired Botvinnik, but his personal great had always been Tigran Petrosian, a World Champion who attacked rarely, commonly made exchange sacrifices, and—most importantly—offered those who played him absolutely no targets for advantage. Wyatt, without the gift of attack, had developed a similar adeptness at anticipating and, so, avoiding trouble. A more thoughtful type might have seen in this approach a personal parallel to his teaching of business without ever working in business, but Wyatt was not such a type.

His little boy, Wyn, had a straightforward relationship to the game that Wyatt sometimes wished he could emulate. Unable to categorize for him the movements of the pieces no matter how many approaches he took, he could at least teach Wyn, finally, to name them, the boy going beyond his usual method of pointing and saying *That one. That one.* For Wyn, the object became to name the pieces and either help put them in their green velvet slots in the wooden box that protected them or achieve his own personal arrangement on the board. When wheeled to the table, he would grab up the pieces. "Bissop," he would say, and drop it into its slot. "Rook. Queen. Horse . . . *no, Knight.*" (Wyn had learned to correct himself on the Knight.) "Pond. Pond. Pond." (Wyatt didn't bother with correct pronunciation of the multiple "ponds.") Wyn often centered the black pieces on the black squares, then, with concentration, the white ones on the white squares. During the course of a day, he would sometimes reach out and move them more, naming them as he did so. "Queen, Bissop, Pond." Wyatt believed Wyn considered it a gyp to have only 32 pieces for 64 squares. No matter how he moved them, he'd never get the whole thing covered.

Wyatt, though spending a lot of time at home preparing lectures and grading quizzes, always came into Wyn's room the last thing before bed-time. The boy's condition was delicate. Slender-framed with insect-like legs that had never been used for walking, Wyn still managed to grow to a size that he could no longer be easily lifted by Z, who didn't have the capacity, or by Wyatt, who feared back injury. "I'm married to an old man," Z complained at his avoidance when it came to heavy objects. "Cousin" Yuri, on his visits from Houston, could sweep the boy easily onto a hip, carry him without effort. Family pictures that Wyatt no longer looked at preserved this "cousin" and Wyn as they visited rose bushes, planter boxes and the screen of live bamboo installed by Z in the back yard on Linden Lane. Wyatt had at one time marveled at the resemblance between this cousin and Wyn that showed even through his little boy's misshaped head that, from some angles, revealed a face nearly as big as his body. A sure sign, no doubt, of the genetic vigor of their shared Ukrainian ancestry. Wyatt checked Wyn's temperature often, his breathing every night before turn-ing in for bed himself. The boy liked to pull the covers completely over his head, which Wyatt couldn't seem to stop, and so he reassured himself nightly by checking, "Can you breathe?"

"Pheeeeew," Wyn would say in an exaggerated fashion. "Pheeeeeeew. Pheeeeeew."

To think of "Pheeeeeew, Pheeeeeew" as a separate sound, preserved from oblivion, was also to recall Z, framed in a doorway, in her black dress with small white dots (unlikely, as the occasion would have been just put-ting Wyn to bed, not worthy of the special dress, but it's how he called it up), saying goodnight to the small-framed figure in his two-level bed, the top level of which the boy would visit only once in his life. She'd be bare-foot, one foot on a knee, flamingo-style, her hip shot, hand resting on it, laughing in a kind of snort that traveled her long, long nose with a special resonance. Or: he would consider his own hand on that hip, in that door-way, the two snickering at Wyn's little joke. "Pheeeeeeew. Pheeeeeeeew." Another one: Wyatt, during those times, did exercises recommended by a physical therapist for neck stiffness. Since Wyn was gone and Z was gone, he no longer did these (though the neck problem persisted), but they involved him lying on his side on the floor, raising an arm ten times to behind his shoulder. And of course, grunting. "One. *Uhn*. Two. *Uhn*." At odd times of the day he would catch Wyn looking at him, and wonder what the boy was thinking, but then Wyn would say, "One. *Unh*. Two. *Unh*." And Wyatt would tickle him.

3
Some Subterranean Creature

The university's men's room stall space so comforted Wyatt that to even call the luxurious, well-lit area he occupied a "stall" contrasted severely with the usual, barnyard-animal association of the word. Nearly womb-like in its enclosure, it had been so many days since he had relieved the burden of waste buildup in his bowels that this facility had been so pro-fessionally designed to accept collection of, that when it came, the mate-rial flowed from him. The effect was better, Wyatt had to admit, much smoother than it ever would have been in some stuffy academic building full of war murals and encyclopedias.

And so, though it hadn't happened for several days, the familiar feel-ing soon enough overtook him. Then, the familiar feeling continued on past mere familiarity. In forty seconds, it began to come out of him in what he took to be large rings. It fell from him in round clods that made *plop* sounds in the small, contained space. As he thrashed atop the seat, the warning signboard blurred, "workers" and "sex" merging. The tiny aces and deuces he'd begun aligning in the solitaire game shook in his grasp. He replaced his phone in his jacket pocket to ensure he didn't drop it.

When it was over, he realized his hands were shaking.

Ultimately, he went to flush. Wyatt didn't feel he'd used an inordinate amount of the very fine paper roll there at his elbow, certainly not considering the circumstances, but the toilet had minor difficulty digesting it all. The water level dissipated, but not until after first rising, then taking its plunge in a manner the professor would have to call unenthusiastic. He breathed easier when all had been carried away, and stood, fastening his belt, but then came a rattle and moan, a shudder like in a car when someone stands on the brakes at highway speed, smoking the tires, causing the rear end to fishtail. This shudder or tremble traveled the row of stalls in a tectonic swell. Perhaps—it being a new building—connections had not been properly sealed. Or: a coincidence, this rumbling that followed so soon after his own efforts. But it felt like no coincidence to Wyatt. Then came another swell. Beginning at his left, as if some subterranean creature had come awake, it then passed, thrust its way as if through catacombs beneath the building, or like the wave crossing a stadium during a football game ("Bowl game," he chuckled), the disturbance and the gurgling noise rushing beneath his shoes, building force as it migrated back towards the men's room door through which someone "of either sex," Wyatt feared, might soon appear, investigating the tsunami-like catastrophe. Washing his hands quickly, he found the comforting long row of stalls now much less comforting as the door of each individually rattled. So many ghosts seeking escape. He departed the men's room, looked across the atrium floor, made certain he had not been seen. In the towering emptiness of the building's cavernous central space, all appeared calm. No teams of specialists approached. He moved to a different part of the ground floor, sat on one of the sofas, crossed his legs and attempted to relax.

This is no doubt an unkind moment to recall his words to the colorful, time-obsessed Paul McBride upon departing the Station Monday afternoon: "I'm doing something over at the university."

If he had come to the town for the sake of his identity, he had planned this stop for the sake of his poetry. But his preformed, invented version of the "University of Sallowsfield" had been, now that he thought back, completely off the mark. Here a much more ambitious, impressive, no doubt highly respected academic institution revealed itself at every turn, which even a cursory internet examination could have told him long in advance if he'd bothered to make one. On a high wall near the sofa where he lounged, a large poster indicated that the university had been declared among the first in Great Britain for the awarding of Education degrees. This was a real college, in other words, certainly larger in campus area than his own school, and it appeared some serious funds had been ear-marked for infrastructure, actualized by TEAM SAL. This, the Lowery Annex, all by itself demonstrated serious investment. He sat and watched as a team of five wearing orange Day-Glo reflective vests and hard hats turned a corner from an adjacent cafeteria and coffee shop area, making for the men's room in something of a hurry. The last among them, shorter than the others, pushed a four-wheeled cart loaded with what appeared to be pumps, hoses, and rectangular cartons resembling fishing tackle boxes. One worker held the door while the others poured into the space in single file as if staging a raid.

This was a truly reputable institution, and Wyatt had, again, a gnaw-ing feeling, that his chapbook—several copies of which he had secreted in his day pack for distribution in the "Creative Writing Department"—his chapbook would not impress anyone here. And should anyone here desire to put on summer writing workshop, that they would reach out as far as East Texas for instructor candidates who had not published in the last twenty years felt unlikely. Scuttlebutt at the time he'd received his poetic laurels worked their way back into his consciousness, a zone from which they had been barred for nearly the same two decades since the appearance of *Water Take Me Down and Also Burn Me*. There had even been a proposal, offered in the single, *Toreador* review, that the chapbook had come about because judges of the Texas Tech Younger Poet Series felt pressure in 1993 to award the honor and publication to *somebody* or else risk admission that the school had nothing at all worthwhile going on poetry-wise, a sad commentary on the level of verse output not only for the Harvard of the Panhandle but the entire greater Lubbock metro. This was a scurrilous claim, one Wyatt had never believed, nor did he accept the reviewer's estimation of the chapbook author himself as a "poseur," attempting to come across as a "wandering outlaw of his own mind."

In addition to his homage to the mythological town where he now found himself—non-mythically—lounging back on a comfortable although not ergonomically correct sofa ("lounging back" being the only acceptable approach to this furniture with its sloping lumbar rest and hyper-stuffed cushions), Wyatt's chapbook contained mostly, as a general category, love poems. He had not had a great deal of experience with love when he wrote them, except, perhaps, love as it had been presented in other poems by other poets, not to mention serial television programs, and that one date with the English major. Despite these experiences, the *Toreador* reviewer found his work on the subject unconvincing. The critic could not accept the emotional freightage of *Water Take Me Down*, whose author, he said,

> *relied solely on a model of love as suffering, generally succeeded by further suffering. Relationships, for Mr. Sallow, leap from their unrequited versions to their suicidal consequences, with each successive attempt at self-harm (undertaken after "great bidding of tearful adieus") unsuccessful—merely maiming for life, let's say, rather than killing—and leaving the narrative persona "now broke without as I am within."*

Oh, please.

The article closed by noting how in a foreword the author had presented "to the world these humble verses meant only for the eyes of friends," the reviewer indicating that if you were one of these friends "you did not need enemies," followed by an impassioned plea: not that readers consider Mr. Sallow a bad poet but, rather, "a monstrous one," and that perhaps it made sense for all poetic instruction at Texas Tech University to cease, with school presses no longer employed to "feed the egos of these fiends."

Wyatt considered the fact that the review had been signed "anonymous" one of the saving graces of his college career in the Texas Panhandle, as how much credence could be given to a critic who refused to self-identify? He remembered this even as he went to the elevator bank, fingering the strap of his backpack as one might suspenders. Getting into the car, pressing the correct button, the doors soon slid shut and the contraption rose, somewhat haltingly, as a mellifluous female voice called out rising numbers. "First floor." "Second floor."

Wyatt, by the way, had not based his entire relationship with X on a single act, delivered as she stepped from the precarious chair in his office while she helped tidy that office . . . stepped downward into his arms and into that surprising kiss. She had kissed him, by his rough estimation, nine other times. All of these had taken place in a particular elevator.

The glass sides of the lift in this university would have made it impossible for Wyatt and X to use it as they had the one from the ground to second floor of the Bellinger and Nord Bookshop in the Turner Mall. X had proposed getting together there at least once per week to set up a "buddy system" of discipline, one that would force them to spend at least a few hours regularly on their "personal work." This meant his poetry and her romantic novel. As for that book, she revealed the title to him though nothing else. Wyatt could only imagine that he played a role in the characterization of this book given all the time he'd sat across from her as she roughly pounded the keys of her laptop. They could reach the second floor and the Bellinger and Nord coffee shop where they most often met to write by ascending a sweeping spiral staircase. *His* idea was that they *not* take these stairs to this venue, but the elevator instead. During the twelve-second to fourteen-and-a-half second ride from first to second floor, from the instant the doors closed until they opened again and revealed the coffee shop tables, Wyatt argued that he should be allowed another kiss, permission for which seemed to have been given by her initial descent from the office chair. To this she agreed and did so with what he'd have to call enthusiasm.

Closing his eyes in the disorienting university elevator, sensing the thrust of its upward lift, almost returned Wyatt to those twelve-second to fourteen-and-a-half second encounters—all nine of them—until the softly accented voice intoned "Fourth floor" and broke the spell.

Stepping out, he grew dizzy looking into the hollow atrium from this level, its central expanse separated from the walkway by a perfunctory railing. Following this passageway, he had little trouble locating the correct department, accessible through a single glass door with the name of "Alfred E. Combs, PhD, Head of Department" frosted at eye level. He should have looked up Combs first, but had come this far, so pulled on the handle.

Locked.

Peering through the glass under the cover of his palm he saw no one inside, only a single desk with computer, a looping screen saver creating lasso patterns in the darkness.

Reprieved, he made his way back to the elevator, feeling that a return to the ground floor and that sofa he'd located at its margins to regroup and plan his next move made eminent sense. Soon enough, "Ground floor" announced the female voice with its wonderful accent, then the device lurched, the doors opening about a third of the way, the floor dropping suddenly at least eight inches below lobby level.

Wyatt debated whether to abandon the elevator or remain securely in it. Like his experience in the Men's Room, he didn't favor being found in this broken device, or—worse—found responsible for its demise. But a partially open elevator door didn't encourage his exit, either. He momentarily replayed incidents of urban legend, persons caught by inexorably closing metal panels, their heads wobbling on lobby tiles as their collapsed torsos visited the penthouse. Anxious, he held his pack in front of him, stepped up and into the atrium quickly, and withdrew his last remaining appendage—the left leg—with enough force to aggravate the hamstring problem. He made his way safely to the uncomfortable sofa, trying to remove elevator of doom imagery from his mind, as the voice repeated "Ground floor," "Ground floor," "Ground floor," over and over through the incompletely closed portal.

Wyatt believed this allowed him to check off visiting the university while admitting the possible necessity for a return trip. Certainly, Hussein could be located to drive him over. He still had to sit and ponder his further moves. He knew, from Jon, that the University Library archive held no family records, which gave him another set of people he had crossed an ocean to happily avoid inconveniencing. Wyatt felt relief at not having to bother another librarian, archivist, student intern or sub-sub archivist who might be pressed into service to tell him Joshua Sallow had departed Torquay in 1896, but otherwise, *nada*. Though having come 4,700 miles and spent a sizeable part of the disposable income he scraped together after sending the portion he always did to his wife, Z (an arrangement he'd agreed to as she established her dental hygienist career) . . . to go to such expense just to sit on this sofa at the margins of this building in this longitude and latitude . . . nonetheless, Wyatt found it childishly simple to talk himself out of completing the tasks he'd taken so much trouble to attempt. He crossed his leg again, bounced one foot, listened as the friendly-sounding elevator continued to announce its arrival through its death-trap maw.

4
Bell, Book and Carefully Crafted Negative Template

Another group rounded the corner from the direction of the cafeteria, this time three men and one woman, all in orange day-glow vests, one carrying a wide waist-belt almost slipping down his torso from the weight of its tools. They began to examine the door of the talkative elevator.

"Edward!" Someone else cried out from the Men's Room door, simultaneous with the raising of a tapping sound from within. "Yo, Edward!"

Wyatt shifted his spine on the uncomfortable sofa. Ran a palm along the side of his head, moved his sparse hair over his ear. He sat. Pumped his foot. Glanced from the consternation of the crew working on the bathroom he'd destroyed to the struggles of the other group crowbarring the door of the elevator he'd jammed.

He wondered if there were a copy of X's book in the University Library. Probably not. A bookshop would be more likely to have such a thing, registered on the *New York Times* top ten for three weeks in the romance category. It had earned not exactly rave reviews but certainly nothing as savage as what the *Toreador* critic had leveled at *Water Take Me Down.* An exotic tale of modern-day New Orleans infused with the gothic intrigue of the eighteenth-century pirate Jerome DeRossier, a Gulf Coast privateer cursed by a renegade Karankawa shaman to haunt the streets and alleys of the Old Quarter throughout eternity, stealing the souls of innocent tourist maidens . . . Anyway, the novel's heroine, Sophie Boudreaux, a compact, dark-eyed, dark-haired Cajun princess who was also somehow an elf (Wyatt, at least, thought she was some kind of elf: or possibly a sprite working for a council of elves)—and in some way, also a detective for an intrepid anti-ghost agency (run by elves), Sophie had been tasked with finding the immortal buccaneer and sending his ravenous spirit into the next world where it more properly belonged. Easier said than done when he so easily blended into the local culture as a chef, bartender, and trumpet player, Sophie chasing him from etouffee restaurant to daiquiri palace to smoky jazz dive night after night. X scored a trifecta of romantic interest in *Sophie and Jerome*: part love story, part ghost story, and all Big Easy bar, restaurant, and rocking nightspot guide. A back-cover blurb called the novel "a stunning achievement"—and it had certainly stunned Wyatt as he poured over the story in an orgy of torment comparable only to the way he took in every detail of the topless picture she'd sent, doing so with similar rapt absorption. He found the female character to have been drawn directly from the personality of X, yet exactly how the pirate ghost related to himself was much more difficult to ascertain. Details of the book and its debonair, dangerous, sexy male specter at times caused Wyatt to believe that their relationship was indeed there, only blanketed deeply under symbolism and allusion. For example, the fact that the plot occurred during the week of Spring Break when a string of innocent tourist maidens were assaulted, pierced on their virginal throats by two bite marks, the exact time of the calendar year when X had stepped down from his student chair and into his arms obviously held significance. (The notion, however, that New Orleans might be filled with "innocent tourist maidens" during Spring Break was a bit of a stretch for some reviewers.) He wondered as well if Jerome hadn't been created as a kind of anti-Sallow: an homage to himself, yes, but in a carefully crafted negative template. Occasionally, though, some gesture, an article of clothing, a fragment of dialogue made him feel that, yes, "Jerome is me. I am Jerome." Naturally, in attempting to "de-spectralize" this ravaging fiend, Sophie had, of course, ended up sleeping with him (why not?), awakening to find him at his electronic Moog keyboard in his bohemian *Vieux Carré* apartment, hunched over his newest composition dedicated to herself, and *wearing a blue button-down Oxford shirt* (albeit open at the collar: a passage nonetheless underlined three times in Wyatt's much-thumbed copy).

Still, this left a character more like his true self, Wyatt Sallow, a largely untapped creative inspiration for X, which is why it had not taken him long to surmise, after seeing her at the train station, that she, who had first suggested he come to this town to seek his ancestral identity, had also arrived, and done so with a similar purpose. How else to begin her task of researching her second book? It took no great leap to imagine exactly who would figure most prominently in that work.

Wyatt pondered these possibilities and wondered if someplace nearby might serve him a drink—a place he could sit and consider the implications more deeply, when X walked through the large glass doors and entered the atrium of the Lowery Annex.

5
The Hours of His Days

Later, walking away from the university, Wyatt had begun to dwell on his downfalls, defeats, and most especially his blunders, and to feel far from home: a wanderer without purpose. Such is the condition of the exile, he thought. Emotionally crippled, banned from involvement in a society he could not understand and that did not accept him. Etc.

An educated man with an advanced business degree, he did not go so far as to equate the experience of an exile with that of a guy who'd flown from Houston to the UK for an eight-day trip to a down-at-its-heels mill town, but no metaphor walks on all four legs. At one time, Wyatt had considered it possible—not likely, but *possible*—that he might have pursued the chaotic life of adventure, romance, and danger as lived by the persona found in his youthful poetry, but the hours of his days had been taken up finishing his thesis, responsibilities of a difficult marriage, caring for his little boy, the vicissitudes of obtaining tenure (which he had done, but barely) and so sue him. He hadn't gotten around to any of that exile shit.

It had to be considered as well that he'd come to this town not as a way of meeting the moment, but of quarantining himself from it, putting off any actual engagement with life. Many on the intramural chess circuit—at least those who knew him well—felt he'd done this with the game. He had, to use the vernacular, "withdrawn from the chess act," something that happened among those who expended hours of concentration and withering strain, suffered from stiff necks, bleary eyes, perhaps done so over years or decades from rawest youth, only to end in seasons of loss: terrible streaks that became, for those obsessed, an insupportable vortex of pain. From this soon followed an unwillingness to create even that necessary, initial imbalance that results from every first move. Say pawn to e4. Arguably, at least he'd proved something with Gail. Some kind of imbalance had been offered.

The woman who'd entered the student center and taken a seat near where Wyatt reclined, though turned with her back to him, certainly favored X. With his fear, his excitement . . . one could say his *shock* and the degree to which his eyesight had, he felt, deteriorated, he had to lean forward and consider, chin on palm, whether this was her or not. Clad head to foot in black, the woman presented differently from the figure in the white slacks of the previous Monday, but either shade would not be uncharacteristic of the mercurial X. Wyatt's great love often sported black when he knew her, loved her, communicated with her daily (sometimes more than once per day, via text). This X, however, seated in the Lowery Annex had moved quickly upon entering the atrium, so he'd managed only a partial view before she sat, then turned away. She carried, as far as he could tell, a lot of camera gear, the camera itself—with a very long lens—suspended from her neck by a wide strap with a striped yellow motif. A square grey equipment satchel rode her hip, hung from a shoulder loop. Photography. That wasn't beyond the realm of possibility: just the category of hobby that would absorb X, in fact, especially after the bestseller. She would be seeking a new challenge. An Aquarius, X could not confine herself to regular interests (or men) for long.

The woman steadied the lens with one hand while she walked, then settled onto the sofa a few meters from him, closer to the glass plate windows that looked over the garden with its stone slabs and poetic carvings.

It was her or it wasn't.

She was short, like X, and Wyatt could begin to see, as he approached her from behind (because approach he did), and because of her close-cropped, spiky haircut, that she had on her neck, in addition to a mole, freckles. Were they the same freckles *his* X possessed? She did have X's trim and solid look. Perhaps less solid, but then, people changed after five years; she wouldn't have been taking part in that muscle-building regimen anymore. The hair spikes as well could have been an innovation, perhaps only hours old. X could express herself differently as a best-selling author compared with her years as the student-wife-dependent of a boring engineer husband in far East Texas.

Wyatt stood in front of her. "Good morning," he said.

He knew then it was not X, although this is not what keeps the encounter from nearly turning out to be not unhappy.

6
Lajitas

"I thought you were someone I knew."

"Yes?" No dimples, but a bright smile and many straight teeth.

He made a half-turn away, as the woman had cocked her head, moved her attention back to tiny white marks that circled her lens. She might be X's age, but no . . . He could tell just from the "Yes?" as people can. One syllable identified her as non-X. The illusion vanished, but that did not end his problems. He made a half-turn back.

"This is going to sound strange," he tried.

"How wonderful," the woman said, giving him her attention more fully. "And here I was, bored out of my mind."

"Ah."

"Now I'll get to hear something strange."

"Well . . . that sounds strange."

She smiled broadly. The woman seemed delighted he'd broken her tedium: as if ready for some new encounter. Or else she merely broadcast waves of irony. Wyatt had gotten into trouble before misreading waves of irony as ripples of sincerity. He narrowed his eyes. Not her.

As someone who spoke publicly seldom unless equipped with a Power-Point and a clicker—his projected bullet statements highlighting environmentalism, contractual relations, reserve bid pricing as he paced the front of a classroom, avoiding eye contact in general—Wyatt understood little of the craft of basic, time-filling small talk.

"And . . . and not that kind of strange."

"Oh. *That* kind," she said. "Ever better. A new kind of strange."

He waved his hands. "I've been looking for . . ."

"Me?"

"Yes. *No!* In a way. You look like someone I know, as I said, but not all that much like someone I know, now that I see you," he managed.

"Someone beautiful that you know."

A joke? Banter? Defensive snark in punishment for his having approached with such a lame opening line? Unfortunately—although it may not have been demonstrated as obvious thus far, Wyatt's gift for snark and banter, though it did exist, could not be depended on to appear when needed. "Beautiful. Yes. Well. Not everyone thinks so."

"Really!"

"I have always disagreed with those people."

She nodded. "So, from over there, you see me, think I am someone you know. Feel you must rise and explain to me how my good looks are a matter of opinion. Am I getting this right?"

Then everything inexplicably shifted. Wyatt couldn't even be sure how it happened. The best way to indicate the changing tone of this conversation, as opposed to attempting to represent only its bare text on the page which, let's face it, might give the wrong impression, would be to point out that at this juncture they both began laughing. Wyatt, for once, felt himself in on a joke he was also the butt of. From sidelong glances he checked on the progress of the crew in orange vests, one of whom had withdrawn what appeared to be a voltage reader and stood uncoiling its wired probes in the door of the elevator, while from the men's room door, a workman emerged with a massive green hose over one shoulder, moving quickly towards the cafeteria at a jog.

"It's not just someone. Or any someone. As you can tell from my accent, I'm . . ." He wasn't sure how to put it.

"An . . . ass . . . hole?"

More laughing. "I'm from far away."

"Ah-*merican* asshole."

"That's right! No. Yes." He tugged at his lapels. Walking up to the woman he'd felt the conversation could go one of two ways, but it had slithered into a third. "A Texan," he tried.

She nodded. "Of course!"

Wyatt's by now nearly pointless giggling confused even him. He sat on the sofa beside her, albeit at a respectful distance. "I'm one, that is. It's not just someone you remind me of, but . . ." What to say? To say about X? "A woman."

"I remind you of a woman!" Both of her hands to her cheeks, she lowered her chin, made out to examine her bosom. (Bigger than X's. Wasn't X.) "And here you were, saying it wasn't that sort of strange."

Leaned back, staring into the hazed sky via the gigantic plate glass the sofa fronted, Wyatt managed somehow to shake out the gist of the story: that she reminded him of a woman who'd told him, years before, he should visit this town. He was able to mention his surname, summarize that branch of the tale. Then added he'd seen this woman or thought he had—and hearing from his own mouth he began to edit the story. "I convinced myself I saw this woman at the station. So, I just have a simple question. Were you at the train station on Monday, around . . ."

"I've been to Texas."

"You're kidding."

"Lajitas."

"Ah. West Texas. Not like where I'm from."

"Oh. Right."

"Different."

"West Texas! Fuck that, eh?"

Wyatt grinned. "Exactly."

"Visiting, Good God, Sallowsfield. You'll be here how long?"

They exchanged numbers, with the woman, Gail, unsurprised he couldn't easily feed her "digits" into his phone. He opened his notebook to a blank page and offered her his ballpoint to jot it down. They agreed to meet the following day, have something to eat.

"I mean," she said, "an actual Sallow. I've always wanted to have dinner with one."

"You're joking."

"Of course, but we can talk about Texas and . . . I don't know . . . how ridiculous Americans are."

"I'm sorry?"

"I've got to run, Wyatt Sallow. Tomorrow evening? Seven-ish?"

"Perfect. I. I'm sorry."

"For?"

Did he even know? He passed a hand down his chest. Sighed.

Gail shrugged. "Call me," and she kissed his cheek, leaving what could only be called a purple and floral scent as she departed the atrium by way of the interior cafeteria entrance, passing the elevator repairmen, and then the workmen at the restroom door, waving to Wyatt one last time before she disappeared.

Beside her number he wrote, "Gail."

7
Gail

His spirits were high. Perhaps, when they had dinner the next day he could find things to mention about himself that would impress Gail, such that he was the author of *Water Take Me Down and Burn Me*, whose title poem describes a horrific drowning incident (in sestina format). He probably would not mention to her that he was able to describe this (not convincingly, according to the anonymous student critic in the *Daily Toreador* who'd gone on to become a respected Dean in a small East Texas college) because he had experienced near-drowning as part of a foolish diving board mistake. One mid-July around the age of twelve, in one of the pine-and-woodsmoke-scented summer camps he'd been dutifully sent to by his mother, Wyatt had followed some new friends up and off the end of a high dive at the camp pool. He didn't know these new friends well enough to trust them with the knowledge that he could not swim, and once he'd stood in line so long, then made that high, high, higher climb on the aluminum ladder whose rough corrugations chafed his feet, he couldn't see not giving it a try at least. The walk out to the end of the thing was more than enough to convince him he'd made a terrible error. One dizzying misstep, a kind of half launch into an incredibly empty and shapeless column of space, then he fell and fell. The water was blue and cool but no longer inviting as he struck it, chlorine stinging his nasal cavity deep into his brain as the liquid—no longer liquid-like—stung his skin from the impact. An embarrassing near-drowning experience followed. Professor Sallow remembered especially attempting to raise himself by pressing against the water's surface with the flat of his hands, but it simply would not support him. However, one of the more foolish camp counselors soon appeared at his side, hearing his choked cries for help and lifting him, pulling him to the edge of the pool. He remembered the man—called "Spyder" by the campers—had been considered an idiot because one evening while this counselor had been chopping wood a spider had jumped on his leg so he struck at it with the ax, cutting a deep gash requiring several stitches. Hence the name.

The camp idiot, Wyatt realized, had saved his life.

He arrived in the center of town more quickly than he thought possible, the railway station hoving into view prematurely as Wyatt rounded a corner, recognizable as he and Hussein had made the same approach after giving up on finding X his first day in town. He could have kept going, on to the Town Central, but he needed to rest. He considered benches in the square. But on the north end of the station stood a cheery enough looking pub, The Top and Tail. Did he have time to stop? At the very least, and not knowing local eating establishments other than the Chinese takeaway, copying out some of the menu offerings of The Top and Tail from its leaning chalkboard into his journal made sense as reconnaissance. He could see tables inside and, unlike many pubs he'd passed, large plate glass windows looked out onto the vista of the town square. Perhaps it could be a place to take Gail the next evening.

Although he did not realize it, Gail was a person who understood how to overcome difficulties. In fact, she had a technique for doing so. Heck, it wouldn't be that hard, even, for her to teach it to him, and who doesn't need to, on occasion, overcome difficulties? She first encountered her method for dealing with frightening, damaging, even annoying situations during the era she'd mentioned in passing to Wyatt when she'd visited West Texas.

The reconstruction of exactly what happened to Gail in West Texas presented difficulties, involving as it did the effects of time, memory, and psilocybin. Gail had trouble decanting what she remembered of the trip to the desert music festival from the thick sediment of what she merely hallucinated remembering. These weren't fantastic, mind-blowing hallucinations, either, but quirky, perhaps true, perhaps faux, recollections that left her with doubts.

She felt certain, yes, that she and her friend Kathy had driven from Kathy's home in Oklahoma City to an outdoor music venue in the middle of a desert in 1998. She was pretty certain as well that, somewhere along the way, tumbleweeds had been involved. These had struck her as odd: a physical embodiment of a cartoonish myth. A weed that traveled. And look! There they were, along the road. Turned out they actually existed on that bizarre continent.

She could not, however, completely determine the outer parameters of her tumbleweed experience. Gail recalled several of these quite large structures rolling in the wind, traveling along, in fact, just beside the pickup truck she and Kathy had used for the trip, as if accompanying herself and her friend to three days and four nights of music and art in a kind of pick-up truck/tumbleweed caravan—Gail, Kathy, and the Large Rolling Weeds "Goin' West" together. That sort of herd movement, thinking back on it, now seemed unlikely: maybe an exaggeration of an actual sighting, strung into a longer narrative by the mind's vagaries. On the other hand, her additional tumbleweed recollection seemed, if anything, even less reliable, as during the gathering itself a particularly large one (had it followed the pickup across Texas, pushed through the entrance gates seeking her out?) passed through the gathered crowd (attendance estimated at 12,000), parted the audience of sun-blasted revelers like a bull through a marketplace, then spun right up to Gail. She reached as if to embrace it, turned, and said to Kathy, "My tumbleweed!" just before it flattened her: mowed her down and kept going, creating mayhem, heading for the main stage and the discordant guitar lines of a forgettable band warming up for Jane's Addiction.

Did any of that happen? Did it merely repeat a shared hallucinogenic matrix woven from later discussions and recollections with Kathy that also, possibly, yes, did involve an actual rolling diaspore root system experienced *somewhere*, but ... ? In a similar vein she categorized the puppy-shaped cloud that she and Kathy watched sail over some distant mountains. There wasn't anything particularly remarkable in that, although the morphing of that cloud into an adolescent dog–shaped cloud, which then became an adult cloud dog, and finally a stooped, bent-backed, and decrepit older hound on its last, wispy legs, all while they both watched, the atmospheric vapor evolving with the precision of a biology textbook illustration of canine development, well ... that was pretty odd. Unfortunately, these days Gail had lost track of Kathy and so couldn't corroborate the tumbleweed, the dog-cloud, the band lineup (had Jane's Addiction played *any* desert music festivals in 1998?) or much else from those three days and four nights, but she had firmly kept hold of a technique she discovered there, a method for "going by and getting by," which she recalled perfectly and trotted out still during times of difficulty.

Gail, spending the hot, hot summer of 1998 in America with her friend Kathy, already in her life had developed a set of guidelines (one might call them rules) she adhered to, especially when it came to mushrooms. Unfortunately, on the day she and Kathy drove into the hard-baked badlands of West Texas for Fantasy '98, featuring fourteen rock and progressive country acts and a simultaneous art festival (where Gail and Kathy believed they could make a killing selling "Bath Herbs," the recipe for which Kathy could claim credit)—all this in the Chihuahuan desert north of Lajitas ... unfortunately she abrogated each of these rules or guidelines one after another. "Start with smallish ones," was the first (Rule #1), but the mushrooms Kathy obtained from her unemployed boyfriend with the prosthetic leg (ideal for smuggling just about anything) and that she brought to the festival in a damp brown sack all seemed to be about the same size. Kathy was a solidly built brunette, had been a foreign student and one of Gail's oldest friends from her days at the University of Sallowsfield, a place of higher education she seemed unable to achieve any real distance from. (Receiving her baccalaureate in education in 2005, she'd remained in the region teaching at various technical colleges and often returned to uni for classes and lectures, most recently photography workshops that allowed her access to extensive darkroom facilities.) Kathy, a Kentuckian by birth, was one of those "heavier" girls who, nonetheless, let's face it, projected the pulsing impression of lightness, a wonder on the dancefloor who could, as men in Oklahoma told her, "downright float," especially during anything remotely foxtrot related, her arm around the neck of the best-looking uniformed guy in the club while her one-legged boyfriend (not a dancer) brooded. (She had, for the armed services, what she called a *penchant*, pronouncing it after the French. She did the same thing with the word *coupon*.) Like Gail herself, Kathy was an ebullient person. "Quite the talker, that Kathy," and so, parking the truck, getting out and stretching, taking the lay of the drought-stricken, parched, and broken land surrounding them, they got to chatting, slathering on sunscreen, and trying on several of the straw hats they'd brought for the occasion. They soon forgot to start with the smaller, chewier, moistest 'shrooms, and began gnawing on them at random as they might a shared order of fries, losing track of how many they'd digested in total. Perusing the gathering crowd, the good-looking young shirtless men, the tumbleweeds, they both set in yawning. Gail began to notice the colorful geometric aspects of the people, sandals, backpacks, hats, trucks, hardpan of desert ... uhm ... that lizard over there—why, the geometric aspects were just everywhere. That scuttling dung beetle pushing its Milk Dud sphere, by golly, looked totally edible—bug and all. She felt she'd been watching the world on a black-and-white set with rabbit ears all her life but, on that day, had won a free Motorola console TV with satellite dish.

This was all before they'd walked away from the truck.

By the time they got to the ticket gate (where they paid a reduced fee for entry because "I have a *coupon*," Kathy announced, and though she couldn't find it, the guy at the gate—reminiscent of a Euro-centric, blond-haired, blue-eyed version of Jesus—went ahead and gave her the discount) ... by this time just how many they'd eaten was a mystery, but what wasn't a mystery was that it had been a few.

Rule #2: *Be in nature.* The ironclad logic of this rule boils down to the fact that mushrooms are themselves *objects from nature.* It made sense, then, that the experience these fungi delivered, one had to suppose, evinced a consonant or harmonic relationship with that world from which they'd sprung. This the Ancient Native Americans with their peyote rituals no doubt understood in their bones, all part of their everyday shared culture. Denizens of the hectic, day-to-day, dog-eat-dog existence of Western citizenry circa 1998 needed a constant reminder, however. Besides, nature made for a much calmer setting in which to hallucinate than, say, an Oklahoma City one-bedroom apartment with no furniture, just tatami mats and a prosthetic leg propped in the corner.

There is nature, however, and there is nature, and no doubt Rule #2 had at its base an assumption of a natural world similar to that described by the Lake Poets in the early nineteenth century. Fandango '98 took place on flat, parched, shadeless hardpan, where temperatures approached 119 degrees Fahrenheit at noon and closed in on freezing by midnight as the rocks gave up their heat the way hijacked tourists in Panama City gave up their wallets. (Gail had traveled Central as well as North America.) This the rocks were liable to do having no plant cover to huddle beneath save horny cacti best adapted for hiding scorpions of the kind that crawled along the bare legs of concertgoers who—most of them stoned—watched the progress of these creatures with gape-mouthed curiosity as they attempted to determine whether anything like that—such a transparent lobster-like rip-off and, *come on*, that upraised, ludicrously threatening tail—existed in reality or only as the shadow of a partly remembered fever dream. Oh, and rattlesnakes. Brown recluse spiders whose venomous sting ate flesh. Feral hogs had been reported. And so, this less auspicious state of nature also flew in the face of the corollary to Rule #2, which was that *the absolute best way to appreciate nature was under the influence of mushrooms.* Gail and Kathy, in other words, had prepared themselves to appreciate their surroundings but those surroundings held no appreciation for them whatsoever.

Rule #3. *Do not—and I mean DO NOT EVER—be in a crowd when dropping mushrooms.* Even in small numbers, humans, with their propensity for both giving off and sucking back energy, emitted dangerous vibes at all times, but multiply their number, add hallucinogens—*et voila!* Intra-species force transferals risked exponential spread, especially if some of those humans began to enter into contact with your bare skin. On this summer day when Gail and Kathy, wearing cutoffs, tank-tops, straw hats and open-toed sandals strapped to the pink scorpion bait that constituted their feet, entered a crowd of 12,000 also scantily clad souls huddled in a forty-acre area north of the Rio Grande, they by no means possessed the wherewithal to pay heed to Rule #3 and inevitably became snarled and tangled in this crowd. For one, the girls held between them a PVC pipe across which they had draped their *sure-fire sellout* "Bath Herbs." With this trawling boom they managed to inadvertently corral at least 6,000 of the 12,000 attendees just by strolling absentmindedly through the mob, while many who saw this approaching juggernaut turned Gail and Kathy into—without their knowledge—a mobile herb-strewn limbo contest that also landed the two in various heaps of bare limbs and torsos, and this more than once.

Gail and Kathy had come up with, as a selling point, a cute name for their "Bath Herbs," but once arrived at the gathering they could no longer remember it, and so called out "Bath Herbs!" as they plowed through the swarm. The products were organic, made in fact from the harvest of Kathy's backyard garden, augmented with sticks and leaves from a nearby school construction site, then tied into "packets" that could easily be arranged over the PVC pipe. "Feel!" they hollered into the multitude as they waded through. "Smell! Think!"

A guy in a knit cap pushing a bicycle confronted them. Had he ridden a bicycle to the Chihuahuan desert north of Lajitas? "Smell what?" he asked Gail.

She took his hand, raised his arm, thrust her face into his sparsely haired armpit. "Better!" she answered. Then gave him one of the packets.

"Bathe with a friend!" Kathy tried as they moved through the crowd, and there was a solid reaction to this, but the sales figures they'd hoped for, perhaps enough to cover the trip, did not materialize. By the end of the first night, they'd accidentally given away all the "Bath Herbs."

They did not do well with the three rules, but fortunately, before they'd arrived at Fandango '98, Kathy and Gail had set up agreed-upon signals. To utter the phrase "Code Nine," for example, would mean it was time to stop, relax, take a reality check. This was a good idea, but went awry, as Gail made the mistake of using this emergency phrase for the first time in an ironic fashion. Surrounded as they were by so many good-looking shirtless guys with black chest hair and bulging pockets who smiled, Gail winked at Kathy, said, "Code Nine," and laughed. And then another group went by (also with black chest hair) so Kathy repeated back, "Code Nine, definitely," at Gail, then rolled her eyes (as one does), so in the end the agreed-upon signal was worthless, which was too bad.

The plan had been to spend at least some time at rest. Sit still and observe as the qualities of the experience began to kick in.

This did not work either.

There was some introspection. Although Gail could not hear the music of the far away bands that sounded nearly like whale sounds from ocean depths, she did *feel* how some of the lyrics pierced the distance, including one line that rang crystal-clear. "Everything . . . everything . . . everything they say of you is true." Gail took this personally to mean that *everything* anyone had *ever* said about her was, in fact, gospel, and this included contradictory statements like "You'll knife anyone in the back to get ahead" (volleyball squad friend in grade school she no longer spoke to) and "You'll never amount to anything" (her stepfather). Didn't the first almost guarantee the second couldn't be the case? She glanced at her now new best friend in the universe, Kathy (so *beautiful*—if a bit chunky) and saw that Kathy's head had been replaced by the head of a coyote with watery eyes.

"They are all having our experience," Gail said to the coyote, indicating the cool, hip, roiling, strong-smelling crowd. "What experience?" answered the coyote. A different guy with a beard and muscular physique (except for skinny arms—"Needs to see an arms dealer," Gail said to herself and commenced a giggling fit) . . . this guy approached, and she began communicating with him telepathically. He got it, too, really laughing at her mentally transferred jokes, although there wasn't much to them. Like a game show hostess, Gail indicated the mountains at the horizon with outstretched hands—as if offering these landscape features behind door number 2. He made a similar gesture towards a part of the horizon that featured—perhaps today and today only—rolling hills. This induced guffaws that made Gail's stomach ache. The desert communicated with her and she understood every word and, more, could tell which words were *italicized*.

Something might have happened with the skinny-arm guy, if a weird roach-eyed girl hadn't come up to him, taken him by a skinny arm, said, "I tried to call you! I tried to call you!"—then pulled him into the crowd.

Well.

Something came over Gail. It was not related to the guy, Bath Herbs, or scorpions, but landed from a different quadrant, took her with such force she had to sit. She planted herself on the warmth of the desert, which burned her ass it was so damn exposed out there. Gail fell into something dark, awful. She tried to find a name for it.

But couldn't.

On the ground, in a dense forest of legs, feet, movement, she felt she could be trampled at any second. She felt a hurricane might come. (Meteorologically impossible.) Or: a limousine. Some guys could get out of it, dressed in black, steal her Bath Herbs, drive away. When she looked, the Bath Herbs and the pipe that had supported them were, in fact, both gone. (They'd been gone for a day and a half.) She felt like screaming.

Gail could never be certain if it had involved a kind of slowing down, a "reality check" of her own devising, that helped her out of this encounter, but she did work through it. Kathy had come over to her, put her head together with Gail's and offered the advice that she should "seek pink energy."

"That won't work."

Kathy nodded. "Then we should consider ourselves to be flutes. The events of the world blow into us. Like the wind. It is this wind that plays the *Tune. That. We. Are.*"

Gail considered. "Do you blow *into* a flute, or *over* a flute?"

So, she set Kathy's advice aside but did then stumble upon the technique. Gail imagined herself a stoplight. One of those red, green, yellow cycling kinds, with bulbs on four sides, as could be found at any intersection, anywhere in the world. She'd seen them in Europe, in America, at an intersection in Antigua, Guatemala, next to a café where she'd witnessed a waiter flirting with the girlfriend of a drug lord and—fifteen minutes later—a waiter gunned down by a very pissed off drug lord. Only, instead of lights, Gail's version was installed with tubes, each tube sinking into infinity, so that—at this imaginary intersection—rather than coming together, things passed through one another: went in one side, traveled the length of infinity, ghosted out the other end. Not only that but, because these tubes were—like traffic lights—synchronized, they engaged their universal bypassing in an organized fashion. Events could travel harmlessly without crossing or crashing into each other. And—this she realized in the desert with crystal clarity—what passes through cannot knock down.

She even paused to say that out loud. "What passes through cannot knock down."

In whatever chaotic circumstance, Gail imagined the infinity of possibilities passing through her rather than bowling her over, and after the space of a few minutes—or, in the Texas desert, what could have been a few hours, it was hard to tell—when she opened her eyes, the world had been set to rights, music playing on a faraway stage, blood on green tiles wiped away with a sponge, the tense encounter in the living room of her first ex-husband's parents finished as her husband's father, snorting in derision, rose from the sofa cushions and stalked away, saying, "You don't do it for me anyway, cunt." Whatever. It passed. The chaos, murder, undesired calf grope ended; the party, concert, avocado lime and ceviche lunch resumed. Normality resumed.

While many give advice such as "don't let it get you down," Gail had found a way to actualize this advice: a method that, at some time, she could pass on to the right person who needed it.

8
Not the Third Man

But not this time.

If Wyatt relied on the assumption that his presence in the town held value, then there remained still much to do. He could not cover it all, he felt, if he began to lose focus. Walking in front of the Henry Scott statue, he noted again its blank, accusatory stare.

A wastepaper basket had been centered on the rectangular pavement in front of the station pub. Once away from the warren of streets, in the open air, Wyatt began to consider the limits to his time. He factored in the possibility, still, that X was here and on a tight schedule, like himself. Should he encounter her, he would have to invest some of his time in an all-out effort to—somehow (especially after that matter with the front door)—get back into her good graces, no matter how impossible.

He investigated the wastebasket, its newspaper, fast-food cups, torn package of AA batteries ripped open and wished he could go home. By this, he did not mean the Town Central, or Turner, Texas, in general, or his home on Linden Lane. (He had returned there seldom since his last conversation with "Cousin" Yuri.) He wanted to open the door and step up into the RV he occupied in the Tranquility Park RV Camp. It was where he'd gone after most of his fiascos, even before the fiasco of his career, or his marriage, or his X. Early in his time with Z, when she'd spent those months in Houston with Wyn, just after the boy had been born, Wyatt would repair to the fifth wheel rather than endure the quiet spaces of his house. Z needed proximity to the ICU while he stayed all week in Turner, keeping his job intact, his insurance coverage sound.

Since he'd been exclusively living there a year by then, it was where he'd gone after he discovered he was not the third man.

He and X had met for lunch, as they often did, at the upstairs coffee shop at Bellinger and Nord, then gotten some writing done together—also as they also usually did, at least once a week. Before sitting down to write, he'd bought X one of the expensive sparkling waters she favored. In the parking lot, sitting for a while before going home, she'd dropped the news on him. Did she know she was going to do that?

Did she know yet let him buy the sparkling water anyway?

In his car, Wyatt followed her van for a few blocks when they left, but then picked a different, random direction. He could see the nonchalant back of her head. There was nothing after that but to go home. He stayed full-time in the RV at that point, a place he could sit in solitude.

He'd learned of not being the third man in the parking garage of the mall where the two of them met so often, the Main Street section. This retail area had been set around a stubby green space, shops representing arcane products surrounding it, most of these presenting as square brick structures. From the tiny Town Green the area did resemble small-town America. The view from an elevated balcony of the mega-retail bookshop where they'd meet for coffee revealed a more laughable movie set facade. Behind each Americana front stood blockish retail space, square, grey, and inelegant as any Soviet-era post office. In Turner, Texas, the mall developer had successfully created a phony small town on the outskirts of an actual small town. To achieve this perch, they rode the elevator. Into this elevator they could steal, hidden from prying eyes, a twelve- or even fourteen-and-a-half-second kiss. They could touch each other, smell each other's hair in enclosed isolation. X it was, by the way, who—waiting barely past the millisecond the door snapped closed—initiated these grappling sessions with a claw-like grab at the back of Wyatt's neck that strained the delicate cervical vertebra there. (He had issues with calcium degeneration that X often structurally challenged.) Her hand on the back of his head, she directed his lips to those places she wanted them for those twelve or fourteen and a half seconds. Her forehead. Throat. Behind the ear. Sometimes on the lips. Wyatt felt his breath, her breath, their two selves momentarily close in a way that registered. It shook him as profoundly as anything had in a profoundly shaken life.

"What was that?" he asked X after one such encounter.

"What was what?"

Wyatt understood the elevator ride to be twelve seconds to fourteen and a half seconds because he'd timed it using a highly accurate stopwatch borrowed from his friend Marc who ran the athletic department's main equipment room. Marc had not been crazy about lending the watch but finally relented. Wyatt visited Bellinger and Nord one afternoon without X. He depressed the circular plastic wafer marked "2." When the elevator doors snapped completely shut—that instant upon which they would hide any occupants from any possible view—he pressed his thumb down firmly on the hefty, plastic-encased watch's start button. Being in the elevator when those doors closed excited him, even without X's presence. When, after the lifting ride, the doors spread enough so that anything—anything at all—could be seen as the panels separated, no matter how small the sliver of vision made possible by this divide between the brushed aluminum surfaces, he quickly hit the stop button. He recorded the result on a "timing clipboard" that the stopwatch snapped onto, clicking into a snug and handy bracket. The "timing clipboard" was also provided by Marc. As it turned out, after repeating the exercise eleven times, the duration was not consistent. Something in the friction of the mechanism or the changing temperature of the afternoon, or possibly the varying weight of the car occupants . . . something created a varying time of transit. Every time he entered the elevator with X after this experiment, he hoped for the extra 2.5 seconds.

Not only the bookstore and its coffee shop drew them to this mall. A nearby multiplex theater gave them a place to sneak away to see movies. He felt they had to sneak since he was still married, although merely a technicality that came with fiduciary expenditures. In truth, he often felt he was the only one out of the pair sneaking during these clandestine encounters. Sometimes—very dark times—he felt that but for the chance to get some writing done on a confirmed schedule, she'd have no interest in him at all. A wrinkle in their multiplex forays boiled down to X's constitutional disbelief in spending money on theater snacks. "Popcorn," she claimed, "costs five dollars per silo—why pay six dollars for a tiny box?" In addition to the kernels she'd air roasted at home and sealed in sandwich bags, she provided at times fudge, at others homemade peanut brittle, and, once, broiled salmon in 8-ounce, leakproof, "Deli-Size" Rightway Tucker-ware containers (Wyatt often studied the product lines of Rightway Inc.)—not bad but not a taste he associated with big screens, previews, and surround sound. She withdrew these from her shoulder "carry-all" that had been aptly named as it provided—usually between Acts III and IV of the filmed screenplays—soda in disposable cups as well. With straws. In the darkened theater, she would reach out—not to take his hand, or stroke his arm, but to offer the homemade snack. Sometimes, when he probed X's open palm, seeking the popcorn (which she preferred doling out rather than handing him, say, in his own sealed sandwich bag) or picking up the Milk Duds she cradled there (purchased in bulk from Costco), he would brush his fingers against her hard skin, feel a thrill of closeness that made him hopelessly happy.

Wyatt felt his passion confined, restricted. To the bookstore, yes, but really to the ride in the elevator, its exhilaratingly compressed opportunity for chaste lust. In the upstairs coffee shop, he would buy her that incredibly expensive foreign sparkling water she favored over coffee—which was fine. She deserved it. Besides, he'd saved so much on movie treats.

Later, heading home, most often, they would sit a while in her minivan in the elevated parking area and chat. And then, that last time they'd met in the parking lot, she told him he was not the third man.

He went from there to his trailer, where the effects of the heartbreaking news hit him right in the kitchenette.

He stood above the joke of the aluminum sink that had been crookedly framed with vinyl. Wyatt grew dizzy in a way that did not pass after a few seconds. Uncharacteristically for someone his age and weight, he did not take this as an opportunity to sit on one of the built-in banquette seats but instead held the sink's edge with both hands. He ended by sitting on the fragile fold-out table. In a way, he feared lowering himself onto his mattress in the back of the RV might mean not rising again. He extended his stockinged feet, his shoes left on the concrete block outside. Several other concrete blocks he'd used to build bookshelves in the back bedroom (or "sleeping nook"), a technique he'd mastered as an undergraduate, though not ideal when it came to bookshelves in a small space. The table's edge creased the back of his legs. Wyatt looked up and to the right, feeling something coming, wondering if it might be something cardiac. He figured up and to the right was the correct direction for a heart attack to approach. He could see, barely, into his tiny bathroom, the corner of the shower curtain, sea horses on it, mold across the ceiling. The fifth wheel felt empty, silent, with the smell of age about it, which Wyatt associated with abandonment, although he had in no way abandoned it. Staying there in some ways felt normal, reprising his earlier bachelor existence.

He did not crouch in pain or hug his knees. Wyatt felt his mouth must be open as, soon, he could taste salty tears running into it. The front door he'd closed and locked, separating himself even from the mid-week noon emptiness of the Tranquility Park RV Camp where he'd moved to leave the memories of the house on Linden Lane to Z, Yuri, and the mice. Mold and coffee constituted the only smells in the small trailer as he'd long used a scentless soap that wouldn't affect the boy's sensitive skin and had tons of it left: cases he just couldn't seem to run out of no matter how aggressively he wasted it. No cleanser aroma hovered in the RV.

From his seat on the table with his head bent backward in a poor imitation of the way Wyn could look easily over his own shoulder, Wyatt saw that the corner of the wall next to the tub had gone to rot, either from a leak or the daily speckling of shower water that sneaked around the curtain. He thought the latter. The mold left a darkness that groped up the wall, and that darkness had an indentation in it, like a mouth.

It wasn't like a funeral. He'd been to several. It seemed the approach of something worse. "This isn't good," he said to himself, and then it fell on him.

Wyatt gripped the table, perceived a sound he'd not heard before and it came from himself.

Analyzing days later, what had been wounded, he believed, was not his ego, although that was part of it. The loveable Wyatt Sallow, perhaps, had taken a hit. That is, the version that could be loved. X had found someone, she told him in the van. She didn't say someone else as one might if breaking off a close relationship. The kind of thing that happens, she explained. She'd grown bored with her husband, and sought passion elsewhere, as he knew (she'd "confided so much in him") and now had found it. Wyatt, beginning after a hopeful few seconds to more accurately grasp her meaning, groped for a way to ask if she'd also grown bored with the person she wanted to have parts of herself buried with, the man she shared twelve- to fourteen-and-a-half-second bursts of elevator passion with, but none of that appeared to be on her mind.

Worse: this person she'd found lived in New Orleans. If he'd been closer—less travel time involved—perhaps she could have managed.

"Managed?"

He'd sensed something could be amiss when, after leaving their table at the coffee shop, X had made a beeline for the stairs, even though they'd attained the second floor via the usual elevator. For this reason, they racked up, in total, putting aside the epic stepping down from his office chair, nine elevator kisses rather than an even number in their time together, although he could add to this one cheek peck.

"New Orleans excites me," she said. She had visited the city a month earlier, seeing family, and that had been the beginning. She spoke of New Orleans much as she'd spoken before of the interests she and Wyatt held in common: the poetry of Millay, Nabokov's novels, Karpov's innovations with the Caro-Kann. New Orleans plugged her into her Cajun ancestry, and she felt charged.

So, this man: Though he lived 500 miles away, X told Wyatt that afternoon in her van in the elevated parking garage, that this man fascinated her. He worked as a musician, although to Wyatt he sounded more like a cook who wanted to be a musician. That is, he earned his living at his brother's restaurant—some seedy dive, but his identity, she insisted, was "musician" and he had an apartment in . . . yes. X would wake up after a night of lovemaking with this cook/musician in the French Quarter. The place people traveled for weekend debauchery was his twenty-four-seven home. He and X rode bicycles in the evenings through the *Vieux Carré* (sounded like the guy didn't have a car, either), went places to listen to live music. "I've never listened to live music before," she told Wyatt.

"We went to that jazz concert."

"When I wake up in the morning, after our lovemaking..."

"In the mall. The combo." But he'd caught it. The musician had no job or car but wasn't grabbing spare elevator moments of bliss, either.

Wyatt seethed.

"...after our lovemaking, I find him bent over the piano. Creating. The problem is," she said to Wyatt. "I have my husband, and I have Jeremy, and...one of them has to go."

Jeremy. That was the name of the New Orleans man.

"It's one too many."

She unscrewed the cap of the incredibly expensive sparkling water she favored that Wyatt had bought her twenty minutes before in the bookstore coffee shop and took a long sip.

The question hung. She hadn't said it yet had. In this scenario, Wyatt was "the third man." But in fact, it was a stretch to consider he counted even as having come in third. Yet he must fit in somewhere. It simply didn't add up. He was surprised to have missed it. So, yes. That was it.

Too many. And himself not even come in third.

"New Orleans," he said. "I'll miss you."

"I'll miss you, too."

To say anything else about it would be a disaster. It was so obvious, now. He resolved to remain silent.

"I guess I'm not even the third man," he said instead.

"What?"

"The elevator. What about the elevator?"

X looked over the parking garage, confused. "Elevator?"

"The twelve to fourteen and a half seconds. Going up, then going down."

Her recollection cleared. To Wyatt it seemed she'd almost understood his concern. She put her hand a last time around his neck. Drew him close. Pecked him on the cheek. "It's not like we won't see each other."

Wyatt, in the months that followed, birthed many pithy, even cutting responses to X's news that they couldn't meet to write together anymore. ("We might see each other, but my time availability is really curtailed, so ...") Other potential though unspoken responses were at the very least thought-provokingly defiant. ("If I'm not the third man, perhaps I'm no man at all.") At that moment he had nothing.

"It may be a mistake," she said and laughed.

Nothing. Nothing to say. Only the desire to prove he was not hurt. He lifted his laptop from the floorboard of her van. Opened the door. Stepped down onto the concrete.

"Ow," he said.

"Wyatt."

He shuffled away.

9
Priyanka? Priyasha?

All in all, these kinds of considerations made it understandable that in the RV he'd do what he did next. Suffering for a while by that time from what Dr. Than called "your erectile issues" (why did they always have to be *his*, not *those* or *those common*?), yet feeling only diversion could save him from the onslaught of solitary thought, Wyatt pushed tears from his eyes, opened the cabinet over the settee, removed his vacuum constriction device, loosened his belt and dropped his trousers and boxer briefs to around his knees. The device's sleeve required, of course, lubrication from the water-based solution he also withdrew from the overhead cabinet. He sniffed and frowned, fitting the oily part over his now completely flaccid self but soon ... by fitting the smoky grey cylinder to its sleeve, uncoiling the looping tube, holding up the device with one hand he began to compress its connected bulb with the other, trying to tune out that primitive air pump's flatulent response until the seal took and, through the discolored cylinder, he'd be able to see himself grow. Rise. His veins take on a more distinctive contrast to his pale fleshy member as the noise of his sadness became lost in the noise of sensation.

Soon, it grew in the device. It was not, even at full measure, a very large one. You never know who'll get one, although when men are deficient in one area, one might hope for them to be gifted in others, but . . . oh, well.

At this point he had no topless picture (yet) of the love of his life, nor was he the type to collect pornographic imagery. As he squeezed the bulb, what could he think of, then, but standing in an elevator, his nose in someone's hair?

Leaned on the table in his trailer, he felt the flesh on his face tugged towards the kitchen vinyl. Gravity, pulling on its clownish TV wrestler mask, threw its leg over his head and squeezed. Exposed, holding out the cylinder, feeling the effects as he pumped at the bulb, Wyatt felt a truth in his throat, a catch from inside his windpipe. That was probably what created the timbre of the screech he emitted. Or maybe it wasn't his throat. He hadn't realized before that sounds could originate in the spine. This must be, he considered, what baby birds experience when they beg for chewed worms. *Please.* He locked his heels against the lower part of the banquette, hunched, yet craned his neck so that mouth and eyes remained flat to the ceiling. His cry must have been loud enough to hear outside the fifth wheel as he was sitting in this somewhat twisted and uncovered configuration when there came another sound, which was a knock at his door.

It was so unprecedented Wyatt could not at first register it. He wasn't certain he had ever heard it before, a knock on that door. But either squirrels had thrown themselves at his aluminum screen, or someone bashed on it with a flat palm.

It's not that he'd never had visitors. No, wait. It *was* that.

It had to be a mistake. Someone at the wrong RV. Or . . . could it be?

X was not the kind who liked to leave things to dangle, their ends loose, and they had definitely—by his lights—let ends drape messily at the mall elevated parking lot. The thought that it could be X, come to check on him, startled him so much he did not bend at the waist, move towards the door, twist the little release valve, remove and then quickly hide—*quickly*—the device by stashing it in some cupboard, let alone wipe his tears with a sleeve. He did none of that, merely froze. No matter, as either he hadn't locked the door after all, or the lock didn't work (possible), as the screaky hinges of the aluminum door engaged, then came a woosh of decompression when the interior panel swung open. Stepping up into his living room/kitchenette came that woman. In her sari. The bindi on her forehead. Walked right in.

Her. From across the windbreak, in the double-wide. Indian lady. A doctor, as in, PhD in History and ... Dr. ... Chaudry? ... Verghese? She entered Wyatt's trailer, filling both the living room and kitchenette, appearing beside him in three quick steps. Barefoot, with a thin gold chain on her dusky left ankle, she had also left her shoes on the concrete stoop beside his.

"Oh, Dr. Sallow."

"Oh ..." *Priyanka Chaudry?*

"I wondered. I wondered."

He nodded through his tears. "Yes."

"It's today, isn't it? Isn't it?"

In a way that would have been shocking had Wyatt not been too far out on his own limb to register anything as shock, Dr. ... Vingh? ... Singh? ... suddenly hugged his throat, brought his head against her shoulder. Her large breasts pinned his elbows. He wasn't sure how to release them.

Priyasha Singh?

He still held his en-cylindered cock and squeeze ball air pump.

"Yes," he stammered. It was all getting a bit too emotional. "I ..."

"You don't have to." She patted his back, as if burping him, then pulled away, placed her hand flat to his chest. "Not anymore." A wedding ring embedded in her brown finger resembled a chain fastened around an oak in mid-century. "You don't have to."

He nodded. Fucking school! No secret of any kind could long survive at Taylor State, although how she'd learned of X and Jeremy, especially so rapidly, he couldn't begin to fathom.

How on earth had she learned so quickly that he'd become not the third man?

She peered directly into his eyes. "Let it out, Wyatt."

He lifted, slightly, the cylinder and bulb. "I'm sorry."

"No matter. No matter. Go ahead."

Nodded, he knew what she meant. "Owwwwww," he said.

"More."

He did so and shook from the awesome sound of it.

This went on for an interminable period, until the doctor wiped tears from his face with the flat of her own palms, spread the dampness back and away from his eyes, towards his ears and stringy hair. Her eyebrows were so rectangular Wyatt wondered if they'd been applied with a stencil. "The fact is," she said, "he was so much like you."

"I've thought that must be so."

"Such a resemblance."

"You've seen him?"

"Everyone has seen him, Wyatt."

Good God. X must have been flaunting Jeremy all over campus. He lowered his eyes. "But I've got a job," he said.

"An important job! You've got to think of your students!"

"I suppose. I suppose." His students. There'd been so many. At the moment he couldn't name any.

Wyatt buried his face in the Indian professor's sari, fearing he would probably soak the fabric. *Priyanka Vingh?* Though they had been acquaintances before her retirement—teaching in adjacent buildings—she had never so much as nodded at him before at the trailer park, remaining for the most part hidden on the other side of a windbreak of brush and pines. He had seen her once through those shrubs, remarkably, hanging clothes on a line outside her double-wide while simultaneously reading a paperback book! She was able, through dexterity, to keep the book in one hand, advance the pages with the thumb of that same hand, while hanging the wash with the other, removing clothespins from her mouth and places she'd clipped them to a sweep of her sari, all without interrupting her reading. He also knew she took care of three small children on occasion, apparently after school. Grandkids? But otherwise he recalled only one other conversation he'd had with her on campus—and by "had" he meant "overheard"—when she'd explained something to a grad student in the mailroom as Wyatt checked to see if he'd gotten an article accepted by a University of Nebraska journal (he had not). She'd been telling the student that she would at times lock herself in the bathroom just to read. "I live alone, Katy! Yet I lock myself in! I need the isolation. The barrier between myself and the ringing phone, the knock at the door, the hungry cat. I need to feel truly and appropriately guilty about stealing away and reading. I need a certain number, like a *body*, of words. To sit on my brains as I sleep."

Apparently, she did not feel the same solitary privacy required for enjoying a book applied to jacking off. Though his balls were clearly exposed, at least the smoky tint of the device left some parts to the imagination, and he could imagine no way to alter his current position without making things much, much worse.

"Wyatt," she said, standing in his trailer, hugging him. "You should not stay here. You should not do what I've done and cover your tracks."

"No?"

"Or become mistrustful of the apparent simplicity of things, even simple people, in simple roles."

She started to lose him.

"If there's something history teaches, it's that people rarely have a single vision. Be more than one thing, Dr. Sallow. What you are, yes, fine, but with the addition of another ingredient. That's why all of this happened. That's why it happened to you."

Although he would not have another conversation with her, as she moved out of the Tranquility Park RV Camp in the next year (he never knew why), on this day she held his face a last time, moved it to arm's length, looked down her nose and into his eyes, as if to make out his small print, and then, with great kindness, said three inaccurate things: "Dr. Sallow. Dr. Sallow. Dr. Sallow."

10
Jeremy

Recently, Wyatt discovered on the internet that "Jeremy" was the most common name in the United States for murderers, information he thought to text to X although he never did. That felt like an eggshell that wouldn't hold his weight. Especially after the really stupid thing he'd done to that door just before X left Turner, Texas, for good.

11
Certain Fantasy

Standing over the waste bin, resolute in his decision that his relation with X would demand his entire attention should he come face-to-face with her, Wyatt opened his journal. The encounter with Gail would most likely come to nothing. But with X here, undeniably he had a true chance to set things right. Dampening his fingers to separate the pages, he tore from the binding the one that was blank save for a single name and a phone number. One thing his years in the chess world had taught him was how to make difficult decisions, even when these were based on an uncertain reality: far better than relying on what had to be certain fantasy.

Of course, if you get those mixed up, this lesson isn't so helpful, but . . .

Placing the journal under his arm, he massaged the page into a tight ball, then deposited it into the bin in front of the Top and Tail, and in this way, a pleasant denouement to the Gail subplot was narrowly avoided.

12
What She Thought She'd Never Say

The Top and Tail displayed a drinks menu prohibitively epic in length, although, technically, it was more an ale, bitters, and cider menu. When asked by a young man with buzzed hair and a dirty smock over his black t-shirt what he'd like, Wyatt surrendered, admitted he came from Texas, and had no idea.

The bartender blew air through pursed lips as if handling his tenth Texan of the day. "You'll want the other side."

This turned out not to be a political or gender preference statement, but an indication Wyatt should follow the man's pointing finger to a different room, paralleling the first, accessed through a connecting passage. Here dining tables crowded the floor, cozy booths the walls, and, at a long black bar, the man materialized again, wiping his hands on a towel and scowling. Quieter, the room had more seating and a full menu on a chalkboard. Wyatt took a recommendation for a local ale and decided he was hungry. In a corner, he sat on a plush cushion, placed his sweating glass on a cork protector, stashed his daypack at his feet, and centered his notebook on the table, becoming again for the moment that bizarre creature of urban naturalism: a guy who writes in public. Wyatt made some desultory notes concerning his day, his trip to the university, his experience with the wave of plumbing noise that apparently had destroyed the new men's room. He did not mention the woman with spiky hair. He also neglected to note how the Creative Writing Department appeared to be closed. He had to interrupt sketching in these recollections to make room for a basket of condiments—mustard, ketchup, other mysteriously bottled items—all flipped upside down for gravity's aid in coercing the substances onto his plate, which also soon arrived, brought by a mature blonde with bangs wearing shorts who called him "Luv."

Bartenders shuttled between the two rooms, each wearing dark t-shirts promoting either a beverage or a heavy metal rock band: skulls with crossbones were definitely involved. Every wall featured railroad memorabilia, including station signs from as far away as Hull, Halifax, and Huddersfield. There was a green model train engine made of tin. The odd rusted railway spike and kerosene lamp. Wyatt faced a row of nearly indecipherably elaborate digital machines that had something to do with gambling. Two youths about college age positioned themselves in front of one called "Mike's Millions" that seemed to pay out: enough for drinks for themselves and two other friends who soon arrived.

Owing to the relative emptiness of the lounge, Wyatt found the atmosphere relaxing. The ale was smooth with a foamy brown head, the battered fish excellent. A bright green item in a cup Wyatt took to be wasabi or horseradish. When he tried it the taste was of ... emptiness. Beside him, a man enjoyed each page of a scuba magazine and sipped at half a pint. His legs crossed, he joggled his worn loafer to Beatles songs from overhead speakers. An older bald gentleman in a Polo shirt moved between the two rooms with a nearly empty glass—although Wyatt had no confidence the same nearly empty glass made an appearance each time. He had never favored crowds, but if the pub were always like this it would not be a bad place to spend afternoons at 5:30. He envisioned momentarily a future retirement, his daylight labors ending at The Top and Tail, perhaps reading Byron or *New in Chess* rather than the scuba mag, but otherwise emulating the man beside him down to the bouncing loafer. The difference would be he could spend his sunset years in a place that—everywhere he looked—showed him back his name.

Y prided herself an Anglophile. It would be late morning in Turner, so Wyatt snapped a picture of his plate, texted it to her, asked about the green substance.

His affection for Y dated to that time he first met her, after her embarrassing announcement concerning Wyn. He attributed their unlikely friendship to something she did not do. She never commiserated. About anything. Her silence was both golden and, somehow, properly proportioned. Y kept just quiet enough. Perhaps, Wyatt considered from time to time, it was genuine disinterest. If so, he could accept that, too. She'd become someone he confided in. He felt certain she would trust him with her great secrets as well, although it appeared she didn't have any. For that reason, in addition to the fact that he had literally no one else in the world who would know or care to hear about it, after the picture of the green substance, he sent her a message: "She is here."

A few moments later, his phone rang.

"I can't believe you're calling me," Wyatt said. He seldom heard Y's voice through a device: they communicated almost solely via text.

"Right?" Y sounded like she might be in another hallway of the train station, about to meet him for an ale, not on another continent about to take notes for a late-morning department leadership colloquium.

He was grateful she called. Y stayed on her phone most waking hours but spoke into it seldom, being of a generation more comfortable with other modes of constant disclosure. There'd been times she'd texted him as they sat immediately beside each other, shoulder to shoulder, in committee meetings. While she claimed to have "no friends," the list of those she stayed in daily contact with was enormous and transnational. Still, he supposed, when it came to "in your face" contact—those who in some way used their anatomical eardrums to directly collect the sound of her vocal cords—maybe "no friends" was accurate.

In fact, Wyatt shared with Y her distrust of talking on the phone. Save necessary communication related to work, he mainly confined his phone calls to annual or even biannual prank calls to Gordon McKenzie in Wappinger, New York. Wyatt, when he was sixteen, served McKenzie a two-slice mushroom and green olive on thin crust with a Pepsi. He happened to see and memorize the phone number on the check the man used to purchase the #7 at Pizza Shack, where Wyatt had held his first—his only—job. He'd called Gordon a few weeks later to place large orders for plastic containers and continued to do so, even though Gordon moved through career positions in nearly every kind of sales other than the plastic container variety. Keeping up with his movements had become easier after the internet. Gordon had recently landed a position with a large fertilizer concern in Wappinger. Wyatt discovered with a kind of shock that he'd lost the thread of Gordon's contact information completely after the man's divorce, and so had to leave his order with his ex-wife the last time he'd made the call. This was less satisfactory, but he held out hope the ex-wife would relent, give him Gordon's number, eventually.

As for Y, one oddity had become associated with her that Wyatt had never heard fully explained. Attractive and slender, with streaks of dyed blond hair, Y had never been seen with her husband. While Wyatt did not exactly dispute the existence of this husband, he had to note how, though she often spoke of him, she never managed to produce him, including on occasions when it would have been reasonable to do so. He did not attend college functions, for example, like the staff awards dinner (which he was *supposed* to have attended). "He dropped me off, won't be coming in," she'd say, or "He'll pick me up after." Yet this husband had never, in anyone's eyesight, been caught engaged in dropping off or picking up. Nor did he feature as a player in the somewhat elaborate photographic essays she posted to Facebook about her activities.

Y felt self-conscious about another personal characteristic. Her left arm, fully functional, had been disfigured in a fire, scars that edged upward and were faintly visible on her throat as well—a fire, however, that she was too young to even remember. She understood she'd been adopted, and that her original home situation had involved a fire, but she knew nothing else about these origins, and had made a point of not investigating them. Y alternately hid the arm under wrist-length flannel shirts and scarfs and brazenly revealed the mottled marks with sleeveless sundresses. As far as Wyatt could tell, it represented some continuous symbol of a long ago, lost, unimaginable pain that, luckily, she did not in any way feel compelled to relive or imagine.

(Notably, Wyatt's female relations, X, Y, *and* Z, were all liable to wear scarfs at almost any time of year. Whether this is revelatory about them, or about him, you the reader may decide.)

"What's wrong?" he asked.

"Does there have to be something?"

"Why the call?"

"Those are mushy peas, Sallie." Y was the only person in his life who'd given him a nickname he could stand. Likewise, Y knew, with her access to HR records, his educational attainments and so did not call him "Dr."

He examined the tiny bowl on his tray. "Why do that to peas?"

"None of your research uncovered anything about this?"

Y also understood, as did virtually no one else at the college, first, that he had made this trip and, second, that he'd done so without looking into it at all.

"I also need to tell you," she said, "we've lost our funding."

Wyatt stopped with his spoon half-way to the peas. His first thought concerned the college as a whole. Enrollment had demonstrably tanked over the past decade, and not just in Applied Business. He imagined the doors shuttered, weeds sprouting between seams in the parking lot pavement.

"The chess club," she clarified.

"Are you . . .?" He felt relieved yet furious. "Chess *team!*" he corrected.

"Right."

"It's barely *got* any funding!"

The college students and the old man walking with his near-empty pint all looked at him. The guy with the worn-out loafers, however, kept tapping out a beat to "Love Me Do," flipping pages advertising both diaphragm and piston second stages.

Wyatt considered the news simultaneously terrible and ridiculous. The chess team represented a fraction of a splinter of student fee allocation expenses.

"In the Fall," Y said. "I knew you'd want to hear about it."

He sighed. "Rationale?"

"The student fee committee feels that since not everyone plays chess, the money shouldn't be taken from everyone's fees."

He raised his eyebrows. "So, you told them not everyone plays football, yet ..."

"Sallie, please." She giggled. "Not everyone plays football in a way completely different from the way not everyone plays chess."

For that, he had no argument.

"They pointed out in the memo," Y said, "that the club ... *team* does not align with learning outcomes, does not conform to program outcomes, nor can its effects be measured in the student success algorithm."

It was the kind of language that had been creeping into the college, around the same time the faculty had been turned into "subject matter experts," and *Business Ethics: Important Sounding Subtitle* had changed from a "textbook" to a "course print companion."

"How's your trip?" she asked.

"I'm seeing what I needed to see. I'm not going to worry that much about the team. I'll deal with Student Activities when I get back."

But he knew he would not. With his RV paid for, many of the day-to-day expenses of the Linden Lane house covered by Z and Yuri, leaving him only the mortgage to worry over, he considered already how to personally cover travel costs to the few regional tournaments the group attended. Being himself nearly the only person who used it, he'd always paid the monthly fee for OtterShark from his own pocket anyway. They had already more clocks and chess sets than they ever used.

Typical, the failure of the imagination. Few understood how the game applied more pressure on players than nearly any other branch of sport. To sit, unmoving, for hours, in a condition of concentration, a condition that slid, at times, into bouts of semi-consciousness, all the while laboring under the most horrifying imaginable possibility (i.e., the possibility of making a mistake). It was grueling. Only one question hung over any chess encounter: Who will make *the* error? It was not like tennis or soccer where imperfections—totally expected—could be wiped out with the next service, the next goal. Giving up seven runs in a baseball inning could be followed by another where fourteen were piled high in answer, a kind of clean slate always over the horizon.

Every mistake in chess, let alone every blunder, hung its weight on the rest of the game, like unforgiven acts.

"And?" she asked.

"And what?"

"Go on."

He, without meaning to, lowered his voice. "The other day. At the station. Right outside. I'm at the station now. She was here."

"Oh, Wyatt."

He felt alarmed. She often called him "Sallie." His name, however, she never used.

"What happened?"

"I saw her. She's here. Or I think so." He glanced around the barroom.

"You think so. That's not too bad."

"I paid a taxi to follow her."

"Good God. Did the taxi find her?"

"I went too! And, no." He rubbed his forehead.

"*And you won't.*"

"I know. I think."

"And your pills?"

"Nothing to do with those. Which I'm taking." He checked his jacket pocket reflexively. Found no pills there.

"Was she alone?"

This brought him up short. "What difference could that make?"

"Just tell."

He had trouble recalling events coldly, as in, solely from the events themselves. It helped him, greatly, to back up a bit. In the same way that a novel could be picked up again after several weeks if one read just a few pages before the place it had been put down.

Had X been alone?

He'd sat on the square, near the saxophone blaring above the background of the band. He'd struggled over the terrible map in *The North:*

A Tough Guide. He'd been absolutely uncertain which direction to take glancing between the graphic illustration of streets and intersections spread on his lap and the chaotic scene before him. He had felt, in fact, *believed* that he might have walked into the wrong town square. He'd noted the statue; the workman in coveralls standing before it; the advertisement on the giant banner.

"She had, now that I think of it, been in a sort of group. As in, amongst other people: not quite the same thing as being *with* them."

"So, what were they like?"

Wyatt considered this scene. A man had been there. He was nearly certain. Two boys. X had children, but they were girls, and older than these children. The write-up on her he'd seen in *People* magazine had not indicated any new love interest—some man with two sons, for example. (As he thought about it, the man on the station steps seemed to have well-combed black hair. The children were much more indistinct.) Although she hadn't married Jeremy, the loser in New Orleans, she'd also given no clue in the article as to any other partner since. But then, such an interest might not make it into *People* magazine, and this had occurred nearly two years ago, the short interview, after publication of the highly popular *Sophie and Jerome.*

"Wait," said Y. "Circle back. You *think* you saw her, but you aren't sure. You haven't like *met* her. Met her there."

"No, but ... "

"In England. Thousands of miles from home. Which would be . . . unlikely doesn't cover it."

"Maybe. When you put it that way."

"So, kind of like the other times."

"Nothing like that," he said. "Those."

"What makes you *think* it was her?"

The woman at the station had the same compact, firm behind as Sallow's X, with not much on top. Full of energy, obvious even at a glance. She'd moved forward through the world with very little notice taken of ... of how the world viewed her, he supposed. A fearless attitude that had always transferred to him while her presence lasted, his conscious awareness of her, which awed and frightened him a little. The energy of a bent sapling about to spring to its original, organic arc. The woman on the station steps was dark and compact, as X was dark and compact, her olive skin managing to be freckled, especially her shoulders. Of course, he hadn't been close enough to register freckles on that Monday afternoon on the square. Anyway: the grinning face, framed by short spiky hair, the dimples. He felt he *could* see the dimples. One of the most prominent and classically attractive features on someone otherwise not classically attractive. Or not to anyone other than himself, Jeremy, her ex-husband, and no doubt several other men.

He realized he was starting to forget what she really looked like. Spiky hair? Had she worn her hair in that way? He sipped his ale. It seemed a detail he'd picked up elsewhere. He might have to get out his torture photo to refresh his image of X.

She had descended the steps, grinning like someone inhabiting the exact place they needed to be. Who else but X would do that?

"Sallie, why on earth would she be there?"

"Researching," Wyatt said. "Isn't it obvious? You read the book."

"I didn't read that piece of shit! You told me you weren't in it at all."

"I wasn't in the text. Only the subtext."

"You're a . . . Good God."

"Buried. But I mean . . . the *next* book. It only figures."

Y emitted an unfortunate sounding snort. "I promise it doesn't."

Wyatt, in spite of the confidences he'd shared with Y, couldn't recall having actually spoken with her for such an extended period. He felt he had reduced the situation's complexities to a simple concept—as he liked to do while lecturing, yet his listener had not understood despite his best efforts—also like lecturing. "There's only one reason, after what we've gone through, the two of us, for her to be here. Our story was . . . for a year of . . ."

"Four months."

He shrugged, though only the table of students could see it, the man with the near-empty pint having returned to the other room. "*And* she suggested I come here. *All her idea.*"

"I see."

"To write about it. Which she is now trying to do for herself."

Y paused. "It's just so . . . seems more likely it would be the other one."

"Other one?"

"Your wife. You sure you didn't see your wife?"

"I *didn't see my wife*."

"She's European, right? Or Siberian or something."

"Do you really think . . . and they look nothing alike. Ukraine is . . ."

"Or, well, the other one is Cajun, right?" Y went on. "I mean, like . . . French?"

"Not the same."

"So maybe you saw a French girl. Came over to Shallowsville from . . . France, I guess."

Against his conscious will he saw a black pawn make the short move from the seventh to the sixth square in the King's rank. Wyatt took a swallow of his reddish ale. "I am not off my medication."

"You're too hard on your wife. This couldn't have been easy for her either. I think you . . ."

He leaned on his elbows. Surveyed the empty white page of his notebook beside the tray of fried fish and dish of lumpy, mashed peas. A ragged tear indicated that a page had been torn away. He examined a layer of grime that clouded the thin wedding band he'd ordered from a jewelry catalog from a company in Kerrville, Texas. "Travel can be confusing."

"Come home, Sallie."

"But enlightening!" he insisted. "It will be worth it. I'm taking notes."

"Of course."

"I might have missed a pill. One."

"Do you remember that time when you saw her before?"

"No."

"In the back of your classroom?"

"That's where she always sat."

"She sat at the back of the game room for chess . . . team." Y's voice was calm. "You saw her in *your* classroom last semester even though she's left town."

"It's not like that time."

"Left town years ago. And never took a class from you. Or when you saw her in Dallas in the hotel restaurant."

"Went for the conference, yes." He swallowed, remembering. Rook. Horse no Knight. Pond, pond, pond. "Millions visit Dallas. She could be one. And could have slipped into my classroom, then left before the lecture was over. Beginning her . . ."

"The other times?"

It was not unusual to believe, or think, that any person might have seen some other person, perhaps even (he gladly admitted to himself) mistakenly, at a store, for example (Whole Foods in Marshall), a carwash (DIY Auto Spa in Turner), the balcony at an operatic performance in Houston (*The Merry Widow*).

"It seems like a lot of times to you," Wyatt said, "because you're the only one I tell."

"You tell everyone."

"It's a small department."

"You told the Dean. That semester they asked for your resignation letter? Breaking and entering?"

"I . . . I needed . . ."

"Look, I want you to leave that town right now."

Wyatt was shocked. He'd never heard her use such a tone. He'd never heard her use the words "I want" in relation to himself.

"It isn't . . ."

"Why do this? Come home."

In fact, he had come to a similar conclusion. When was that? It probably wouldn't be that difficult to arrange with Singapore Air. Jesus. What was his purpose here? Except, of course, that everywhere he looked, he was liable to see his name.

And Y was on him like . . . like . . . He tried to come up with a simile for the way he was getting grilled by his friend.

"I've got to get off the phone," Y said.

"You're on me like . . . Also neurotic," Wyatt said. "Paranoid about using the phone." He smacked his spoon onto the surface of the mushy peas. Then the food item resisted with a kind of "pop" when he pulled the spoon away. Bits of the green substance both rose in hillocks and fell into valleys from the rounded impact of the cutlery implement. The pasty undulations in the dish resembled his surroundings here in the North of England, in fact. Green curves rose in its gelatinous mass. At other places across the tiny bowl the substance revealed impacted dimples.

A rough chin.

Wyatt lay his head at table level to peer at the shape that formed in the green blob.

"Goodbye," said Y.

"Chess team. The funding. It's because of her, isn't it? They're angry…"

"No one cares about her. Signing off."

"Wait! The peas," Wyatt said.

"The what?"

"Are they known for… are they used, in addition to their use as a food source, for… for implementing…?"

"Huh?"

"Figures?"

"Signing off, Sallie."

He blinked at the shape in the little bowl. Dropped his phone into his jacket pocket. Wyatt felt spent but grateful to have someone like Y in his life. A college was a small, dark world, he thought. A small college, even darker. He lifted the little bowl closer to his eyes. He was, yes, lucky to have Y, who'd put down her phone after speaking with him, pushed back from her desk in the reception area of Applied Business. She stepped down the hall to Dean Zepeda's office, where two other Business School faculty congregated, sipping the last of the morning coffee. Dean Zepeda was an okay guy. Y kind of had a crush on him. Gossip was such a great way to open the door to people's attentions in a small college. He'd done his undergraduate work at Tech the same year Professor Sallie had attended. He felt a tinge of regret, occasionally, for the way he'd anonymously eviscerated the guy's little book back in the day.

She leaned in Dean Zepeda's doorway. "He's seeing her again," she told those collected in the office for the late-morning department leadership colloquium. And then she said something she thought she'd never say. "He's seeing her in the mushy peas."

PART TWO

1
Rachel

Her name was Rachel Shrimpton, and she was not a hippy, although her long dresses and straight shoulder-length hair—neither of which styles she ever abandoned—made her the next closest thing to a hippy for Sallowsfield. A now-retired teacher of elementary school often found haunting the hillsides, looking out over the town—especially fond, as a matter of fact, of the ridge below the Victorian structure atop Tower Hill—she had been, in her active pedagogy years, given to creating her own curriculum, none of it found in books. One of her innovations, the so-called Favourite Things exercise, she introduced during a field trip to the Bately Jungle Experience on an afternoon in 1974. Rachel used the Favourite Things exercise only that single time. As she stood to one side, listening to all the favourite thing possibilities her year five students drummed up, she noted with some alarm how none were anything at all like any favourite that might come to mind for herself. She felt this reflected more on her than the students.

For example, as the class droned on, she could not push from her memory a half-week stay with a favorite uni friend, a ski trip they taken together to Switzerland. Before the trip they had made a pact and—strange it had played out this way—that pact boiled down to a promise of engaging together in an experiment with physical intimacy of a Sapphic nature. Amorous congress. Sexual closeness. Rachel recalled that Sharon had read a then-famous article titled "Acts in Service to Venus, (as it were)" by one "Magda Mondragon" and had got it in her head as a thing to try, so the pact stipulated "the trial" would last the duration of their half-week together only. They could see how they liked it.

Zermatt was striking. The rustic simplicity of warmly lit timber and beam shops belied the pricey Patek Philippe watches and Cartier bracelets in street-level window displays. Rachel and Sharon rented a sparely furnished but well-supplied chalet that overlooked the town and featured a rough stone fireplace they utilized to create a roaring blaze on their first night, and when her favourite college friend, Sharon, sat beside her on the rug, Rachel Shrimpton knew immediately she had no desire to be touched by this friend nor engage in amorous congress either. The best she could describe it, having had a boyfriend who was a pillock but adventurous enough in the back seat of his Daff 66 Super Luxe, was that Rachel felt she had traded Victoria Sponge for a plate of toast. Or: she'd got a terrific discount on clothing—blouses, skirts, trendy accessories—to discover she already owned them all. It was nothing personal, in other words. She felt it best she mention this as this friend leaned over, began to rock her head on Rachel's shoulder, gently stroked her arm. So, she did. She told her.

"Oh," said Sharon. "Okay."

Rachel got up from the rug and went to boil water for instant noodles they'd packed.

The next morning, a blizzard snowed them in. Rubbing one spot clear on the upper left of the loo's double-paned glass they could spy whiteness blanketing the trees and mountain passes. From nowhere else could they see anything, as a shadowy bulk covered all other windows in a glaze of grey. They felt they best remain in the rented chalet for the morning at least, stoking the fire. Then the blizzard kept up. It kept up four more days, the two of them trapped with the spare though tastefully apportioned furnishings in a space that became as metaphorically icy inside as the air was in the out-of-doors. Neither felt up to breaking through this chill, though both tried. Neither felt capable of locating the thread that would allow them to spool out the friendship as it had been. By the third day neither said a word. "Strange," thought Rachel Shrimpton as she watched the Favourite Things exercise play out among her year fives. She kept returning to the fourth day in that frigid space, the vacation ruined, money wasted, friendship shattered. Huddled, isolated on a broad-cushioned sofa, she had gazed for nearly an hour at a frosted window, until a great calm descended, deeper than any she'd felt before or since. "That it would be that fourth day," she thought. "That hour, that window. My 'favourite thing.'"

Then, after what happened at the Bately Jungle Experience, she never in her twenty-year span of teaching repeated the exercise again.

2
Tony

Anthony "Tony" Crane had been thirteen at the time of the field trip. A sickly child, Tony was plagued by a blood condition that he still takes regular injections to manage as anyone knows who reads *Buzzcall Britain Blog*. (Noteworthy, even at that age: his already good looks and thick head of black hair.) A frightening black zippered pocketbook of needles and syringes had been stashed in the back of his schoolroom just in case and accompanied him wherever he went. Although not exactly, to use mid-'70s parlance, *crippled*, it was understood he would not be hiking the 19-acre Bately Jungle Experience with the other kids, so there'd been arranged a wheelchair, the syringes carried in a canvas bag attached to the handles. Oh, how he was the envy of every kid on that field trip . . . except Simon. Simon was a true blue. A good friend. Why, Simon had shown young Tony how to make the V sign, for example.

This was not in any "oh, here's how to do this and how to do that and here's what it means" sort of way. No. This was a finely crafted, almost unfathomably profound insult delivered symbolically as near-performance art, the third and pinkie fingers curved simultaneously and tightly in a manner that left the arrow-straight index and middle members soaring above their foundational establishment like twin monuments to offensive abuse. The opposable thumb tucked firmly—unopposed—away from view of the intended insultee seemed nearly a parlor trick. *Where was the thumb?* Delivered with a kind of flourish like gestures that oft accompanied old-fashioned curtsies and hat doffings, *this* index finger/middle finger pairing was presented crisp, clean, powerful. The method of it fascinated Tony, who knew somehow what it meant, but as yet possessed no literal picture of how the activity signaled by the hand might actually work. At the time of the Bately excursion he had no clue how experienced he might become (Tony, that lad), and really, let's face it, on that occasion, the occasion of the zoo trip, he didn't know anything about anything.

Most important: Simon did *not* show everyone how to throw the V sign in this pristine fashion. It was only he and Tony who had perfected the move.

At the zoo, good old Simon for the most part pushed the chair, although on occasion another student would give it a go for the honor. How the incident came about was like most such disasters: suddenly. Somehow Simon and Tony became separated from the rest, and then Simon stepped away from the wheelchair—only for a moment—to visit a nearby water fountain that required sticking one's head in the opened jaws of a plasticine hippopotamus and gargling up a stream that emanated from one of its hollow teeth. No thank you, Tony said, so he remained where he was, alone in the wheelchair for the moment. It was, he recalled, very near the enclosure of the African Crested Porcupine. Or Porcupines. He couldn't tell, as the fenced area appeared to be empty anyway, the spiny creatures perhaps escaping the noonday sun in that shadow zone beneath a laurel. A pear-shaped man stood at the fence, holding the wire mesh, his fingers through it, his back to Tony. His shirt pooched out where rolls of flesh encroached his waistline. A lady came past with a maroon pram. Tony—although not certain why, the act having been performed almost before the capability existed to consider any motivation, sitting alone as he was in his wheelchair in front of the African Crested Porcupine enclosure—showed this lady his practiced hand gesture.

She had curly blond hair and wore a blouse that featured horizontal black stripes. She reacted unfavorably. One might say inappropriately.

Bystanders jogged to where she stood with her pram, thinking that walking over to her wouldn't be quick enough, fearing the worst, as she, to put it mildly, made a scene. "Howling" would be one way to label the sound that came out of her. Animals across the Bately Jungle Experience responded in kind, the din rising around her and the assembled zoo-goers like a discordant orchestral swell of tuning that preceded a sonata performance. The flamingos even noticed, turned their heads sideways to the commotion, though they added nothing.

The woman let out the kind of resounding screech that might be heard upon the discovery of an amputated leg on a driveway rather than a noise you'd make realizing you'd been given the "up yours" signification. It didn't stop, either. Her scream pressed on, came in successively louder installments separated by the slightest of gasps for air. Tears formed at the outside corners of her eyes. Though loud enough, Tony supposed, he had to admit later he could hear it only in the margins of his immediate consciousness. There was such a flavor of unreality about this scream, much like the impetus—from *nowhere*—that had occasioned him to produce his insulting gesture in the first place. His own attention narrowed to a laser focus. He felt he could see only his own raised digits against a blurred backdrop. This attentiveness was such, and of such a power, that the waves of noise served only as more evidence concerning the fingers' obvious nexus as an antennae-like source of immense influence. Later, studying sociology in college, he would learn about objectification, the dehumanizing of people, but he was at that moment capable of doing this even with himself. Tony became an object of attention rather than a boy, a person, a being with agency or will, a creature with a case holding expensive hypodermics attached to his chair he'd have to be injected with in the event of seizure. Everything outside of this core seemed counterfeit.

He continued to show her the sign. She continued to scream. The baby in the maroon pram began to scream, too.

His teacher, Miss Shrimpton, and the other students and Simon with hippo water dripping from his chin, all eventually congregated around the commotion. Miss Shrimpton had a kind of instinctive understanding, just by looking into Tony's eyes, that this was a reflexive action for him—as in the way people grip electrified fences when they really should let them go—and that telling him to knock it off wouldn't suffice. Nor would that method work for the hallooing young mother who rocked in the throes of a postpartum hormonal deluge of some kind. As someone in authority, perhaps the only such person within eyesight or earshot at the moment, the teacher knew she had to act. Tony wasn't a vindictive boy. His entrancement with the fingers came across as a form of "spell" rather than the actions of a showoff.

This teacher, incidentally, paved the way for his becoming an actor. Arguably a star.

Fair enough. Co-star.

Rachel Shrimpton and her students rolled Tony away from the mother, and the pear-shaped man stopped searching out the porcupines and turned to comfort the blond lady with her carriage by applying the usual "It's alright luv" kind of language. "Stupid lad" and the like. "Psssh, psssh, psssh," he said to the baby, pursing his lips like a baby pig's, which worked pretty well. The man wasn't in good shape but, as an experienced father, knew how to handle both woman and child, although exactly what interiour scars either of them might have carried from the Bately Jungle Experience to this day Tony would never know. Simon took up the chair, a look on his face either of guilt or just fear that somehow the blame for this would land on him. Simon did not abandon his friend, however, and in fact, Tony's visited his house in Hull a couple of weeks back, the two of them having lagers, watching Hull City play Sunderland while Simon's Jamaican wife made cacciatore. Simon and Jannah both still call him "Tony."

The teacher decided on a course of action. It must be noted that at no time did she appear to contemplate punishment or retribution. She'd seen the look of transport on Tony's face. Something was wrong, a condition that required not penalty but cure. After quick consultation with the class, she rolled him alongside a bricked flowerbox. Tony sat, drained of energy, brittle and scooped out by the powerful finger experience. Casual auditors of this story might think that it was the successful focusing of personal power upon those fingers that had given him the performance bug. They would have it backward.

His class filed by, one by one. At the teacher's suggestion, each told Tony their "favourite thing." As in "My favourite thing is four square," a girl told him, a game played with a rubber ball. "My dog," said a boy.

"Ponies," said Davida (who Tony, even at that age, somewhat fancied). Some were predictable, falling into the category of, you know, what one usually says when asked about what might be one's favourite thing, having to come up with a serviceable response though allowed no time to consider, answers like "rainbows," "sausages," or "koi ponds." Tony felt his student colleagues with *those* answers had to be kidding, lying, or panicked because they couldn't think of anything. He had a sense even then those weren't *really* the favourite things of most who passed by, but more just what they would agree to admitting in public. Poor, poor lies.

What had been the teacher's aim? Her motives are lost to time. Actor and Sallowsfield native son Henry Scott, thinking back, considered it must have been some hippy-ish, New-Age attempt to demonstrate—to someone who had lost sight of the fact—that there *were* good things in the world, things that had *value*, value to real people like his classmates. And people simply couldn't be treated the way he'd treated the mother with the maroon pram, as she and the baby—make the leap with me here—had feelings too. When you raise your middle and index finger, then turn your palm towards yourself, exercising the iconic power which that gesture entails, there are consequences.

No matter the theory, witnessing all of this, Tony in his wheelchair felt positively evil. If his act required going to these lengths to instruct him in the way of "goodness," his classmates, teachers, chaperones, and even his friend Simon, they all must all consider him evil as well. He didn't know if his reaction should be anger, remorse, or what, but then Simon—good old Simon—came up, the last in line, the mate who had shown him that finger symbol in the first place. Simon stood before him and in a way that Tony absolutely believed, in a manner bespeaking the greatest heartfelt reality concerning how the precarious evil of the world must be confronted, and confronted with sincere goodness, said, "My favourite things are hugs and kisses."

Then Simon winked at Tony.

Tony wet himself.

Both giggling and sobbing in his own piss Tony knew he'd spend his life attempting to deliver a sensation . . . a sensation *half* as powerful as that powerful-and-purposeful-though-contrived release of feigned sincerity Simon demonstrated on that day. He hoped to do so before audiences everywhere, which he arguably accomplished, achieving eventually a viewership of over two million in the UK alone.

3
Edgeland

Late Thursday afternoon (as we return in time to the present or, as Joyce said somewhere, *the pressent*) . . . Late Thursday afternoon, that is, Hussein drives Professor Sallow up a climbing sequence of switchback lanes into the outskirts of town to the Edgeland Arms, then stands with him at the front desk, a stamp of legitimacy for the benefit of the beautiful Muslim women who had been left in charge there. It's a legitimacy the grass and twigs still in the Texan's hair, as well as his overall wrinkled demeanor and broken luggage might otherwise argue against, not to mention the fact he wears different colored socks with one sneaker and one dress brogue. But he hadn't, he wants to tell these women, transformed into this disreputable figure on purpose. *No fair!* Wyatt wants only to be in the safety of his room with the door closed and bolted. In addition to events on the hillside, he has no idea where in town Gail might live. What if she spies him on the streets of the Edgeland District, avoiding their meeting? (He's due to call her in just an hour.) He is still certain that throwing away the number the day before made sense. What if he'd met with her, then X had caught sight of them? Seen him out with Gail? The two of them together. How would he be able to explain? As had happened more than once over the board, some move that at the time had simply *felt* right had turned out to be—under the weight of serious analysis—sure enough, the best decision after all. Depositing Gail's number in the bin had worked better than keeping it, much as Knight to the Queen Bishop's sixth rank sometimes just *feels* more fruitful than Knight to the King Bishop's sixth rank.

In contrast to the certainty of his actions regarding Gail, on the drive to the hotel Wyatt had grown progressively more rattled, like someone replaying the trauma of daylight hours at night, legs moving in spasms as they reconstructed violent encounters in half dreams. "I did that?" he asked. "I could have been killed." There'd been that rock—a boulder, some might say—against which he'd nearly dashed his skull (again, his leg, really). True, and there'd been the way he'd landed on his side. Had he landed that way on his spine instead he might have been worse than killed. He could be on that hillside now, staring paralyzed at the sky while ants made their way across his torso. He thinks of Hussein's tale of the ants and the baby and shudders. The impact of the fall and tumble had scrambled the seasons of his life, caused him to shuffle present and past. How easy to draw it out of a person—a life. As smooth as a coin removed from an ear by a favorite uncle.

The Edgeland Arms, converted from a mansion, has a foyer the size of a small living room, a check-in desk at the end of a hallway that's tucked into a closet, and a layered aroma that reminds Wyatt of his grandmother's pantry. In his room, he finds two small but crisply made beds, the sort he hates to disturb by sleeping on. A green curtain sweeps around a footed bathtub with shower pole in the small bathroom and, through a passage with no door, the window in the attached sitting room overlooks Edgeland Street, displaying the fronts of similar hotels and boarding houses on the lane's opposite side. Before this window, a bare writing desk stands like an invitation to take out his notebook. Before he has to return to Manchester, he looks forward to spending time there, gathering his thoughts, getting some writing down about the trip, its joys, its disappointments. He worries. Maybe not enough has even happened to him to warrant any writing. He can see no shape or weight to the random jottings he'd scribbled so far. "You should just go there," X had said. "And write about it." He rubs his lower back where Tower Hill had leaped up and beaten him and considers it might well be disappointments that received the lion's share of space going forwards in the notebook's remaining white sheets.

The sitting room is decorated in 1950s-style Americana, with unframed 45 rpm records thumbtacked onto the walls (The Big Bopper, Richie Havens) along with pictures of Elvis. He wonders if other occupants stay in rooms with different decorative themes. There is most wonderfully a slender three-ringed binder, its plastic laminated pages displaying xeroxes about everything anyone would need to know who wished to navigate the Edgeland neighborhood and, for that matter, Greater Sallowsfield entire: bus schedules, taxi phone numbers, lunch tips, fine dining opportunities, sites of historical interest.

It is exactly what he'd needed five days before.

4
Aisha

Wyatt could get comfortable and enjoy the setting, but one of the beautiful Muslim women keeps coming to his door. She knocks so softly each time he's not certain, at first, he hears it. Initially, she inquires if he wants breakfasts included with his stay, and when he says no she nods and leaves, only to knock fifteen minutes later, informing him that, unfortunately, he had paid for breakfasts already when he checked in downstairs but that she would return ten pounds to him—she holds the bill in her hand—since it's not fair to have paid if he didn't want to eat in the morning. Wyatt says rather than do that she should certainly keep the money and he'll come down to breakfast, although fifteen minutes later she arrives again, this time with 5 pounds, saying he'd inadvertently paid for the full breakfast rather than the regular. He agrees that going ahead and taking the full breakfast is probably for the best. "It is very tasty," the woman says, nodding and keeping her five pounds, nodding again, then exiting. He wonders if he has missed something there: whether the woman wants to get him to agree to something.

Mainly, Aisha Bhat is just forgetful and stressed out. Rounding the corner of the high desk on the ground floor of the Edgeland Arms after visiting room 2-8e three times to sort out the breakfasts, she touches that desk's sharp edge lightly as she commonly does many times during her day, often leaning against it as it's far too high to set a chair behind. She wouldn't be able to see over it, at least not using any of the irregular chairs the hotel featured. The Edgeland

Arms has been furnished in a style she dubs "Late Hodgepodge." There are no two chairs alike in the whole place. She hopes she can spend some time behind that raised table built into the cupboard that serves as an office, as she needs to figure out exactly what to do with the credit card information she'd taken from the man in 2-8e. She hopes she won't have to disturb him again about the charge card or anything else she remembers at the last moment.

The telephone rings. She allows it to do so five, six . . . eight times. Surely that's enough for anyone who might be calling. They should give up, call later, hopefully when her cousin who owns the hotel arrives back from his trip to Nottingham ("visiting a sick friend") so he can answer and deal with it. It's her seventh day on the job. As she pulls out the credit card slip of "Mr. Sallow," shrugs, then places it again in the basket they keep beneath the till for such purposes (as much of Edgeland Arms' business is on a cash basis), the phone rings another, ninth time, then a tenth! Her cousin surely has the wherewithal to arrange for these calls to be forwarded to his mobile. He's missing a lot of business relying on the likes of her to answer questions. An eleventh ring! This cannot go on, as her other, much older cousin (three years older though also beautiful) works as a maid and housecleaner at the Edgeland Arms and she will would no doubt soon be sticking her head in from some cranny or nook, staring at Aisha in an accusing manner.

"Edgeland Arms. We hope you enjoy your visit with us." The last part is a slogan her cousin wants associated with the hotel. He calls it *branding*. "How may I help you?" Aisha grabs a nearby biro to take down this person's number so her cousin can maybe give the caller some actual help (the cousin "visiting a friend," not the older, unmarried yet still attractive one presently running a vacuum upstairs and given to accusing glances).

"I am looking to rent a room in your establishment."

"You know . . ." She makes a *chop-chop* gesture with her hand. "The registration desk . . . *department* is indisposed. If I could take your number?"

"I don't want to register. I'm just looking," says the man. "I want to make sure that the Edgeland Arms will be suitable."

Aisha thinks very hard. "It is. I'm sure of it."

The man makes an uncertain noise on the other end of the line. Something like: "Nnnnnh." "I would just like to know," he goes on, "if there's anything else you can tell me about the suite."

"We don't have 'suites.'"

"Of course not. Did I say suite? It's just that I want to book a long stay. Several months."

It happens that the Edgeland Arms at that part of the week has exactly three of its nineteen rooms taken. A truck driver with some of the most frightening tattooed figures on his forearms that Aisha has ever seen (although she has to admit he is a nice enough fellow, polite, asking at breakfast—he'd sprung for the *full* breakfast—if he could possibly . . . if it would be okay to use the remote to turn to his favorite cable news on the flat-screen in the dining room since, after all, he was there by himself). Then there is a Hindu family—a man, a wife, and three children—who did not pay for any breakfasts but spend time in the small foyer playing a quiz game with cards. The children are sharp and boisterous. And now there is Mr. Sallow.

With an occupancy this low, even preparing the full breakfasts is a break-even endeavor at best. If someone were to stay several months . . .

"I'm certain my cousin, who owns the Edgeland Arms, would like to speak with you."

"It's just . . . I see here you don't allow smoking or pets. Is that true? That you don't allow smoking or pets?"

Aisha feels she needs to give an answer, although, in fact, she has no idea. She's never seen anything—like a warning signboard for example—that says NO SMOKING, or PETS PROHIBITED. But then she'd only worked at her cousin's hostel/hotel for a week before he left her in charge of the tall desk, the mystifying credit card swiper, and the entire staff (her cousin with the paranoid stare), the two of them barely able even to cook up the full breakfasts every morning for one (soon to be two) persons. But in that time, she's never seen anyone smoke in the hotel. It isn't done so much anymore, is it? Wouldn't everyone just *assume* that it was a terrible idea to smoke in a hotel? Nor has she seen any animals.

Aisha felt decisive. "Do you smoke, sir? Or have a pet?"

"I do not. No to both."

"Well, that's alright then."

"Although I occasionally drink ale, and while having the ale, also enjoy a fine cigar."

"I'm sure that's acceptable, sir. That would not be a problem." Aisha has so little familiarity with tobacco products, she thinks if it is indeed a *fine* cigar it will probably be placed in some other class of burning objects, such as incense. "If I could . . ."

"And I don't have pets . . . to speak of. Although . . . I'm an entomologist."

"Congratulations, sir."

"Thank you. An entomologist at the university. And at times I must bring some of my researches home. You understand."

"Of course," she says. She has no idea. She does feel like the voice on the line seems too young to be any kind of "ologist."

"Ho, ho, ho," he chortles.

This reminds Aisha of something. She can't recall it. Like something she's heard on TV.

"I bring home cases of them, in fact."

"They are spacious rooms, sir. Also, we serve breakfasts."

"When I say cases, I'm really speaking of something sophisticated. Better to say enclosures. About the size of a refrigerator."

"Oh, my."

"Each has a generator, which I will need to run all of the time. It generates heat for the roaches inside."

"Roaches!"

"Which is why I'd say while I don't have *pets* to speak of, I did want to tell you about my cases, my generators, and the roaches. That won't be a problem, will it?"

Aisha rubs her forehead. This is truly getting to be an inquiry for her cousin. "Did you say that the cases are sophisticated?"

"The cockroaches don't, you know, get out."

"Wait a minute."

"There's that time ten thousand escaped, but that was just once. Ho, ho, ho."

"Wait . . . are you . . . do you run a restaurant? Or . . . Philip? Philip is it you?"

Aisha recognizes the voice of someone she'd gone to high school with and the trademark saying of his readily recognizable father from the local chat shows, the Jerk Chicken recipes and . . .

The person on the line begins to laugh. No, wait. Sounds more like he begins to cry. Sob. "Is it?" asks the voice. "Is it me?"

Before Aisha can inquire further, he hangs up.

5
Yardbird Suite

Wyatt drops onto the bed and sleeps until evening, too late to find any-thing for dinner, so has a sticky shower (uses his green, jungle scented shampoo to wash his body—the effect unpleasant—as there's no soap any-where in the tiny bathroom) and then returns to bed. At his age, one roll down one hill is enough for one day. It might be mentioned that across town someone waits for him to call. She doesn't wait all that long, truth be told. After a while, Gail forgets it has been set up, and even thinking about it later in the evening as she watches *8 Out of 10 Cats Does Countdown* she merely wonders if she's given the man—can't remember his name, although at the time it had seemed memorable—the right number, or if she has the right night in mind. Isn't this just like her? She tucks it out of her thoughts. It's not anything she needs pink energy for, let alone any sort of infinite pass-through universal traffic signal.

His sleep is not easy, the hillside rolling behind his eyelids much of the night, but the next morning, in contrast to that trauma, Wyatt experi-ences something he can describe mainly as waves of peace and comfort. These lap over him downstairs in the breakfast room Friday morning as he devours fried eggs, following this with bacon, small pork sausages, tomatoes, mushrooms, and baked beans scooped onto triangles of brown toast he takes from an ever-replenished silver rack brought to the table by a lean, scowling woman with a jaw shaped like the state of Florida (though still attractive). He sips instant coffee made palatable by two teaspoons of sugar while cool air from the lane blows the curtains of the breakfast room window. He thumbs through the three-ring binder provided in the sitting room. "WELCOME TO EDGELAND ARMS," reads the first page. "We hope you enjoy your visit with us." Inside, the first laminated page con-tains emergency numbers for the hotel, Wi-Fi passwords, and information about his own two rooms and their furnishings: like where to find clean towels in the cupboards, where to put "anything you would like washing," instructions on the use of the room's green plastic coffee maker. More startling, on the next page he finds nearby bus stops and lists of their var-ious destinations. The bus system strictly terrifies him, as does anything new, but he sees an opportunity to free himself from the tyranny of Hussein's "you're like a member of the family!" politeness for at least a day. He'll stick with his outline, though events of past days indicate to him clearly that he does not need to, and he'll make his way by himself to the Thornfield Museum.

Headed downhill towards the bus stop, Wyatt hears some of the most beautiful and complicated birdsong of his life. It is nearly bird jazz. He stops short, stands by a stone bridge where, in a single tree in the corner of an empty lot—he can't locate the bird itself—this music unfolds. The bare yard contains a metal folding chair under its lone tree, and he has to believe someone put it there as a resting place for enjoying the song of this particular songbird: it's as good as a concert. Whether some species commonly features this complex tune, or it's an individual warbler—some genius Charlie Parker of the avian population—he has no clue. Wyatt removes his phone, records some of the sounds, although after a while the melodies came in snatches rather than the streaming fall of notes he'd caught when he first approached the stone bridge. Maybe someone at his college could identify it when he returns home.

He doesn't know if it's a sparrow, a bird X has a relation to, of all things. "Y" had once called X a hideous woman, but Wyatt had such a variety of experiences with her—they had written together, played chess together, eaten lunch, kissed enough times to register right up to the gateway of double digits (especially if one threw in that cheek peck), and held such a variety of conversations as well that he feels this evaluation inaccurate, believes also that anyone who had shared even one of these experiences with X would agree with him.

The sparrow thing he accepted as part of her sweat lodge affinity, though he had never investigated that, an enthusiasm he did not share. In Texas, to seek out purposely a cramped heated space, for Wyatt gave the impression of a flirtation with a special kind of insanity. She called the sparrow her "totem animal." It seemed a mundane one.

"I won't tell you," Wyatt said, "my name for your totem animal."

"Is it something like 'feathered vermin'? 'Mice with wings'?"

"Something like." He never felt certain he could judge her seriousness. She had a serious affection for a truly awful film starring Sandra Bullock, for example, as he learned when he thoughtlessly ridiculed it one afternoon and set off an atomic chain of moping that lasted a solid week. "Would 'mice with wings' offend you?"

"I know a lady who calls them LBBs. Little Brown Birds. That's okay. But no. What you said wouldn't be okay."

"Understood." Wyatt often found he censored himself around X, opting on this occasion, for example, not to admit he had adopted his father's name for the common birds, regularly employed by those "in aviation" (whether they ever got in airplanes or not): "sky rats."

"When I first learned they were my heart totem, in a heart totem workshop, I was not thrilled."

By nature, Wyatt considers himself to have a good sense of humor (questionable), but exercising this humor while traversing the eggshell thick pathways that surrounded X created dilemmas. (Not so serious as logical, safety, legal, and even religious dilemmas that arose, let's say, when denying employment to men with beards in chemical plants where emergency spills on occasion necessitated closely sealed gas mask implementation: discrimination or compensating circumstance? Discuss.) He knew it would be dangerous to risk any line of inquiry about this sparrow thing.

"How *did* you say you learned about your animal?" he asked nonetheless.

"Heart totem workshop."

Wyatt bit his lip.

"We asked ourselves, what animals are we drawn to? What animals appear in dreams? Or, when you go into Nature . . ."

Wyatt understood X's use of the word to involve a capital letter.

". . . in Nature are there animals you see more often than others?"

Sparrows in East Texas were as common as . . . well . . . *sparrows*. He feared he would lose his grip on his reactions. Perhaps, not laughing, but what if he snorted derisively? He attempted to hold it together.

"More often than others?" he squeaked.

"Those might be the ones that can teach you. Sparrows are near my heart. I made a quilt about them. You never ask about my quilts, do you?"

There were so many things to ask X about, without question he hadn't gotten to the quilts. And he didn't on that occasion either. A person with so many talents, she was certain to encounter disappointment at times.

She influenced him, however. When playing X, what appeared as brilliant moves on her part were often, via later analysis, shown to be more the results of desperate stupidities on his part, mistakes she had no problem seeing and taking advantage of. Partly his mind teetered on edge from the stakes of playing a person rather than OtterShark. Partly it was straight-forward X: his own missteps and egregious blindnesses, produced merely by being in her presence, left her with patterns to exploit, set effortlessly before her. What benefit could Wyatt serve to X as a coach? Her success seemed baked in, and on some level the simple result of having a complete familiarity—through long exposure—with uncertainty.

Uncertainty simply did not faze her.

None of this made X hideous. Y was incorrect on that point. Certainly, another good reason X was not a terrible person would have to include how her own intervention with the college had allowed Wyatt to keep his job after the Sheriff's report, which, of course, allowed him to continue on as a source of mortgage payments for Z.

He resumes his approach to the bus stop, the very cool cat of a bird falling behind him, blowing mad.

6
Henry

Wyatt, believe it or not, catches a bus and takes it into town.

Thanks to the maps and instructions on the laminated pages of the three-ring binder, he has a good sense of where to find this bus, and even where that bus might go. He continues down the hill towards a corner where six (he counts them) streets meet in a confused, dovetailed spoke arrangement he can see as he descends towards it after leaving the stony bridge and the amazing bird. He passes a sofa stuffed down some basement steps. So: sofas get stuffed down basement steps, even in a town that has his name on it. Where orange cones and yellow tape block a right turn intersection a sign reads "Diversion Ends." Truer words never spoken. Behind him, a woman calls from a doorway. "Eric!" she yells several times before he turns to sneak a peek at this "Eric" she's so angry with, but the woman in a white headscarf, her hair pulled back tight, bears down on him along the sidewalk. He's prepared to step aside when she stops, looks up at him.

"You're not Eric."

"No. No."

She nods. "Thought you were." She points a gnarled finger at him. "And being rude."

Before he can apologize, the woman turns on her heel. He continues towards the bus stop under a cloud of guilt, but a vehicle indicating "CENTRAL" on its ticker-tape signboard arrives as he steps up to the battered plexiglass bus stop. This Wyatt understands—thanks to the three-ring binder he's taken along (after asking permission from the lovely Muslim woman with the head covering who had—he is happy to report—hounded him into a terrific breakfast)... this bus he understands to be the first step towards arriving at the museum.

Only one rider gets on the bus before Wyatt, and she lays a card against a plastic pad to pay, while he must ask, "How much to Central Station?" and offer a note.

"Nothing smaller?" The driver is South Asian, older, in a white shirt with official-looking epaulets.

"Sorry." An apologetic morning.

The driver doesn't state the price but drops some change in a tray. Wyatt takes it up in curled fingers, then slinks to the first seat he can find, near the front, feels the day veer askew after all. Diversion ends. Seated in the front of the bus he's able to overhear the conversation that starts up between the driver and a man carrying a large duffle who gets on at the very next stop. Wyatt has the feeling he's seen this man before, maybe in town, but after his "sighting" at the train station, almost another one at the university... after his conversation with "Y," he's no longer certain of his powers of individual recognition.

The man takes a seat across the aisle and one row forward. Zipping open the duffle, he removes some items. He pulls off his shirt, then his pants! Uhm, trousers. He proceeds to change clothes right there on the bus. In his underwear, he steps into an orange jumpsuit, sweating a little.

"How's the new system?" the man asks the driver, nonchalant. Do they know each other? See each other on this route so commonly they've struck up a relationship? A relationship so casual it allows for private toilette on public transport?

"I don't know." The driver laughs. His manner with this man in the orange jumpsuit is not the same as his demeanor towards Wyatt while counting out change. "It's my first day."

"First day driving!" The man continues to ransack the duffle. "I'll get off here, mate."

More laughing. "With this company. The new system is the new system either way for me."

The man fastens a wide tool belt, sans tools. "Right. Either way."

"I've driven here for twenty years."

"God, man!"

"Four companies!" The driver sounds amazed himself. "All different systems." He smacks his lips. "I just turned sixty-nine. Retire next week."

Wyatt considers. The man had spent twenty years traveling a town that has his, Wyatt Sallow's, name displayed on every corner. Yet he doesn't know, seated behind him, that, well . . . there he is. He would like to find a way to mention it. Perhaps just start by being polite.

"Your first day and last week?" Wyatt asks.

"Are you pretty well set?" asks the man in orange. "Looking forward?"

"So looking forward to it."

Wyatt snorts, rubs his mouth beneath his nose. "So . . ."

"You look familiar," says the working man to the driver. He pulls boots from his bag, steps into one, then the other, leaves the laces loose. "Have I seen you somewhere?"

They ignore Wyatt in a way so total it's not technically ignoring as that would require registering his presence first. The bus is noisy. There are wind and road background effects. At his next opportunity, he'll speak louder.

"I've been driving here for twenty years."

"You're not on TV, then."

"Hah."

"You're not some host or something. Drive busses for jollies. To shock people. Hidden camera."

"Hah! I've been driving twenty years."

The man now successfully wears the orange jumpsuit with work belt and boots and snakes his limbs through the armholes of one of those bright yellow vests workmen all seem to have. He nods. "I've been away meself. Do I look familiar? People say so."

The driver can only glance from the busy road momentarily. Wyatt begins to study the man.

"People think I look like someone," he continues.

He does look like someone. Square jawed with thinning black hair. Hardly any eyebrows. This had been part of the reason his getting dressed in front of Wyatt hadn't seemed so alien as all that. The man resembles someone he did already know.

The driver, by peering into an overhead mirror that shows him the whole aisle, agrees. "You do! I can't say, though."

"Henry Scott," says the man. "People think."

"Ah! I don't know. Well, sort of."

"Sort of!" The man is put out. "Very much, I'd say."

"Okay." A half-block passes as the bus moves towards the town's clustered center. "Don't look like the statue, though."

"Makes it hard to go to the DIY shop. Or even the aquarium shop. People always stopping me."

"Statue has more hair."

"Ouch!" The man rubs his head. "Know how to hurt a guy."

"Could have been a wig on the show. They do wigs."

"Not always."

"Not thin like your hair."

The man laughs. "Okay! Okay!"

"Don't sound like Henry Scott."

"It's you, they say. It's you, isn't it! So I say, 'Yo Captain.'"—this last delivered in a droning, robotic monotone. "I mean, how else answer, right?"

The driver slaps the wheel and laughs. "You sound like him a little."

"Listen." The man leans forward. "That statue is shite. Am I right? Doesn't look like me at all."

The driver laughs more. "Yo Captain. Doesn't look like you." He slaps the wheel again. "Need to fix that, don't they?"

"How can I look like it if it don't fuckin' look like me?"

The driver thinks the guy is hilarious. "I don't pay attention. To TV. Football sometimes. Otherwise . . ."

"Here I am, born and raised in this town." The man in orange presents a formidable and dramatic high dudgeon, points at the floor of the bus. "Where you have driven twenty years."

"Twenty years."

"And you don't bother? Because, really, I am him."

"Are you!"

"I am Henry Scott."

The driver nods. "Good to meet you."

"No, really."

"Love your statue."

"Statue is shite, man. Yo Captain."

Wyatt peers. He, like the driver, is not much for television. He's seen *Off to the Planets* a handful of times (As opposed to *Rocket Cadets* that he can recite by heart), but Scott's character is memorable. A kind of yellow-skinned robot or android. Wyatt can't remember the robot or android's name on the show. Now he watches the jump suited figure from behind in a three-quarter profile, weaving to the bus's undulations as it grinds into town. From this angle, the man's bald patch broadens at the crown, leaves only wisps of black hair. Wyatt doesn't think of the robot as having a bald patch. But surely, it's been a few years since the series was canceled.

They do have makeup for such things. Still, he also seems like someone making a joke.

Of course, a professional actor would have no difficulty presenting as a man making a joke.

"It's me," says the man. "On your bus, and you don't know it."

"I didn't know!"

"Or care. And here I am. Me standing here."

"I'm so surprised you don't have a car, Mr. Scott." The driver slaps his wheel again.

"Still, you doubt?"

When the man raises his eyebrows very high, indeed he looks quite a bit like the statue. Older, certainly. "You look older than the statue," Wyatt tries.

"You'd probably like to have his bank account," says the driver.

"Mate, it's me." The man gazes blankly. "Wish I didn't have his child maintenance."

The driver cackles.

The workman's hands on his knees are alarmingly well-manicured, not dirty like Wyatt would have expected from an actual workman.

Can it be?

Wyatt often encounters these kinds of mysteries. He had, he felt, seen it with X, who, while not the most attractive woman in the world, and in spite of his own obvious obsession, he did consider a highly capable person. Not skillful, which requires work and practice, but something else. Talented. A talent. In possession of an enviable quality that could be seen, recognized, but that escaped understanding. Such was X, and this explained her effortless abilities at the game, the easy way she created items such as quilts, drawings, her ability in the year following their relationship to dash off a best-seller. A horror-romance about love in the Realms of the Great Hereafter (and the New Orleans nightlife district).

The man on the bus. Wyatt thinks he can tell. He has something.

"If you're . . ." the driver starts. "Which, of course, you are. You are. But if you are . . . why are you here?" Another mirror glance. "And in orange?"

"What could it be?"

"A role," says Wyatt. "Could be studying . . ."

"A role," says the driver.

Neither man looks Wyatt's way nor indicates they register him. Wyatt's mouth is dry, a side effect of his round, yellowish, morning pill. He feels he possibly doesn't exist—a side effect of the night-time, elongated, pink one.

"Could it be a role?" Henry Scott asks himself out loud. "Why yes. Yes, Henry, you might be studying for a role."

"As a mechanic or bin man," from the driver.

"Perfecting my role. What better place?"

"A plodder," says the driver. "You've got it, sir! You've perfected it. A menial."

"Scott" is offended, or effectively acts offended. Or: is a mechanic of some kind, in a jumpsuit, having a lark on an early Friday. The more Wyatt thinks about it, the more he considers the likelihood that Henry Scott happens to be on the very first bus he rides in this country . . . it doesn't seem highly probable.

On the other hand . . .

"There are no small roles," Henry Scott says. "Only small people."

With that Wyatt understands the actor is there, on the bus. No repair-man would say such a thing. He's mistaken, of course—all sorts of repair-men say all kinds of things, as do musicians, wives, pirate ghosts. But Henry Scott now stands, lifting his duffle. "Plus, I'm here to see me mum. Next stop." He ducks his head to watch oncoming intersections.

"As you wish, sir," said the driver.

"My name is Sallow," Wyatt says.

"All disguises, right?" From the partially zippered duffle, Scott snakes out a bow tie, holds it under his chin. "All disguises?"

"I believe you, sir."

The bus slows, lowers, and settles in its frame. The door swings. Henry Scott descends before the complaining brakes clinch the vehicle to a complete stop, his manicured fingers release their grasp on the chrome handrail. "I think you heard me," and then he's gone.

And that. That right there. What had been nagging at him. Idiot! Wyatt deliberates only a few milliseconds before realizing he must act.

"It's him!" Wyatt stands.

"What's that?" The driver examines a clipboard, removes a ballpoint.

He has things to say to the man. Who had, yes, not only played that android character but—Wyatt remembered it now, floating up from scraps of disconnected pop culture: *People Magazine* at the urologist's office, or *Entertainment Tonight* around the holidays, the only time he ever got home early enough to watch television. Or maybe even the name flashed across the credits during all of those thousands of viewings. "He's Retro! He's the voice of Retro! Not just the android. In *Rocket Cadets*. He just gave the . . ." Wyatt moves to the doorway.

The driver doesn't seem to comprehend.

"I'll get off, too."

"As you wish."

6
Remembering Phoebe

On the pavement, the covered bus stop is situated beside a benched gathering area for one of the town's two community colleges, its square, officious buildings squatting against the hillside, some of the windows cranked open at this hour to allow refreshing morning air. The bus departs almost before Wyatt's cognac-colored brogues leave the footboard, its doors snap shut as it moves away with a diesel whine. Brown exhaust clouds spurt behind, leaving an acrid smell.

Wyatt has an odd, disjunctive, sliding feeling. Something... something about how surprised, even proud Wynn would be to hear he had found the voice, the voice of that cartoon hero... no, *villain*. Retro was the villain, but one the boy had spent so many hours with, listening to. Wyn would... but no. In fact, this encounter with the actual Retro—the voice himself—didn't matter, and couldn't, on any level, as Wyn would not be able to abstract, in all probability, that the cartoon rocket had a flesh and blood counterpart talking in his, the evil Retro's, voice. It would be impossible and (here Wyatt shakes his head from side to side, looks around. A single newspaper page turns in the wind beside the curb, mostly coupons. A bus-stop advertisement in a black frame: special on Lekali Timur Masala at Gurkha Sizzlers.)... impossible even more because Wyn is gone gone gone and... and he still wants to find the man, Henry Scott, and just tell him, tell him about Wyn, his voice, the hours of *Rocket Cadets*.

He wants a word. To explain. How he's come to be here. The actor will have some appreciation for it, if librarians, hotel clerks, train station personnel did not. Rain starts to pepper the sidewalk, but not so he has to pull the folding umbrella from his pack. A Black girl tries to use an automated teller against the college's brick wall, but it doesn't want to cooperate. He does not see Henry Scott anywhere.

He just wants to say...

... what?

Anthony "Tony" Crane, a.k.a. Henry Scott, spies from the darkened door of the student union, watches the guy in tweed peer about like a lost mole. He's used to exercising caution when it comes to excitable types or others who want some kind of association. He watches the man's confusion, wonders what he should do, as he'd wanted to get to an aquarium shop before too much of the morning burned away. Needs only a part for a pump for his mother's brackish water tank. She's got five tanks, these days: a saltwater, a freshwater, a coldwater, one just for bettas (which must be disorderly fucks to need their own tank like that), the brackish, and . . . wait . . . technically, then, there was that breeder tank as well. So, six. Certainly "Tony" had done well by his mother, getting her a house, a reliable car, and enough mad money just to do whatever she wanted which apparently centered on the aquatic world. "Better than cocaine," thinks Scott. "Tanks for the memories." The aquarium shop's one stop earlier—he'd missed it—so he'll have to backtrack. But he couldn't resist the bus, the duffle. It had been a week since he'd come to town from the Comic Convention in Leicester. That's how it went these days. Fewer and fewer Sci-Fi, media, movie, or television conventions, which left comic books. Still, the crowds there lined up for autographs, chanted his name at an *Off to the Planets* panel discussion and partial reunion. (He and Raymond Guillory, who'd been Captain of the S.S. *Calendar*, now with a wife paralyzed from a neck injury caused by a quack chiropractor, and so turning down nothing, the two of them being among the only core cast at the gathering, the rest of the panel a handful of one-episode journeyman actors and actresses: second-communications-officer-in-Series-3-Episode-5 level talent.)

"Tony" doesn't think he convinced the bus driver, but that was perfect. He had clearly pulled off a masterful "Man who looks like Henry Scott but isn't." One hand in his duffle, he fingers the bow tie. Feels the vinyl zippered wallet containing his hypodermics. *Matrix, Matrix!* they'd yelled in Leicester. He'd played the bus gig too long, but just has a couple of blocks to hoof it for the aquarium emporium. He begins to feel foolish.

He frowns. It had been earlier in the year at a DIY shop, buying mom a hinge for the half loo cabinet when, queuing up, someone had recognized him. Somewhat. "Do you know you look just like . . . ?" Scott had a variety of responses for this, including the ever-reliable "I get that a lot." This had been a busy DIY Centre day, though, and the other people queueing, guys mostly, all turned. Stared. Gave the looky, looky. "Not really," most agreed. "No more than I," said one. "Ehhh," said the kid behind the counter.

But this shop he'd been going to ... for ... he had to think about it. He'd been there first with his father nearly fifty years before. They knew him in this B&Q, had seen him grow up. Mr. August always had a kind word or a reach out to rough up the hair he used to have. Mr. August who'd followed his career with pride. Or ... at least the previous staff there had known him. None of those people seemed to be around now, and Scott feared asking where they might have got off to.

"I am him," he'd insisted.

"You wish," said the guy in front of him.

He couldn't convince them. It had shaken him, and between travel engagements, hustling, feeding what was left of the *Off to the Planets* machine what it required (psychic fuel, personal identity shoveled in one end so licensing and residuals continued to stream out the other), whenever he found himself in town after wrapping the occasional *Rocket Cadets* voice gig, helping out his mum and all, he'd taken to riding the busses. Usually with the duffle. Almost always pulling out some kind of conversation starter—like the bow tie or slipping the blank-eyed contact lenses in and starting up conversations with riders, or public wardrobe shifts, for example. Some clowning. Just to see what happened. Just to trot out the performance juice. Broadcast the sincerity.

Somebody'd notice and put it in *The Examiner* soon he reckoned.

At Leicester, he could still draw a crowd, even at a pub corner table after, but most often these days he worked his way to his hotel room alone after the festivities. The women in the room that were interesting to him at all had either not been born when the final mission of the S.S. *Calendar* had gnarled its way across the reaches of the outer galaxy ("Take her to gnarl unit five, Commander Matrix"), or else had arrived costumed up like veritable off-planet beings themselves, taking on the personae dreamed up by scriptwriters for four quid an hour twenty years before and, frankly, pretty much mad as rats in a can. The worst: the ones who didn't want Matrix at all. How old were they? "Say it," they'd whisper in dark hotel rooms that smelled of disinfectant. "About how you think," they'd breath. "How you think I heard you."

Sad.

He's taken his duffle out on the busses for the third time that week.

"Henry" hangs about the doorway, watches as the tweed-clad figure, with a sort of visible sigh, walks towards town, his backpack slung over a thick arm. Scott relaxes, turns, begins examining the student union foyer. He used to go to this college. So long ago. And so little accomplished in the meantime, really. What did any of it . . .? Who did it . . .? Who . . .?

Took his first real acting classes here. Teacher named Spielman. Phoebe Spielman. He played Bernard in *Death of a Salesman*. Henry Scott doesn't remember that bank of drink machines, though. What about the sandwich machine around the corner? Still there? Nothing stayed the same.

7
OtterShark

Every time he transfers to another bus, Wyatt pours random amounts of money into a silver tray, speaks his destination, accepts what comes back. At the central bus station—which also has a place for him to leave his chapbook—he examines the digitally posted schedules mindlessly, awaits a connection. He thinks about—and this for the first time in a long time—removing his phone and playing a game with OtterShark. But the last occasion he'd done so, months before, playing white as he had, and up by the exchange, there had been only one possible way for him to lose, and he had managed to find it.

No fair!

After X, something had happened to his game.

Wyatt didn't recommend using the application to his team, in spite of its strong analytical abilities. It embodied too many empty calories. A time waster. Time that could be spent on improvement. Wyatt often felt much of his coaching came down to "pulling back" his charges from exciting but unhelpful practices, like quick rounds of Bullet chess or relying on a computer for analysis before an attempt had been made using the player's own human brain—a worthy exercise even if performed inaccurately. He first downloaded OtterShark onto his office computer in 2004, the same month Wyn was born. Primitive compared with its present iteration, the program still delivered all the calculation abilities of the gigantic Deep Blue hardware that had given Kasparov such heartache a mere seven years earlier, available, however, for home use. He had all expectations that it would improve, too, and get better. These proved well-founded. Magazines had touted OtterShark as the next best thing to playing a person, which Wyatt saw as positive since his interest in actual opponents had already begun to wane. Parallel in his mind he wondered how Wyn might also improve as he learned the game: Wyn and OtterShark developing together over the years.

This was fantasy. All of Wyatt's memories of Wyn at the board are of him placing the pieces in their green velvet slots. The Rook. The Bissop. The Horse no Knight. Looking on intently with an enthralled grin as the Queen matched her negative form in the box.

Wyatt parcels out Wyn, nearly rations him into short scenes that serve to replace his hoped-for, longer engagements: the battles of wits that didn't happen. These, he's sure, would have been memorable classical encounters with the clock set to 45 minutes as Wyn—deficient in many ways but perhaps, perhaps, capable in others—fought it out with him. Wasn't that how it often worked? Wyn could have pattern recognition abilities above the "neurotypical," and these could be latched on to and improved. Wyatt imagined a day Wyn climbed above the expert level, received a FIDE certificate, clutched it with pride in his splayed fingers. Going into the upper reaches of club play, Wyatt would understand when it became time to set aside his own coaching as Wyn began to learn imbalance, concentration of forces upon a single piece, the necessity of retaining tension until the perfect opportunity, things a better coach could provide, a coach he would find and hire.

Instead Wyatt recalls some sweet, yes, but no triumphant afternoons. Pulling into his driveway after classes, the sun low, he noted as he reached to lower the garage door that Z and Wyn were behind him, down the long street, figures in the distance on one of their afternoon walks. (Z could not pronounce the circular feature they walked to—the cul de sac—as anything other than an unintelligible burst of consonants faintly resembling "cuddle sack.") They took these walks twice a day in good weather, in the summer waiting until the afternoon hours when light remained but the heat had somewhat abated. The air between Professor Sallow and his family would be clear and unwavering at that time of day, none of the shimmer their street took on in the oven-like noon, the turning circle obscured by rising air that converted the pair into something resembling figures in news police footage pixilated to hide their identity. Z, removing her hand from the protective foam on the wheelchair's handlebar, would wave to him lackadaisically, move the big-wheeled chair forward with its orange padding, its straps splayed to either side. A hand rises from the contraption, too, and—from far down the street—it's Wyn seeing him. Recognizing. The boy's vision seemed perfect, although difficult to test for. The tail of his Daniel Boone cap whips in the wind as he rolls forward, approaching. That hat. A thing Wyatt finds "ridiculous" and "wonderful."

Wyn has his legs crossed in front of him in the chair; he's limber, double-jointed and folds himself into whatever available space, not a problem. He pushes back in the orange padded seat, extends his arm as far as he can towards Wyatt, turns his head on his flexible neck backward towards his mother (Wynn could nearly lay his head on his back.) and the rac- coon tail faces forward like a snout. Turning back, the mantis-like hand trembles out towards Wyatt, who hears as they approach, hissing through flaccid vocal cords. *"That one. That one."* Pointing at him. Wyn's cheeks sag, his mouth falls into its perpetual triangle as the tongue moves over the lower lip.

Wyatt drops his briefcase behind the car, runs, nearly, in his loping gate, to meet them at the end of the driveway, lower his head, get close to the pale cheek.

You can't go down a road without encountering an intersection, so such vignettes are often paired with times he'd grown tired at the end of a long day. He was the working part of the team. Bringing in the mortgage payment, food money, insurance coverage. Once he'd been spread out on the card table in the living room, working through complicated variations in a Spassky/Petrosian '66 World Title match as Wyn, down the hall in the bathroom, moaned and complained in his shower. The cicadas trilled in Wyatt's inner ears and seemed to amplify the little boy's attitude. Wyatt lost the thread: a movement of the Queen's Rook to Queen Knight's file in the English but why? Z raised her voice in the bathroom, patience obliterated after a long day, reverting to some rough slick stream of the not-quite-Russian-not-quite-Polish people spoke in her native land, which was too much, her losing patience at the same time Wyatt lost patience.

"Stop it! Stop it! Stop it!" Wyatt thrust open the bathroom door, his words discharged like volleys against the off-green tiles. Wyn cowered, covered his ears with the backs of his hands (he seldom used his palms for anything) crouched low, naked in the tub, a plucked and broken bird.

"I am sorry," said Z. She stood stiff with arms at her side. "I am sorry."

"Take down your hands! Away! Don't cover!" His words didn't make sense, really. Wyn must not have thought so either. Jerkily, the boy moved his hands out towards Wyatt. As if to strike.

Red.

Had he really done it? With the back of his own hand, batted his son's frail, bird-boned arm away? When he noticed himself, he found he'd pulled back his own right arm. To what?

A good time for Z to have reached out, taken him firmly, fiercely by the wrist. Stopped him. But she did not.

Wyn did pull down his hands, then, looking miserable. Wyatt, like someone catching themselves drowsing while driving at freeway speeds, snapped stiffly. Snatched up some of Wyn's tiny socks from the bathroom rug, slapped them into the wicker hamper. Behind Wyn, the chrome handles Wyatt had paid to install gleamed against the tiles. Were they still there? "Pick up! Shower!" He nearly screamed and Wyn raised the back of his hands to his ears again.

"I am sorry," said Z. "I am sorry."

This wasn't the worst he'd done, either, as he just couldn't stop (and why?). Couldn't let it alone but instead, before he turned and left the bathroom, said the thing he said.

Unforgiveable. But, tangled in some combination of these memories (his boy was not a symbol, his boy soiled his diapers, could not follow two step directions, was—at times intentionally—hilarious, Pheeeeeeeeew. Pheeeeeeeeew) he decides against pulling out his phone to play a game against OtterShark, only sits and waits with guilty hands hanging between his knees.

When the bus that would take him to the Thornfield Museum opens its doors, Wyatt, with a glazed expression, rises from the plastic station chair, bypassing as he does a column where a flyer is attached at its four corners by blue masking tape. The flyer asks in bold, demonstrative typeface if anyone has seen the person pictured in the flyer and that person is X.

8
A Roly-Poly Punchable Clown

The Thornfield stands in the center of lightly wooded acres now utilized mainly as a dog park. Still private property, the ancestral home of Alexander Thornfield and family, the museum structure dates to the late nineteenth century and reflects a fortune made, then lost, in textiles. Wyatt rests by the museum's front doors near a stone lion and a concrete urn repurposed with sand for extinguishing cigarette butts. He pushes inside, pays the fee, and walks slowly through the cool, windowless gloom.

Wyatt can discern no plan or pattern to the ground floor exhibits. The museum's core consists of items the Thornfields had collected for generations, their acquisitive impulses proceeding with little evidence of interest in either chronological completeness or historical importance. One room displays old bicycles, arranged—or disarranged—randomly so far as he can tell. Another is devoted to "cabinets of curiosity," several of these specializing solely in preserved beetles of enormous size and frightening horned aspect ("Wouldn't want to meet you down a dark alley," Wyatt tells one particularly vicious appearing specimen, bending close to examine it.), as well as, along one long wall, a variety of bird species. (Did any once fly over the head of a Sallow ancestor? Who knows? Who knows?) The dusty-looking specimens sleep in nests of linen, their beaks universally tucked towards chests, eyes sewn shut. A single Amazonian shrunken head, similarly sewn, scowls from its glass case. Wyatt ponders the complexities that once spun inside the now tiny skull. Beliefs. Passions.

Frustrations with impossible family members. "How, sir," he asks, "did you come to be here?"

Wyatt receives the unfortunate impression from a down-curled lip that the misplaced rainforest inhabitant wonders the same of him. He moves on.

One positive: no one hears him speaking to the Amazonian. The museum is not popular. He sees no other individuals in the building save the young man and woman behind the entrance counter handling ticket sales and the Thornfield Museum gift shop.

Soon, Wyatt finds the corner he seeks, a museum feature he's read about in the *The North: A Tough Guide*. It's less impressive than even the disparaging guidebook has let on. Here five smudged cases contain drawings, maps and the occasional photograph arranged to narrate the story of the town's foundation and development through time. One display, labeled "In Dismal Sallowsfield" examines the earliest written record of the place's existence, the title pretty much giving it away. To its left, eighteenth-century accounts report on "The Feeble Village." A 1757 paragraph written by John Wesley, excerpted from his extensive travel accounts, is memorialized with a longer quote. "I rode over the hilltops to Sallowsfield. A more feral people I never saw in this island realm. The men and the women, too, filled the streets, seeming prepared to roast and eat us all. It is undeniable that I have found here nothing to admire." Dioramas memorialize the arrival, abandonment, and then re-arrival of the regional railroad (there had been municipal disagreement over whether rail would "catch on"), the expensive, dangerous and laborious drilling of canals through nearby rough terrain over many years to create a transport route (a short-cut no longer in use save by canal boat enthusiasts literally and Christian missionaries figuratively) and, ultimately—with much sweeping aside of erased years in between—construction of the ring-road in the 1950s displayed in triptych form. Wyatt had similar hopes for the Thornfield Museum that he'd held for the Sallow File in the "S-Se" cabinet in the library, and these had now been similarly dashed.

He discovers an offbeat "Sallowsfield in Modern Media" exhibit. It takes him a few moments to figure out its exact intent. The case is filled with quotes from radio and television and demonstrates how the town possesses one of those slightly "funny" names, requiring only mention to garner giggles from a certain class of audience. A cheap laugh. The long-running comedy series *Way After Its Time* had been filmed in the valley and nearby villages, and often invoked the name. In one episode, a crusty character opines that, upon breaking his arm, he'd had it cast in plaster at the hospital. A photo of this character in his moth-eaten cap features a speech bubble: "Why is it called plaster of Paris? Shouldn't it be plaster of Sallowsfield?" Wyatt learns how sit-com scripts allude to the municipality often, usually in ironic juxtaposition to some shortcoming. As in: "Leonard insists we've got arts and culture here, but c'mon—it's not like we're in Sallowsfield." Producers could exchange "Arts and culture" with "letters and learning" or "science and research" to achieve a similar effect. Then there was the comedy series featuring a man who worked in a razor factory who made plans to travel to a professional gathering: "The Sallowsfield Stubble Festival."

Wyatt turns a corner to find a surprise. *Finally*, exactly what he'd sought from the moment he'd heard of the Singapore Air bargain. In fact, if dramatizing him in a fictional narrative interested X, she would almost have to appear—as part of her research—in front of this very display, perhaps stand where he now stood. Unable to stop himself, he examines the thin grey carpet. It reveals no clue that her feet had once been there, either in or out of her silvery low-heeled shoes. Or: could she be on her way? Possibly soon? Could X momentarily step past the cabinets in the passageway ahead and approach him with her notebook? (Wyatt gives himself credit for encouraging X to keep a notebook. "Would a photographer go out without a camera?") He glances towards a nearby doorway. Looks to see if she appears beside the glass cabinet of dried fungus, lichen, and mushroom specimens arranged alongside printed period illustrations of fungi, lichens and mushrooms.

Although X's appearance at the train station surprised him, in the past he'd had intimations of her nearness, at times sensed her imminent approach before it happened. It was in a way a form of "manifestation" he felt he could practice; nearly *calling her into being*. This symptom, Dr. Than insisted, 10 mgs of the yellowish round ones every morning could easily abate. But wasn't a "manifest" in *Business Ethics: Important Sounding Subtitle* defined as *listed deliverables, set to arrive at a destination*? Why consider it odd that he'd sense her presence, or essence, upon her looming arrival? He'd pick up on her emanations just before she appeared, in other words, strolling, nonchalant, into this passageway, as she had in his classroom, at the car wash, at Palo Duro Canyon State Park.

"I thought I'd find you here," he could say, should she appear.

Does he feel that presence now?

Wyatt peers down the hallway. It ends at an intersection with the museum's entrance. He attempts to conjure her. Then, sure enough, something moves. Against the darkened background, a man in orange dungarees enters stage left, carefully walking backward, causing Wyatt momentarily to believe that Henry Scott—or his impersonator—has followed him from the central bus station to enact a bizarre pantomime for his benefit only. The grey backdrop behind this man falls away in a trailing shimmer as he continues to move his feet, revealing a now much brighter space transformed into a wavering tunnel with a pear-shaped figure set in its vortex: this silhouette resembling one of the blow-up toys children hit that spring up again, weighted at the bottom. This punchable clown replicates itself in a shaky infinity, an intersection of space that's emptied out before Wyatt's eyes. He feels the hairs on the back of his neck clinch. Another man, also in dungarees but wearing dusty boots and needing a shave, enters, copying exactly the first man's bizarre sneak-step though facing forward in his case. The frame they tote between them contextualizes the scene that snaps, then, into a more realistic tableau. Workers hoisting a gilt-framed mirror. Straining under the weight of the thing. They are taking it to some other part of the old mansion, no doubt.

They move beyond the passage's dark opening.

Wyatt recognizes the roly-poly punching bag as his reflection.

9
A Gentleman and a Weakling

Wyatt would realize X is not appearing at the end of the hall of the Thornfield Museum had he at that moment been in New Orleans, Louisiana, where she stands beside the Riverwalk Gazebo and A-1 Parking, her eyes overlooking dark waters. X is in New Orleans but no longer with Jeremy. The sun rises over the Mississippi, and she watches light play across the features of a Rastafarian-type in a billed velvet cap who wades into chocolate-colored liquid, ankle-deep. He steps into the river to meditate and pray amidst bobbing plastic bottles, chunks of Styrofoam, unidentifiable detritus from shipping containers. This man fixates on the patterns they form, designs they weave, especially when caught along the rock retaining wall that keeps the Mississippi out of the Market. It's a place—minus the Rastafarian—she'd written about in her novel, and where she—her hand shielding her eyes from the sun—has returned to seek inspiration: some mission her elvish female protagonist (member of a Spectral Containment League) . . . some mission her heroine, Sophie, can take on as an assignment to once again foil the exploits of the city's demon, jinn, dybbuk and/or voodoo witch population not to mention fulfill the parameters of the three-book "Sophie-driven" series for which she's received a large publisher's advance, each volume showcasing the crafty girl's battle against a different (though seductive) demon, jinn, dybbuk, etc. since dispatching the ghost of the pirate captain Jerome. (Hiding in the warrens of the *Vieux Carré*, disguised as a down-on-his-luck musician and fry cook, given to sitting unshaven in the morning, composing on his piano as his seduced nightly victim awakens groggily, wondering how this man, this *force* could "unearth such a powerful attraction in her," yet also "drain her so spellbindingly of vital energy," and who . . . *who* among the city's population might come to release her from his curse?).

X dips into her ubiquitous shoulder carry all and withdraws . . . not a journal notebook and pen, but a dictation recorder half the size of a cigarette box. This has replaced for her the far too tedious task of jotting notes. Thumbing its switch, she captures her impressions. "A Rastafarian-type in a billed velvet cap," she says, "wades into chocolate-colored liquid, ankle-deep." But it's not so good. Pretty lame. Unfortunately, X can't find the inspiration she seeks for her next major work. The lack gnaws at her, as she considers herself an inspirational person. She has told many people many inspirational things, like:

A hotel manager in Roma: "I like doing things for you. And to you. And around you and with you and on you. Especially on you."

A trainer she'd hired at a gym to help her lose weight. "I need to feel you close, and soon. I have been thinking about you all week."

An attorney in Houston who helped with her divorce. "I'm arching my back and thinking of you." (This in an email.)

A phone call to a different attorney in Houston who hadn't been involved in her divorce at all but whom she met at a party thrown by her divorce attorney. "Imagine I'm wrapping my leg around yours, so my toes touch your calf. Whispering in your ear. Telling you how I'd like you to touch me. Please. I can smell your hair and feel the warmth of your neck and your breath on my skin, and . . ." and so on.

Jeremy, a New Orleans musician/short-order cook: "I wanted to crawl into your mouth, to be in those words, the lyrics you whispered I couldn't understand. I touched my tongue to your teeth and lips, but it wasn't enough."

A male nurse at her grandfather's nursing home: "I climbed into you and haven't left yet."

A psychotherapist. Not her psychotherapist. Just someone who happened to be a psychotherapist she met who worked for the jail system in Corpus Christi: "We need to have an epic grotto adventure."

Her chess coach in a small East Texas college she'd flirted with but found unattractive: "I plan, if I can, to cut my hair and burn or bury it with you."

The chess coach had been an interesting case, although he had not in any material way helped her game. It had all ended badly. A man estranged from his wife over some sadness, X felt he'd developed an attachment to her, certainly nothing she'd encouraged. They did have the odd smooch. He'd been one reason she'd started in on the manuscript that later became *Sophie and Jerome*, true, although his actual advice about writing had been of little service. ("Show, don't tell!" he'd exclaim, never quite filling in how it would be possible to show readers anything they hadn't been told about.) Yes, he'd begged for that racy picture one time. Flattering. Such a sweetie (she thought), but so old! She finally relented by shipping him something tame via email after obtaining his promise he'd delete the image. She thought it might cheer him up and he was too much of a gentleman and a weakling not to erase it. He seemed hurt when she explained she'd be leaving her husband for

Jeremy, but nothing earth-shattering. He had no reason to believe they'd ever be together.

He was over forty!

By the time she'd left that husband, sent her daughters to live with in-laws, broken up with Jeremy, and had her manuscript in the hands of a New York romance publisher, she was back in Turner for a few weeks, moving out of her house, preparing the big move to the Big Easy, a duplex in the Garden District. Then she discovered while nudging the front of her garage with enough force to dent the sheetrock, that her brakes were in sore need of refurbishing. After a (she admitted it) foolish, shaky, slow drive that made her perspire profusely fearing at any moment something would call for her to stop and she wouldn't be able to, she'd gotten to the shop where her mechanic informed her it might take five hours for repair. Who did she still know in town who could pick her up for lunch?

He'd been a professor of business studies at the college, too, in addition to chess coach—now she remembered. Even after the Jeremy business, he'd stayed in touch. Had gone to her home to feed her dogs, the dear. So, she called, and he'd bought her the lunch as she waited for the brake pads or shoes or whatever it had been. Sitting across from her, the coach had kept his eyebrows level. He seemed to be swallowing his black beans (they'd gone to a Mexican place) in measured spoonfuls. Gawd. That sort of thing would have driven her crazy if she'd had to put up with it beyond one lunch. She spoke of New Orleans, her concerns over petrochemical plants in the Baytown region, her concern (which was new—a new passion she'd given herself over to, as she so often did give herself over to such things) that an ecological disaster loomed on the horizon: a black cloud of poison floating in to kill everyone on the Gulf Coast. She'd read recently as well about earthquakes that would destroy California cities, global warming that would melt polar regions and cover half the country in seawater, viral pandemics. Professor Sallow was such a poor conversationalist, the time pretty much always had to be filled with her riffing on news items, as had always been the case between them.

"All your talk of the future makes me hopeful," he'd said.

She laughed. He seemed surprised she'd laughed.

"You seem to be discussing a future," he said, "that does not, or not explicitly, not include myself."

"That's so true, Wyatt." A strange thing for him to say. She had, after all, also talked about a future that did explicitly include fatality, disease, and destruction. His reading this as positive should have been a warning sign. "But, look, stay in touch," she said. "We should talk more, the way we used to."

Later, in the early morning hours, he'd come to her house, broken down her door by throwing himself against it. She understood he'd maybe gotten off his meds.

She did not press charges.

She did not wonder what he was up to now.

Let's see. Who else?

Her psychotherapist: "I love looking at you after we've fucked. Your eyes are slits. Barely opened. So relaxed. A look of comfort and satisfaction."

10
Kylie

Wyatt glances at the fungus cabinet a last time, satisfies himself X won't be manifesting soon. If she would walk around that corner, maybe follow the workmen with their mirror into the passage . . . what a relief it would be, at the least, to report her presence to Y. He polishes his glasses on his shirttail, tucks this in, then bends to read the display concerning "How Places Get Their Names."

On a stylized map of the region including linguistic analyses of variants on small bronze plaques, he is able to discover the origins of several area place names. The plaques—to give a visual indication of just how far back these linguistic traces go—are shaped like medieval weapons such as spearheads, or the spiked business ends of maces. They lay out a variety of possibilities when it comes to the names. For example, a village could be labeled by those who first settled there. A family of Sallows, in other words, or a clan, setting up a sphere of influence by identifying it with themselves:

a reasonable if not ground-breaking approach to place-naming. A different plaque points out how "locales may acquire a new name from later conquerors"—which could have been the case had a roving band of Vikings surnamed "Sahller" (or even "Selja") entered the region in the ninth century, claimed that shallow valley below present-day Tower Hill as their own home, or—more likely—performed a duty, possibly mercenary in nature, for which they were then paid with land: a "field" (Norse: "feldt").

Sahllersfeldt.

The display notes a third possibility: hybrid alterations and combinations, names containing elements of different languages, perhaps descriptive, mixing the vernaculars of both original settlers and later invaders (the "Sals" conquered by, but then assimilating the "Lows" over the course of a century).

The analysis does not preclude other options. The word "sallow" is commonly associated in contemporary times with the color "yellow" and, most especially, an unhealthy skin (especially face) complexion. Even, less commonly, with unclean items in general. The Middle English noun "salwe," would be an original approximate spelling for what's now called the "sallow tree"—a type of willow, in which case, rather than traced to a person at all, let alone one who earned a *feldt* by the spilling of blood with sword, lance or mace, the town's name could readily and peaceably trace itself to the proximity of one or some of these trees, a common enough botanical species in that climate.

All of the above is speculation on Wyatt's part, however, as this informative educational diorama complete with convincingly portrayed medieval weaponry does reveal the name origins of the towns of Kiljoy, Underblow, Beanpot, Leap, and even (the original childhood home, though Wyatt does not realize it, of *Off to the Planets* co-star Henry Scott before his family moved to Sallowsfield) Slickwang. There is no mention of the philological origins of the largest town in the vicinity at all. Sorting through the educational display twice, then again, he fails to locate any . . . *any* mention of how the place got its name, including any mention of the name (or word) "Sallow," its historical or cultural variants. He grows more certain that, for the thousands (let's say hundreds) and more who'd ever set foot in this edifice and seen this display, this lack would not have been noticed by anyone but himself.

By the time he scours the back reaches of the ground floor seeking any information concerning the syllables bestowed on him by his father, his surname, he's decided to bypass in disgust the second floor (or "first" as it would be known here, given over to the Luddite revolution and supposedly containing actual sledgehammers used to destroy actual mill frames), and heads to the ticket and gift counter he'd passed on the way in. He inquires from a bespectacled young man about "the name of the town itself."

The young man's pitted chin hangs low momentarily, lips barely parted. "I'd have to ask."

He obviously works at selling gifts and stamping tickets, is not a historical reference librarian, but that he would ask someone about this inquiry shows promise. Such a large museum, set on such a grand and canal-adjoining stretch of landed (and dog-covered) property, would have to feature an on-site director or researcher. Perhaps a community board. Wyatt can leave his phone number, email, have the young man—or someone in authority—get back to him with the answer to this simple inquiry.

The young bespectacled man turns to an overweight young lady seated behind the counter on a tired-looking aluminum chair. She's flush of cheek, full-figured and about the young man's age. She stares blankly ahead, focused far away (though the ticket area is small and cramped).

Wyatt recognizes immediately the girl from the library, leaned on her elbows over the ancient volume of . . . some kind of archaic lore, complete with a bronze latch, triangular lock and tiny key. He recalls the beatific look on her flush cheeks.

"Kylie?" says the young man.

"What?"

Wyatt is cheered. He might get to the bottom of his inquiry, finally, with the right question posed to such a mysterious authority. He recalled how the librarian had handed over the important looking tome without being asked. The gift shop cashier, however, seems at first loath to disturb her concentration.

"Kylie." Almost whispering. "What's the town named for?"

A long pause. "Town?"

"Yes, this one."

"Named for?"

"Or after. Named after?"

Another pause. "Who cares?"

"Ah." He returns his attention to Wyatt. "We don't know."

Wyatt felt beyond disappointment by that time. Ready to leave. Right. Who cares? "Do you think there might be anyone—"

"Could be the color," says the girl. "Or a family named after the color."

"The color! The color itself." The young man appears in a hurry to turn away from Kylie. He shakes his head. "But I don't think so."

"Or the tree," she says..

The pair of them depress Wyatt further.

"I know what Pendle Hill is named for." The girl, ignoring Wyatt, continues her distant stare. She does smile. "Witches. That's my family name. 'Pendle.'"

"Except," says the guy, "the word 'pendle' itself means 'hill,' so 'Pendle Hill' is like saying 'Hill Hill.'"

Kylie expands her eyelids, cants her face to one side, raises one brow. "If you neglect the *witch trials* that took place there." She stares at her colleague with malevolence.

Kylie, when twelve years old, was already a 200-pound, five-foot-two, mean bitch and furniture destroyer, at least so called by her stepmother, Naomi. Kylie could at that age lift, throw, and break into kindling almost anything, including stools, drawers, and end tables (usually doing the plasterwork no good, either, where these items intersected with it). Other destruction resulted from times she flopped in anger, as on a sofa or mattress, her weight doing a number on coil springs and cushions. An armchair in Naomi's living room, an heirloom from her grandmother, retained a permanent imprint of Kylie's arse. She'd managed to break the wheels from her steel railed bed by the age of fourteen, which wasn't a great tragedy as it only made it lower, and this had to be considered an improvement over what she'd done to the wooden bed that had been Naomi's as a child—and her mother's before her—pulling the headboard over onto her younger stepsister's sleeping body and ripping out the sideboards in the process.

Naomi did love her troublesome stepdaughter, up to a point, and understood Kylie's anger issues as she shared a few of them, especially those stemming from the girl's father being taken to prison for defrauding Her Majesty's Revenue and Custom. He'd been caught in an evasion scheme while defrauding the remnants of the Thornfield family who owned the Thornfield Museum, specifically the two remaining Thornfield twins—a "boy" and a "girl," which remained the only way Naomi could think of them although they had both now reached seventy-two years of age. The pair didn't share a brain cell between them in Naomi's estimation, and belied the saying that "a fool and his money are soon parted"—as these fools were parting with their inheritance on an excruciatingly leisurely schedule, lazily dissipating the tail-end leavings of their family's textile mill empire until it amounted to a run-down mansion full of decaying birds, dusty dioramas and a shrunken head. Rumor had them likely to sell off the estate lands as well, throwing the museum's future into uncertainty. In the meantime, the connection had been good for obtaining Kylie the part-time gift-shop gig which helped some with bills and the girl's expenses of candlesticks and books about auras, covens and odd spells. Arranging this job had been downright charitable act of the Thornfields considering Kylie's dad had cost them more than £126,000, although the possibility remained that their act of kindness toward the girl had been more one of senile obliviousness.

Kylie, still steaming after the young man (Kenneth's) comment about "Hill Hill," rolls her eyes, begins to recite one of her spells, although it sounds to Wyatt and Kenneth like a string of irreducible gibberish.

"I think she's cursing me," says Kenneth. "Again."

Wyatt remains still. He wonders if an inquiry into the town's name might be directed to someone other than the angry fat girl. "You don't look worried," he says to Kenneth.

"I try to excuse her. She's on a diet."

"*I am not on a diet.*"

Kylie, no longer twelve but twenty-seven and coming in at eighteen stone, still lives with her stepmother, Naomi, although her stepsister has escaped . . . that is, moved off to Derby Uni where she stays over summer terms, too, rather than come home where she'd have to deal with Kylie who eats all of the time, hides food in her room, hides food under the bed, in closets, not to mention regular refrigerator raids in the night after Naomi, exhausted, has dropped off to sleep. Naomi believes going to Derby is probably a better way to escape Kylie than going to prison, but she's too old to re-sit her A-levels.

In school, Kylie hid her exam reports without showing Naomi, her responsible guardian, nor returning a signed copy to her teachers, though in the end neither Naomi nor the educational staff called her on it. She often did the schoolwork, then neglected to turn it in as she'd become fond of it, stacking up projects and papers on a corner of her crowded desk in her filthy room, or otherwise concluding she had too little interest to bother finishing the assignments. Or both. Her lack of decent GCSE results made the search for a better position than museum gift-shop attendant a vortex of impossibility, a situation Kylie blamed on Naomi who obviously hadn't taken her interests to heart, although she—Kylie—never had anything bad to say about her felonious father (he had, some in the remnants of the Thornfield "empire" believed, gotten caught on purpose, considering a stint in Wandsworth better than staying home with Kylie).

Growing up, she couldn't be left on her own even for an hour, so, again, why the Thornfield twins felt she could be trusted with their museum Naomi wasn't sure. Maybe they hoped for a fire and massive insurance payout. Daily, Naomi expected Kylie to arrive home with her eyebrows singed, the TV chattering news bulletins announcing that the Thornfield House—its moth collections, piles of bicycles, broken looms—had burnt to ash. That bit about "even for an hour" was a tested hypothesis, by the way, as one day, when the girl was sixteen, Naomi simply had to get her car in the shop for tyres, and asked Kylie to babysit her younger sister. It ended up being fifty minutes. When Naomi returned, the living room stereo could be heard from the postbox in the roundabout seven houses from her own. Inside, Kylie had sprayed a pump dispenser of green toothpaste across the bathroom tiles and across a hall into Naomi's bedroom (Kylie had been "wondering," she said, "how far it would go"), the worms of green paste even staining a sheepskin rug that had belonged to Kylie's departed (to Wandsworth) father, its rehabilitation requiring not an expensive trip to the cleaners but an extortionate trip to the furriers. Kylie had started shooting the cat with the green toothpaste, which the cat didn't like for some reason, this necessitating that the girl chase the animal around the house at high speed, squirting and splurting, which explained why the mattresses had been removed from the beds (the cat having sought sanctuary beneath them), why every lamp in the place had been knocked over, and why a knick-knack shelf filled with ceramic frogs lay sideways on the baseboards, chipped and broken amphibians surrounding it, their eyes wide with terror. Not too bad but Naomi considered it had just been fifty minutes and shuddered.

Naomi had already explained to Kylie—now, as mentioned, twenty-seven years old—that later in the summer her stepdaughter needed to go spend some time with her biological mother in Stockton-on-Tees. Naomi had not quite yet got around to a suggestion to go along with this explanation, i.e., that she also look for work in Stockton-on-Tees, forget about the dead-end museum job. Daily, this seemed a better and better solution to Naomi, notwithstanding that Kylie's biological mother's new husband (number four) was a sculptor who had never owned a television, needed silence to work, and—when he did listen to music—listened exclusively to African Anthropological drum tapes. "He'll *love* Kylie," Naomi said to herself often and, who knows? Maybe they'd all hit it off. If the girl left, did not return, delivered a respite of years or a decade, a period of tranquility impossible to imagine from this point in time, Naomi had little doubt that someday in the future she'd still turn up at the doorstep, four hundred pounds, carrying a baby, and it would be her problem all over again.

For now, Kylie continues with her eyes closed reciting a chant or curse of the kind Sophie Pendergrass, Elfin Council member of the Spectral Containment League, New Orleans Division, and heroine of *Sophie and Jerome* would never go near—the blowback from such black magic being far too dangerous. Wyatt, though he feels rude simply leaving, turns to simply leave. He does not mention anything about his personal interest in the town's name, anything about his own name, nor does he purchase a souvenir with his credit card as the name there would have, embarrassingly, revealed all. Not mentioning it doesn't help, however, as Kylie—having obviously paid more attention in the genealogical reading room than appeared at the time calls "I know your game, Mr. Sallow," before Wyatt can push out the heavy front door.

"I know you do." He exits leaving only Kenneth with the brooding girl. Poor Kenneth. If Kylie gets her way, some day the curse would (arguably) play hell with his prostate health.

11
Evan

As another bus brings Wyatt halfway back towards town, he recalls he hadn't at all looked into the Luddite displays in the Thornfield: a topic that had taken up months of his life as he'd worked hard writing a thesis to avoid having to work hard in a business internship to obtain his MBA. The trip to the museum might have provided something he could have at least used in class. He had instead walked out the door.

He decides to purposefully lay low the rest of the day. Go someplace he has not planned nor included in the outline on the final page of his notebook. A destination encountered at random. Hidden in this decision, of course, could be a secret desire that "reverse psychology" will work when applied to the universe, that his aimless wanderings will in some way cause X to appear just as his searching the streets, shops, and sidewalks had so spectacularly failed to cause her materialization.

He stops at his rooms to apply deodorant and attempt to rinse off some of the green, sweet, jungle-scented shampoo that still coats his body, then sets out. Wyatt has an idea there are restaurants on nearby Duck Lane, a few blocks from the Edgeland Arms, although he has less of an idea concerning how to get there. All roads seem to end at a massive cemetery. He has little hope of finding any "Sallow" memorial stones in that place so does not bother to look. It would have been possible to head down the hill, hike past the bridge, walk back up the other side, but in his mind, he pictures a more direct route. Finding it would alleviate the long trudge.

After moving randomly into the surrounding neighborhood—he's gotten past the cemetery, some of the stones ancient and leaning—he eventually hangs a left. An anonymous street, townhouses on both sides, appears to be a circle, taking him back to Edgeland. He wouldn't have found the path to Duck Lane at all, but two couples turn in to a shortcut at an elbow of the road where a light pole indicates a break, so he follows. Paralleling a wall of red stone, a very sound footpath broken by bricked steps descends into the neighborhood's lower elevations. The four going before him give the impression of heading to some event together: maybe, like himself, in search of dinner, though crowd noises from a distance cause Wyatt to consider the possibility of a sporting contest. He lands on a busy road beside an off-license and follows it to the right along a pavement that circles a council estate: a block of flats with round, open areas between that are bare of grass and interrupted with overturned tricycles, trash, fallen clotheslines. Wyatt crosses to the "low" side of the street, sees an eating establishment and, only a few buildings before it, behold. It is the famous Donnelson's Ice Cream that Hussein had mentioned to him as a not to be missed attraction of the town. He pauses, considering. Ice cream. A bit sweet. A bit late in the day.

Before he can decide the silver aluminum door of the famous ice cream parlor shoots open in a way that sounds injurious both to its hinges and a bell that must be attached somehow to the interior of the frame. A young man exits, moving towards Wyatt, brushing past him at high speed. The guy jerks his shoulders in such a way that his torso twists away from Wyatt just in time, then he stalks down the street towards the off-license, his shoes slapping pavement. Looks vaguely familiar. Dark goatee. Slicked back hair. Slight eye bruise.

So easy to get run over in his town.

Evan had been inside, holding up the line with questions about the flavors, cones, scoop sizes. There were generally fifty-six or more flavors on any given day, but Sarah Donnellson, who stood before him behind the granite counter in her apron with a silver tumbler frosted with moist droplets didn't really see that as a problem. That's just Evan, in't it? She knew how to put a stop to that, hold up a hand. "Choose," she'd say, although she realized as well that this would only move him into other, more generalized requests. Spur of the moment petitions, like: "Just cold water, then, Mrs. Donnellson. But can I drink it out of that silver tumbler you use to mix the smoothies?"

She gripped the tumbler tighter. "No."

"So, tell me then. Have you ever seen anyone get into a fight over the ice cream?"

"Luv, what kind of fight would someone get into over the ice cream?"

"Like someone here asks for vanilla." He glanced at the line forming behind him. "But I say, no, no you want Sweet Minty Choco. And we can't agree."

Mrs. Donnellson had watched all the boys in the neighborhood grow up and retained a nurturing fondness for all of them. Evan, of course, was new. "Is that why Philip give you that black eye, Evan? Was it over the Minty Choco?"

"Fuck Phillip."

Mrs. Donnellson set the silver tumbler on the granite counter with enough force to make it ring.

Moments later, Evan narrowly avoided some old git with a backpack on the pavement as he swung out of the parlor for the last time ever, headed quickly down the street. Not quick enough as the aluminum door hadn't quite swung shut to block the shout.

"Comer-inner!"

12
Graham

Adjacent to Donnellson's Wyatt passes a small eating establishment several times before convincing himself it's the closest, if not the only, place to grab a bite around here if that bite is not to be ice cream. It seems, as well, the kind of place incredibly unlikely to draw in someone like X for a meal if she's in town. (She's not.) He hasn't seen any other place quite like it on his trip. Wyatt gathers what turns out to be more force than he'd reckoned he'd need to push open the oft-painted red wooden door of the Duck Lane Fish Bar.

It's impossible not to mention the attractive power of the appealing oversized grinning blue fish cartoon painted on the restaurant's darkened windows in making this decision. Its toothy smiling demeanor reminds Wyatt of Charlie the Tuna. It leans a fin casually on a surface (as if on a bar—he sees what they did there), flashes a grin worthy of a silent movie star beneath its oversized Ray-Bans. More important, Wyatt has seen in one dusty window corner, nearly touching the casual fin, a viscerally familiar logo together with an advertisement for the "Pizza Shack Special."

"Fish and pizza," Wyatt murmurs. "Together again." But it's the specific franchise symbol that seals his decision. He always frequented the Pizza Shack franchise on Academy Boulevard after classes on Tuesdays and Thursdays, not so much for the food as the dark red-tinted ambiance, faux Tiffany stained-glass booth lighting, and high veneered paneled partitions that allowed him to eat alone in a way that didn't spotlight the fact he ate alone. The Pizza Shack logo in the window indicated he might expect the same here as he found bi-weekly in Turner, Texas, thousands of miles away behind its screen of pines, a place calling out to him now as more attractive and well-suited to his life than he'd imagined.

Wyatt had often considered the title of his second book—one centered on his more scholarly interests—might well be *Everything I Need to Know about Business Ethics I Learned at Pizza Shack*, as, other than academic pursuits, the only business he'd ever engaged in happened throughout high school at one of the franchises near his home: an experience he found both low-wage and high stress. The job, and especially the actions of his manager (Tod Guidry) often appeared in his lectures. "What are the implications for employers who allow schedule changes—pertaining to *prom night* let's say—that create double shift early morning counter duty for one employee merely because this employee *has no date for the prom*?" He had little recollection of applying for the job—or the reason he felt he needed to do so—but Wyatt thought often of the occasion of walking into the restaurant on his first day of employment and the bizarre behind-the-scenes access suddenly afforded by his introduction to the oven, toppings and storage areas. Despite the years, the miles, the dreams gone by, pushing open the door of the Duck Lane Fish Bar makes him feel approximately sixteen years old. Definitely, a high point of his continual patronage of the Pizza Shack in Turner was that walking into it served as a comforting reminder he no longer had to work in it. He would not have to lend a hand with the shovel-like peel that fed pies into the massive ovens, would not have to chop vegetables or fill topping trays, carry boxes to his own car in zippered therm-sealed bags for late-night delivery to surly customers or—the worst—deal with that cash register.

That cash register. It never reconciled correctly on the nights he manned the insane device.

Taken together with the twisted, meandering scattershot approach he'd made in arriving at the Duck Lane Fish Bar through narrow passages and across council estates, he can think of no more promising spot to hide away from the possibility of any encounter with X. He can rest his mind in a familiar-seeming place.

Inside, however, is a cramped, grey-walled area—no paneled booth bathed by red light in sight—mostly given over to food production, although by neither eye nor nose can he detect evidence of food produced. No pebbled crescents of condensation cling to the plexiglass of the pristine steam tables. No warming lights glow over the empty stainless racks. At a broad counter the only person in attendance could have come from the staff of the Pizza Shack in Turner, a business that had what could only be considered an unhealthy affinity for white, mainly male employees recruited from the community rather than the more multi-cultural candidates from the college. This particular male seems to have entered at least his third decade, however, with bad skin and hair that hangs into his eyes and curls into his collar. Wyatt nods to the man, reminds himself he doesn't seek any kind of complication, just wants to order, take a seat at a shelf-like table set along one wall, eat and leave. Maybe he'd take the pizza back to his hotel, listen to the radio, relax. (The television at the Edgeland arms did not produce an image, but he could tune to local radio stations on it—something Wyatt hated to bother the attractive Muslim girl about, especially after all those encounters covering breakfast.)

The man, though not wearing anything like a maroon Pizza Shack polo shirt with white paper hat (just a flannel with rolled-up sleeves), does have a name tag. HELLO I'M GRAHAM. "Good afternoon, sir," he says. Friendly enough.

"Well, Graham. I think a medium pepperoni to ..."

Wyatt stops.

"You have an accent, sir," says Graham behind the counter. "From America?"

Wyatt doesn't really hear. "No," he says. "Texas. I'm sorry, where—?" He indicates a bulletin board, the only object decorating the grey-green-painted walls of the Duck Lane Fish Bar. "—where did you ... ?"

A single sheet—a kind of flyer—has been displayed on the framed board, attached to the cork background, not with pins but secured at its four corners by blue masking tape. It's X. It's a xeroxed, poor reproduction of her, the love of his life, bare to the waist. That is, he knows this is the case since he had personally examined the photo often enough. But thankfully in this version, she is displayed in this poor reproduction only to the armpits, the portrait having been tastefully cropped. X might be wearing a simple strapless dress for all anyone standing in the Duck Lane Fish Bar might casually assume.

Wyatt recognizes her even poorly reproduced, much as plane spotters or birders, they say, can identify their subjects by mere silhouette, plucking identity out of a blank background. He must strain to find the wry grin, the dimples, that damaged chin, but it is her. Behind X, the background wall with its portion of Art-Deco nude art has been wiped away, replaced with whiteness. Along the top, a caption asks: HAVE YOU SEEN HER?

Graham follows Wyatt's eyes to the board. "Have you?"

There's no ready answer.

The empty corkboard contains nothing save the single large-captioned, poorly reproduced flyer showing X, its request for information, and a phone number—one of the characteristically long variety from the region. Although he doesn't raise his phone to check, he's pretty sure it's Hussein's.

Not good.

Wyatt is certain that if X, were she in Sallowsfield, and were she to see this flyer, would be . . . he has a hard time coming up with the word. She'd blame him, certainly. For having this private, personal picture still, undeleted after these years, for one. Worse, for sharing it. Hussein had said: "I've got somebody working on it." Too late, yet how many nights of exquisite torment might he have lost if he'd deep-sixed the photo? Twenty? A thousand? What could be the harm, to keep a single copy only, and only on his phone? And if he told no one about it, and sent it to no one, why . . .

Oh, right.

"Sir?"

Some edge of concern in the man's voice causes Wyatt to backtrack, recall his purpose. The empty steam tables to Graham's right contain, as mentioned, nothing that looks like food—neither pizza nor fish related—nor was there anything that looked like a bar.

"Medium pepperoni."

Graham appears unconvinced. "You're certain?"

"That's it."

Graham dutifully writes the order on a pad, takes Wyatt's money, gives change from a modern-looking digital cash register. The till snaps shut with an audible *bing*. He rips the top page from his pad along some perforations and places the single sheet on a ledge beneath a cutaway window space behind his left shoulder, then, excusing himself, walks through a doorway into a back area where—in that same window—his hand takes up the torn sheet he's just written. Looking through this order window Graham sees the man in the tweed jacket peering steadily at the bulletin board that's upset him so much. He seems highly distracted. It's obvious he wears a wedding ring. Possibly has a wife at home who's trouble. Constantly alone and constantly whining because—no doubt—this man is busy. Out in the world attempting to establish himself. Possibly trying to help get a relative's business off the ground. It's clear the strain on him. That wife, no doubt, ready to crack at any moment. Developing *enthusiasms*. Developing *disorders*. Certainly isn't like the usual "customers," who mainly only drifted in and ask to see his uncle or his cousin or even just ask to see a SKY DEMON. Graham lifts a wall phone, dials a number stuck beside it on a yellow post-it note. "Graham at Duck Lane," he says into the handset. "Medium pepperoni, thin crust."

He hangs up.

The sacrosanct back room of the Duck Lane Fish Bar contains no freezers, no cans, jars of condiments, shredded cheese, or anything that might be obviously edible. Stacked to the wainscoting along one wall are colorful flying tops, still in their black and gold packaging. The inventory lists upwards of five gross (they probably should be keeping better inventory) of the SKY DEMON spinning toys in that room, nearly all of his uncle's ready cash invested in this sure-fire product. Like a yo-yo, but . . . *flies*. Graham has seen the stockpile appreciably diminish. Thank God. It's hard to deny the appeal. The SKY DEMON means fun at reasonable prices. Get started today. Spin it up! Use those two sticks connected by twine and, gosh, it's hard to stop! Do two on a twine. Juggle three (if you dare)! Try the "Sleeper," the "Forward Pass," go "Around the World."

"Hey," Graham says under his breath, adopting a voice he has heard in American gangster films. "Wanna try the 'Reverse Slack Trapeze,' *muthafuckah?*"

Wyatt drops onto one of the stools next to the ledge-like table (there are no chairs in the Duck Lane Fish Bar), ponders X looking down at him from the corkboard. He's not hungry anymore. He recalls the angry dog that had his name, considers slipping out his notebook, making some kind of entry about this unexpected development, but what to say? The man, Graham, doesn't call out an order to anyone but returns after a few moments to lean on the counter. There's a hardback book close by Graham's elbow that he hasn't touched. Perhaps he feels it's rude to read while a customer awaits his medium pepperoni.

A much older man with grey hair and a white windbreaker emerges from the back, his mobile at his ear, chatting in a low voice. He nods to Wyatt, then opens a back door and departs into a sun-dappled back alley. Under the man's arm is some kind of plastic item—a tool? A plumbing fixture? It's wrapped in black and gold cardboard packaging. The man in the white windbreaker doesn't seem to be taking else anything with him (like, for example, a pizza delivery), just that item. Wyatt can't read the gilt lettering. After ten minutes, the above sequence repeats, this time a younger man appearing with a black and gold box and a mobile at his ear. The way this more youthful person steps towards the back door leaves the impression he's certainly going to do *something*, in spite of stifling a half-yawn as he departs. No one appears to be either cooking or delivering pizza . . . or fish for that matter.

"Has there been any word?" Wyatt asks.

"A few more minutes."

"Sorry." He aims a thumb at the sheet of paper tacked with blue tape. "Anyone seen her?" It occurs to him that's the wrong question. "I mean who is she? What happened to her?"

Graham looks at the flyer. "Expecting word any day, sir. Reports are coming in."

"*They are?*"

"Oh, well." Graham's brought up short by the man's fierce reaction. "I suppose reports are. Don't really follow it. That's not us doing the asking."

By *us* Wyatt takes him to mean the staff and crew of the Duck Lane Fish Bar.

"I think the police brought the flyer."

"The *what*?"

"I *think* the police brought the flyer." Who brings flyers? Graham doesn't know and furrows his brow. There are a couple of officers, friends of his uncle's, who drop in regularly, but he has no idea who brought it. "Do you know the woman, sir?"

"Why would you say that?"

Graham grins. "Exactly." He raises a forefinger to his lips. "Mum's the word."

Wyatt swallows. The phrase *Never saw her before in my life* comes to mind, but he makes do with "Just curious."

Graham shrugs. "You know what I know, sir." He figures whatever upset this man—and he appears nearly driven to the edge of the brink of despair by the look of him—has to do with a woman. Has to. Explains his fixation on the flyer. Probably in too deep in some fashion. Maybe a girlfriend in addition to the wife. It isn't just his fixation on the missing woman's bare-shouldered portrait that leads Graham to this conclusion, as he discerns other indications: facial tics, uncomfortable jaw movements, a rolling of the arms and grasping of each elbow with the opposite hand in an effort to hug himself as a form of self-comfort. Probably there's someone out there not giving him a moment's peace, angry he won't leave his wife who's at home. A wife frittering away her time on sketchbooks, trips to the library. Living all day on a piece of cheese. A *slice* of cheese, from a pack of pre-sliced, cello-wrapped slices. And then, this girlfriend, in addition, is no doubt texting him. Getting pissed off when he doesn't answer right away—*I am not attached to this phone, Sigourney, I walk away from it at times*. Getting pissed off and taking up his time when he needs that time to do things like work on his uncle's SKY DEMON business, which his wife certainly doesn't seem to think is important, either, and what does she think is important anymore?

Between the wife and the girlfriend, it's difficult to even get in a few hours helping the uncle and the cousins cover the pizza and fish orders for three stores when there's only one cooking fish and pizza.

Graham touches the cover of the hardback at his elbow. No doubt this man in the tweed jacket, who doesn't appear a violent person, not a violent man, has taken his frustrations out from time to time. Not on the woman. Never. Maybe he's just gotten frustrated one night, gone ahead and, well . . . maybe *just wailed the shit out of his own acoustic guitar.* Like, put his foot through it or something, then grabbed it by the fretboard, broken it over the sideboard, *bang, bang, bang.* An Alvarez-Yiari 3415C, maybe.

Which just makes the wife shrug like all she cares about his music, she has her "art," her "wooden boxes," her "jewelry classes." Building shit and drawing shit and *creating* while she's wasting away herself on cheese, just to take it out on him.

This girlfriend is probably doing to this guy what such girls do as well. (Who can understand them?) That is: the threats. Only, it doesn't come off as a threat, does it? Like: "I'm going back to Leeds," or something. Sure. Hold that one over his head. Going back to Leeds 'cause her father is ill, her sister pregnant (again), her nieces' grades dropping. One of the nieces, she's lying about attending, now, plus smoking, riding in cars with (if Graham remembers the tirade correctly) *thirty-year-old men,* and "I might as well go back, isn't it? My purpose here is none. I don't have a purpose here. That's why I've never settled. I've got boxes I haven't unpacked in my apartment, Graham."

"I said I'd help unpack."

"The legs are coming off my table, Graham."

He had no idea what that meant.

"Only, 'Don't come home for my sake, Siggy,' Mum says. 'It's your Dad, though. He misses you so much.' And if I go back, I won't matter either. I don't matter anywhere. Do I, Graham? I might have *this* much effect." Sigourney lifts a left little finger, pinched halfway down its length with right thumb and forefinger. It turns pink. "But I'll be able to do something right."

"So, we won't be going to Edinburgh, then?"

"*Of course we're going to Edinburgh. You said you'd take me. You said. It's just going to be such a sad trip to Edinburgh, is all. Our final trip . . .*"

"Thank you," says the man in tweed.

"Sorry?"

"For telling me about the flyer."

"Since you asked."

"*Simple, idle curiosity,*" Wyatt emphasizes.

There are zero amenities in the cramped dining room, evidence this is a takeaway business, not designed for those who, like Wyatt, come in off the street. Probably also explains why the door is so difficult to open: perhaps it is seldom moved on its hinges. No tables, chairs, tablecloths: just the metal ledge across from empty steam tables and a couple of stools pulled up to it, the stuffing coming out of the cushion of those in places where gaffer tape hasn't succeeded at holding it in. Another clue to the unusually deserted condition of the restaurant is the surly and quiet nature of the young man, an indication, to Wyatt, that not many people pushed through the red door in person. The guy's not used to dealing with the public.

He wants to know more about how X came to be on a bulletin board but understands Graham has little to add. Wyatt sits. The colorless, muddily contrasted version of X grins for reasons that can never be uncovered.

The other two men also connected with the Duck Lane Fish Bar—separately—return, then separately leave again, speaking on their mobiles, carrying those oddly shaped triangular items in black and gold packaging.

As for his own order, "Soon," says Graham. Wyatt wonders if there is, perhaps, something wrong. Not existentially, but a malfunction in the equipment, else the power had been turned off to the ovens for some reason. Finally, Graham remembers something that needs to be done behind the scenes—or pretends to remember this—leaving Wyatt, who might have used the opportunity to slip back onto Duck Lane and find a pub or fast-food shop had he not already paid—leaving him to sit at the ledge, pull out his phone, look over the original of his torture photo.

He had for a short while friended X on social media, but presently she's blocked him. Cut him off. On his phone, in the color original that still includes the background wall and the breasts, X looks square-shouldered and happy. This of course is the worst. That a person can remove you from their life yet find happiness.

Wyatt wonders what she makes of the town. What she thinks every time she raises her head and sees his name.

"And what are you doing in Sallowsfield, sir?" asks Graham, who returns, takes up a position again next to the empty steam tables, but hasn't brought with him from any recess of the restaurant a pepperoni pizza, medium or otherwise.

Wyatt, feeling unbalanced from the flyer and pondering the depth of his troubles does not at all wish to tell him his purpose. As is his approach at times in class, he responds to the question with a question. "What do you think a Texan should see who comes here?"

Graham's response is quick. "Edinburgh."

Wyatt considers. "*The* Edinburgh?"

"Eight hours by train."

"So, the best thing to see in Sallowsfield is . . ."

". . . in Scotland," Graham insists. "My friends and I drove there in less than five hours. Museums. Fairs. Castles. They have it all. A lot better than here." He holds his nose.

Wyatt considers the Thornfield Museum, the Christians he'd met at the street fair. The Rook-like tower on Tower Hill.

"This town," says Graham, "is a good place to retire. Not to visit. Laid-back. Lots of pensioners. Small enough to get around without a car, without breaking a hip."

Wyatt thumbs through other pictures on his phone, waits as the older and younger man arrive and then depart again. He had begun to pray his pizza would arrive, not out of hunger but just so he could leave. He has only two more days in town before his travel day back to Manchester and the airport. Some of the notes from his ethics class came to mind, especially the definitions. Like for "business" itself. *The pursuit of transactional activity with the intention of making a profit.* So far, the Fish Bar had made a profit from Wyatt but had yet to follow through on its transactional responsibilities. If any other exchanges have taken place, he's unaware of them.

Graham observes the guy is wrapped up in some kind of deep thought, probably just got told by his girlfriend she had some big news. "Big important news, but don't worry," she'd have said on the phone. "Changes is all. Big changes. I'm lucid about them. Completely lucid."

And she probably wouldn't have told him about these big changes until they could meet in person. Until he could come over *yet again one last time* "It's just not the kind of thing you want to exchange in a text, is it? Or email." So now this guy hangs on, becomes more and more played. Having to drive over to Sigourney's—or whoever's—to find what the fuck is going on, rather than just getting told. The woman breaking into his day *again*, though he's very, very busy, has several tasks his uncle wants him to get through. Like finishing this book Uncle Thomas had given him to study. *Sales Through the Roof!* Full of great advice. Good tips on reading body language when making sales, for example (the reason he picked up on this man's self-elbow grabbing behavior). Or advice like "Don't find customers for your products, find products for your customers." They'd done this! The SKY DEMON. If ever this region had need of a flying spinning juggling toy, the SKY DEMON was *it*. If this man, this American, were anything like Graham, at about that time, as he headed to her house on the Mining Road bus route, he'd be thinking "What am I doing this for? I should be busy. I should be finding products for my customers! This better be good!" And, perhaps, hoping for disaster. Secretly. Yes! Then, and only then—and Graham has to admit that his selfish peevishness does, somewhat, come first in his life where business is concerned—he begins to think, well, what if her father really is bad off? Has gone into a hospice or something? What if he's dead, and she's brushing up on being brave and "lucid" in this new condition of the world. This after she and the father had such a falling out they didn't speak for eleven years. So, then Graham begins to feel like shit. Like maybe Sigourney *is* leaving then. *Wants* to leave him. It makes him sad, even. Teary-eyed to consider it. He and Sigourney have been through it. Lord, Siggy. *That* one. Even not knowing, ever, where to place his foot, put his next step on the shifting sands, it had been something. A hell of a three months, no question. Might make things easier with the wife, of course. She might pick up on his new calm demeanor. She might stop attacking her own body, wasting away her own body to get back at him.

Sigourney. Now she'd be gone and gone without ever, not once, appreciating his position. Not realizing it was *her* doing the sabotaging, had been for months . . . well . . . one month. And yes, fine, we can go to Edinburgh, then. Edinburgh would be the one good thing she gets out of this, even if she has to do it as "the other woman." Before she goes back to Leeds. It would be proof to her—confidence enhancing proof—that she really can plan something, pull it off. We'd be good traveling companions, possibly, if not good partners. Or lovers. We can be friends to one another in the future. But, shit, who am I kidding?

Graham's mind races.

Who could ask for a better vacation than one incorporating the apoc-alyptic forced ending of a difficult and tempestuous temporary illicit rela-tionship combined with furious sweaty animal fucking turbocharged by accusatory whining (nonstop), booze, castles, and museums?

But it was nothing like any of that. Once he got to her apartment, he learned it was her big plan, now, *not* to go back to Leeds. That had been the change. The lucidity. She would *not* get a job there—a good job. She had, in fact, decided against it. Against it entirely. The night after they'd spoken, she drank a lot, couldn't sleep, thought about calling, calling to say how she was going to drink herself into oblivion. So, that's what she did. Got plastered. And then changed her mind about Leeds. That's what the "change" was about, and by the time Graham got to her apartment it was all "I'm worthless, no one will hire me in Leeds, I've screwed up my whole life, certainly never for a good job, I'll go back, back to Leeds a failure, and I *hate* going back there, so I won't, everyone there, they look at me like I'm a failure because *I'm not married,* and I thought if we were married, if you left your wife, she's just like a *skeleton,* Graham, for shit's sake, saw her at Tesco a few weeks back, be better for *her,* my parents would like it, that is, the two of us together, it would look like I'd accomplished something, but you just keep me in limbo, that's what I can't stand—*the limbo*—why don't you get rid of me, but you can't get rid of me, I believe in us, *I believe,* I felt we had something, something special, I wish we could get it back, could start over, start over but there's nothing to look forward to, nothing but *DEATH...*"

... and so on, until at some point the sense of her words begins spi-raling around, plugging back into ground already covered, then covered again, then the sentences taking off, jumping one track to fit another, earlier chain of rant. By which time Graham asked if there was anything to drink. Anything. Beer. Wine. Bombay gin. "I've got water," Sigourney said, so Graham got a glass of water, and listened, unable to work into the conversation any sort of idea of their true history the way he saw it. (That is: his version—when had he *ever* said he'd leave his wife? When had this *ever* been anything but what it was, and no promises?) Unable even to mention how that time when he had hinted at the faint, slight, barest of bare possibilities resembling less than a half hope that he could, perhaps, at some point in the future, the distant future at that, leave his wife—how that time she, Sigourney, refused to accept the idea. "*You're lying*," she screamed. Literally screamed. Especially since it was an idea he'd come up with after she'd subjected him to one of her long dragon-fire-word-fests, and she "didn't want him to be influenced by anything but his own desires," yet how she'd also never stopped ranting long enough for him to consider making the step without that influence on the cognizance of his own desires, whatever the fuck those were. Yes. The longer this sort of thing went on, the less able he became to deal with it at all, deal with it, that is, in any manner other than escape, and he took up his glass of water, felt the smooth liquid go down his throat, swallowed in neither hope nor despair . . .

"Are you a museum person?" Graham asks.

Wyatt considers it. "You know. I think I've only been to one."

"Edinburgh is *full* of museums. They're so. . . ." He sighs. "Restful."

Even xeroxed, cropped, somewhat blurred, X's face and form do not belong in the Duck Lane Fish Bar. She looks out of date: like a post office wanted poster from the 1980s. Wyatt wonders if he had ever been important to her at all? Too late to keep this photo out of circulation, to do what he'd agreed, delete it. Or was it? Too late, but what about for his own well-being? A gesture. Right here in the Duck Lane Fish (and Pizza?) Bar.

As it has other times, his thumb hovers above the trash can icon in the phone's lower right corner. Wyatt looks up before pressing it. Out the tinted windows, two ghostly figures, a couple, glide past. Young people with a pale, stooped and generally unemployed look about them in ragged jeans, t-shirts, both with hands in pockets.

"It's the secret of travel," Graham says. "Planning and research. Know what to see and how to quickly get to everything before you leave."

Wyatt to himself: *And make sure you don't get stuck in a pizza and fish bar.*

Although he can't see who placed it there, a flat cardboard box arrives in the window behind Graham, who lifts it and holds it out. Wyatt decides to go ahead and eat there on the ledge and drops his phone into his jacket pocket.

"Need a drink to go with?"

"No."

He can't imagine where the pizza came from. There's no pepperoni. It has such a cardboard-infused taste he ends up not being able to finish it, anyway, so doesn't miss the salty meat product. After twenty minutes of chewing, he grins and thanks Graham for the meal and leaves with the box and a promise to "finish later tonight," although a trash bin alongside one of the estate buildings would get it very soon—the Edgeland Arms didn't seem like a place to take leftovers on second thought.

"Take care of yourself," Graham says when Wyatt leaves. "Be careful."

Take care of himself.

Be careful.

Here? In this town? Where could there be danger to a man?

CHAPTER SIX

OPEN GAME

1
Nick

Nicholas Luis ("Nick") Zepeda Villarreal, PhD in Economics, Texas Tech University, 1995, presently Dean of the Department of Applied Business at Taylor State College in Turner, Texas, does not have a dimmer switch. When he learns Silly Sal's wife or ex-wife ... *whatever she is* ... works now at the Culberson Dental Group on the bypass, he cancels immediately all plans to find a better clinic for his toothsome needs (he's never left the Culberson Group without gum pain, often lasting several days) and instead calls, makes an appointment not just with any hygienist for his six-month checkup, but insists on *her*, Ms. Sallow, and schedules his appointment around her availability though it means canceling a meeting of his summer PRINCIPLES OF DATA ANALYTICS seminar. There is little chance he wouldn't arrange his priorities this way. Zepeda had known of Sallow, of course, long before sitting in on his hiring committee at Taylor some nineteen years earlier. Had he placed his thumb on the scale concerning that hire not out of faith in the man's teaching or research abilities, but simple faith in his being an oddity and a trust in fate? Sallow was obviously destined to land close to wherever Zepeda might find himself, as fire ants are destined to invade San Augustine lawns. Nick's glowing testimony concerning his once fellow student's appropriateness for Taylor State (all lies) did not, he supposed, serve "student success" (the most recent iteration of an ancient academic buzzword), but there *was* a managerial proposition, originating in Japan and called there *Baka* Theory, that the economist in him found irresistible. This idea held that purposefully hiring fools for one's team inevitably produced a situation of energizing catalytic synergy. Workers in whatever field who simply didn't know any better often pushed a company beyond its expectations, sometimes even by their blunders. As in: How to forge a team of problem solvers if there are no problems?

Why wouldn't it work for a department in a small college?

By these lights, in overcompensating for the mistakes of the *baka*, a collaborative, almost symbiotic magic is released, the energy resembling that called forth by the wily trickster coyote—fools at times effectively illuminating barriers and obstacles for whole societies by notably tripping over them. Stupidity and bravery likewise had an inseparable nexus, as studies had demonstrated. That cash-strapped Sallow had emerged from his RV to suddenly travel alone to an unlikely European town did not surprise Dean Zepeda at all. As they say in Osaka: *The idiot does not flinch.*

Zepeda's anonymous evisceration of the young poetic production called *Water Take Me Down and Also Burn Me* (what a title!) had been an epic and oft-recalled spark of hilarity that had lightened the otherwise dismal drudgery of his final year at Tech. (He'd never revealed his authorship. He'd be a secret assassin or a famous one, nothing in between.) He had by pure chance and loyalty to a thin blond fellow student (Courtney) found himself on a student panel judging the Texas Tech Younger Poet Series where he first saw the manuscript, realizing instantly the fatal attack he *could* write and publish in the *Daily Toreador* if only given a chance. But it would have to win the series award first. Gratefully, no one on the panel knew anything about poetry. They met Zepeda's fire hose of technical jargon in favor of *Water Take Me Down* (". . . enjambment of the sprung verse hides the subtly hidden slant rhymes *within* the anapestic meter while . . .") with open mouths and nodding heads. He assumed the faculty went along out of a misguided sense of student empowerment (a popular concept at the time albeit one that, like "student success," ebbed and flowed with the waves of academic whimsy). Maybe they never looked at the thing.

In other words, he ensured Wyatt Sallow's poetry collection won the contest because he had already developed a killer review ("... of images deposited like half-melted Easter eggs discarded by previous bunnies, while ...") and needed an excuse to publish it in the student newspaper.

He had to check out Sallow's "bride," the charmer who had, by scuttle-butt, convinced him he was owed romantic attention as part of the human experience before—by snatching that attention away—reducing the man to his present, soul-less, cash-poor status.

Colleagues thought well of Zepeda at Taylor State, yet he'd always been cut from the same troublesome cloth. When he'd first left California for college in Lubbock, he'd also left a girlfriend in the Bay Area. Someone he'd been living with but who would attend school out there, make the community college circuit. For a year or so he and Suki kept in touch, wrote each other, called at least once a week ... but came to pass the inevitable result of distance. On Valentine's Day, Zepeda *forgot* to send even a cheap card. Other matters (Courtney) had kept him busy, and he didn't think about it until he'd gotten that very nice card himself from Alameda, plus a lovely gift from Suki (a real fountain pen), at which time, though, *come on.* Too late to do anything in return. He'd look like a schmuck.

A week later he had a dream.

In this dream, his girlfriend, Suki, was seeing another guy. So what? Free country. All that. Just a dream, besides.

The next night, he had the dream again.

The next day he was on a plane to Oakland. He maxed out the credit card his parents had given him to use for, yes, flights to and from Cali, but scheduled ones, near holidays, not random dream-inspired excursions. He carried on this plane a spray of flowers bought at the Lubbock Preston Smith International Airport flower kiosk (also with his parents' Visa). Nick called Suki's roommate, Alice, to come to get him at the Oakland International so that it would all be a surprise.

It was a surprise. Suki was not happy to see him whatsoever. She stood in her apartment living room with her wet hair wrapped in a green towel and confirmed the accuracy of his dream; she had been dating someone.

Norman was his name. They had a date that very evening, and Nick should seriously just go back to Lubbock. A scene ensued. The future Dean refused to leave. He stayed in Suki's apartment with Alice when Norman came over to pick up Suki and the two of them went on with their date. "Is there some reason you didn't tell me about Norman?" he asked Suki's roommate, Alice.

"Can you think of one?"

Leaving Alice's bedroom a few hours later, the wilting airport flowers on her night table still vaseless in wrinkled tissue paper and his torso wrapped in the same green towel, he believed, that Suki had used to dry her hair (lifted from the tank of the toilet in the apartment's single bath), Nick began to rifle a pile of bills and other documents he found on the kitchen table. He located a simple blank note card with a telephone number on it. No name. He couldn't tell if it was Suki's writing or not. But it was Norman's number. Had to be. Zepeda simply knew this, though no evidence supported it. Using the apartment phone, he dialed.

A male voice explained Norman wasn't home. Out on a date. "Oh, man. Too bad. I'm a friend of his. Really wanted to see him. Only in town a little while."

Within the hour, Nick ended up at Norman's apartment, talking with his roommate Woody. Why? Because he had no dimmer switch? No. More just that he had made the decision to go and talk to Norman's roommate Woody. And Nick Zepeda has a rudder. As in, when he makes a decision, that decisive move points him off into a particular direction, whether it has to do with departmental budgetary allocations, staff hiring, curriculum alteration or the vexation of old girlfriends. When Nick Zepeda decides something, he doesn't need to—let's say—look around. Check the temperature of the room. Ask: "What does everybody else think?" whilst scanning the faces around the boardroom table for evidence of disappointment. He has steered his course. And later, fine, if at some point, some part of that decision doesn't work out, if money is lost or the state accreditation board is breathing down his neck or someone's upset or someone needs to be fired, Zepeda doesn't throw up his hands, say, "My bad! Let's go back! Change it all!" He considers the long view. Understands—in a way that comes from experiencing leadership and decision making as a *process*—that it's never quite so simple as "make the right decision and don't make the wrong one." Understands that things aren't always clear. That choices arise from a set of imperfect possibilities.

Hence the helpfulness of the rudder.

Woody, the roommate, and Norman, Suki's date, were both pre-laws. Thick casebooks stacked high on the living room table supported two empty Chinese food cartons. Nick and Woody had a few beers while a National League playoff game went in the background. "That Norman. Who's he out with this week?"

"Japanese girl."

"Between his 'other engagements,' I suppose." Nudge of elbow in upper arm of Woody. "If you know what I mean."

"Seems kinda serious."

Five innings of small talk, careful inquiry, and utilization of the occasional innuendo revealed the worst. Norman was okay. A normal kind of pre-law guy. Disappointed, but glad to have met Woody—also a pretty cool guy—Nick returned to Suki's apartment and crawled in bed with Alice.

The next morning, believe it or not, an even bigger scene ensued. Women! Nick and Suki tore into each other. Woody, who'd put it all together by then, arrived, tried to persuade Nick to leave. "Why isn't Norman here trying to convince me?" "Uhm . . . because you're crazy?" said Woody. Alice wailed they should leave Nick alone. "He has no dimmer switch!" (She didn't know about the rudder.) Woody threatened to call the police. "And tell them what?" said Nick. So then, in the way of these things, everyone calmed down. Nick left for Lubbock that evening. He should have visited his parents since he'd flown to Oakland on their dime and would have to borrow more to come back for Christmas, but he didn't feel like dealing with them.

"See how fate took a hand in all this?" he'd ask, speaking, years later, to some of his colleagues in his big corner office. "How did I know the dream was real? Yet it was. More: how did I know that was Norman's number on the card? I mean, if it's someone you're dating, someone you're interested in, do you keep their number on a blank card?"

"I can't remember any phone numbers at all anymore," said Wickham, the English prof. He raised his cellphone. "If it's not on here, forget it."

"As said," Zepeda continued. "She's at Culberson Dental Group now, where I get my teeth done. And I've got an appointment. I'll get the scoop," he said. "It's fate."

2
"Z"

Above her surgical mask, Z narrows her eyes, wrinkles her brow. She has a lot of brow to wrinkle, her hair pulled back severely to reveal a nearly Neanderthal forehead. She is also, the stories are true, very tall. Zepeda knows he'd met her before at some function—that condescending accounting department toady, Tyson, had thrown a soiree in his tiny condo—but he remembers few details. He recalled a long nose, ostrich legs, a disabled kid. A scarf, although it didn't seem the right season for a scarf (there it is). But how had Silly Sal ever rated any wife anyway? And what did Sallow expect? Zepeda recalled her mail-order status. Married him, no doubt, to enjoy the novelty of living in a house with a roof.

Z examines the prematurely grey man, her clipboard tight to her flat chest. She remembers him, too, vaguely, from some party or other, although she and her husband had not attended many, unable to leave Wyn even with trained babysitters, although at times Yuri was available. At times not. "Yes, yes I guess I am," she says to his first question. "I suppose, technically, I am Mrs. Sallow."

Nick wants to ask more. She does still sport a ring. He'd heard through the grapevine she'd kept . . . taken over Sal's house with a Ukrainian boyfriend. Kind of hard to ask about that. Zepeda prepares to dig further—maybe something like "Haven't seen you recently and was wondering . . ." but she beats him to any interrogations.

"How is Wyatt?"

"Ah." An opening to feign ignorance about their living arrangement, but he recalls then something so out of Sallow's character, he, without thinking, puts his feigning of ignorance aside. "In Britain," he says—sounding astonished at the statement himself. "At the moment."

"*Where?* Wyatt is?" Z stands, her hand resting on the tray of wrapped and sterilized picks, brushes, and water guns. "Are you sure?"

"No one . . . is sure," he admits.

She nods, fastens the man with a bib, leans him backward and raises him to begin her usual regimen, the sort that as a professional byproduct cuts small talk to a minimum.

In Odessa, homes have roofs. People have cars, work in advertising agencies, spend nice days in city parks. Trained health workers, however, such as dental hygienists, make standard government wages that equal roughly 200 dollars per month. Z had studied English since grade school with a view towards changing that, including such romance magazine phraseology as "your shirt smells so good," and "cute butt." The ubiquitous Ukrainian marriage agencies were scams—a way to make money, basically, at least according to her friends, but she sensed also in the con something that could be turned to her advantage if she were careful and if she could find a worthy candidate. She felt confident. Z had, largely owing to a drifting, goal-less adolescence, lived for a time with a cult in a collective housing arrangement, the group funding her dental training as it did most members' professional degrees and licenses. The Leader, however, stopped producing quasi-spiritual tracts of enlightenment one day when he died: choked on a chicken wing. Z had to admit she was much happier with her present religion of Buddhism although occasionally reflected on how the Buddha had also, by some reports, died while eating. Mushrooms in his case. But the Buddha—being the class Buddhistic act he had so truly been—had explained to his followers with his last words that they should "Follow the law, and not the man," before passing into *nirvana*.

The Leader's last words, by all reports had been "Shred the documents."

And so, the collective disbanded but not before its members had collectively accumulated and assimilated several useful techniques for boosting group membership using the promise of genital satisfaction. These approaches worked well especially in bars and airports but best of all in airport bars. Z felt only a slight modification of the methods, customized for what "marriage-minded" Westerners expected, would probably do it. In fact, Wyatt's experiences with Dnipro Girl, as he explained to her later, convinced her she'd been correct.

He admitted to her on their first "date"—lunch at a cafeteria—how addictive it had been to look over the women on the DG website. Sallow soon had a list of twenty that he was willing to actually meet during his gamble of an investment: a one-week stay in Kyiv. As contacting the girls cost money for every email, he wisely limited his electronic communication and requested actual meetings, face-to-face, upon arrival—an approach that really messed with the Dnipro Girl business model as it relied so heavily on clientele who never got so far as actual meetings. "Few girls agreed to this," he told her as he sampled a beef and cabbage pierogi. There were also cherries and bowls of cottage cheese. Wyatt Sallow admired everything about the cafeteria, from the cheese *paska* to the battered chicken to the framed black-and-white photographs of cathedrals, and most especially the reasonable prices. "You're the first who's brought me anywhere that has reasonable prices," he said.

In fact, Z turned out to be the second and last woman he met face-to-face in Kyiv. She realized he did not fit the American norm, since most who used the websites never even made it across the ocean at all, just used the internet to receive the attention of more women than had ever expressed interest in them in their lifetimes. "All the women have kittens," Wyatt explained incredulously as he described the emails he'd exchanged. "*All* of them love to knit."

"I'm a dental hygienist. I'm allergic to cats."

"All desire to walk on beaches and cuddle at home on cold evenings."

"I desire to use my training and be paid for it."

Wyatt enjoyed finding someone in Kyiv to talk to, even if the talk consisted mainly of disparaging Ukrainian women. "Two . . . *two* separately explained to me how God divided every human soul in half, scattering the bifurcated parts across the wide earth, and that only by searching on another continent could a true soul mate be found."

Z blinked. "I desire to use my training. Productively."

Like all the men she'd actually met through Dnipro Girl, she had studied his profile closely and tailored her no-nonsense approach individually to Wyatt. Her time acquiring new converts to the cult had taught Z the importance of personalized connection. Also, the importance of oral sex, but this and personal connection were two sides of the same *kopiyka*, no? Z noted, for example, that Wyatt mentioned in an email exchange that he had an RV. Her only mental picture of these consisted of the sleek aluminum Airstream (not like Professor Sallow's block-shaped fifth wheel at all), so when she found a t-shirt celebrating the famous American icon at a flea market, she snatched it up. She understood that any man who actually arrived at the offices of Dnipro Girl seeking a flesh and blood partner had undoubtedly reached the end of his mating rope and so had chosen to undertake what she later—after many seasons of enjoying the violent *burya* of American football—came to recognize as the "Hail Mary": matchmaking reduced to a last gasp prayer act. Last gasp acts of prayer had been a cult specialty as well, so: the unicorn plush toy. For these losers, finding a wife of any kind would approach the likelihood of discovering a living example of the horned equine at a livestock auction.

Dnipro Girl officed close to Independence Square, and when examined through the trick one-way mirror, Z found Wyatt . . . well, no *worse* than his pictures, a change from the other men she'd encountered through the agency. He did seem kind, relatively educated, and astonished to discover she showed up. As they walked to a cafeteria, a little girl on the street came up to him, pressed her ice cream cone directly onto his jacket, laughed, and ran away. Against the grain of American outrage she'd come to expect from these established, narrow men, he laughed, too. Perhaps he favored cheap and ugly clothing for practical reasons. "Scamps," said Z and withdrew tissues from her purse, got on one knee though she was wearing one of her best skirts (black with polka dots), and proceeded to wipe him off. The Texan chuckled. "Good word," he said. "Scamps."

As they chatted over lunch his surprise at seeing her began to make more sense. He'd arrived at Boryspil, been met at the airport by the agency van driven by two bearded men, and informed that, unfortunately, the apartment he'd rented for the week had been closed due to a gas leak, so he'd be placed in other accommodations that happened to cost twice as much. Wyatt, hampered with language difficulties, could devise little response beyond agreement, and so arrived at his roach-infested lodgings, dropped off after also being informed that the trip in the van cost 1,600 hryvnia, around sixty dollars. (Z knew that a taxi to the city center worked out to around seven dollars.) Over the course of the next few days, he received messages that girl after girl he'd made appointments with had canceled, all due to unavoidable but not highly detailed family illness circumstances. Glum, he'd watched the people in the streets out his apartment window, certain he'd been robbed and tempted to take to the city himself, to at least see part of it. It appeared as classically apportioned as drawings might be in a coloring book of Paris, albeit with none of the colors filled in. Called finally to the DP offices (never meeting "Anastasia," the lady who ran it and whose picture was featured on the web), he sat by this point in a bare conference room in nervous trepidation while two young men with beards—different from the two who'd picked him up at the airport—served him a canned cola and a bag of chips. He waited ninety minutes for the appearance of "Victoria." Unfortunately, "Victoria" sent word that she could not make it for an unavoidable reason having to do with the illness of a sister. There would be three, *three* (holding up the fingers) meetings on the following day, however, so they took him back to his apartment in the van for a mere thirty dollars. On that following day, "Natalia," "Ulyana," and "Natasha" also failed to show, and so this poor Sallow character began to wonder if the framed mirror at the rear of the conference room had a one-way reflective surface and if the ladies had arrived, taken one secret look at the back of his head (the bald spot obviously a point of personal shame by the way his hand often moved to it as he spoke), and decided to pass.

On the third day, however, he met Khrystyna, a brunette with an infectious smile and horn-rimmed glasses whose English was much more rudimentary than indicated by the two emails she'd sent. The jpeg picture she'd attached was also different enough from the in-person Khrystyna that Wyatt suspected it to be from a decade before, a Photoshop alteration, or possibly just a picture of a different, more beautiful woman. The eighty-dollar taxi ride to a French restaurant near the Park Imeni Bohomol'tsya set him back a few hundred dollars total after drinks and a meal but, by this point, he figured Khrystyna would be his only expense, possibly his only chance for an actual relationship from the expensive trip, and so shoveled good *hryvnia* after bad, tried to find aspects of the lady that attracted him, yet longed to return to Texas as soon as possible and take up lonely bachelorhood again. On the return taxi ride—same driver as luck would have it—Khrystyna took a phone call on her cell, chatting in Ukrainian for twenty minutes, but this turned out not to be rude as she explained that it had been her mother who was on the verge of having an operation to save her life and no doubt the entire family would have to sell all of their possessions—*all* of them—to cover the expenses.

"I knew I was being scammed then because health care here is free."

"It is free," Z explained and put her soft hand over his chapped knuckles. "Except for expenses like medicine, doctor visits and hospital stays. But yes. And the taxi driver was probably her brother."

"Scamps," said Wyatt Sallow.

If memory is the paradise from which none are exiled, Wyatt's recollections of the afternoon at the Aroma Kava cafeteria is still one of his most cherished, especially his sensing with a kind of wonder through the passing minutes that, surprise, in his life, for once, something good had happened to him.

This, by the way, in spite of all that happened later.

They traveled the next day to the heavily populated left bank of the river visiting parks, bookstores, and then—upon returning to Independence Square—the largest McDonald's Wyatt had ever seen in his life. Z had arranged quirky excursions for the afternoon, including an open-air architectural museum that featured folk crafts, and she watched him stand, hypnotized, by the descent of the blacksmith's hammer as the man created a horseshoe from blank metal. Z wore the same black dress with white polka dots on this second day. She explained that she'd like him to meet her parents but as they lived in Odessa that wouldn't be possible on this trip. In reality, her father had passed away in a mental health facility, and she hadn't spoken to her mother or sister for years, they'd been so angry about her joining the cult and still refused to see her. "I feel like I should check into this apartment they've stuck you in," she said and so, in that way, on his last night in Ukraine, he and Z made love, awkwardly, on the plyboard-hard mattress as roaches scuttled the baseboards, Z feeling nonplussed that it went in such an unwieldy manner when, after all, she'd been in a sex cult for Christ's sake, always considering herself adaptable to any occasion. It just had to be done.

Wyatt returned to Texas. After a handful of weeks, much tender exchange of texts, emails (one of these from her insisting, in spite of the awkwardness, "You make love to me like we are meant to be."), both the emails and texts featuring long strings of emojis (especially on Z's part who got on board the emoji train early—she thought they were cute) and the news that she was pregnant, Wyatt made arrangements to accelerate her emigration to Texas, filed for the Fiancé Visa and had successfully moved her into the Linden Lane house by the start of the Spring Semester, 2004. Z's boyfriend, Yuri—one of a pair of twin sons of the now chicken-choked cult leader—arrived in the U.S. on a separate flight one week later. Yuri ended up remaining in Houston, as it turned out, far longer than planned, overstaying his travel visa owing to complications, mainly those brought about by Z's first glimpse of her son asleep behind thick plexiglass panes in an isolation chamber at the Houston Medical Center, a long silver needle inserted into the flesh of his skull. Then had come the confounding stress of doctors explaining new-born open-heart surgery, and her flabbergasted reaction that the operation was actually covered by her new husband's insurance. (When handed a paper suit, scrunchie shoe coverings, and mask to approach Wyn's incuba-tor for the first time, she asked, "How much?") Explanations of "the disease Jerry Lewis collects money for" soon followed, as well as lessons over the operation of a feeding tube. When Wyn came home, Z explained to Wyatt their good fortune. Her cousin who'd visited in December and accompa-nied them to Aspen had immigrated to the United States and could help out from time to time, something that brought the professor no joy (an aura of untrustworthiness about the fellow—that mustache) but family was family. Time passed. Wyn's vocabulary increased from subtle grunts to more pro-nounced statements like "uh-oh," and even a pure Texas "yippee."

Expensive treatments continued. Z found she needed to postpone her original intention—a plan she'd only partially ever considered in the first place but now understood as something only to be held in reserve—which had been to build a life independent of the strange business ethics teacher. This approach she'd researched carefully years before in her Odessa apart-ment. Foreign brides in America, sources insisted, could easily claim green card status in the lackadaisical country—possessing as it did a gigantic bureaucracy, absorbing immigrants the way leafy plants absorbed carbon—and they could do this by claiming they had been assaulted by their hus-bands. Something called "VAWA" or "Violence Against Women Act" came into effect for such cases, a good idea if Z ever heard one. This appeared foolproof and did not depend on said husband having ever lifted a finger in anger, only on a signed affidavit of complaint and a lot of crying. Z felt all of this fell within her abilities. As Wyn's expenses increased, however, months, then years passed. The milquetoast yet infinitely responsible Wyatt had gone ahead, hired an attorney, obtained a green card for her anyway and, one and a half years after that, full citizenship in a ceremony taking place in a high school basketball court in the suburbs of Houston where she discovered and chatted with *ten* other Ukrainian women, three of whom were familiar with "VAWA" but, shrugging, had decided against invoking it. Though not exactly enamored of the strange academic, she developed more and more enthusiasm for the minuscule hospital copayments that came with his employment, and there was nothing stopping a citizen from simply divorcing when the time was right. Then Yuri could be first sent out then brought back into the country (his joke of an original 90-day visa having long expired) using the same Fiancé paperwork she herself had entered with.

But the time was never right. Years passed.

As he got older, the severe weakness of Wyn's muscles extended to those that helped him circulate his blood, that helped him breathe and swallow, and eight years later, Yuri still cooling his heels in the city, smoking too much, gaining weight, her husband the professor having just departed to give a quiz review in one of his classes, Z walked into Wyn's bedroom to find him barely moving in his bottom bunk. ("Of course we will get him bunk beds," she explained to Wyatt. "It's primal. The need to climb.") She stood over him only a moment before convincing herself that a coldness creeping over her meant something was wrong, wrong, wrong (his cake in the fridge, white frosting, almost his day, almost his day) and an ambulance was called.

After the funeral, the ambulance, she learned, they had to pay for. Fourteen hundred dollars. What a country.

Having re-established her hygienist credentials and finding employ at Culberson, Z is uncertain these days whether she wants Yuri around at all anymore. With her career, a new nationality, the fulfillment of all she'd dreamed of when scouring her computer in those cramped Odessa days, the focusing mindfulness of the chanting she does every morning and every evening before her mandala, Z is surprised to find herself daily becoming more and more quietly miserable.

She scrapes, grinds away with a small drill, injects water at high speed, ends with floss and a fluoride rinse. Spit. Dean Zepeda needs a periodontist, Z decides, after probing with a measuring device, and recommends one in Houston "as around here they are not so professional." Nick hinges his mouth open and closed, squeezes his chin, massaging the lower jaw on the right side. He tends to doubt it's that serious. When she hands over his chart she asks, "He's really in Britain?"

"You didn't know?"

Typical of Wyatt to tell his friends nothing about their separation. He is so maddeningly silent. She's been thinking about contacting him. They are still married. Yuri had fallen into a pattern of beer drinking and wasting his time on low-paying, cash-only jobs, mainly freelancing in the audio-visual industry (a vital area of training and expertise, after all, for most cults). This is a male template Z recognizes from her years with the Leader and, frankly, from her neighborhood growing up. She does not want to deal with Professor Sallow—impossible—but has juggled in her mind her uncertainties over whether Wyatt might help her out if asked. She'd applied to dental school. Z understands his guilt over things he'd said to her but has a hard time believing his pliancy will last forever. What kind of a person does such things? Maybe just one more time? Wyatt undertaking transatlantic travel demonstrates something new with the strange, strange man, including the fact that he could, despite everything, now possess more disposable income. Or possibly it's simpler. He may just be changing.

Reliable. Yet Z had no illusions. Illusions, in fact, would have been very strange to have at this point. He'd worked hard, yet arguably those duties were a convenience when it came to distancing himself from more direct responsibilities Wyn represented. "Represented" was it—the issue. Wyatt Sallow tended to treat the boy as a kind of concept. Not flesh. Not spittle, shit, vomit, tears.

If he could help her with dental school, he should.

"I didn't know," she admits. "But if you see him, tell him hello."

In the parking lot of Culberson's, Nick slides onto his broiling hot car seat. Really needs a different color interior for his next vehicle. This black leather. And what on earth is up with Sal and that gal? Nick can't say, especially at the end when she peels off the surgical mask. Ms. Sallow is not so unattractive as he recalled.

His gums ache.

Her attitude takes him back. Good God. So many bizarre hidden flavors of intimacy existed side by side in life's melting chocolate box. Even in his own life. A year after his precipitous journey to their respective apartments, Suki and Norman had gotten married! You could have knocked Nick down. More years passed. Nick met Dorothy, stumbled across her—literally—trying to find a bathroom at a party in Austin in 2001. There'd been three girls asleep on the floor in the apartment of his friend Glen's living room, "But I chose to trip over you," he often tells her. "Could have been Jen. Could have been Cassie." Suki, securing a quasi-governmental job with the United States Postal Service, traveled the country often, conducted cross-training at distribution facilities. One day Nick received an email: she'd be having sessions for a week in the town where he now lived and taught economics to undergrads, Turner, Texas. She'd be at the Marriot.

There were a few mix-ups. She never mentioned her new last name, so he couldn't ask for her at the front desk. One afternoon spent hanging out in the lobby and—then, there she was, stepping in sandals across the faux Egyptian rug by the natural rock fireplace next to the coffee kiosk. "Out of all the gin joints in all the world," she said, walking up to where he attempted to email her on his phone.

They saw each other every day that week. Lunch. Drinks. Several times she invited him to her room, but he declined. On the last day, her plane departing early the next morning in Houston, they came very, very close, but he pulled back.

On or off. Yes or no. For Wyatt's boss, there could be nothing in the middle, probably a godsend for everyone in the department.

3
The Toy Balloon

He pulls against the resisting control yoke, its steering-wheel shaped like cat's eye glasses, adjusts a ribbed lever at his right hand that fine tunes what he vaguely understands to be the "trim" and does ascend, then, climbs gently though the weather threatens. He wants no jostling, certainly not until they've cleared those peaks ahead. God. Wyatt must thread space between jagged rocks and a shelf of overhanging clouds (stirring, he pumps his legs in the tangled sheets as the curtains begin to glow) but the raccoon is safe.

He yawns. Opens his eyes. Wyatt understands at times it's best to allow the tension to remain, make moves that improve the position, maybe, but put off forcing an issue. Allow the weight of the pawn, as it were, the one staring down that other pawn on that central square . . . allow that *lever* to rest in the hand, rather than releasing the coiled force prematurely. "What should I do?" he wonders. Maybe just stay here in the fetal position. Sunlight washes from the sitting room where he'd left the curtains open to Edgeland Avenue. The best knew *when* to do something, and, conversely, when to hang back. The beauty of this principle, transferred to life, is its justification for any inaction.

A breeze lifts the curtains over the writing desk. Tires whoosh the street. His dream had involved . . . yes, it had been a raccoon rescue mission.

Plucked from an isolated mountain pass where it faced certain frozen death, or . . . snatched from the many venomous flashing fangs of a tropical viper pit, the raccoon was lifted, taken, gone . . . flown away is the point, transported from danger and towards security, food, warmth, medical attention. Wyatt would fly him to a place where he could be toweled off, comforted, the plastic nozzle for his nasogastric intubation tube cleared and serviced, perhaps attended to in a holistic way—the *whole raccoon*—by a panel of experts from Houston. From somewhere, someone thanks him. "Thank you. Thank you," he hears. He can't rest. Typical of the logic of *the mission*, rather than strapped in a seat behind Wyatt, let's say, seatbelted and secure (there at 11 o'clock: a lightning storm approaches), the nocturnal mammal, clinging outside the plane, rides a landing gear. Well, shit. Why does he have to ride a landing gear? His limpid legs and tail flap behind him in the prop wash. (Wyatt throttles back, attempts to reduce speed yet still provide lift. But did racoons even have tails? The mountains!) The creature's grip is white-knuckled around hydraulic joints and tubes of that damned landing gear. Wyatt gingerly touches the wheel in front of him, uses his feet to manipulate other . . . controls . . . glances quickly to his left, afraid to look. There, under the wing, the little guy hangs on, the slow turning rubber tire not at all helpful against its rump as it fights to remain attached, avoid falling into the tops of trees thousands of feet below.

"Of course they have tails," he says, rubbing his face. What would Davy Crockett have been without those tails?

Wyatt remains in bed. Yes. Definitely, it's possible to see inaction as strategic biding of time. He had witnessed mornings, afternoons, entire weeks in recent summers when he wasn't teaching, fly past completely without accomplishment, all by virtue of this approach. Utilizing it this morning makes sense. He remains with his legs drawn upward, attempts to decide what he's experiencing: a time-biding reserve of auxiliary power or a simple, curled-into-himself *grand mal* episode of procrastination, not helped by the vivid agoraphobic memory of the terrified animal in his dream.

An additional thought that does not help: supine poses when one has spent a third of one's savings to travel 4,700 miles for a specific purpose seem *so* egregious. He really should get up. It's taken him so much to get here. On the other hand . . . hello? Pacing? It matters. Saving and banking energy for when it will be required has advantages.

It strikes him how major questions in his life are often simple, certainly compared with major questions presented in *Business Ethics: Meaningful Subtitle.* This day does not involve nondisclosure agreements, shop floor safety, whistleblowing or even unfair pizza restaurant crew scheduling. It does not involve philosophy. It boils down to a single inquiry. One.

"What should I do?"

He recalls that the "large breakfast" is, true to the proprietress's word, "tasty."

An overall nagging thought plagues him as he goes down to eat: that this trip and everything he's learned from it could have been accomplished in a day. Perhaps a morning. The town should have been *on* his itinerary, not comprising his entire agenda. He would have little to show for his money and effort and would have to talk up—*inflate*—each aspect when he got home, else remain silent on the trip. He replays in his mind the places he's been across town, much as he used to attempt to improve his game by examining exclusively his blunders, replaying contests through the Otter-Shark analysis computer.

What had been learned that wasn't encapsulated in the story Hussein retold from *Taming of the Shrew*?—only its reverse? He'd arrived expecting himself to be—at least here, this one place—a kind of prince.

With effort, he makes himself presentable after a heroic run at finishing the "full breakfast," takes up his backpack with its cargo of chapbooks, and—vowing to find a place that sells bar soap at some point in the day—begins the walk down the hill towards the university, its massive red-brick dormitory building that can't be missed from the elevated Edgeland neighborhood. He plans to once again drop by the department, peer through its glass door, discover no one there, then retire downstairs. A possible drawback: he could stumble across the black-clad "Gail," which would mean a big explanation, or, worse—her silent passing of him in a hallway. A lapse on her part? A vicious snub? Walking to the university he finds himself on the lookout for two brunettes: one to hail, hold, perhaps throw himself at the feet of. One to avoid.

He needn't bother. One at that moment just drops off to sleep in her king-sized bed in the Deuce Hotel, New Orleans (every bit as trendy yet half the price of the nearby Ritz-Carlton), her bags stacked, including the carry-all stuffed with snacks and bourbon from a corner liquor store, next to the untouched mini-bar, ready for morning departure to the Hamptons; the other adds "loo rolls" to the end of her shopping list, preparing for imminent departure to Tesco.

Wyatt leaves the elevator on the fourth floor of the student center about an hour after lifting himself from bed, still stiff from his tumble down the hill. His mind is blank. If he can't find this professor, Combs, he could seek out the Literature Department to inquire when the man might be in, hopefully finding that empty as well. Uncertainty fills him over what to do with the rest of the day. Still, he looks forward to facing that emptiness, leaving the campus as soon as possible. He rounds the column of blank air, looks four floors down into the computer-loaded atrium, glances through the plate glass office door of the Creative Writing Department he'd glanced through on his previous visit. A man sits behind the single desk, typing. Wyatt pauses. His instinct is to turn around. A nearby loveseat looks comfortable, placed there, he has to assume, for student use as it's so near a wall plug. Students need wall sockets these days, can't do without them. He can, himself, charge his phone there. The man looks busy. He might be writing. He might be toiling away at his own creative works, taking these moments he can set aside from his teaching and administrative duties to do so, and to disturb someone like that . . . while not technically criminal, Wyatt knows enough of the kind of trance that's entered when swimming in the pool of language to understand an interruption won't be appreciated. It makes sense to, first, return to the hotel room. Research this man. The name on the frosted glass he sees again is Dr. Alfred Combs. He could search for Combs's CV online. In fact, it would make the most sense to send an email first. He still has a couple of days in town. He can set up an actual meeting with a meeting time, and in that way present himself as less of a burden for the no doubt harried professor. Wyatt composes the email in his head, although there are difficulties. Everything he can think of by way of introduction sounds amateurish. No, dropping in, face-to-face, has advantages. Pull that chrome door handle, walk in. But his chapbook could serve more as distraction than credential, with its cover photograph of the Appalachian waterfall. Why the Texas Tech production team had decided on this image Wyatt always assumed could be traced to an inexperienced intern who looked at the title, felt incorporating "Water" that was in some way "moving down" would work fine, and had thrown the thing together. The obvious problem would be his last name on the cover, with Combs then understanding why he's here, in this town. Instantly seeing the foolishness of it, Wyatt makes out his own, large face superimposed over the typing man's form in the glass office door. Combs looks harried, probably gets his meetings set by appointment. That in itself might make for another argument in favor of a sudden appearance. Grinding his teeth, throwing back his shoulders, he tugs on the door handle, which does not move.

Something in this obstacle recalls the raccoon on the landing gear, the slowly spinning tire. Once, standing by the Xerox machine on the second floor of Krall Hall in his department, trying desperately to feed it his ID number to make copies of a class handout and properly charge those copies against his personal account, a colleague's son, home for the summer, had come into the workroom holding two thin wooden sticks like those used to make kites. The boy proceeded to hit Wyatt across the arm with them. They stung! He snatched the sticks. What to do? It had been unprovoked! But…yell at his colleague's son? Who he didn't know? Where was his standing to do anything other than take the beating? Though it might be better for the kid in the long run if Sallow were to stroke the sticks across his bottom.

"Don't," he'd said, then handed them back.

"Don't!" The boy brought the stinging sticks against Wyatt's arm again, hard, then ran for the hallway door.

Why think of that boy?

The metal door handle withdraws from his hand like a lost toy balloon at the circus.

"Yes?" Dr. Alfred Combs says. He must have noticed Wyatt's hulking form in the corridor. He's come to the door.

4
"And the chess coach."

Wyatt hates it that he doesn't even know the man's genre. That could have been looked up easily. It could have been done on his phone from the fetal position at the Edgeland Arms if he'd had any sense, and he mentally pounds himself on the forehead. "Wyatt Sallow," he stammers and unslings his backpack. "MBA . . . Texas . . . chapbook . . . conference in the city so I thought . . . pop over and . . ." He hopes it adds up to a reason to be standing in Dr. Combs's doorway. Wyatt names his college.

"We're in finals." Combs looks around the atrium. He accepts *Water Take Me Down and Burn Me* in his stubby fingers when it's offered. Thumbs through it and nods.

"It's not an important conference," Wyatt says. "For small colleges."

"What's the name of it?"

There simply isn't one. "Small College Conference."

The man smiles.

"International."

Combs fans open the chapbook, aims the Appalachian waterfall at Wyatt and points out his name. "Searching for roots or something."

"I admit . . . It hasn't panned out."

Combs laughs now. "Sure. Based on present-day orthography. Nothing to do with the way the language has . . . well, I'm sure you know."

"I do. I do, yes." He nods quickly. "Family stories."

"We're in finals. But listen, I'll take this. Thank, you."

"Never mind." He tries to retrieve the chapbook, but it's snatched back.

"If I get a chance, I'll let you know what I think, uhm . . . Sallow."

"Nobody likes them much. The poems." He looks at the floor.

"'In Sallowsfield!' An American. Who's never been here." The man shakes his head. "What college did you say?"

Wyatt tells him again.

He holds up *Water Take Me Down.* "Do you teach your own work in your class?"

Wyatt sees no reason to lie. "I'm in the Applied Business Department. I teach ethics."

"Ethics! In business!"

Wyatt nods.

"In America! I do love it." Combs grins. "I hate people who assign their own poems in their classes."

"Right?" Wyatt understands he's about to be dismissed. "Alright then."

Dr. Combs appears ready to retire back into his office.

Before departing, Wyatt, off-handedly, throws in one other duty he performs at the college.

"What's that?"

"Or as some would put it, team faculty advisor."

5
Melissa

When the character—Combs checks the author's name again on the stapled book—Somebody Sallow, leaves, it takes a few moments for him to realize where he'd seen the man before. He's only partially correct as he does not place him as the figure reading the menu in the doorway of The Angle four days previously but does note the resemblance to his father and that he'd recently seen someone else with that resemblance. Where had that been?

Hell, the man looks like he *could* be descended from the population around here. Who knows the vagaries of DNA through the ages? Combs is sure, at least, he'd no expectation of encountering a chess coach from Texas by coming to the office on a Saturday morning.

He knows he'll despise the poems in the book as he despises everything handed to him by those who walk up and, often in embarrassment like this man, hand over their work. Combs doesn't take this occupational hazard personally. A glance at the doggerel-like sing-song of "bass the shallows yield," which the man has through some abomination rhymed— *rhymed* mind you!—with the name of Combs's own native town ensures that, sure enough, it's not good. Bad stuff. The very first poem in the chapbook is titled "... To Sallowsfield!" Exclamation mark and everything. His own institution of employment is, true, a middling one as such go, but one where Combs has attempted over the years he's been there to raise the stature and awareness of the Writing Department (while circulating his CV in hopes of garnering attention from a larger school). That Sallow hadn't been a writing prof, even at the minuscule college he mentioned, was too bad, as Combs sought constantly details of the American model when it came to his discipline. If they hadn't invented writing degrees, they had certainly best succeeded in industrializing them, plus managed somehow to turn the word "workshop" into a verb. Still, he sees this figure from Texas as an opportunity. After all, a poet—even a poor one—is not someone who knows something, but who is something.

Combs opens the chapbook, inserts his nose along the stapled spine, breaths in the aroma of the pages. A personal quirk he applies to any new work of literature. He shrugs, flips it onto a desk littered with poetry volumes, end of term papers, folders, the occasional paper cup from the execrable tea machine in the dining hall, and, in one corner, a chess set, parked presently in the middle game of a Kasparov vs. Karpov encounter from the 1980s. Combs loves this gifting of games from the past: *delivered* reborn at the board via the algebraic system. Strategy and tactics, yes, but more importantly, the movements of minds can be recreated, analyzed, with luck understood. Was any recorded grandmaster game, then, much different from a poem—also subject to similar analysis by generations of readers? Perhaps the notational representations of these contests were a cleaner form of poetry, a distillation of pure mind as opposed to classical verse with its cargo of imagery, metaphor, allusion. Messy. (Combs does not think his colleagues would abide by this interpretation.) Still, if he *had* been—Sallow, that is—a writing professor, their meeting would no doubt have been briefer and Combs's interest more subdued. As it was, he had set them up the next morning at Havril Park, a backdrop sure to thrill a colonial. (And throw him off his game? We'll see. We'll see.) That aside, as he sinks into his chair, Alfred once again considers . . . not so much his father, but Melissa. How when she had picked him up after the viola lesson, women being from Mars, men from Venus or wherever . . . how it had been nothing new aside from the general unexpectedness of such an encounter. A thing which might not happen, but *could* happen on any given day, not only the day of his father's death. Was it because of his dad's illness the night before? Was it because of the brain in the jar? He'd *expected*, almost, terrible news.

After telling him, Melissa did not turn down his street, but continued straight, driving far past his neighborhood, in a direction away from home. Alfred, suddenly no mere boy but rather, as he'd put it in an early poem, "a dead father's son," sensed change in the atmosphere on the outskirts of town; a difference in the hue of the shadow cast by Tower Hill. Events, he perceived (not for the first time) could unravel completely, and relatively simple acts could make this so. Pulling at a particular thread. Lifting a certain blouse. A word could do it. Words he now knew better how to utter. "Please," for example. That word coming from him at that moment could ignite the air like fireworks.

Past the blocky corrugated Kimbrough Plumbing building, past broad flats of moving grass, they drove through the as yet undeveloped suburban edge of town, Melissa saying nothing, looking ahead with her head cocked, steering with a wrist on the wheel, her long off-red fingernails (Combs, in the later poem, called them "gingernails") tapping the gear stick. When there were no more houses, there was no more road, but Melissa aimed carefully at a kerb-less gap and nudged the Cortina off the tarmac between two trees. She worked the car into this break with one eye closed, the way TV cowboys sighted rifles. It had not occurred to Alfred, thinking it over later, that a car could be driven off a road. Somewhere behind them stood the corner shop run by the first Chinese person he'd ever met in his life—a man who sold him a chicken heart and then a cow heart from the tiny meat counter: organs Combs dissected with the aid of a book, scalpel, and tweezers. The book—really a pamphlet that came with the scalpel and tweezers—unlocked the complex secret interiors of frogs, earthworms, grasshoppers. It managed to do so though it was much thinner than even—here he plucks it from his desk—*Water Take Me Down and Burn Me* ... for Christ's sake.

The tree-line offered privacy but not enough as Melissa continued edging forward into a vacant lot of high grass and reeds beside the curved drainage tributary of a canal. One day they'd break ground for a huge retail center, but in 1977 it stood empty, high grassed, and the tires of the Cortina went over dry earth ruts and popped them like a field of light bulbs. Wax paper bread bags and empty lager cans and beer bottles hung in the dense weeds that came nearly to the door latches. She swung the car behind yet another line of reeds that rose like a narrow fence. Albert had the feeling she'd brought the car here before. He felt at first that she sought someplace to get out so that the two of them could wander in the grass, their hands in their pockets, investigate the sky, contemplate. But she turned off the engine. He heard himself ask for what he wanted, heard himself say "please," and Melissa wriggled from her denim vest, lifted her t-shirt, showed herself as someone might expose a tattoo for examination, or hold up an interesting bruise. He buried his face in her, cried into her, explored her as he would some creature related to humans but otherwise so alien that to touch its back was a discovery.

He'd harbored childhood theories of thinking about it before he knew. Combs had later written poems about this. (Of course. Of course.) These ways were often weightless, acrobatic, and foolish. Togetherness was immediate, unmistakable, and, no doubt, confined to one or at most a very small group of persons one could "fall in love" with. No maddening smell or acrid taste appeared in ignorant dream love. Reality proved that some areas were difficult to reach, especially in the front seats of a compact car with a gear stick right there. And then: drawing some body parts closer meant distancing others. Weight on forearm. Neck strain. A girl without a shirt, without knickers, *still weighed something* when she climbed on top of you, lad. Odd nobody mentioned. Whipping around so violently it seemed she might snap off at the neck brought not only ecstasy but a kind of detached concern. These days, his own wife had evolved into a nearly untouchable being. Though a beautiful woman he had grown disgusted with her, seen photographs of women buried centuries in peat bogs more fuckable to his eye. But that time with Melissa (who afterwards, said, not convincingly, "So good.") remained always, in his mind, the kind of experience a newly dead father's boy ought to have and in the place he ought to have it. Not ideal. Not reproducible.

Imperfection did not take long, as they arrived, within the hour, at his house. An ambulance stood on the kerb, his mother at the porch, smoking and grim. She shielded her eyes from a naked afternoon sun. He thought of Melissa with a protective tenderness when he followed her to the house, not least because she'd put on the Anarchy t-shirt inside out, the tag showing. Part of him worried at the future, part of him was concerned that his mother would see the tag, and they'd be in trouble.

None of that happened.

Melissa, he understands, married a man from Keighley, had a child, went to work in a nursing home, lost custody of that child to that man. One day, with access to the facility's medicine cabinet, she swallowed a bottle of something and that was the end of Melissa, and He'd. Written. A. Poem. About. That. Too.

6
Certain Dark Things

Inspirational messages Z sent to Wyatt in the weeks before she arrived in Texas:

An email already waiting for him when his plane touched down in Houston: "You're so good with so many things, such a variety, including but not limited to the things you do when we're both naked and alone."

A text the next day: "Hi, handsome."

After a few weeks of being apart: "Look at how many books I've read that you mentioned when you were here. I don't think I was trying to impress you. I think it was my way of getting close to you in whatever capacity. I never thought I'd get this lucky."

Firing up his desktop computer at work before class one Thursday. "I crave your body, your cock, your arms, tongue, your cute butt. Baby you are the one. I'm crazy about you. I either hate to tell you or thrill to tell you I am pregnant."

And, a day before he met her at Houston Intercontinental:

"You and me. I like the sound of us. You make my heart happy."

7
"Or some kind of park, anyway."

Wyatt doesn't have to spend the rest of the day at loose ends, nor does he have time, that afternoon, to lie in the fetal position. He forgets about trying to find soap: first things first. He does climb into the newly made bed in his second-floor room, the counterpane's corners stiff and well folded. He places his notebook on his lap, its spine bent backward, cracked to keep its face open at two blank pages. He has only a few moments to give over to regret for his actions. How bad could it be? It won't matter how it turns out, just that he makes an accounting of himself. It's to be a friendly game in some sunny park, but it's also momentous and dizzying. Wyatt has, after nearly five years, agreed to play a person, and he feels he's going off the high board again.

He withdraws his pen from his pocket in case it's needed. He doesn't want to be taken up short. Removing his phone from his jacket, he activates the downloaded app version of the software called OtterShark.

1
Rashmika

Of course, he doesn't have to show up.

Business Ethics: Meaningful Subtitle has no problem defining a virtuous act: *doing the right thing for the right reason.* Straightforward enough and to the point, but unfortunately the "course print companion" then throws in *habitually, and on purpose*, which creates a nuance Wyatt has to interrogate when it comes to the present circumstance. He's not sure he's going to appear for this game with Professor Combs in a way that comports with either of those predicates. He has already aligned potential excuses that could get him off the hook. For example, Wyatt—if he thinks about it hard enough—does sense the beginnings of a sinus headache behind and slightly towards the right side of his left eye. Minor physical ailments exaggerated, then used to beg off of agreed engagements, have *habitually* served him far more often than the mere path of virtue.

Finally, could one deny that the most logical conclusion to draw from Petrosian's "present no target" strategy would be "play no game"? Nothing bad could come from not being there. He'd backed into it, against reason and good sense, having had as his goal the gifting of a single book, and this with no expectation of anything in return. A game with a person was the last thing he could have imagined when exiting the fourth-floor elevator at the Lowery Annex. And yet, exhausted and bleary-eyed, he'd called Hussein early that chilly morning to pick him up and take him to the place called Havril Park.

Rather than virtue, right or wrong, Wyatt considers his appearance at this place has more to do with contracts: the promise-making impulse of humanity (a much bigger section of the textbook), along with its some-times-overemphasized moral stance against promise-*breaking*. Boundaries are invoked in a contract along with thresholds, invisible gatekeeping functions (as Hussein slows the cab, Wyatt sees the park has a single entrance under an arched brick walkway), these constituting the glue tacitly or explicitly securing the cohesion of society. Besides it isn't some construction bid, purchase agreement, prenuptial, or reassurance of "Yeah, you can pick it up tomorrow," but a promise that concerns the game. It seems more inviolable.

Still, he doesn't want to play.

He wondered if Combs were that rare breed: the player coach. Obviously, the man had a full-time literary and teaching career. Dvoretsky, upon taking up the mantle of training a generation of grandmasters, quit playing even friendly, casual games. Wasn't that for the best? A prerequisite, almost, for the necessary clearing of the mind required when advising others in this most difficult of endeavors?

At any rate, he doesn't arrive for the contest fit or rested. Wyatt had spent a disturbed night, unable to sleep, considering at every toss in his stiff Edgeland Arms sheets that he should go ahead, get up, play out some more opening possibilities, review tactical patterns or puzzles on OtterShark, reassure himself he could recall the Tarrasch variation of the French should Combs draw white and work into that position. Or: if Combs drew white but played the Queen's pawn opening, there was the Slav to deal with, its tactical variants. But continuing his last-minute studies would only have prolonged the beginning of sleep while shortening its overall duration. As a coach he understood rest as the best palliative to ensure un-lapsed concentration: an understanding that made him not at all restful, unfortunately, only frantic for sleep. Wyatt remained in bed, tossed more until the same thought cycle began anew.

At 3 am he checked his watch, sighed, blocked the number on his cell phone, and made a prank call to Wappinger, New York.

It hadn't helped.

"I can't wait to see this." Hussein draws into one of the few traffic pullouts along Havril Road that will allow him to park the taxi for an extended time.

"No way."

"Two grandmasters."

Wyatt is horrified. "First of all, that is a *thing*." Assumptions that he held a PhD were one thing. Being mistaken for a grandmaster . . . "And . . . I don't want you there."

Hussein frowns in the rearview, his eyes dark orbs below the dark sunglasses nested in his hair. "Is it about the posters?"

"No," Wyatt lies. "And I'd call them flyers."

"I explained it wasn't my fault. My cousins got hold of her. How is that on me?"

The image, Wyatt notes, has become the person. "They got hold of *her* because you gave *her* to them."

"How could I know what they'd do?" Hussein slaps the wheel.

"Did you tell them *not* to do that?"

"Like that would work with those guys."

The photo, sent via Hussein's phone to a family member, then passed on to more than a dozen other family members, many in the livery business although others representing every kind of service industry in the region including corner stores and house cleaning agencies—this picture had been duplicated mainly by Hussein's unemployed brother-in-law on the Xerox in Hussein's uncle's office. From there X had been circulated by hand along with rolls of dull blue colored tape that had appeared across town in great abundance, and her visage then attached to any surface that could accept adhesive. "That brother-in-law," Hussein says. "One of those wazzocks who assumes if they do something for someone, they'll get rewarded. If it's not about the posters, what do you care if I watch?"

Wyatt knows he can't show up with a gallery. When Combs asked him to meet in the park, he imagined an area with benches for groups. He'd visited such game spots in many cities: New York and Chicago had active ones, although Turner, Texas—not surprisingly—did not. It's hard to imagine one here, but he doesn't want to break any local etiquette.

Most of all, he doesn't want the taxi driver to see him lose.

He is going to lose. The sluggishness of his movements rising from bed, the stiffness in his spine, heaviness around the eyes—these factors plus his incessant yawning and inability to concentrate deliver a sense of doom. To have his chances reduced to such a negligible possibility nearly relieves him. This morning, the park appears to be about the width of a sidewalk, an impression that adds to his suspicion he's not processing visual imagery well. Worse, when his fingers go to his jacket pocket, groping for the familiar cylindrical shapes, they don't land on his pill bottles. Had he taken them that morning? When was the last he had taken them? Wyatt opens the car door and places a foot on the pavement. "I'll call when I'm finished."

"I have a picture, too," Hussein says. "I meant to show." He tilts his lean frame towards the dashboard, flips the glove box, hands not a digital image but a paper 5×7 photograph into the back seat.

Wyatt is shocked. Was this some kind of repayment, or . . .? A (literal) "tit for tat" for what had happened with X's photo?

The color picture is not professionally lit but shot into a mirror using what appeared to be an ancient disposable camera—visible in the girl's, or woman's, hand. She kneels alone in the frame, the mirror reflecting her body in profile, one knee on a lacquered floor. Dark skinned and completely naked, she's profoundly pregnant. Her belly's massiveness makes other aspects of her nudity—large breasts with hanging, dark-nippled tips, the frank black pubic triangle, the fist digging against a bare buttock—seem beside the point.

"My sister."

Wyatt has no ready response.

"As in my brother-in-law's wife."

"The asshole who put my picture all over town and—"

"Different sister. Different asshole."

Wyatt attempts to hand it back, but Hussein spreads both palms wide. It looks like he will refuse to take it. Perhaps ever.

"So you're showing me this . . ."

"It was in a letter my sister sent my wife from Halifax. She's moved to Halifax, the sister. See, Wyatt?"

He did not.

"When my wife opened the letter—it was a long letter, Dr. Wyatt, as it concerned how she was leaving my brother-in-law ..."

Wyatt, operating on little sleep, feels his brain wobble. At times he considers that his mind, his thoughts, need a certain bandwidth to operate. There was room for a relatively limited amount of actionable information in its subtle pathways, especially in the morning. This morning, with its looming showdown, gives him an even narrower zone of operations. He holds the photo delicately between two fingers and again moves his other hand flatly into his other jacket pocket where the pills might have migrated. Nothing.

"So, my brother-in-law, he's kind of wild. Can't keep a job. Can't keep it in his pants. My sister, Rashmika, she gets convinced he's cheating on her. Sleeping around."

"Another 'call a cab' story?"

"No. One day at lunch—she works at a bank—she and one of the tellers go out to her car in the parking lot. My brother-in-law had been at a bar the night before with his friends and took her car. This bar, Wyatt, was called Confetti's.

"Kashmiris go to bars?"

"You follow? A bar called Confetti's where at midnight they drop confetti from the ceiling? Unfortunately ... or fortunately, depending on how you look at it ..."

Wyatt wants to get moving. He can't see from the street where on earth anyone could set up a board in this tangle of trees and green undergrowth.

"... unfortunately, in bed that night, she notices there are shiny glittery spots all over his bum. 'You must have had your trousers off at some time at Confetti's!' He laughed it off. So, this next day at lunchtime she and the teller go out to examine the back of the car, and there's confetti there, too, plus lots of white fibers. 'She must have been wearing a cashmere sweater,' says the teller. Then they find a stain."

"Hussein ..."

"Guy left a *stain*! '*Fuckin' 'ell*,' says the teller. So Rashmika calls her husband, my brother-in-law, and he says he'd spilled a milkshake back there."

Wyatt still has a foot on the curb. "I better ..."

"She leaves him, Wyatt! High and dry! She's seven months pregnant, Rashmika is, but doesn't care. And then, yeah." Hussein takes back the picture, flicks it with a middle finger, bends it backward, examines it wistfully. "Then she sends the letter, and in the letter is this. This picture. My brother-in-law is basically out on the street, hustling to survive since she had the only real job in the family. And she had the baby. Her daughter. She just keeps on." He shakes his head.

Wyatt waits. "How on earth is this *not* a 'call a cab' story?"

"It's a *'women will do anything'* story, Dr. Wyatt. You can't expect the expected from any one of them. Can I tell you good luck, then, or is that allowed?"

"Appreciate it."

Wyatt crosses the narrow street to a stone wall interrupted by the arched gateway. Parked alongside this entrance, a bizarrely painted van advertises fire and burglar alarm installation, a figure obviously ripped off from Munch with "STOP THIEF!" in a dialogue balloon emanating from his horrified mouth. Wyatt examines a sheet of typing paper creased lengthwise that Combs had sketched for him to show the spot for the meeting. He's once again struck slow-brained and confused as Hussein motors away. He doesn't see how, beyond some non-Newtonian folding of space and time, that entire layout indicated on the drawing could be included in this small physical park area. Other than the sidewalk and wall, there is nothing but a deep ravine. From his position, he looks down onto the tops of trees and out into the far horizon. Stepping through the arched doorway reveals that the park is not, as the drawing's two-dimensional presentation indicates, flat at all, but clings to a steeply descending hillside, trails and walkways snaking downwards through stony outcroppings, moss-covered brickwork, ancient-appearing porticos, and staircases. Combs's drawing presents nothing of Havril Park's poetic, exotic, *slanted* aspect unless tilted downward at its left edge. Wyatt understands why the poet and professor had taken such care, the tip of his tongue slightly extended as he sat at his desk, laboring on the map for 15 minutes. Below him, he sees a labyrinth that, indeed, might be impossible to navigate without guidance. He begins to consider that the accident of missing his medication that morning might have been a happy one as he can't afford vertigo managing this terrain.

Why hasn't Combs met him at this gateway? Or, in a market coffee shop? Was he being psyched already? Wyatt looks again over the slightly lower than chest-high wall into the wooded abyss below. In the arched gateway, an 8½ by 11 flyer has been fixed with blue masking tape to a circular column over a functional-looking olive drab trash receptacle. HAVE YOU SEEN HER? He pulls it down to rip into two equal pieces before depositing it, tape and all, into the container.

Down a half-flight of steps and he's on another pathway, below the level of the road. From here he takes in a better overview of the park and the valley beyond. Wyatt continues descending, pausing to lean over at yet another level to look into another wooded abyss. Scanning the horizon, he makes out the rook-like edifice atop Tower Hill. Clouds spot with moving grey ovals the far-away landscape that had injured him so badly. How great if X were to call him at that moment. "What are you doing?" she'd ask.

There is no one around. Birds sing overhead. Staircases and paths proceed in terraced arrangements, then ahead of him loop and turn to disappear into a rocky, boulder-strewn, deciduous jungle resembling a gothic movie poster. Soon, still following Combs's map, there are footbridges constructed in medieval motifs and carpeted in a fur of damp green moss. A clashing anachronism: the set of handrails on the next staircase are constructed of some utilitarian metal pipe, painted grey and connected with plates and elbow bends. Before he's gone five steps down another bank of stairs, his left hand cautiously skimming this rail, his fingers scoot under an angular, black helmeted beetle with a rhinoceros-like beak, the dry and spindly legs of which stick to his fingers as he hollers, shakes, then blows fiercely with pursed lips in an effort to dislodge the thing. Wyatt and the beetle do a simultaneous groping dance in the middle of the stone stairway, but his feet, luckily, keep their purchase. The bug drops from his knuckles, finally catches in a blur of brown wings, lurches through the thick air towards a clump of foliage in a rocking, buzzing, arc. Wyatt, despite the degree of incline, feels it prudent to step with caution from there on, evading the handrail altogether.

He doesn't make much progress. Fallen leaves and coils of green moss carpet the pathway below his feet. There is a pervasive hanging gloom. Heavy overgrowth blocks the sun to such an extent that as he descends, he detects a damp cardboard box and mildew smell, like an abandoned basement. This is where Combs wants to play? The atmosphere fights his efforts at staying alert. He yawns. Still just barely in the middle of one of the park's upper terraces, he watches clouds through overhanging branches, pauses to take some pictures with his phone of particularly twisted and expressive trunks and rocky outcroppings, and considers his loneliness. Phone reception has dropped to a single bar. Perhaps this had been Combs's main intention: a supreme isolation that puts the opponent beyond the assistance of sophisticated software. A more likely possibility is that he's in the wrong place. Looking at the map, then his phone, he scowls, considers separately a few intertwining vortices of worry over events that might or might not happen in the minutes ahead, although most of them came down to arcane questions, such as *Can I trust his unfamiliarity with the Caro-Kann against e4 if I play Black?*

A man in checkered shorts appears: not Professor Combs. His crew cut gives him a military demeanor although he's actually a fire and burglar alarm installer. His dog—all nose for, it seems, nearly half its length—walks alongside and glances at Wyatt with suspicious eyes. So, people do come here. Wyatt nods, steps towards one of the retaining walls to let the pair pass.

"Don't jump," says the man.

"Right?" says Wyatt.

Man and dog walk on.

Before he loses all cellular service, he pulls out his phone again. She's in his contacts, although he knows the number has changed. "My X." Wyatt shrugs. Sends a text. "Are you in Sallowsfield?" He hits SEND before he can reconsider and stop himself, and, using the hand-drawn map as a guide, continues to pick his way down the side of the hill, tentatively fingering the grey pipe handrail only on occasion.

2
The Board is Set Already

He descends into the setting of a Poe story, reminiscent of the opening paragraphs of the "House of Usher" with its surfaces "rotted for long years in some neglected vault." Wyatt passes three more arched doorways echoing the main entrance, each marking passages to structures he has to assume no longer exist. Each arch contains a blue-taped flyer that he removes and deposits in a side coat pocket. Notes on Combs's drawing wave him away from turning into several paths. ("First Arch: No. Second Arch: No.") Stepping under the third, then along a molding bridge, he disturbs a board meeting of crows who clack skyward from a pile of stacked limestone, fly towards the sun. After this comes a scene of utter abandonment and desolation, the rectangular outline of some cottage. It could have been decades since anyone walked this deep into the park, an impression that remains for Wyatt right up until he finds another HAVE YOU SEEN HER? flyer taped to a square brick structure resembling a fireplace mantle without a fireplace. Wyatt considers tossing all the paper under the next bridge as his side pocket is filling but balls it tightly and shoves it in deeper instead. A damp chill hangs. He's glad he hadn't left the jacket in his room. Wyatt feels anyone who's been choking down a dose of reality for a while might find true relief in this space if it weren't for the flyers.

X would love it.

If it weren't for the flyers.

Wyatt descends, feeling he must be getting close to the floor of the valley. Although most landmarks align with the map in his hand he suspects again, and is ever more comforted by this suspicion, that he has been driven to the wrong park. After the man with the dog, he doesn't come across a soul, let alone hear the banter of people playing board games, nor can he locate any areas well adapted for such activities. When he feels he nears the end of the indicated trail, tall trees to either side, the paths and switchbacks he's followed on his way down all but invisible now behind him among ferns, walls, ravines, gullies, and boulders, there—at a circular clearing—Professor Combs sits at a round concrete picnic table, bathed in dappled light. Dropping in as he had, from the upper elevations, the first thing Wyatt notices is the professor's bald spot.

Good.

The board is set already on the picnic table, the pieces removed from their wooden velvet-lined case. Combs wears a grey suit and vest.

The two shake hands, exchange pleasantries. Combs makes a noise on the order of "Beautiful morning," holds his own ribs as he breathes in deep, but Wyatt concentrates on the chessboard, constructed from bluff tile squares set permanently into the concrete picnic table. He rests at the bench and wipes his brow with a sleeve, his legs aching from the stair-stepping. One tap on Combs's closed left fist when both are extended and the fingers flex to reveal . . . the White pawn.

Wyatt masks his disappointment. He'd spent much of the day before and on into the night considering his responses as Black.

It's been a long time since he'd held chess pieces, more often these days touching a screen or grasping a mouse. OtterShark had been programmed to emit snicks and plops when moves were made, but it wasn't the same, and Wyatt had long before muted that unsettling feature. Combs's set is, to the judgment of his palm, at least triple weighted, also wooden carved, and not Staunton designs. Russian? The pieces manage a look of fragile brutality, thick at their bases, tapering as they rise, spindles on the royal couples no bigger around than a number 2 Ticonderoga. Slanted saucers cut into the orb of the Queen in a Saturnian mode. Wyatt raises a finely shaped Knight, moves his fingers across its smooth neck on one side, the carved sweep of its mane on the other. The Knight's neck whips backward fiercely.

"Latvian," Combs explains. "Tal's favorite. Reproductions, of course."

"Of course."

Tal.

He is doomed.

They sit after the Knight is returned to the center of its initial square, nod, shake hands again. No clock. Without thinking much about it, Wyatt plays his Queen's pawn and begins to build his usual Colle-Zuckertort tabiya, remorseful only that in addition to having been dealt by chance the upper hand, he will be unable to use any of those elaborate defenses he'd spent a day reviewing in preparation for an unexpected opening from Combs, who responds with a sensible King's Knight development. Will Combs joke, comment upon the positions? Will it be more muted, a space where they interact as opponents, not acquaintances, isolated in a cone of antipathy in the lowest reaches of this unused medieval park?

The space where they sit is a semicircular clearing at the bottom of the twisted walkway and is abandoned save for the two men—no other players at any of the two other squat picnic tables, no kibitzers. The other tables, for that matter, have no inlaid tile boards. The one set into this slab stands barely illuminated at these submarine depths, even as the sun begins its rise over the hills. Wyatt begins to wish he'd brought Hussein just so someone else could report on the fantastic setup. He begins to wonder, as they develop their pieces without haste, if he's overestimated his opponent, who is moving towards a King's Indian Defense, but in an unusual order—either subtly applying pressure in a new way or clueless as to opening theory. Wyatt feels disoriented observing the pieces in three dimensions but only for the first few moves. It all comes back to him. Fluttering leaves dapple light on the tile inlays and across the fantastic Khrushchev-era figures. Though not uncomfortable, he fears he's missing an important defensive consideration, realizes he can distinctly smell Combs's aftershave as the man fianchettoes on the King side, an act so conventional he feels the urge tug at him to alter his beloved Colle, push past his own comfort zone. Almost immediately, instinctively, he resists this momentary compulsion, and seeks a way to stick with something straightforward.

As his turn comes, for not the first time that day—or in his life—Wyatt acts without a clear imagined notion of success or the willed offering of risk. He swallows lightly, and—his King pawn resting still in its home place—slips his Queen's Bishop into the square four ranks above his King's Bishop.

Which is to say, like a coward, he plays the London.

3
A Different Era

Wyatt waits with his hands loose in his lap, blinks, looks around as Combs considers a response. The sun strikes dust and unidentified specks on his glasses, so he wipes the lenses on his shirt and squeezes the red places atop his nose where the frames pinch. This steep hillside doesn't look like one he could scramble down—or even safely tumble down—as he had

Tower Hill, with or without luggage. He had looked down the slope of that ancient hillside that afternoon—from this depth Tower Hill is no longer visible behind the forest screen—had looked down and across a rugged but much different, more open terrain, the town occupying the landscape below as if swept into the valley's lowest reaches with a broom, pushing out in suburban fingers that stretched along creeks, gullies, old canals. He had stood there, deliberating while the clouds stacked against a deep blue, and a small plane labored overhead. From his current position on a quiet concrete bench at the base of Havril Park, his careen down the hill seems to have happened months before rather than . . . three days? When it came to his trip, the encounter with the hillside feels like the introduction to an era of his life, not the middle of an eight-day excursion.

He'd felt his own paunch under his tweed jacket that day and nearly touched his waist then and there, across from Professor Combs, resting in the shadowed bottom of Havril Park. He is in terrible shape. A boy and his father had a drone on the hilltop. There were steps but blocked at the time by two young people helping an old lady slowly down them. Clouds scudded the sky, dry twigs blew at his feet, a candy wrapper moved past the wheels of his luggage. (*Smarties*? What on earth were *Smarties*?) Leaving the trail, he had begun his descent in much the way he'd done many things: believing, but not knowing for sure, that it would be a good move.

"Do you realize," said Dr. Combs, obviously feeling the game would be a casual one, "that you, like all people on Earth, have eight great-grandparents?"

4
Sisyphus/Granite

The path down the side of Tower Hill had quickly become no discernible path at all.

Wyatt had found himself skirting, nearly circling the northeastern edge of the hilltop, crabbing downwards in spite of observing no clear point of descent. Soon he noticed a family—the ginger-haired father in blue flannel, but also a mother, three children—all clambering along the slope to his left. There must be a path, else what were *they* using? He felt the comfort of not being the only person attempting this act and began to follow their serpentine line, although the going was tougher than he'd imagined standing at the hilltop. At the edge of the rim, behind him and to the right, a slender woman in a long dress seemed to be noting his progress.

Originally, looking down this slope—the tower looming behind his left shoulder—the road had appeared much closer. But his burden proved an obstacle. Already in several spots, the wheeled luggage simply would not wheel. Tufts of grass and inexplicable ruts like plowed furrows caused him to lift the heavy suitcase/pack by its handle. This grew wearisome to the shoulders. Wyatt noticed how, try as he might, much of his own weight, owing to the pressure of gravity, became concentrated on his downhill leg and knee, whichever leg and knee happened to be lower at any time. He began switching between limbs, making each, in turn, the weight-bearing volunteer. Occasionally he lifted with his back to bring his luggage over the ridges of grass and soil and soon sweated profusely. He considered removing the jacket, tying it around his waist by its sleeves. He came upon areas that were steeper still and, glancing upwards from where his eyes had been concentrated at securing his next step (attempting to place each foot on some solid patch) he noted the family no longer traveled in a line in front of him. From turning back and forth, making first the left, then the right the downhill leg, he'd slowed his progress while—with his head turned away—they had gone back and currently climbed *up* the hill, leaving him the sole prospector of the rugged slope.

"You're never alone in the Rocket Cadets," Kitty Canaveral insisted more than once to a downcast Bobby Booster, but Wyatt did feel alone, exposed, on display above the town. He suspected the mother had abandoned this shortcut first and forced the rest to follow. The father glanced at him, only momentarily, but long enough to project to Wyatt his intent:

Fool.

The man turned and continued to climb with his family up to actual trails and walkways. Just to hop his backpack/duffle over relatively small clods and ridges winded Wyatt severely. He'd underestimated the exertion required, yet it was far too late to change course, turn back to the hilltop, and drag the monster *up* the slope. He considered, too, stopping to unzip the thing and placing his notebook inside rather than carrying it, although it seemed to help his balance as a counterweight going over some of the terrain.

It could be said that he continued to "step" down this decline, but this soon became more like a controlled—or semi-controlled—"skip," not easy while tugging at the handle of the luggage/pack. His wrist began to ache, its jointed connection twisting in unaccustomed ways. His wrists, in fact, were most accustomed to locating a place of rest as he fingered a computer keyboard. The gradient increased, and Wyatt attempted to discover the delicate balancing point required to ensure his feet would not fly out from under him. "I might break a leg," he said aloud. Occasionally he found rises in the land that had to be negotiated via cuts made across them, these often very distinct scars in the reddish soil.

Soon, he leaned over his stomach every few steps, used his hands to help with "stepping" by reaching to steady himself. The grass felt brittle and dead. Sweat pooled a rectangular shape across his back. In a while, the stepping that had become more like crawling turned into a sort of dash interrupted by the occasional scoot.

"Do you know the names of those grandparents?"

Combs performs a simple developing move, and Wyatt, dropping from his reverie of the hillside catastrophe, squares his shoulders, returns his attention to the board and the figures in carved Latvian boxwood.

5
What's in a Name?

Play continues with regular though not overlong pauses. Pawns have explored into the center to leverage against each other in détente—springs yet unsprung—while escalations loom when Combs brings his Queen to the sixth rank. Wyatt responds with his to the third in the opposing position: not the engagement of contrary force it appears so much as a staring match, neither side willing—yet—to trade away that powerful piece . . . or *anything*. Wyatt understands these tensions as a feature of the London, not a bug, and remains unworried except to the extent it's obvious Combs understands the same. But from here, at some point, Wyatt might even have an advantage. He also understands Combs as possessing a modicum of restraint: a dangerous quality. Still Coach Sallow feels he has a structural superiority he knows to be sound: something that can pay dividends although even being here, engaged in action at all, makes him queasy.

"Everyone has eight great-grandparents," says Combs again. "Even you."

Wyatt considers it. "Eight great-grandparents. It's true. Has to be."

"Except in case of incest. Then you might have fewer."

Wyatt narrows his gaze to his opponent's side of the board, the sixth rank. Something up there. "Of course."

"Not so many, and not even that long ago in the scheme of things, yet you can't name them."

Wyatt may have to completely push back from the board to give such a question its proper due, which he doesn't feel like doing at all. What is this? Is the game so insignificant to Combs? If so, that might be good news. It would give him plenty of additional excuses to perform poorly.

On the other hand, if the poet were *that* cavalier, Wyatt could beat him, and the prospect of that, here, 4,700 miles from home, after being away from the board for so long, contains a seed of thrill. He knows such seeds keep people at the confounding game for years, despite all manner of frustration and defeat.

Wyatt chuckles in a way that sounds insincere, even to himself. "You know what, I actually *can* name one." He pauses long enough to allow a sliver of his brain to shuffle its way back to the Borough Library five mornings before. "Joshua Sallow, my great-grandfather, left Torquay for Newfoundland in 1896." He smiled. "Although the truth is, I didn't know that before last Tuesday."

Combs nods. Both men move in turn. The professor from Sallowsfield acts first to clear some tension in the center, moves a black pawn diagonally to snatch a white one with the motion of one hand. Wyatt, ready for such an eventuality (surprised it comes so soon, going for a palm along a thigh before a cheek has yet been kissed), retakes in a similar practiced gesture. It feels good to touch the wood, move the captured pawn to the side of the board, not simply see it disappear from a screen save as a miniature thumbnail pawn reminding both opponents of what's been captured, what exchanged. The two, small sidelined figures stand outside the field of action. They remain, mainly because of their squat brutality, recognizable products of the Soviet Bloc, but now, Wyatt senses even in this shimmering of dappled morning, they are somehow only wood, their quest for the final file and promotion—what Nimzowitsch labeled their "intention"—literally drained way. He can't recall thinking about that concept since childhood. Something about each Latvian pawn on the board suggests capability, while those removed present as the arrest and incarceration of that capability.

Play calms. Wyatt can't see how the trade helps his opponent. Maybe it was just a thing to do. But it's getting harder not to believe something else entirely has begun to evolve on the Black side of the board, and that this has been only a preliminary clearing, the purpose of which he can't yet see. Moves after this take longer. They, the moves, begin to present as—not fingertip brushes anymore, perhaps a foot, moved over an opponent's toe, kept there, as if accidentally. Wyatt edges into the maddening optometry visit the game often sets up in his brain. "Is this better? Or is this better? Is this better? Or is this better?"—to which one side of his brain eventually responds: "Show me the first again."

"*I think you heard me,*" says Retro Rocket, apropos of nothing, and Wyatt thinks of Henry Scott with regret.

A disturbing silence descends. Behind the quiet, Wyatt can, if he tunes in on it, hear the cicada-like rhythm section of his brain song, playing, it seems, not in this ravine, but as if from another, nearby valley. He had, back in his playing days, felt strange considerations from time to time in rooms full of talented people, as in tournament situations: a feeling that blunders hung in the air. Or worse: that a single blunder—like the condition for a grand mistake—circulated the cafeteria hall that had been converted for their purposes, and that this blunder could, like an evil sprite, land at any moment on any particular board. If such a thing will affect him in this space—which he deems far from impossible—it lurks already, perhaps, behind one of the columns encased in a latticework of vines or will crawl out—like a troll—from the arched stone bridge.

"I can't name any of my great-grandparents either," Combs says, erasing Wyatt's mention of his forebear Joshua with a palm. "That's the point. I think about this. I got a poem out of it. How we wipe clean from thought whole generations. And why?"

"Uhm." Wyatt catches mainly Combs's intriguing idea that a poem could be "got," as a sort of bagged prey. Perhaps a prize. He hadn't considered it that way. Could he—at the very least—"get" a poem from his tragic relation with X? Or: from seeing her—*thinking* he had seen her, at the train station?

Would that constitute a payoff for his misery?

"We're patrilineal," Combs says, raising his voice as if making a discovery. "We care about our names, don't we, Dr. Sallow? But not *all* of our names."

Wyatt feels a professional imperative to correct him on the "Dr." part, but more fervently wishes the man would cease chattering.

6
The Blunder

The poem of X. No doubt he'd begun to take as guaranteed their elevator rides, that they would continue for years. Decades. For Wyatt, these moments (in twelve- to fourteen-and-a-half-second bursts) presented as rare, even chemically induced, instances of undeniable attraction: the substances inherent in pheromones, hormones, and sweat, sebaceous, and salivary glands, commingling in the two of them in a way science could no doubt graph if the pair of them but turned themselves in to a lab for study. If anyone could not believe that two figures like the frumpy Wyatt Sallow and his olive-skinned, intense, erratic X could sustain such intensity for twelve to fourteen and a half seconds as the elevator at Bellinger and Nord traveled up or down its single flight, then they had never experienced that kind of molecular-level interaction. They hadn't a clue. Who in their right mind would give up such a thing? Wyatt met X at the elevators to taste her, sniff at the aura congealed around her. A hotel, yes, might have been more conventional, his fifth wheel would have made sense, but the elevator was so strange, mobile, unfamiliar . . . *inconvenient*. Perhaps the fact he was still married (technically) heightened the excitement, even for her.

On the later occasion after she'd left her husband, after she'd pointed out to Wyatt that he was *not* the third man and found herself needing lunch as her car was in for brake repair, she'd made the call to him. While they'd waited for the shoes to be replaced, the grinding of the discs, they'd had Mexican food. Wyatt and X discussed disasters—large, small, ecological, social—and then he'd dropped her off at the shop to retrieve the repaired vehicle.

She'd said, "We should do this again. We didn't quite finish discussing . . ." whatever they had been discussing. He'd agreed and driven home.

Her husband was out of the picture. Jeremy continued his underemployed existence four hundred miles away in the City of New Orleans. Wyatt called her an hour later. "My X." She didn't answer, but he left a message, inquiring if she'd like to have dinner. He felt it a perfectly good, decent, reasonable message, including a reminder of her idea that they do it again, as they'd had such a good lunch that afternoon and had discussed so many things. He believed the next message he left, an hour after the first, was also a good one. While he waited in his fifth wheel he spread out on the settee, read the newspaper with his legs crossed. Disaster filled the pages that day for some reason. Airplane crashes. Superfund sites. Under-the-table payoffs. These were the sorts of things he could probably raise as issues in class, so he jotted the content of a few paragraphs into his notebook, then surrounded those jottings with boxes. Now and then he would call X and read a few of the passages into her messaging service.

Six o'clock passed. Eight. What had happened to X? By eleven, Wyatt's stomach roared. His messages moved through pleading and into begging. So stupid. Even he knew begging didn't work. Ever. It was something he'd heard on good authority, yet he had never been backed into this particular corner before. He couldn't stop himself. Was there someplace they could go to *eat* he asked cravenly into her answering machine. One of the newspaper articles looked back at how the emission of phosgene gas had cooked the lungs of Indian citizens in Bhopal in 1984.

When she did call, after 1 am, Wyatt had passed out on the settee. He could hear his own messages in the background. "How did you *think* of all this stuff?" she asked.

"Where were you?"

"You're *crazy.* I was shopping."

"For food? I'll be over."

In the background, his edgy, strained voice. "*Cooked lungs! Right now, that sounds tasty.*"

"There was a *sale.*" She laughed in that way she had. He never felt certain of the sincerity of her laughter. It resembled the mirth of animated cartoon dogs. "Hang on," she said. "Look, can I call you back? Can I call in three minutes? I'm getting ready for bed. I'm going to brush my teeth."

Wyatt agreed, then went to get his keys, climbed into his Mazda, began the drive over to her house which he knew to be only a little more than three minutes away and . . . believe it or not, none of this was the blunder.

7
Present No Target

Positionally, it's give and take, although only the two pawns remain outside the 8×8 tiled arena. After the inquiry over great-grandparents, the opponents maintain silence, though the birds increase their chitter as the sun rises. Both sides make perfunctory retreats in front of perfunctory threats both sides recognize as obvious. Territorial occupations shrink, valuable central property they'd taken care to initially seize becomes subtly abandoned. This, the middle game, were it a conversation might have been the sort neighbors engage in across hedges while watering lawns. Wooden surfaces click each other in a flurry of trades and simplifications on the King side as a darker note chimes in from elsewhere on the board. Wyatt can sense it but not reason it out. There are demonstrations, but no veils pulled away. The series leaves Black with the bishop pair, but Wyatt a pawn up. Personally, he'd never found Combs's advantage more than theoretical. ("If your opponent has the bishop pair, it's a problem," he tells his students. "Especially for them!"). He wants material. He *senses* something bigger, however—upsetting—and needs to hunker down to consider it. It has to do with an exposed rank before the Black King. He can, through an uncovered check, threaten more than one act simultaneously, endanger that strangely canted Saturn ring on the bulbous head the Queen wears in her Latvian translation instead of a sharp-waved crown, but . . . nobody would fall for it, and it would only, again, result in a check, perhaps an exciting looking pin, then nothing. The game is too balanced to risk rash action. Like a statement that could seriously backfire if it weren't taken in the right sentiment, the correct light, everything could turn in unanticipated ways if he got overly fancy without being sure.

Interesting was not necessarily good. Beautiful was highly overrated. The point became to prevent interesting beauty: keep the contest tense, controlled. Provide no opportunities for *art*. When any player developed the freedom to move creatively, the game's curtain had lowered (that moment when, among those who knew what they were doing, the loser resigned rather than face the inevitable). It was *over*, because one side had simply gained too much of an advantage, couldn't be stopped from exhibiting flair, but they had not in this game come close to deciding which side that might be.

Then . . .

He can't see any problem with it. One of Black's hanging pawns is soon gobbled. Without consequence! ("When in doubt, take the pawn!") Suddenly, by all lights, Wyatt has to consider himself winning. Plus there are visible, possible improvements ahead, built into the variety of overall possible plans, and these could downright assure him of eventual victory, he feels. He imagines the worst: a drawn-out end game with few pieces left on the board but himself possessing the advantage. *Up two pawns.* He looks forward to making these improvements and hopefully soon, as he also knows the most common time to lose all objectivity and logical thought is when ahead.

Wyatt doesn't mind difficult positional play. He doesn't have a problem with involved calculations, where one piece becomes the spoke for the threaded possibilities that unravel (and ravel) in seven different directions. He cannot, absolutely cannot, however, abide having the upper hand. More and more in his dealings with OtterShark such advantages always preceded an unexpected digital trouncing.

When it came to the software, Wyatt sometimes believed he demonstrated a will to lose.

Sure enough, it only takes a few moves for him to realize that the upper hand has done him raw again, though it's far too late that he sees.

Combs will, yes, lose a bishop but gain the exchange with Wyatt's rook. And . . . *unstoppable*. Because of taking the extra pawn. Of course. That capture had moved Wyatt's Bishop out of a defensive position, gained a tempo for black, created one of those looming disasters that could not be defended against. He feels bile rising in his throat. He's overcome by a strong desire to stir. Stand. Possibly shoot the bird at the board. He can't move.

Wyatt, in his misguided desire to beat a human being at chess has broken his—and Petrosian's—ironclad rule: present no target.

He forces his eyebrows to remain still and does not glance at the square Black's bishop needs to attain. He's certain he's correct. Thus far, the play on either side can be considered competent, but Wyatt realizes he still has no real sense of who he's up against. He's let his guard down. It's this damned park! Combs had brought him to this abysmal green abyss to throw him off. Latvian chess set my ass.

He knows he's going to lose.

Wyatt grieves for all the time he wasted the day before even worrying about it. A better-balanced personality would have enjoyed this trip much more, taken the town for what it was, lightened his heart. Winning had taken over his every thought from the second Combs suggested the encounter. Now he'd lost a game *and* a day.

If Combs plays the bishop fork, then . . . well, he'd still only come across as a competent player (as any competent player would find it, would play the bishop fork), but it would place the Brit an exchange ahead, turn Wyatt's position grim if not hopeless. He might as well resign. Maybe before Combs moves. He contemplates it. It's hard to imagine even drawing. Or, he can keep going. Keep as much beauty away from the other side as possible. Turn it into an ugly win for Combs at least. Wyatt begins to regret not attempting the discovered check, just to see what might have happened, although that's a fool's attitude.

A kind of blindness descends, making it worse: the experience turning sour as he scans ... *scours* the board with bleary eyes, unable to formulate a plan that would work after the loss of the rook.

If Combs overlooks the move, there would be a way.

8
Scooting is Considered
(but unfortunately then abandoned)

At Tower Hill, Wyatt felt muscles he hadn't felt in a while, given his sedentary, professorial lifestyle.

If he'd known his legs were to be used to descend steep hillsides, he would have taken better care of them: not the first time in his life he'd drawn a similar conclusion. On nearly biannual occasions as he sat in waiting rooms anticipating the call of his name for a professional poke and prod from his Vietnamese doctor, a re-upping of his prescriptions, this had crossed his mind. The sensation of the hill approached a complete relinquishment of control, however, much more than the agency he turned over to Dr. Phu duc Tranh, yellow pills, pink pills, and diazepam. It was as with snow-skiing (Z in her parka, glowing and pregnant. Yuri in the lodge beside her, guzzling mulled wine). Similar to the challenge of the slopes, the challenge of the hill came in stopping. Occasional misjudgments meant he jammed his leg into the landscape when he'd wanted to traipse lightly across. He angled violently sidewise in a way that made his hip creak, sent him skittering west to keep upright, luggage trailing like a dragged anchor. The far horizon jiggled. After attempts to steady himself by bending and using his hands, his back began to ache. He gave that up, partly in case anyone saw him (he did not want to come crawling down this hill), but soon he had to maneuver his center of gravity over his feet to keep from landing on his ass. Every instinct made him lean towards the hill, but he could feel his shoes lose traction badly when he succumbed to the impulse, and twice he remained bipedal only by leaning on the luggage handle. Holding out his notebook as counterbalance helped some and he imagined an observer—that wraith-like figure on the hill-top—watching his method, believing the black volume a kind of revealed and then retracted semaphore flag. When he finally came to a temporary stop halfway down on a narrow indentation that broke the otherwise relentless 60-degree incline towards the road below (which seemed not much closer), he saw that the handle of his luggage had become slightly bent and jammed. When the time came to telescope it back into its closed position, he'd probably need a hammer. Wyatt considered surrender, not crawling but *scooting* down, the bag held across his belly like a pillow, at least in that way to way avoid dangerous stress fractures or blowing a knee. His calf muscles ached. He was forty-five years old.

Moving forward again turned out to be a mistake as soon he was jogging down Tower Hill, the luggage handle twisting behind him—his forearm twisting behind him, too—and then (and why was this even there, he had to wonder) he stepped into a gully.

9
Combs Plays the Bishop Fork

Combs plays the bishop fork.

10
Pangboom Calling

Wyatt's international prank call to Wappinger, New York:
"Is Gordon McKenzie in?"

"Gordon doesn't live here. He's my ex-husband."

"I'm trying to place a large order with his Rightway Tucker-ware distribution business."

"Ah. Wrong number."

"Is there a number where I could reach him?"

"I should say you have the wrong number *again*. As I told you last time you called."

"Been about a year."

"You called last month. I don't have contact with Gordon. We are estranged."

"It's a large order."

"We're estranged, and unless something has changed radically that I don't know about, he has no Rightway Tucker-ware distribution business."

"It's for fifty sets."

"I can't help you."

"Are you *ever* in contact with him?"

"The last time I was in contact with him, I told him about your last order of Tucker-ware, and he looked at me like I was crazy. I believe you have the wrong Gordon McKenzie."

"I know he's the cheapest in town. If I could just leave my order with you and you could get it to him."

"It's not possible. Mr. . . . okay, you've told me, but . . ."

"Selhisi. Selhisi Pangboom."

"Of course."

"I left my order with you last time, I believe."

"Well, I wrote it down. I gave it to him at our daughter's wedding reception and . . ."

"Oh, congratulations. Congratulations on that. Well, thanks for passing it on. I did receive the order."

"*You did?*"

"And I appreciate it. If you won't give me his number, if you could just take my order again. My name is spelled as it sounds."

"Good God. Let me . . ."

"Are you ready?"

"I'm . . ."

"Just tell him Selhisi Pangboom called and he'll know what it's in reference to. And tell him I need five . . . that's *five* of the sausage kits, and fifty-two of the four-to-a-set, two-quart containers with lids. Opaque lids."

"I'm . . . fifty-four of the two . . ."

"Pangboom, with a 'P'."

11
"By all means avoid being even creepier."

Five minutes after setting down the phone—he kept one eye on his watch which, in those days, he wore on his wrist rather than depending on his cell's digital readout—Wyatt had already turned off the access road and into X's neighborhood, down Flagstone, turned onto Allendale, the direction to her house recollected from the time he'd driven her to the airport to fly out and meet her engineer husband in Saudi Arabia or the U.A.R., plus the times he'd gone over twice a day to feed her dogs. But now, at that hour in such a small town Wyatt did not wait for traffic lights to change. X lived in Turner's gated community, so he expected to see the African American guard in his shack, but it stood empty, the barrier lifted—which seemed counterproductive: wasn't nighttime the right time to *lower* barriers, keep that guard shack manned? No matter: it meant another piece of business he could avoid, the African American stepping to the curb, calling ahead to X, asking X if he should be let in at all, which would ruin the surprise of it. Not that X liked surprises.

Maybe he should have thought of that.

Lights blinked in loops across the townhomes along the entrance to the community. Electric candles burned in windows. It was almost Christmas. At X's, however, all stood in darkness, the porch light extinguished. Didn't she usually leave that on? Wyatt knew from the trip to the repair shop that her kids visited with their father over the holidays. Why tell him that? Why reveal her solitude? She'd also told him she planned to go to bed. That she'd changed into her nightgown. Or had he imagined the nightgown? And was it so strange she'd drop those hints? Couldn't their attraction remain as powerful as it had been? Wasn't it all an indication of some kind?

He understood this thing with "the Jeremy." A distraction. Younger, exotic, a *musician* (and cook), but Wyatt doubted its seriousness. He glanced at his watch again. She couldn't have gotten in bed in the last eleven minutes, could she? Where were the lights? What was going on?

He almost backed out of the driveway, made a three-point turnaround, went home, but instead turned off the engine. It would be even creepier to have come all this way, pulled onto the "property" as it were, and then not stopped. At least he should knock after this breakneck drive. Not to do so would be the act of a disturbed individual. Something a much younger, much crazier man might do. A musician, perhaps. A helicopter made a parabolic arc overhead, towards the south, probably Beaumont, and he thought of emergencies, airlifts, big size trouble, bad, bad news.

When he knocked, the dogs started in.

He hadn't forgotten about the dogs but hadn't alarmed himself over them either. They knew him. He spoke to them through the door. "Bert!" he said in a kind of stage whisper. "Ernie. Ernie, it's me."

His strained and rasped whisper didn't comfort them, but he felt a louder entreaty might alert the neighbors. He could hear the dogs' nails clicking on tiles, scratching the inside of the door which already had its share of nail scratches. He'd forgotten about their nearly endless aptitude for yapping and howling. They were a couple of undersized mutts X had rescued from the pound in a moment of compassion (she'd give them both away by the end of the year), and the two of them yapped, growled, and whined. No doubt they wet themselves in excitement, anger, surprise, agony, not recognizing his voice. Wyatt wished X would get to the door already. He was hungry. He knocked three more times. Waited.

Nothing happened. More barking.

He tried to line out the possibilities for what might be going on inside while he pounded the door and the dogs barked. He'd driven over to give her a nice surprise, but now whole systems of tragic consequences played out in his mind.

He stood on the porch with his ear against the door—listened for sounds of movement in addition to the dogs, perhaps some discussion in the background. Was someone else in there? He couldn't hear anything. The dogs sliding on the tiles yammered, and he called out her name.

A different dog, one block over, began barking, possibly hearing these two. The helicopter returned, then yawed in a different direction. As far as he could tell, no one in any of the homes or townhomes paid attention to him or the noise he made. No shadowed forms appearing in windows, no blinds blinked open. He pummeled X's door a last time before leaving the porch to make his way around the house. Maybe find some window to crawl in—or, wait—no. At least peek in. A vent to shimmy through. *Something.*

The dogs stopped barking.

12
Andy

Andy asks his bull terrier, Alan, what he thinks about nostalgia. "It's like, I remember once thinking it was a waste of time and energy, right?"

Alan lifts his small eyebrows but doesn't look at Andy. They sit atop a mossy slab near a buried circle of brick that had once marked out a fountain pad and pool, filled first with trash from homes at the top of the ravine in the 1950s, then leveled with dirt when Havril Park had been (somewhat) rehabilitated in the 1970s.

"I look back on my days of thinking that way with a kind of warm . . . reflective fondness. At other times, though, I wish the past would go away. Just go away. Ever feel like that?"

Alan does not respond on this topic or the topic of lost love: Andy's actual subject.

Andy turns when he sees a figure dressed in black sidle behind himself and Alan on the way down the hillside. He's carrying . . . no, wait. Almost certainly *she* carries a large black folio. Andy thinks it's a woman, probably a young woman, in spite of the hoodie that hides her face. You can usually tell.

"After all," Andy continues. "If you enjoy your own company at all, you probably ought to take some effort in building a relationship . . . with yourself. That's what I aim, Alan. As in: aim to do. It would seem right. Right? That you might want to take as good care of yourself as you do others? Oughtn't it? Because that's the thing. I just care about others too much. Don't I, Alan?"

He scratches Alan's head, who does not disagree.

13
Probably a Hoity-Toity Sandwich Anyway (like watercress)

After exchanging the bishop for the rook and dropping the pit of Wyatt's stomach into even lower regions, a tempest of quick moves causes the game to—as he often thinks of it— "descend" towards its final outcome. Not a good one. Combs goes after simplification; the pieces come off. The Texan finds himself playing along rather than risking an even more escalated material loss. Pawns and pieces begin to line the sides of the concrete picnic slab. The power concentrations on the board are reduced, yes, but Wyatt understands how the inverse also works: everything remaining as the ranks of bystanders hulk in the margins (here he picks up a captured black pawn, grips it as he surveys the damage, turns its wooden grain between his fingers), every survivor has increased its store of dangerous potential. A few tactical schemes raise their heads. Wyatt can just see what Combs might have in mind. Meanwhile, his own plans are thwarted at every turn. He begins protection moves and withdrawals, tells himself he's in a controlled retreat. Absorbed in the progressing horror, Wyatt notices forty-five more minutes have passed, and that Combs has wandered away from the table to light a cigarette, waving the smoke away from the visitor with a hand. Combs extinguishes the butt under his shoe, then drinks some water from a plastic bottle he'd stowed in a canvas picnic bag. "Sorry, I didn't think we'd be here so long as to need two."

Good. Very good.

Wyatt no longer seeks a path to victory, though he understands that a defeatist attitude is, in fact, the surest and quickest road to defeat, yet . . . there is a glimmer.

Combs, arching his back, gestures at the board. "It's a kind of universal truth, no? I mean: the present isn't exactly in question. Not only can we look at it," and here he pauses, to do just that, as if examining the board not only from his position on the black side, but from either margin as well, "but we can know . . . *everything.*"

"I'm not sure," Wyatt says, both legitimately struggling and beginning the process of modest self-effacement he hopes will wear well after this loss.

"You are sure! A pawn does this. A knight that, then that. You know every part of it."

"I'm . . ."

"What's uncertain is the future. What will the situation be in a move? Or two? *Twenty*?"

Wyatt nods. He can't deny it. He's not someone who can devote hours of study to the game, and so has pared his chess world, his chess experience to particular areas and possibilities that he uses over and over, as he's pared his brittle class notes to a single Business Ethics three-ring binder. He's gained his place by playing within himself, committing almost to muscle memory such patterns as the Colle-Zukertort and implications of corporate espionage. It isn't that he can't alter his plans, or even that he wouldn't see a novel opportunity should one arise and present itself. In fact, for someone with such a careful approach, he'd gotten into an incredible number of novel opportunities. X herself didn't seem to see life in terms of such limitations, but Wyatt knew his results improved when he withdrew, remained in his zone. He can probably blame his already inevitable loss this morning—now early afternoon (he is growing hungry, and wonders if Combs has brought sandwiches—most likely *a sandwich*—in addition to the single bottle of water) . . . he can blame this fiasco on his stepping away, foolishly, from the Colle-Zukertort in the first place. Combs hasn't been such a powerful opponent as all that.

The action concentrates on a focused, particular place that happens to be a corner of the board, the ranks closest to Wyatt on his Queen side. He sees a Queen exchange possibility—a terrible idea given the situation—but he has a problem imagining any other path forward. He could then, at least, trust in his own power to gobble pawns with the rook that remains. Keeping that rook active is the key. But the way to do even that is not clear. He reviews possible results. If it were Wyatt in a situation similar to Combs's, ahead so much materially, he would absolutely wipe the queens off the board. From where he examines it, hovers over it with his back bent and shoulders slumping, the corner grouping makes a wry face. OtterShark, rendering the position in two dimensions, would show the Queens as two long-lashed eyes, the black one winking at him. The King and a pawn make up a cauliflower ear and weak neck, his last rook jutting like a glass jaw. The rest of the board registers as an amorphous cloud. Sweat forms at his brow. He can worry about everything else later and so brings his own Queen against the black one whereupon Combs ignores it and does that fourth thing Wyatt hasn't considered out of the three he had, captures the hanging rook he'd now left a clear attacking path toward, right there on the same file. It's over. Too much. Doomed years before, probably, when his confidence had been doomed. There was no getting used to it.

It was the kind of losing that makes it difficult to breathe.

14
Trajectory

Stepping into the gully, watching his shoeless foot emerge while his knees buckled, and luggage drifted overhead, blocking the sun for a moment, he recalled as a kind of conceit not that he'd fallen and struck the hill, but that from his position of hanging flight, the landscape had risen slowly to strike him.

When his foot first dropped through the surface of the murky water it created no splash or ripple, his leg penetrating farther and farther like a slow-motion arrow shot into the carcass of a sheep. The chill of the liquid did register and caused Wyatt to recoil. He happened to have fallen into a crouch-like position before dropping into this unexpected hillside feature, so his surprised reaction sent him out of the ditch in a powerful, though unbalanced leap. Wyatt could not say his foot ever reached the bottom of this murk-filled depression or even estimate its depth, as his other leg had flexed so strongly, that the now shoeless appendage withdrew with a kind of "pop" giving some indication of the viscous and unpleasant nature of the stuff. As he'd been holding the handle of his luggage/duffle tightly, this came with him in a reflexive pull or lift that caused it to also clear the mire but begin a heavily tottering mid-air tumble. Tugging at the handle set up an added levering force like what an atlatl gives a spear, and the lurching, falling, tugging forces combined to launch his collected tourist possessions over his head, the handle slipping from his grasp, spinning wildly like a flipped hammer. Although this happened too quickly to cause alarm, for what would have to be considered a pregnant second both Texan and luggage separated from the ground, Wyatt moving onto his back, his head pointing downhill, the backpack/luggage blocking the sun and placing him in a cone of its oval penumbra that crossed him as it soared overhead. The buoyant experience had been similar to one Wyatt unfiled from ancient memories stored in a now long unvisited "stack" annexed in his brain's library: a trampoline in his neighbor Annie's backyard when he was, Good God, three years old (And where was Annie? The maddening truth: even if she'd died, she had to be somewhere), and this, plus the simultaneous centripetal spin of his luggage, the top heaviness of his bodily frame and wild flailing of first his right hand as it attempted to ensnare the telescoping handle when it came around again—for the pack was spinning just that fast overhead—while his left arm windmilled, his black notebook gripped tightly in its fist, all combined with the downward slope of the terrain that fell away from him as he moved past this unseemly water hazard located where no such hazard had any right to be, it all placed his body on a loose momentary glide-path he was certain had the potential of ending in disaster if he did not make arrangements to land in some way that would not affect his spine, neck, or cranium.

Wyatt rolled in mid-air. The man-made buildings of town grew faint in his awareness as they spun in the background, a part of him seeking a grassy spot on which to land, another part aware of the wildly spinning suitcase/duffle's dangerous path. Its lopsided twirl might well be attributed, he believed, to the fact that he had placed in its bottom *Sallowsfield: An Undeniably Admirable Place* and a couple of Luddite volumes. Somewhere within its spinning folds, the shoulder pad and supporting waist belt system wrapped around the zippered torso of the luggage/duffle like the sewn arms of a straitjacket. But the handle and its grip—like a kind of satellite, whipped around the greater mass of the pack once, then another time. Wyatt, almost watching himself do so and yet still not impacting the grassy soil, extended a hand to once more stop that handle, but again missed. His body curved into a protective "L." A small white left sneaker and a muck-covered right sock rose before his face, the sock trailed by a broken necklace strung with glistening brown ditchwater beads. Beyond this, between his own legs and to the upper right of the twisting luggage tumblering his books, his blue button-down shirts, jackets, dress shoes, dirty socks, dirty white cotton boxer briefs, nineteen copies of *Water Take Me Down and Also Burn Me* ("Why take my shoe?" he considered in the space of a millisecond), beyond those legs and luggage the wide feathered wingspan of a bird of prey circled the hill. Had he a rifle he might have sighted between shoe and sock, held his breath, pulled the trigger, and taken it from the sky, though he was not a person who commonly murdered avian creatures (one more thing that had made him, growing up in Texas, even more of an outlier than the outlier he had been), then another revolution and the pack/duffle's logo Sisyphus/Granite hove past, too blurred for him to see the figure there leaned against the oval stone. In this accelerated intake of images, the stone seemed more a house, the figure a ghost throwing itself at a wall. Dispirited, he flew. (For without the fragile spirit what is a person, but a sack of meat locked in some trajectory?) He had to assume the vacuum constriction device, its tube like a transparent rocket fuselage ("Toooob") turned inside the pack, inverted, then inverted again.

If the space between his shod and unshod feet appeared like the far length of a rifle barrel, that deadly opportunity to bag the motionlessly gliding eagle was lost as his own shadow grew beneath him. Almost certainly his own eyes bulged in his head (he had no way of seeing this) as the ground approached and he stiffened, attempted to lean into the mountain. The ground came on. He could stiffen for impact, cover his head protectively with his arms, lead with a shoulder as he had one evening near Christmas in Turner's gated community, trying to help—no, *save*—the woman he loved, or he could try the opposite: let himself go limp, hope that the versatile elbow, leg, upper arms, and knees could shape him into some shock-absorbing configuration. This he had tried when approaching the blue pool water, hoping the approach would better float him at summer camp (it had not). There's his student (Named Vasquez. That was his name. Charlie Vasquez!)—his student advising him on "blocking through the man," his family so poor he once admitted they smoked grapevine because "we had no cigarettes, sir."

At the gated community it had almost not happened at all save for a change in the air as he stepped off the porch, the sound of his own shoes scuffing concrete, causing the suddenness of the quiet in X's subdivision to startle him. Those were not dogs that would stop barking. Ever. These were the small, yappy kind that, if not barking, were about to bark. Yet they had fallen silent. If X had come, snuck up on them, grabbed them by their collars (did they have collars?) dragged them to a bathroom to lock them in, they would be barking as they went, barking when they got there, noisily sending their voices off the shower tiles, even the enclosed space amplifying them. The house had one of those hollow paneled doors—he could tell by the way it gave under the flat of his hand when he slapped at it, attempting to raise X's attention within.

If her attention could be raised.

It could be that X had simply found something other than tooth brushing to do. It could be that she did not wish to answer his knocks. Other possibilities rose in the dark night. He created scenarios and played them out. X, the love of his life, who he had been speaking to on the phone only ... he checked ... nineteen minutes before, refused now to answer his entreaties. Her car sat in the driveway. Her dogs, two of them, of a yappy breed—highly, even corrosively yappy—had ceased their noise suddenly and without explanation.

So (stiffening his body) he broke down her door. He was afraid. He believed he had no time to hesitate.

In one scenario, the young black security guard—*missing* from his shack where he was supposedly guarding over the gated community—this guard, who with (possibly) keys to all units in this subdivision (Did they do that? Was that possible?) had broken into one of the homes, had done so with ill intent, had done so to commit mayhem, possibly murder. "I am not a racist," Wyatt thought as he steeled himself.

"I'm breaking it," he said out loud. "I'm breaking the door," he said again. "Give me a reason not to, if you have one, because I don't see any other way."

Of course, another way, as anyone could see, would be to walk back to the car, drive home to his fifth wheel, check on X the next morning, discover then the perfectly rational explanation for it all. (Took a sleeping pill, conked out. On the phone with Mom in Calcasieu, couldn't hang up. *Did not want to see you.*) To *not* take that escape route was outside of his normal range of behavior. Yet overlooking little problems could result in even more trouble . . . leaving, walking away, assuming everything would be alright . . . Wyatt felt in his marrow that night the fatality of such an attitude. On the other hand, breaking down the door did not thrill him. He did not want it. Wyatt set his shoulders. Even as he took his running start in hard-soled shoes—not at all the best for this work—he understood the likelihood, probably a 99% chance or more, that everything inside that home was fine. *Fine.*

What about the other 1%?

An engine tick at highway speeds on I-45 South. A Knight on the sixth rank threatening in six directions. Some mild night fever that will pass, surely. (99% chance. That 8 am quiz review on nondisclosure to get to.) A man who ignores such ratios, delays a moment to cover the last percent, such a man can lose it all, so he broke down the door.

In spite of widely distributed rumors the following week, he was absolutely sober. As it turned out, breaking a door was not beyond him. He should have worn different shoes, although he hadn't left the fifth wheel thinking to break down a door, so had to make do with the soles he had. Wyatt got a running start, tried to stop thinking and just do. He concentrated on bringing his shoulder against the door.

He had to make several runs at it, more than four, tearing first the molding. The deadbolt grabbed, held, could have stopped the entire process except eventually it sheared *through* the panel (a quality piece of hardware, just attached to shoddy material). The top half of the door broke in vertical slivers of wood where his shoulder hit, such that the bottom panel, attached at the lower hinge, jutted out, pushed his feet from under him, made him lose his balance. He slid down the door, scuffed his knee, but he was through. It had been loud.

With the lock broken he could push the door inward, found it would go about five inches—the chain inside caught and held better than the bolt had—so he reached, groped in that dark space, tried to find a way to unlatch it. Inside was darkness, and he called out.

"Sophia!"

No answer.

What else to do? Wyatt took another run. He lowered his other shoulder—realizing, now, that it could be accomplished. He jumped at the moment of impact to get as close to the chain as possible, which *snapped away*. Something about the twisted manner the door sat in its frame had caused only one hinge to part as the last locking device gave out. The door still hung in its space, as if weightless, but only barely. He had to hurry.

He rubbed his shoulder. Tried to pull that door out of his way, but his grip had weakened. The impact had taken something out of him, and he ended up bruising his shoulder badly, but now he knew: Wyatt Sallow could break down doors.

In the gloom of the hallway were shapes and forms, and he pulled on the knob to work the door against the places that it was still bound to somehow, then he heard a gasp or breath inside. It was X. He could see her. She sat in the hallway that he remembered to the right of the entrance. Down at the bottom of the wall, along the floor, her knees pulled up closely to her. Light from some window showed where she slumped, the dogs in her arms. They looked at Wyatt in a shivery manner. Their eyes glowed. All three had their noses turned up. The dogs looked at X, worried. They were all alive.

"Are you okay?"

X wept. Everything in that house was afraid.

"Sweetie?"

"Just go," she said.

"Are you alright?"

"The police are coming."

"Yes?" Wyatt did not take this as a warning at first. Had some intruder gained entry, wreaked havoc before he'd arrived? Had she called a hotline?

"You didn't answer the door," he said.

"Go. Police."

"Is someone in there?"

"You broke my *door*," she said. She buried her face in her dogs, who pumped their front legs on her lap.

Wyatt couldn't get past the wreckage, couldn't reach or touch her, but wanted to do something, provide comfort.

"You broke my fucking door," she sobbed.

"No, I didn't," he tried, and she began to scream, which gave the dogs permission to bark again.

He walked to his car for what seemed like a very long time. She didn't stop. From inside the house, he could hear her screaming, saying that she had already called the police. That they would be there any minute. "I can fix it," he told no one in particular.

She screamed and screamed, so he opened his car door, got in, and drove away from the woman who told him to go, but he'd done it, gotten through to her at least in some fashion, so he decided—if "decided" is even the right word . . .

. . . so he decided that bracing himself for impact was best after all as the ground approached. (*"Kiiiiiity*??" Robby Rocket cries out as his female space-traveling friend leads him, inadvertently, into a path of near collision with a crowded belt of jagged and craterous asteroids.) When the blow came it could have been worse, he realized, but he did not have time to congratulate himself ("That was a close one, Kitty") before the telescoping handle of the pack speared the hillside by his chin, buckled, and he moved the arm holding the notebook over his face as he tumbled on a grassy slope, protecting his head from falling books, shoes, washed and unwashed articles of clothing, figuring he was going to get his skull bashed in, killed by his own luggage/pack even though he'd survived a bad hillside tumble.

In a surprising development, he was not crushed. Wyatt rolled. Raising dust as it also tumbled, the pack spun away from him, turned awkwardly several times. Wyatt and pack pin-wheeled ten yards closer to the road, the luggage well ahead and Wyatt—with more appendages slowing his way—not liable to catch up. Together they teetered to a stop: both sitting upright. The pack demonstrated its bent appendage, looking now like a crooked elbow of a man offering a business card to a new acquaintance. Organic particles fell around him in the air. Blades of green grass hung in his eyes and when he pushed these away: there—the only boulder on this entire grassy hill, no doubt, as jagged as an asteroid, and he had nearly found it, just six inches from his leg.

Wyatt stood, felt a pain in his heel. Moved his limbs. Placed weight upon his legs and felt around his ribs. Like his sneaker, his ballpoint pen had been irretrievably lost. He looked back up the slope.

15
Jaws of Defeat

Wyatt stepped over a pipe fence, found himself on a vaguely familiar-looking road, and felt there was an intersection nearby that led into town, towards which he ambled with his shoulders rounded much in the way he had slunk low in his car and watched from the end of the lane when the police arrived at X's house, and then, not very much later at all, a man with short hair showed up in a black SUV, X's husband—or ex-husband—came to stand in front of the shattered door with his arms crossed, then went in, ducking under the yellow police tape. X stepped outside, too. She glanced both directions up the street, but didn't see him, turned in the dark, police lights flashing against her white robe. She moved away from him.

Wyatt sighs over the chessboard. Breathes in the greenness of this hollow space between oaks and ferns. It was not just this loss. This contest. Somewhere behind him, the invested years, the time he'd spent—hours, days, decades. Gone. Just to bring him here. To a place where he *still could not see* the threats. Could not visualize the disaster that hunched towards him, dragging its veil.

Somewhere, a truck labors up a hill. The sun is nearly overhead, and despite the leafy cover begins heating his bald spot. He can resign, but ... instead pushes his queen, the only power he has left. He pushes the queen to the eighth rank for an uninspired check. It's not threatening a back-rank mate. Some buying of time is all until he resigns. Maybe he can think of something. But no. Work the Black King around into some sort of drawing position or a perpetual check, but he doesn't see it.

Combs moves his King. Wyatt checks him again on the seventh rank, still searching for some way out. Combs returns to the eighth. They go back and forth in this manner between the two rows.

After the third time, Queen and King shuttling, Combs emits something like a little squeak.

It's not until the sixth move after the blunder that had cost him his remaining Rook that Wyatt realizes (although of course, it had been there all along) he'd managed to work an isolated pawn to the sixth rank, closing off a square of movement for his opponent. Combs says, "Damn," very much under his breath, in the way one does not so much when cursing as when seeing something unexpected. Understanding a condition that had hitherto been outside perception.

Combs proposes the draw, and Wyatt, staring at the board, tries to wait an acceptable amount of time before thrusting his hand to shake the professor's. It doesn't seem possible.

Is it? Had Combs missed something? But the English professor and poet appears calm, even happy as he stands and stretches again, as if he'd just participated in some enjoyable activity rather than nearly two hours of concentration focused on the besting of an opponent—someone he *had* bested and, in fact, vanquished in all possible manner—only to have that victory snatched away.

"Ah," Wyatt says.

After some pleasantries, and Wyatt's out-loud analysis of his foolishness concerning the bishop fork (omitting a play by play of the much more embarrassing blindness involving the other hanging rook), Combs offers to walk with him back up the stone staircases, although he's brought some papers to grade and might spend a quiet hour or two at this spot, one of his favorites, to read through the poems of his students. Perhaps it had been no more than that: a place. A location Combs wanted a visitor to see.

Wyatt offers to hang about, help him carry the . . . well, there isn't much, but he could shoulder that canvas bag that holds the chess pieces, only Combs waves this away politely. "We'll do it again sometime," he says, and Wyatt can't imagine a thing more unlikely, but mentions that should the man ever find himself in Turner, Texas, to look him up. He doesn't bother to reach into his wallet for business cards as he'd given the last of those away years before, and the department, owing to cutbacks, hasn't ordered more. The two shake hands again and Wyatt, after a last look, in a leisurely manner begins to climb up the way he climbed down.

Soon he can no longer see Combs. The path he'd descended appears less gothic and bizarre with more daylight as he rises through the park. He rests on several landings, takes in the scenic overview. At some point, he can find through the trees once again the tower on the hill. The man with the strange looking dog remains in the park—has been there for hours. He and the pooch sit under an arch, look into the valley. They both seem wistful.

It doesn't occur to Wyatt to check his messages until after he's called Hussein and stood a few minutes, whistling softly and leaning against the arched entranceway of Havril Park. The world seems so new. He pulls out his phone. The text is from his estranged wife, Z.

> *Greetings and salutations. I have a question*
> *and was wondering if you had a minute*
> *to talk sometime. Maybe 2 minutes.*

CHAPTER EIGHT

END GAME

1
Yuri

"We come from a balanced culture. You wouldn't understand." Yuri followed Wyatt, who moved toward the front door of his home for the last time save trips to pick up a few "ends and odds" (as Z would say): times he'd hunt up towels, cutlery, and the like when the two Ukrainians would not be around. "Not as it is here. So, all or nothing. She doesn't blame you."

"Fuck her," Wyatt said. He wanted escape but the man trailed him even out that door. Wyatt could smell alcohol on him, and on a day like today.

Well, maybe it was the best kind of day.

"Balanced as in, we don't pile up all your good on one plate." Barefoot, Yuri walked Wyatt to his Mazda. "You know, the sort of plate that's on a scale. Like the Justice scale."

"Maybe later."

"Pile up all the good and then . . ." Yuri pinched his fingers together, raised the pitch of his voice. Down the hazy street were the cul-de-sac and the entrance to walking trails. "All the patience, the support. Then you put on the other side just one. Just one. That terrible thing you said."

"I'm sorry about it. Goodbye."

"I know you are. I know! And that's why we don't hold it against. Just the one bad thing, against all the good? It wouldn't be right."

Now Z wanted to get in touch. Wyatt, in the back of the cab as it headed to the station, figures both that it is too early to return that text—3 am in Texas at the moment—but more that he should not appear too eager. He has his phone on his knee already to determine the time in Turner, and readily moves to picture files, thumbs through the months and the years of them that he's saved. A trip they had taken to Galveston—their only vacation together with just the two of them, Wyn staying with Yuri for a weekend, and some photographs of them taken in the hotel room. He pauses at a picture of Z walking frankly from a shower in a white bathrobe, the hotel's insignia sewn over a large breast pocket. Her slenderness shows through the draped garment, the length of her legs. Her feet are bare. The things that had attracted him from the start (despite the overlarge ears, that nose, that forehead) are not marred by a demon-like retinal glow the phone's camera has captured. He hadn't looked at it in five years or more. An honest man would admit that his Ukrainian bride represented the closest thing to a relationship he'd ever had. Maybe Yuri's true colors were beginning to show. The years were piling on. Perhaps she was tracing out the prospects of someone approaching, now, her forties. "Old" as she'd always said of him. Hard to find partners for women at that age, or so Wyatt had been told. Hard to face the "declining years" with no partner, too ...

The terrible thing he'd said before stalking out of the bathroom that wretched night, "Take care of what you brought into the world," was, as Yuri had pointed out, unforgivable ... yet unique—a one-off insult hurled when he'd been tired. When the situation at the college had worked against him. At the end of a long day. His Spassky vs. Petrosian game interrupted. Of course, he'd regretted it immediately, horrified. What happens to people? But now, if something had come to pass with the ridiculous, underemployed Yuri. If she began to see herself in a more vulnerable position or doubted her ability to attract another man ...

Wyatt could not consider these pretty prospects for why he should, possibly, maybe consider taking her back, but they were prospects. They had never divorced, after all. He looks at her long legs in the picture. He recalls that there is on one corner of the square in Sallowsfield not a

Ukrainian but a Polish restaurant. There would be pierogis. For the first time in the entire trip, he realizes it. Z would love this town.

2
The Empty Square

Rain falls on the town like hash marks on a pen drawing. The taxi's windshield wipers thock from side to side. It had rained all morning, a gloomy day, yet he'd still awoken in a tsunami of relief. Wyatt recalled the draw upon opening his eyes. Queen to the last rank. Surely there was no key to his final hours in town that would deliver a greater thrill than that Hail Mary Queen to the eighth rank, so he hadn't gone out to do any more sightseeing. In general, as he'd forced his belongings into his battered pack/suitcase, he felt his trip hadn't been wasted.

Hussein did not arrive that morning at the Edgeland Arms. Wyatt felt a vague guilt being driven by this man he'd never met before, another of Hussein's uncle's employees. Stockier with less hair and much poorer English, he was friendly enough. Had he angered Hussein? Had the driver sent someone else as a snub? Or: was he embarrassed because of the debacle with the flyers broadcast so widely of Wyatt's lost (and naked) love?

Or—and this seemed most likely, given the way people normally assigned weight to the items they placed on their balancing scales—was he furious, that he, Hussein, had not been able to watch the "big match" deep in the bowels of Havril Park, especially since it had ended up as a draw. "A draw?" Hussein had said the day before when he picked up Wyatt at the arched entrance. "All that for a draw?"

"Yes, and thank God."

The new man drives. Taped to the back of the seat a rate per mile chart edges against an advertisement for a lamb restaurant and a xeroxed picture of X with oddly smudged eyes above her eternal question.

The taxi rolls down a hill, towards the bend in the railroad tracks that ends in the faux Victorian-era station. Wyatt tips the driver a few pounds. Is X even in this town anymore?

"U.S.A.!" the man says, fingering his coins.

Of course, X is not in this town, but he's missed only by a few minutes Gail Gillespie coming out of the gigantic doors of the station, jogging down the front steps onto the square, looking trim and energetic in white jeans. She's arranged a few more pictures in the atrium as the university had an agreement about displaying student work. In that space hung framed photographs. Some were in color. Others—the best—black-and-white images of the station's metal and fiberglass platform covers and frameworks taken from intriguing angles by Gail herself, as well as a few that captured accent views of the new, angular, Lowery Annex. She couldn't help noticing someone had interspersed between the framed photos other artwork, and frankly had doubts these were associated with any class at uni. Oh well. Gail examined them: pencil drawings torn from a sketchbook and attached directly to the painted grey wall with blue masking tape. One displayed a hand, dainty save for its thumb, outsized and looming. Another: a girl with strange teeth glancing coyly over a bare shoulder. Bent low to see it better, close to the skirting boards, Gail frowned at the image of two stocky figures hunched over a circular table, a bird's-eye view, their bald spots emphasized. Either shrubbery or ghosts surrounded them—it was hard to tell which—and apparently, they played chess although the individual pieces resembled more oddly shaped tools like spanners, gigantic bolts with nuts cinched on them, scimitar-like probes. The checkered board, if scaled to the human figures, would have to be wider than a Volkswagen.

She's been gone seven minutes by the time Wyatt enters the same atrium, approving how whatever leak or spill that had left a puddle on the floor on the day of his arrival has been seen to and the concrete dried. On the loaner shelf, he places one copy of *Water Take Me Down and Also Burn Me*, which means he'd brought nineteen of them across the ocean and would carry back seventeen. He moves towards the platform but then turns on his heel—his luggage, without its handle (he's managed to remove it with a hacksaw borrowed from the Edgeland Arms cleaning lady), now rolls so poorly he can't whip it around but has to do a three-point turn and skid it across the dry concrete. He retrieves the chapbook, opens it, bends the stapled spine backward such that, showing on the top of the now spread-wide volume is ". . . To Sallowsfield!" He looks it over momentarily, notes a HAVE YOU SEEN HER flyer he doesn't bother to peel from the wall beside the shelf, then heads to the platform. Probably because of the flyer, he doesn't glance at the photographs or artwork.

Wyatt duckwalks towards his train, bending to grasp his duffle/pack by one of its looping straps. At the turnstile two men in rail uniforms, not the same who'd helped him the week before, reassure a woman with a young girl at her side.

"Not here today, but he's okay."

"Day off is all."

The car is one-third full of passengers, most from the South, heading to Manchester on a Monday morning. Suitcases are stacked in an area by the car's door—two bicycles as well—but Wyatt finds a seat that barely fits both himself and the luggage/pack. It's just before 9 am when the train lurches, then rolls. Abandoned red-brick mill structures with plywood eyes back away from his peripheral view. Rain flecks the window. Some homes near town go by. In one lower story window, a computer screen or television glows. "I do not know this place," Wyatt says.

He considers the cab ride over. No Hussein. A pity, but . . . it's only now he thinks of it: through every block and lane between the Edgeland District and the station, in myriad instances, printed on signs, written on the shop windows of businesses, bus schedules, the lighted ticker-tape labels of busses themselves, in advertisements, on promotions. . . . Odd. It had been there, he was sure. His name. Over and over. Yet he hadn't noticed seeing it. Not once this morning. Before, he'd considered that if he retired in this town—so unlikely, but where else?—he could enjoy the pubs, take walks, and as an added surplus see his name everywhere in his declining years. But it wouldn't work like that, would it? In a short while it would fade from his notice. That was much more likely. He'd been here only a week and a day, and it had already disappeared.

The platform itself has a lovely offering of his name on a blue back-grounded signboard as the train slides away that he can probably see if he turns his head quickly, but no: the platform is gone.

The porter moves down the aisle, asks for tickets, says thank you with his soft voice. A boy with *Northanger Abbey* is ensconced in a seat across from Wyatt. A young couple—the girl heavy-set but beautiful—discuss their "big class project," and it must have been a graphics class, as they hold the assignment on their laps, examine and admire it proudly, a box of cereal they'd designed together. Behind Wyatt, a man in a pork pie hat and Hawaiian shirt, his stylish earring dangling almost to his shoulder, flips through a magazine. His companion is now gone.

Wyatt's phone is in his hand, and when he activates it, the picture there is not of X. It's Z. Full length, against the backdrop of the room door in the Tremont Hotel in Galveston. Check-out times are framed behind her. The door that cut them off, away from prying eyes for one and a half days of their marriage. Z is a tall girl, slender. He's not sure. Does it help or hurt that the photo has caught the retinal reflection? She wants to talk to him for a minute. Possibly two. Thinking of her reminds him of the Latvian Queen.

Then he sees it.

That's all it takes, a consideration of that Queen, the one he'd moved to the eighth rank, and he's almost certain. Yes. Because of the way it had all panned out, Wyatt noticed much later than he should have how that isolated white pawn kept Combs from moving his King from harm's way. Except. Except.

Wyatt is not the sort who can play blindfolded, but the game is recent, and . . . right there, the empty square. Labeled f6, most commonly, in front of the King's Bishop pawn. Empty, certainly, for the entire game as no pawn had moved into it, and the Horse (no, Knight) had gone to the seventh rank instead, tucked in front of the King, much earlier.

It's the sort of move OtterShark would light up and indicate with sirens (if it had sirens), showing how, with a simple shove of the King into that empty square, the advantage could have shifted completely back to Black. Not a draw.

Had Combs done it on purpose? Picked up on the despair emanating from his poorly dressed overseas colleague? Was that why he hadn't been upset when he'd so ignobly snatched a tie from the jaws of victory?

It doesn't matter!

Wyatt refuses to wipe away the sense of calm relief he's clung to since the day before, the one he'd awoken to, that had colored his travel day in a positive light, made him think about the possibilities of life, made it possible even to miss Z. This rather than the gloom that comes from throwing oneself onto a bed and weeping after an especially devastating, rape-like tournament loss against someone who'd gotten the upper hand. That the draw had been somehow allowed rather than . . . well . . . perhaps it was like winning an election with a stuffed ballot box, or receiving a windfall in cash, unearned; like extra money removed from a blind beggar's cup.

It doesn't matter. It doesn't matter.

The man offered. Wyatt accepted. A draw. Always would be. Wyatt does not, he reassures himself, feel pain over the good fortune of others, nor rejoice in their tragedies. He's not that kind. The sore winner can be a spiteful character, but there was no sore . . . uhm, draw-er. Was there? He doesn't believe in it.

Oh, empty square, that should by all rights have had a piece—the King—occupying it, but had remained, instead, occupied by nothing. The blind spot on the board around which everything else raged and battled and that both of them should have paid the most strenuous attention to yet had not. Oh well. He'd discussed often with his students how a contest could evolve around a single piece or pawn, a concentration of forces, those attacking, those defending. But . . . but . . . so it could all hinge (it's coming to him now), could all seize upon a space so dear, so empty . . . the posing, strategizing, obsessive focus and calculation an excuse, not a contest . . . busywork that made it possible, even palatable to game what wasn't there. No King, no Bissop, no Horse (no Knight) no Pond, no Pond, no Pond.

He thumbs past the picture on his phone of Z in her bathrobe, finds the picture of X, naked, dimpled, grinning. He looks upward and to his left, out the train-car window.

3
Brian

The train moves. Behind Wyatt Sallow in the car, a magazine page flips, a man looks up. It's him. He is the man in the pork pie hat. Raising his head, he sees the man in tweed look upwards and to his left. The man in the pork pie hat smiles, because, of course, he recognizes that one, now, has seen him, of course, previous week, thinking back. Yes. Brian Sallow under that hat. Drummer for the (not popular) group Drowned Out. A writer of lyrics few get to hear. A teacher of music in the fifth form at Torquay these days. He is the man in the pork pie hat. His shirt is Hawaiian. His earring is long. The brunette who traveled down with him? She's gone, isn't she? Might be back. Who knows?

Where are we? Where? Of course! Never been, never stopped in. Ironic given the name. Heard there's not much to see. Still, whenever passing, Brian salutes, always does, given the name. Doffs his hat (which he does now) as houses and an exhaust store go past. "To Sallowsfield," he says (to himself). "You're not my town but I am your man." Cocks his head. And that one. In the tweed. Fossicking with his phone. The man in tweed turns his shoulder in a heavy-hearted way, yes. Fossicking with his phone, but looks out the window, too, and smiles. He smiles! What's out there?

Out the window, there's a hill. On the hill, there is a tower. Then the carriage passes under a red brick arch, into a black tunnel, races toward Manchester Piccadilly and all the other stations on the line.

ACKNOWLEDGMENTS

I'm grateful to those who helped me with *Sallowsfield*.

David Samuel Levinson's encouragement, friendship, and editorial advice have been a great influence. Editorial polish from Michael McConnell is also much appreciated. Friends and colleagues offering invaluable advice through multiple drafts include David Mercier Parsons, Kelly Patton, Dede Fox and Cassandra Tomchik.

Author and educator Molly McBride Lasco survived several versions of the novel and I'm thankful for her patience and wise feedback. My two UK Whisperers, Sue Hartle and Sue Neill, have been invaluable in keeping me from saying anything too boneheaded about the North of England, although if anything boneheaded has snuck in it's on me and the oft-perplexed Wyatt Sallow, not those sensitive and supportive readers.

Thanks to all at *Texas Review Press*, including its founding director Paul Ruffin (1941–2016) who had faith in me, and current director J. Bruce Fuller who's kept the faith. Thanks also to *TRP* copy editor W. Scott Thomason and Publishing Specialist Karisma "Charlie" Tobin.

While I don't always heed it, when writing I do always listen to the voice in my head ("Is this going to start soon?") of my mentor Daniel Stern (1928–2007).

Many thanks to artist Brandy Beucler for the wonderful bollard illustrations, Magda Berg for the photography, and my good friend the poet Sharon Klander for being so good with titles.

Much gratitude to my wife Kazumi and son Dylan who, in more ways than one, gave me leave to go to Sallowsfield, as well as to my amazing half-siblings, Jack Hudder and Judi Hudder Lane, who always wanted to go.

ABOUT THE AUTHOR

CLIFF HUDDER received an MFA in fiction writing from the University of Houston in 1995 and a PhD in American Literature from Texas A&M University in 2017. He has been an archaeological laborer, a film and video editor, a photographer, air compressor mechanic, electrical lineman (apprentice) and educator. In addition to articles on regional and American literature, his short stories have appeared in several journals, including *Alaska Quarterly Review, The Kenyon Review*, and *The Missouri Review*. His work has received the Barthelme and Michener Awards, the Peden Prize, and the Short Story Award from the Texas Institute of Letters which inducted him as a member in 2017. His novella, *Splinterville*, won the 2007 Texas Review Fiction Award and his novel *Pretty Enough for You* was named a top ten Texas favorite of 2015 by Lone Star Literary Life. He is Professor of English and Chair of Psychology and Sociology at Lone Star College-Montgomery in Conroe, Texas.